SIMON & SCHUSTER'S

YOUNG READERS'

ILLUSTRATED

DICTIONARY

REVISED AND EXPANDED

P9-DEU-522

Simon and Schuster Books for Young Readers
Published by Simon & Schuster Inc., New York

SIMON AND SCHUSTER
BOOKS FOR YOUNG READERS
Simon & Schuster Building
Rockefeller Center
1230 Avenue of the Americas
New York, New York 10020

First American Edition 1984
First published in 1984 by Kingfisher Books Ltd.
Copyright © Kingfisher Books Ltd., 1984

Published by the Simon & Schuster Juvenile Division
SIMON AND SCHUSTER BOOKS FOR YOUNG READERS
is a trademark of Simon & Schuster Inc.
Printed in Portugal by Printer Portuguesa, Sintra
Also available in Julian Messner

10   9   8   7

ISBN: 0-671-50821-0

Simon & Schuster edition edited by Jane Hyman, elementary principal and former
reading specialist in the Randolph (Massachusetts) School System.

Library of Congress Cataloging in Publication Data

Grisewood, John
    Simon & Schuster's young readers' illustrated dictionary

    "Simon & Schuster edition edited by Jane Hyman"—T.p. verso.
    Summary. A dictionary with approximately 5000 definitions and introductory
material on how to use it.
    1. English language—Dictionaries, Juvenile. [1. English language—Dictionaries]
I. Hyman, Jane. II. Title. III. Title: Simon and Schuster's young readers' illustrated
dictionary. IV. Title: Young readers' illustrated dictionary.
PE 1628.5.G74   1984   423   84-5128

Introduction

ABOUT YOUR DICTIONARY

What is a dictionary? It is a book like this one, which does two main jobs:
1. It explains the meanings of words.
2. It shows you how to spell words.

Alphabetical Order
A dictionary helps you to find the words you want. How does it do this? All dictionaries list the words they explain, or define, in alphabetical order. This means that the words are listed in the order of the letters of the alphabet. To use a dictionary you need to know this order. The words entered under each letter of the alphabet are themselves in the alphabetical order of the second, third, etc. letter of that word. So, for example, under the **F** entries, **fabric** follows **fable**; since the first three letters, "*f*," "*a*," and "*b*" are the same, you must look at the fourth letter, and "*r*" comes after "*l*."

Guide Words
You can look at the top outside corner of each page for the **guide words**. In this dictionary, the first guide word on the left-hand page tells you the first word on that page and the second guide word on the right-hand page tells you the last word on that page.

Entries
A word with all its information is called an *entry*. All entries in this book are in bold black type. So are other forms of the same word. For example, **abduct** is an entry word in bold black type and the other forms of the word, **abduction** and **abductor**, are also in bold black type.

Pronunciation
Sometimes the entry is followed by a pronunciation guide; the part of the word to be stressed is in bold letters, the rest is in sloping or italic type. For example, in the pronunciation guide for aborigines, (*abo-**rij**-in-ees*), the part of the word to be stressed is **rij**.

Part of Speech

After either the entry or the pronunciation comes the word's part of speech, printed in italics and in an abbreviated form. For example, *n.* stands for noun and *vb.* stands for verb. The parts of speech are also given after other forms of the same word.

Helpful Sentences

Some words are easier to understand if you see them in a sentence. Many words in this dictionary have a sentence to help you understand their meaning. These sentences are printed in italics, like this: *John, vase, and cat are all nouns.*

Which Word Do I Need

Some words are spelled the same, but have more than one meaning. If a word has two or more separate meanings, each meaning is numbered with the part of speech following the number. For example, *abrasive* 1. *adj.* ---2. *adj.*--- 3. *n.*---. If a word has separate meanings but both meanings are the same part of speech, the part of speech goes before the number. For example, *abdomen* n.1.---2.---.

ABBREVIATIONS

The abbreviations used in this dictionary are as follows:

abbrev.	abbreviation
adj.	adjective
adv.	adverb
Austral.	Australian
conj.	conjunction
e.g.	for example
etc.	etcetera (and so forth)
i.e.	*id est* (Latin, that is)
inter.	interjection
n.	noun
pl.	plural
pl. n.	plural noun
past. part.	past participle
pron.	pronoun
Sc.	Scottish
vb.	verb

A dictionary is a very useful tool. Learn to use it well.

a, an the indefinite article, used before a noun. *A person. An apple.*

aardvark *n.* an African mammal that resembles an anteater.

aardwolf *n.* a burrowing animal from Africa that looks like a small hyena.

ab- abs- *prefix* meaning away from, without, e.g. **abnormal** different from what is normal.

abacus *n.* a frame with sliding beads, used for counting.

abandon *vb.* 1. stop doing something. *They had to abandon the game.* 2. leave and not return. *They had to abandon the ship.*

abbey *n.* church and other buildings where monks or nuns live; a great church.

abbot *n.* the man in charge of the monks in an abbey.

abbreviation *n.* a short way of writing either a word or a group of words. *Tom is an abbreviation of Thomas.*

abdicate *vb.* give up a position of power, usually that of king or queen. **abdication** *n.*

abdomen *n.* 1. the stomach (in people). 2. the rear part of the body (in insects).

abduct *vb.* kidnap, carry off. **abduction** *n.* **abductor** *n.* a person who abducts.

abhor *vb.* detest, feel hatred for. **abhorrence** *n.*

abject *adj.* miserable, degraded.

able *adj.* having the power or strength to do something. *Are you able to help me?* **ability** *n.*

aboard *adv.* on a ship, aircraft, or train. *They went aboard the ship.*

abolish *vb.* stop or put an end to something, e.g. slavery.

abolitionists *n.* the name given to people in the 17th and 18th centuries who worked for the abolition of slavery.

abominable *adj.* disgusting, unpleasant.

aborigines (*abo-**rij**-in-ees*) *n. pl.* the first people who lived in a country, especially the first Australians.

The aardvark breaks open termites' nests with its strong claws; it then pokes in its long sticky tongue and pulls it out covered with insects.

abort *vb.* cause to miscarry; put an end to, e.g. spacecraft mission.

abortion *n.* operation to remove fetus from womb.

about 1. *adv.* more or less; roughly. *About an hour ago.* 2. *prep.* around; nearby. *She wandered about.*

above *prep.* overhead, higher than something.

abrasive 1. *adj.* having the property of grinding or smoothing down. 2. *adj.* (of a person) rude; upsetting people. 3. *n.* a substance that grinds or smooths.

abreast *adv.* side by side. *Keep abreast of me.*

abridge *vb.* shorten, condense.

abroad *adv.* in another country.

abrupt *adj.* sudden; hasty.

abscess *n.* a boil; a collection of pus.

5

A

absent *adj.* not there.

absolute *adj.* complete.

absolve *vb.* free someone from blame.

absorb *vb.* take in water or some other liquid. *A sponge absorbs water.* **absorbent** *adj. & n.*

abstain *vb.* hold back or restrain oneself from doing something, e.g. eating, voting, etc. **abstinence** *n.*

absurd *adj.* something that is ridiculous or comical.

abundance *n.* a plentiful quantity of something. **abundant** *adj.*

abuse *vb.* 1. use something wrongly. 2. be rude to someone. **abusive** *adj.*

abyss (*a-biss*) *n.* deep pit or gorge. **abysmal** *adj.* bottomless.

academy *n.* a higher or specialized school; society for art, science, etc. **academic** *adj.* scholarly; theoretical.

accelerate (*ack-sel-erate*) *vb.* go faster. **acceleration** *n.* **accelerator** *n.* device, e.g. gas pedal, for increasing speed.

accent (*ack-sent*) 1. *n.* local way of pronouncing a language 2. *vb.* emphasize; stress.

accept (*ack-sept*) *vb.* receive or take something which is offered to you; agree to; believe.

access *n.* entrance, approach. **accessible** *adj.* that can be easily approached or reached.

accident (*ack-sident*) *n.* something that happens and is not expected, usually something bad; a mishap.

acclaim *vb.* praise; welcome.

accommodate *vb.* provide someone with a place in which to live. **accommodation** *n.* lodging.

accompany *vb.* 1. go along with someone or something, perhaps on a journey. 2. play a musical instrument alongside another instrument or voice. **accompaniment** *n.*

accomplice *n.* helper, partner (particularly in crime).

accomplish *vb.* achieve, carry out. **accomplished** *adj.* skilled, talented. *She is an accomplished violinist.*

accord *vb.* agree, be consistent with.

according *adv.* (with, to) asserted by. *According to him the report is true.*

accordion *n.* musical instrument carried by means of a strap over the shoulder, played by pumping air from bellows, and fitted with keys like a piano.

account 1. *n.* a record of money owed, received, or paid. 2. *n.* a description or report of an event. 3. *vb.* explain, give reasons for.

accumulate *vb.* collect; pile up; continue to gradually increase. **accumulation** *n.*

accurate *adj.* correct and exact. **accuracy** *n.*

accuse *vb.* charge someone with wrongdoing.

accustom *vb.* make used to, familiar with.

ace *n.* 1. the name for "one" in cards. *The ace of spades.* 2. someone of great skill, such as an aircraft fighter pilot. 3. a successful unreturned serve in tennis.

ache (rhymes with *cake*) *n.* a pain that goes on for a long time, like a toothache.

achieve *vb.* succeed; reach a goal or target. **achievement** *n.*

acid (*as-id*) *n.* a substance which tastes sour, like vinegar. *Strong acids can burn you.* **acidic** *adj.*

acknowledge *vb.* admit to; recognize; accept something as one's own. **acknowledgment** *n.*

acme *n.* highest point or stage.

acne *n.* red spots on the skin, common among young people.

acorn *n.* the fruit or nut of an oak tree.

acoustics *n.* 1. the science of sound. 2. the effect of a building on

Acorns

sounds, particularly music, produced inside it. *The acoustics were so bad that I could not hear the orchestra properly.*

acquaintance (*ack-wain-tance*) *n.* person who is known, but who is not a close friend. **acquaint** *vb.* make aware or familiar. *Let me acquaint you with the facts.*

acquit *vb.* (in law) declare not guilty; set free.

acre (**a**-*ker*) *n.* a measure of land (4047 square meters or 4840 square yards). *A football field has an area of about one and a half acres.*

acrobat *n.* a person who does balancing tricks, often in a circus. **acrobatics** *n.pl.*

acronym *n.* a word formed from the initial letters of other words, e.g. NATO, which stands for North Atlantic Treaty Organization.

across *prep.* from one side to the other. *Kate walked across the road.*

acrostic *n.* a set of words, often in the form of a poem, where the first letters of each line spell a word.

act 1. *n.* a thing done. *There are some acts you do every day.* 2. *vb.* behave; play a part or pretend. *He acts the part of a pirate in our play.* **acting** *n.* art of performing. 3. *n.* part of a stage play.

action *n.* 1. a deed. 2. a gesture. 3. a lawsuit.

active *adj.* busy, full of energy. **activity** *n.*

actor *n.* person who acts in plays, in films or on TV.

actress *n.* woman who acts in a play or film or on TV.

actual *adj.* existing in fact; real.

acupuncture *n.* kind of medical treatment in which thin needles are used to puncture various parts of the body. Developed by the Chinese about 5000 years ago, it is still in use today.

acute *adj.* 1. sharp, penetrating. *He had an acute pain in his shoulder.* 2. coming to a crisis. *The situation is acute.*

AD *abbr.* short for *Anno Domini* (Latin for "in the year of Our Lord") used with dates after the birth of Christ.

ad- *prefix* (also **ac-** before c, **aff-**, **all-**) meaning to, toward.

adapt *vb.* change something to make it more suitable for the purpose. **adaptation** *n.*

add *vb.* put things together to make more. *Colin added all the numbers together to find the total.* **addition** *n.*

adder *n.* a small poisonous snake found in northern countries; a viper.

addict *n.* a person who is obsessed with a habit – especially drugs – almost beyond cure.

address *n.* 1. the place where a person lives and to which letters are sent. 2. a speech.

adenoids *pl.n.* small lumps at the back of the nose that help to prevent infection. When enlarged, they can make breathing through the nose difficult.

adequate *adj.* enough; sufficient.

adhere *vb.* stick to something. **adherence** *n.*

adhesive *adj.* sticky; able to stick to things. *Adhesive tape. n.* a substance that sticks things together; glue.

adjective *n.* a word that describes what something or somebody is like. *The black cat.* "Black" is an adjective. *The water is cold.* "Cold" is an adjective. Most adjectives can be "compared," e.g. cold, colder, coldest.

adjourn (*ad-jern*) *vb.* postpone (a meeting), suspend, move elsewhere. **adjournment** *n.*

adjust *vb.* arrange; put in order. **adjustment** *n.*

administer *vb.* govern; run something. **administration** *n.*

admiral *n.* very senior officer in the navy.

admire *vb.* think well of something or somebody. **admiration** *n.* **admirable** *adj.* worthy of admiration; excellent.

admit *vb.* 1. allow to enter. 2. confess; own up as true. *He* *admits his mistake.* **admission** *n.* being allowed into somewhere; the money you pay to go in. **admissible** *adj.* what may be admitted or allowed.

admonish *vb.* warn, usually mildly.

ado (*a-do*) *n.* unnecessary fuss.

adobe (*ad-doh-be*) *n.* sun-dried brick; also building made of adobe.

adolescence *n.* the period of life when a person moves from childhood to adulthood.

adopt *vb.* 1. accept somebody else's child as a child of your own family. *The couple decided to adopt the boy.* 2. take up, accept (an idea etc.).

adore *vb.* worship; think highly of someone or something; love.

adorn *vb.* cover with ornaments. **adornment** *n.*

adult 1. *adj.* grown-up. *An adult person.* 2. *n.* a grown-up.

advance *vb.* move forward, proceed. *n.* a movement forward; a loan of money.

advantage *n.* gain; a better condition or circumstance.

advent *n.* the coming or arrival. *Ice cream sales increased with the advent of warmer weather.*

adventure *n.* exciting happening or experience.

adverb *n.* a word that tells us how, when or where something happens. Most adverbs have the ending *-ly*. *They walked home slowly.* "Slowly" is an adverb.

adversary *n.* opponent. **adverse** *adj.* hostile; unfavorable.

adverse *adj.* unfavorable.

advertise *vb.* tell people about something you want to sell. *People advertise in newspapers, on television, or by sticking up posters.*

advertisement *n.* a printed notice in a newspaper or a message about goods or services on radio or television.

advice *n.* something said to you to help you decide what to do. *We took our teacher's advice and borrowed the book from the library.*

advise *vb.* tell someone what you think they should do. *What do you advise me to do?*

aerial *n.* something through which radio and television signals are sent out or received.

aero- *prefix* meaning of air, aircraft, e.g. **aerobatics** stunts in aircraft.

aeronautics *pl.n.* the science of flight.

aerosol *n.* substance, which can be sprayed under pressure from a container.

affair *n.* business; that which has to be done. **affairs** *pl.n.* business in general. *The affairs of state.*

affect *vb.* make someone or something different in some way. *The hot weather affects her health.*

affectation *n.* insincere, pretentious manner.

affection *n.* a great liking.

affinity *n.* an attraction.

affirm *vb.* state positively, formally or confidently.

affix *vb.* attach; fasten to.

afflict *vb.* cause pain of body or mind. **affliction** *n.*

affluence *n.* wealth.

afford *vb.* have enough money to buy something. *He can't afford that car.*

afraid *adj.* 1. frightened. 2. sorry. *I am afraid this shop is closed.*

Afrikaans *n.* dialect of Dutch spoken in South Africa.

aft *adj.* toward the stern of a ship or back of an aircraft.

after 1. *adv.* behind. *They followed after.* 2. *conj.* later in time. *After they left.* 3. used with other verbs: *Look after my bags* (take care of them). *He takes after his father* (he is like his father).

aftermath *n.* period following a disastrous event; the outcome.

afternoon *n.* the part of the day between morning and evening.

afterward *adv.* later. *We watched TV and afterward went out to a play.*

again *adv.* once more; another time.

against *prep.* 1. next to; resting on. *Put it up against the wall.* 2. in opposition to; versus. *Which team are we playing against?*

agate *n.* a semiprecious stone marked

by bands of color.

age *n*. 1. length of time a person has lived. 2. a length of time in history, such as the Stone Age and Bronze Age.

aged 1. *adj*. (**aj**-*id*) very old. 2. *vb*. to become older. *He has aged a lot since I saw him last.*

agenda *n*. list of things to be done at a meeting etc.

The HP42 Hannibal – one of the last of the famous biplane passenger aircraft.

agent *n*. 1. someone working on behalf of someone else. 2. a spy. A double agent is a spy who tries to serve both sides. 3. the representative of a musician, artist, actor, etc. *His agent has found him a wonderful part in a new play.*

aggravate *vb*. make worse; annoy. **aggravation** *n*. annoyance.

aggression *n*. an attack without cause or provocation. **aggressive** *adj*. eager to attack; great energy. **aggressor** *n*.

aghast *adj*. shocked, amazed.

agile *adj*. nimble, quick. **agility** *n*.

agitate *vb*. disturb, shake up; make nervous, stir up unrest. **agitation** *n*. **agitator** *n*.

agnostic *n*. a person who believes that nothing can be known about the existence of God.

ago *adj*. & *adv*. in the past; previously. *Ten years ago.*

agony *n*. great pain or suffering. **agonizing** *adj*.

agrarian *adj*. relating to farming and land management.

agree *vb*. say "yes" to; consent. *If you agree, I will come, too.*

agriculture *n*. farming.

aground *adv*. (of ships) stranded on the bottom of shallow water. *The ship ran aground.*

The F-111 strike fighter, the first swing-wing warplane.

ahead *adv*. in front. *Dad went ahead to get seats for us.*

aid *vb*. help. *n*. the help that is given.

aim 1. *vb*. point a weapon at something. 2. *n*. something you try to do. *Jane's aim was to learn French.*

air *n*. the mixture of gases we breathe. *vb*. expose to the air (to dry); make known. *They aired their views at the meeting.*

air-conditioning *n*. system for cooling and cleaning the air in a building.

aircraft *n*. airplane, airship or helicopter, etc.

airline *n*. organization that owns and flies aircraft.

airplane *n*. a flying machine driven by an engine or engines.

airport *n*. place where aircraft land and take off.

airscrew *n*. propeller of an aircraft, etc.

A

airship n. a lighter-than-air craft that is powered and can be steered by its pilot. Airships are sometimes called "dirigibles" from a French word meaning "to steer."

airtight adj. so tightly shut that air cannot get in or out.

aisle n. side of church nave, separated by pillars from main nave.

ajar adv. partly open. *The door was ajar.*

akin adj. related, similar to.

alabaster n. a stone similar to marble.

alarm 1. n. a warning sound or signal. 2. vb. frighten; arouse to sense of danger.

albatross n. a large seabird that spends most of its time in the air over the oceans.

albino n. & adj. a person or animal without natural coloring matter (pigmentation) in skin, hair and eyes.

album n. 1. a blank book for keeping photographs, stamps, etc. 2. a collection of songs (on a long-playing record).

alchemy n. a medieval form of chemistry. **alchemist** n.

alcohol n. 1. the name of a group of chemical substances, mostly liquids. 2. strong drinks, such as beer, wine and spirits. **alcoholic** n. person addicted to drinking alcohol.

alcove n. a recess in a wall.

alder n. a tree belonging to the birch family.

ale n. a kind of beer.

alert 1. adj. paying attention. 2. vb. attract someone's attention. 3. n. watchfulness. *Be on the alert.*

algae pl.n. a group of plants that includes seaweeds and other water plants.

algebra n. a branch of mathematics in which letters are used to represent quantities.

alias n. an assumed name.

alibi n. a term used in law when a person or persons accused of a crime says that they were somewhere else at the time it was committed.

alien 1. adj. strange; foreign. 2. n. a stranger; a foreigner. **alienate** vb. turn away; make a stranger of.

align (*al-ine*) vb. bring into line. **alignment** n.

alike adj. 1. looking or acting the same. *People say my sister and I are very much alike.* 2. in the same way. *We were always treated alike.*

alive adj. living; not dead.

alkali n. the name of a number of chemical substances, such as ammonia, which have the property of dissolving other substances, but which are distinct from acids.

all adj. each, every; the whole of something.

Allah n. the name for God among Muslims.

allegory n. story with a deeper meaning than the literal one.

allergy n. a bodily reaction to some normally harmless substance. *She has an allergy to eggs.* **allergic** adj.

alleviate vb. make easier, relieve. *The pill quickly alleviated the pain.*

alley n. a short narrow passage between buildings.

alliance n. a union, especially of states, political parties, etc.

alligator n. a reptile like a crocodile that lives in parts of the Americas and in China.

alliteration n. the same sound frequently repeated in a poem or sentence. *Peter Piper picked a peck of pickled peppers.*

allot vb. share out. **allotment** n. a share.

allow vb. let someone do something, permit. *He allows us to play in his garden.* **allowance** n. fixed sum (of money) allowed.

alloy n. a mixture of metals. vb. mix metals together.

allude vb. refer to briefly or indirectly. **allusion** n.

allure n. & vb. charm, have the power to attract.

alluvium n. sand, soil, gravel, etc., washed down by a river.

ally (**al**-*eye*) *n.* a friend, or a country that helps another.

almond *n.* a tree cultivated in warm climates for its edible nuts (almonds).

almost *adj.* very nearly; not quite.

alone *adj.* by itself; with no one else.

along *prep.* the length of something; from end to end. *Jill walked along the path.*

aloud *adv.* in a voice that can be heard.

alpha (**al**-*fa*) *n.* the first letter of the Greek alphabet A.

alphabet *n.* all the letters of a language arranged in order. **alphabetical** *adj.*

already *adv.* by this time; previously. *Have you finished your work already?*

also *adv.* as well as; in addition to something.

although *conj.* even if. *Although he was ill, he went to work.*

altar *n.* the table with a cross on it in a church. Communion table.

alter *vb.* change something. *You should alter the dress to make it fit.*

alternate *vb.* happen by turn, one after the other.

alternative *adj. & n.* a choice between two things.

altitude *n.* height above the sea level. *The aircraft flew at a very high altitude.*

alto *n.* second highest of the four voice parts.

altogether *adv.* completely, utterly.

aluminum *n.* a silvery metal which weighs less than most other metals. *Aluminum is used to make cooking pots and aircraft.*

always *adv.* at all times; all the time.

a.m. *abbr.* the hours between midnight and noon from the Latin *ante meridiem* meaning "before noon." *Nine a.m. is nine o'clock in the morning.*

amalgamate *vb.* combine, mix. **amalgamation** *n.*

amass *vb.* gather together; accumulate.

amateur *n.* a person who is keenly interested in sport, music or some other activity for pleasure, not for payment; unprofessional. **amateurish** *adj.* inexpert.

amaze *vb.* astonish, astound. **amazement** *n.*

ambassador *n.* a person who represents one country in another country.

amber *n.* a golden-yellow fossil resin from prehistoric trees; the color of amber, used for the lights between green and red in traffic lights.

ambi- *prefix* meaning both, e.g. **ambidextrous** able to use both hands equally well.

ambition *n.* strong desire to succeed; the object of such desire. *Her ambition was to be a vet.* **ambitious** *adj.*

amble *vb.* walk at an easy pace.

ambulance *n.* a vehicle for carrying people who are ill or injured.

ambush *vb.* hide and wait for someone so that you can take them by surprise. *n.* a hiding place for a surprise attack.

amen *n.* an expression used to show agreement, especially at the end of a prayer.

amend *vb.* correct, make improvements.

amethyst *n.* a semiprecious stone; a purple variety of quartz.

amicable *adj.* kindly, friendly.

ammonia *n.* a strong chemical, often used for cleaning purposes.

ammunition (*am-mu-***ni**-*shun*) *n.* bullets and other projectiles that are fired from guns.

amnesia *n.* loss of memory.

amnesty *n.* general pardon, especially of prisoners.

amoeba *n.* a one-celled animal that moves about by changing its body shape.

among *prep.* in the middle of; together with a group.

amorphous (*am-***or**-*fuss*) *adj.* shapeless.

amoral *adj.* neither moral nor immoral; without a sense of morality.

A

amount *n.* the total sum; a quantity. *He needed a large amount of money to buy the car.*

ampere *n.* a unit for measuring the strength of an electrical current.

ampersand *n.* the sign (&) which means *and*.

amphibian *n.* an animal that lives both in water and on land. *A frog is an amphibian.*

amphitheater *n.* in Roman times an arena surrounded by tiers of seats, used for sporting events.

amphora *n.* (plural **amphorae**, **am**-*for-eye*) a Greek jar with two handles.

ample *adj.* enough, plenty.

amplifier *n.* electrical equipment used to make sounds louder.

amputate *vb.* (surgical) cut off a limb. **amputation** *n.*

amuse *vb.* make someone smile or laugh. **amusement** *n.* **amusing** *adj.*

anachronism *n.* a person, event or thing that is historically/chronologically out of place. *Napoleon rode to Waterloo in a jeep.*

anaconda *n.* the longest and heaviest snake in the world. Some have reached 30 feet in length.

anagram *n.* a word or phrase made up with the letters of another in a different order. *Alps is an anagram of slap.*

analyze *vb.* examine in detail. **analysis** (plural **analyses**) *n.*

anarchy *n.* without government; disorder.

anatomy *n.* the science of the structure of the body, learned by dissection (cutting up) of dead bodies.

ancestor *n.* forefather, a person now dead, from whom one is descended. *His ancestors lived in this house for hundreds of years.* **ancestral** *adj.* **ancestry** *n.*

anchor *n.* a heavy iron hook on a long chain. *An anchor is dropped into the water to stop a boat moving.* *vb.* secure a ship with an anchor.

anchovy *n.* small fish of the herring family, and with a strong flavor.

Amphibians such as this newt spend part of their lives in water and part as land animals.

ancient (**ayn**-shent) *adj.* very old or very long ago.

and *conj.* a link word expressing addition to what has gone before.

anecdote *n.* a very short story, account of an amazing or amusing nature.

anemia *n.* a lack of red blood cells. **anemic** *adj.*

anemometer *n.* instrument used to measure air speed or pressure.

anemone (*an-em-on-ee*) *n.* cultivated or woodland flower of which there are many species.

anesthetic *n.* a drug used so that people do not feel pain during an operation.

angel *n.* a messenger from God. **angelic** *adj.*

anger *n.* bad temper, fury, rage. **angry** *adj.*

angle *n.* the space between two straight lines or surfaces that meet.

Anglican *n.* member of the Church of England or an episcopal church in communion with it.

Anglo- *prefix* meaning English, e.g. **Anglo-French Treaty**.

anguish *n.* extreme distress.

animal *n.* any living thing that is not a plant.

animosity *n.* extreme dislike, hatred.

ankle *n.* the joint between the leg and the foot.

annex *vb*. seize, take possession of (territory). **annex** *n*. additional building.

annihilate *vb*. destroy completely.

anniversary *n*. a day on which an event is remembered each year, like the anniversary of a wedding.

announce *vb*. tell; declare; make known; present (a person or event). *She announced that she was leaving at once.* **announcement** *n*. **announcer** *n*. (especially in radio) a person who reads the news.

annoy *vb*. make someone cross or angry, irritate.

annual 1. *adj*. happening every year. *Christmas is an annual event.* 2. *n*. a plant that lives for one year only.

annul *vb*. abolish, cancel.

anoint *vb*. smear with oil, especially in a religious ceremony.

anomaly *n*. exceptional or irregular condition.

anonymous *adj*. without (the person's) name. *The author of this poem is anonymous.*

anorak *n*. a waterproof jacket, now usually made of plastic material, with a hood; parka.

anorexia *n*. a chronic lack of appetite for food.

another *adj*. one more; a different one. *Have another glass of lemonade. That is quite another thing.*

answer 1. *n*. & *vb*. reply to a question. 2. *n*. the solution to a problem.

ant *n*. a small insect that lives with many other ants.

antagonism *n*. hostility, dislike. **antagonist** *n*. opponent. **antagonize** *vb*. cause dislike, hostility.

Antarctic *adj*. & *n*. (of) the south polar regions.

ante- *prefix* meaning before, e.g. **antenatal** before birth, **anteroom** a room leading into another room.

anteater *n*. a toothless mammal of South America. It has a tapering snout specially shaped for getting ants, etc.

antelope *n*. an animal like a deer with upward-pointing horns.

ANTELOPES

A

Hartebeest

Greater kudu

Sable antelope

Four-horned antelope

A

antenna (plural **antennae** *an-ten-ee*) *n.* 1. one of a pair of feelers on an insect's or a lobster's head. 2. an aerial.

anthropology *n.* the study of all aspects of people.

anti- *prefix* meaning against or opposed to, e.g. **anticlimax**, **anticlockwise**.

antibiotic *n.* a drug which helps destroy harmful bacteria. *Penicillin is an antibiotic.*

anticipate *vb.* 1. expect. *We did not anticipate that you would get here so quickly.* 2. do something first. *Do not anticipate the question before I have finished asking it.* **anticipation** *n.*

antifreeze *n.* a substance used to lower the freezing point of water in car engines.

antique (*ant-eek*) 1. *adj.* very old. 2. *n.* a very old object. *Antiques are often valuable.*

antiseptic *n.* & *adj.* a substance, such as chlorine, that kills certain kinds of germs. *The doctor cleaned the child's cut knee with an antiseptic.*

antithesis *n.* the opposite of something or contrast of ideas.

antler *n.* the branched horn of a deer.

antonym *n.* a word which has the opposite meaning to another, e.g. long, short.

anvil *n.* a block on which a blacksmith hammers metal into shape.

anxiety *n.* uneasy feeling of uncertainty. **anxious** *adj.*

any *adj.* some. *I haven't got any money.*

anybody *n.* (also **anyone**) any person; no matter who. *Can anybody tell me the time?*

Anzac *n.* & *adj.* Australian and New Zealand Army Corps in the First World War.

apart *adv.* away from each other; distant. *Our houses are two miles apart.*

apartheid *n.* in South Africa the political system of total separation of Europeans from other races.

apartment *n.* a set of rooms used for dwelling in a building.

apathy *n.* lack of interest, indifference.

ape *n.* 1. a large monkeylike animal with no tail. 2. *vb.* imitate, mimic.

aperture *n.* opening or gap.

aphid *n.* tiny soft-bodied insect which does great harm to plants.

apologize *vb.* express regret for doing something wrong. **apology** *n.*

apostle *n.* any of the 12 chosen by Jesus Christ to preach the Gospel.

apostrophe (*a-pos-trofee*) *n.* a punctuation mark, like this ('). It is used when letters are left out (*don't* means *do not*) or when "s" is added to a word to show ownership. *That is John's bicycle.*

appall *vb.* horrify or shock greatly. *She was appalled by his rude behavior.*

apparatus *n.* equipment designed for a particular use.

apparent *adj.* obvious, clear.

apparition *n.* unusual or unexpected sight; a ghost.

appeal *vb.* 1. call for, make an earnest request. *The police appealed for witnesses to the crime.* 2. be attractive. *The idea appeals to me.*

appear *vb.* 1. come into sight. *A man appeared through the mist.* 2. seem to be. *A microscope makes things appear larger.* **appearance** *n.*

appease *vb.* calm, soothe.

appendicitis *n.* painful inflammation of the appendix.

appendix *n.* 1. part of the intestines. 2. addition to a book, at the end.

appetite *n.* the desire for food; hunger.

applaud *vb.* clap one's hands as a sign of enjoying something; praise. **applause** *n.*

apple *n.* the edible fruit of the apple tree.

appliance *n.* a piece of equipment for a special purpose, e.g. an attachment to a vacuum cleaner for cleaning difficult corners.

apply *vb.* 1. ask for something. *He applied for a job in the local factory.*

2. be relevant. *That rule does not apply in this case.*

appoint *vb.* choose someone to do a particular job.

appointment *n.* a time agreed for a meeting.

appreciate *vb.* value highly, think much of; rise in value. *Paintings appreciate rather than depreciate in value the longer you keep them.*

appreciative *adj.* showing gratitude.

apprentice *n.* a person learning a craft or trade from an employer. **apprenticeship** *n.*

approach 1. *vb.* go near. *They approached the house.* 2. *n.* access; the means of getting to a place. *The approach to the house was through a forest.*

approve *vb.* express a good opinion of.

approximate *adj.* nearly correct. *I can give you the approximate cost.*

apricot *n.* an orange-yellow fruit with a big, hard seed.

April *n.* the fourth month of the year.

apron *n.* a piece of cloth or plastic worn in front of and over clothes to keep them clean.

apse *n.* a semi-circular end to a church.

apt *adj.* suitable.

aptitude *n.* talent or ability.

aqualung *n.* breathing apparatus for swimming under water.

aquarium *n.* a place where fish and other water animals and plants are kept and studied. **Aqua** is the Latin name for water.

aquatic *adj.* growing or living in water; taking place in or on water.

aqueduct *n.* a channel or pipe for carrying water, often a bridge, across a valley.

arc *n.* a curved line; part of a circle.

arcade *n.* row of arches supported by columns.

arch *n.* a curved structure of stones that can support a load, used to cover an opening such as a doorway or the ceiling of a church.

arch- *prefix* meaning chief, principal, e.g. **archbishop**, **archvillain**.

archaeology (**ark**-*i-ology*) *n.* the study of history through the things that people have made and built. **archaeologist** *n.*

archaeopteryx *n.* a prehistoric bird about the size of a crow, with teeth like a lizard.

archaic (*ar-***kay**-*ik*) *adj.* ancient, no longer in use, antiquated.

archer *n.* a person who shoots with a bow and arrow.

archery *n.* the sport of shooting with a bow.

archipelago (*ark-i-***pel**-*ago*) *n.* a group of islands; an area of sea containing many islands.

architecture *n.* style of buildings. **architectural** *adj.*

archives (**ark**-*ives*) *pl. n.* public records; place where the records are kept. **archivist** *n.* person who keeps the records.

Arctic *adj.* & *n.* (of) the North Polar region.

ardor *n.* enthusiasm, warmth. **ardent** *adj.*

arduous *adj.* difficult to do.

area *n.* 1. the size of a surface. Areas are measured in units such as square feet, square yards and acres. *A football field is about 5300 square yards in area.* 2. part of a country or the world. *They come from the Detroit area.*

arena *n.* a sports stadium; originally the enclosed space in which the Ancient Roman games took place.

argue (**arg**-*yoo*) *vb.* dispute; give reasons why you support something. *They argue their case well.* **argument** *n.* reason put forward. **argumentative** *adj.* fond of arguing.

The part of the circle in red is the arc.

A

A suit of armor

arid *adj*. dry; parched with heat.

arise *vb*. get up; come up for consideration.

aristocracy *n*. nobility.

arithmetic *n*. sums; the science of numbers.

ark *n*. 1. ship or large boat, particularly Noah's Ark. 2. the wooden chest in which the Jewish Tablets of the Law were kept (the Ark of the Covenant).

arm 1. *vb*. give weapons to. *They will arm the soldiers with the latest weapons.* 2. *n*. part of the body from the shoulder to the hand.

armada *n*. a Spanish word for a great fleet of armed ships.

armadillo *n*. a small South American mammal protected by a shield of bony scales.

armed forces *pl. n*. the army, navy and air force of a country.

armistice *n*. a truce, an agreement to stop fighting.

armor *n*. a covering, usually made of metal, that protects the body in battle.

army (plural **armies**) *n*. a large number of soldiers.

aroma *n*. a smell – usually pleasant or belonging to something in particular.

arose past of **arise**.

around 1. *adv*. on all sides. *She looked around but could see nobody.* 2. *prep*. in a circle; in all directions. *We walked around the old town.*

arouse *vb*. wake up, stir to action.

arrange *vb*. fix or organize something; put things in order. **arrangement** *n*.

array *n*. arrangement, display. *There was a lovely array of flowers on the table.*

arrest *vb*. take a suspected criminal into custody.

arrive *vb*. reach a place. *The train arrived at the station.* **arrival** *n*. reaching a place.

arrogant *adj*. exaggerating one's own importance; conceited.

arrow *n*. a pointed stick that is shot from a bow.

Boltheads for the crossbow

Longbow arrow

Crossbow bolt

Arrowheads for the longbow

arsenal *n.* a place where weapons and ammunition are stored or made.

arsenic *n.* a chemical element, a form of which (white arsenic) is extremely poisonous.

arson *n.* a name used in law for the crime of deliberately setting fire to property.

art *n.* drawing, painting and modeling, and the things that are made that way.

artery *n.* one of the tubes that carries blood from the heart to all parts of the body.

arthritis *n.* painful inflammation of a body joint causing severe stiffness.

arthropod *n.* group of animals which includes insects, spiders and crabs.

artichoke *n.* name applied to two different plants: (Jerusalem) plant with edible tuber; (globe) thistle-like plant the flowerhead of which is eaten.

article *n.* 1. any object. 2. a passage in a newspaper, encyclopedia, etc. 3. the words "a, an" (indefinite article) and "the" (definite article).

articulate *adj.* 1. clear and distinct of speech. *vb.* speak clearly. 2. having joints. *An articulated truck. vb.* connect by joints.

artificial (*art-i-fish-el*) *adj.* not natural, made by people and machines; not grown. *Natural rubber comes from the juice of a tree, but artificial rubber is made from coal.*

artillery *n.* the big guns used by an army.

artist *n.* a person who draws, paints, or carves. **artistic** *adj.*

as 1. *adv.* to the same extent. *Please do it as soon as possible.* (Also used in proverbial phrases. *The baby was as good as gold.*). 2. *conj.* because. *As she is sick, you will have to go.*

asbestos *n.* the name given to a group of minerals that occur naturally as fibers. Because asbestos does not burn, it is used for fireproof materials.

ascent *n.* the act of going up a slope or hill.

ascertain (*ass-sur-tane*) *vb.* find out, make sure.

ash *n.* 1. the powder that is left after something has been burned. 2. a tall tree with grayish bark and tough white wood.

ashamed *adj.* feeling guilty or disgraced.

ashen *adj.* pale, ash-colored.

Ash Wednesday first day of Lent in the Christian Church.

aside *adv.* apart; on one side. *I shall put this book aside for you.*

ask *vb.* put a question, enquire; make a request. *She asked her boss for more pay.*

asleep *adj. & adv.* the state of sleeping; not awake. *They were all asleep in bed when the phone rang.*

asp *n.* a small poisonous snake.

aspect *n.* a view, a look; the direction in which a house faces.

asphalt *n.* a brown or black tarry substance, used for surfacing roads.

aspidistra *n.* indoor plant with broad pointed leaves.

aspiration *n.* ambition. **aspire** *vb.* aim high.

aspirin *n.* a drug used to reduce pain.

ass *n.* a donkey, especially a wild one.

assassinate *vb.* murder a public figure. **assassin** *n.*

assault *vb.* attack someone. *n.* an attack.

assemble *vb.* collect together a number of people or things; put the parts of something together to make a whole. **assembly** *n.*

assent *vb.* agree. *n.* formal consent.

assert *vb.* declare, maintain.

assign *vb.* appoint; give someone a share. **assignment** *n.* a task.

assist *vb.* help someone. **assistance** *n.*

association *n.* a group of people or organizations that works together. **associate** *vb.* join, connect.

assorted *adj.* mixed, various.

assume *vb.* 1. take for granted as true. *We assume the facts are correct.* 2. take upon oneself. *She has assumed far too much responsibility.* **assumption** *n.*

A

assure *vb*. promise, make certain. *She assured me that she had posted the letter.*

asterisk *n*. a star-shaped mark (★), often used in books to refer to footnotes.

astern *n*. at or behind the stern, or rear, of a boat.

asthma *n*. a medical condition which causes wheezing and difficulty in breathing.

astonish *vb*. amaze; surprise.

astound *vb*. surprise, shock.

astray *adv*. in the wrong direction; lost. *My notes seem to have gone astray.*

astrology *n*. the study of the stars in order to predict the future.

astronaut *n*. a traveler in space.

astronautics *n*. the science of space travel.

astronomy *n*. the study of the sun, planets, moon and stars. **astronomer** *n*. a student or expert in astronomy.

astute *adj*. shrewd, crafty.

asylum *n*. refuge, shelter. Once a place for treating people with mental illness.

ate *vb*. past of **eat**.

atheist *n*. a person who does not believe that there is a God. **atheism** *n*. disbelief in God.

athlete *n*. someone who is good at sports or games that need strength or speed. **athletic** *adj*.

atlas *n*. a book of maps.

atmosphere *n*. the air around the earth.

atoll *n*. a coral island with a central lagoon, or lake.

atom *n*. the smallest particle of a chemical element.

atrocious *adj*. cruel, wicked; very bad. **atrocity** (*at-tross-ity*) *n*. wicked act; (*casual*) ugly object.

attach *vb*. fasten or join one thing to another.

attack *vb*. try to hurt a person or capture a place. *The soldiers planned to attack the castle.*

attain *vb*. reach, arrive at, accomplish. **attainment** *n*. accomplishment.

In a solid state, atoms pack tightly.

In a liquid, atoms move about.

In a gas, atoms move about a lot.

Everything is made of atoms – all solids, liquids and gases.

attempt *vb*. try to do something. *Jack will attempt the climb tomorrow.*

attend 1. *vb*. be present. **attendance** *n*. 2. *vb*. give thought to. *Please attend to what I am saying.* **attention** *n*.

attic *n*. a room just below the roof.

attire *n*. clothes, costume. *vb*. to clothe.

attitude *n*. way of thinking, opinion.

attorney *n*. 1. lawyer. 2. person authorized to act on behalf of someone else in legal matters etc.

attract *vb*. pull toward; have an appeal for. **attraction** *n*. **attractive** *adj*.

auburn *n*. a reddish-brown color. *She had auburn hair.*

auction *n*. a public sale at which the asking price is raised until a buyer is found. *vb*. sell by auction. **auctioneer** *n*.

audible *adj*. loud enough to be heard.

audience *n*. people who watch a play or listen to music together; a formal interview.

audition *n*. trial hearing of a musician, actor, etc.

auditorium *n*. part of concert hall or theater where audience sits.

August *n*. the eighth month of the year.

aunt *n*. the sister of your mother or father. Also your uncle's wife.

austere *adj*. stern; without luxury; severe. **austerity** *n*.

authentic *adj*. genuine, reliable.

author (**aw**-*ther*) *n*. a person who writes a book or a play.

authority *n*. 1. power over others. 2. an expert. *She was an authority on Shakespeare.*

auto- *prefix* meaning self, e.g. **automobile** (self-moving).

autobiography *n*. the story of a person's life written by that person.

autograph *n*. someone's name written in their own handwriting. *Georgia collected the autographs of famous authors.*

automatic *adj*. working without being looked after, like an automatic washing machine.

automation *n*. the control by machine of the process of manufacturing goods.

automobile *n*. a passenger car.

autopsy *n*. post-mortem, examination of a body after death.

autumn *n*. the season of the year between summer and winter. **autumnal** *adj*.

avail *vb*. help, benefit.

available *adj*. obtainable, ready to be used.

avalanche *n*. a great mass of snow and rocks sliding down a mountain.

avarice *n*. greed for wealth or gain.

avenge *vb*. take vengeance; get satisfaction for a wrong by punishing the wrongdoer.

avenue *n*. a road with trees on both sides; a broad street in a town.

average 1. *adj*. normal; usual. 2. *n*. a mathematical word. To find the average of 2, 4 and 6 you add them together and divide by 3. The answer is 4.

averse *adj*. opposed to; unwilling.

aviary *n*. a place in which birds are kept, often a large cage or a building containing cages.

aviation *n*. (science of) flying in a powered plane.

avid *adj*. eager, greedy.

avocado *n*. a pulpy green fruit with a large stone which grows on several kinds of tropical trees.

avoid *vb*. keep out of the way of someone or something; fail to do something. *He decided that she was deliberately avoiding him.*

await *vb*. wait for someone or something.

awake *adv*. not sleeping.

award *vb*. give someone a prize or distinction. *n*. a prize.

aware *adj*. conscious; knowing. *Aware of dangers.*

away *adv*. 1. at a distance; far off. *Do not throw anything away.* 2. continuously. *Sing away.*

awe *n*. respect mixed with fear. *The soldier stood in awe of the general.*

awful *adj*. terrible; dreadful; nasty.

awkward *adj*. clumsy; uncomfortable; difficult.

awning *n*. covering, often of canvas, to protect against weather.

ax *n*. a tool for chopping wood.

axle *n*. the rod on which a wheel turns.

ayatollah *n*. a Moslem religious leader.

azure *n*. & *adj*. the unclouded sky; sky-blue.

B

babble *vb*. chatter, prattle.

baboon *n*. a large kind of monkey.

baby *n*. a very young child. also **babe**.

baby-sitter *n*. a person who is paid to look after a child or children while the parent(s) are out.

bachelor *n*. an unmarried person; someone who has taken first university degree – *B.A.*, *B.S.* (Bachelor of Arts, Bachelor of Science), etc.

backdrop *n*. part of stage scenery hung across the rear of a stage.

back 1. *n*. the part of the body from the neck to the buttocks. 2. *n*. the side opposite the front. 3. *vb*. move backward. *Ask her to back up the car.* 4. *vb*. support. *I back your decision.* 5. *vb*. bet on. *She backed a loser.*

backbone *n*. the bones that run down the back of a skeleton; the spine.

backer *n*. a supporter.

backgammon *n*. a game for two people played on a board with 15 light and 15 dark pieces which are moved according to the fall of dice.

background *n*. the part of a scene or picture that is behind all the rest or in the distance; a person's education, etc.

backstage *adv*. behind the scenes at the theater.

backward *adv*. toward the back, opposite of forward. *adj*. directed backward; slow in learning.

bacon *n*. smoked or salted meat from a pig.

bacteria *pl. n*. tiny living things that can only be seen with a powerful microscope.

bad *adj*. not good; faulty; wicked.

badge *n*. something worn by a person, usually with a picture or message on it; an emblem. *Badges often show that a person belongs to a school or club.*

badger *n*. a burrowing nocturnal mammal with a white mark on its forehead.

badly *adv*. incorrectly; to a serious extent. *The house badly needs repairing.*

badminton *n*. a game that is played with rackets like tennis, but with a shuttlecock instead of a ball.

baffle *vb*. bewilder, mystify.

bag *n*. a sack or pouch; a handbag; the animals or birds a sportsman has shot. *vb*. capture, seize.

bagel *n*. a hard glazed doughnut-shaped roll.

baggy *adj*. hanging loosely.

bagpipes *n.pl*. a musical instrument with a windbag and pipes.

bail 1. *n*. money or other security given to free an accused person before trial. *He was released on bail of $1000.* *vb*. (out) secure temporary release of; drop from aircraft by parachute. 2. *vb*. scoop water out of a boat.

bait *n*. food used to attract fish or animals so that they can be caught. *vb*. set a trap; tease.

baize *n*. woolen cloth, often green, used to cover a table.

bake *vb*. cook in the oven.

baker *n*. a person who makes cakes and bread and sells them. **bakery** *n*. a place where bread is baked and may be sold.

baking powder *n*. a white powder used in cooking to make cakes light and spongy.

balalaika *n*. triangular stringed instrument.

balance 1. *vb*. keep steady. *Roger balanced the book on his head*. 2. *n*. an instrument for weighing.

balcony *n*. a platform or gallery attached to an outside wall.

bald (rhymes with *called*) *adj*. without hair. **baldness** *n*.

bale *n.* a large bundle. *vb.* pack into bundles.

ball *n.* 1. a round object, often used in games. 2. a dance.

ballad *n.* a simple poem or song that tells a story.

ballast *n.* a heavy material, such as sand or water, used to fill the storage areas of an empty cargo ship.

ballerina *n.* a female ballet dancer.

ballet (**bal**-*ay*) *n.* a stage show that usually tells a story with dance and music.

ballistics *pl. n.* the study of the movement of bullets, shells, and other projectiles.

balloon *n.* a bag of thin material filled with air or gas.

ballot *n.* a method of voting secretly.

ballpoint *adj. & n.* a kind of pen with a ball in place of a nib.

balm *n.* a healing ointment; a soothing influence. **balmy** *adj.* mild.

bamboo *n.* giant, woody tropical grass.

ban 1. *n.* a prohibition; something that is forbidden. 2. *vb.* forbid; outlaw. *Cars are banned in the park.*

banal *adj.* commonplace, trite. **banality** *n.*

banana *n.* a long, thin tropical fruit with a yellow skin when ripe.

band *n.* 1. a thin strip of material for fastening things together. 2. a group of people who do things together. 3. a group of musicians.

bandage *n.* a strip of material for covering a wound. *vb.* tie up with a bandage.

bandicoot *n.* a rat-like marsupial of Australia and New Guinea.

bandit *n.* a robber, often working in a group or band.

bandy 1. *adj.* having curved legs. 2. *vb.* hurl from one person to another.

bang 1. *vb.* beat violently. 2. *n.* a sudden loud noise.

banish *vb.* send away from (a country); exile. **banishment** *n.*

banister(s) *n.* rail(s) up the sides of staircases.

Hot-air balloons use the difference in weight between hot air inside the balloon and colder air outside to obtain lift.

banjo *n.* a stringed musical instrument with a long and round body.

bank *n.* 1. sloping ground. 2. land along the side of a river. 3. a place where people keep money; a business that specializes in money. **banker** *n.* someone in the business of banking.

bankrupt *n. & adj.* (someone) unable to pay debts. *vb.* make bankrupt.

banner *n.* a flag.

banns *pl. n.* official announcement of an intended forthcoming marriage read aloud in church.

banquet (**bang**-*kwet*) *n.* a feast or official dinner with speeches.

baptism *n.* the Christian ceremony of christening someone, usually a child, by pouring water on their forehead. **baptize** *vb.* give baptism.

bar 1. *n.* a long piece of hard

B

material. 2. *n.* counter at which refreshments are served; a room with a bar serving drinks. 3. *vb.* to stop someone going through. *The man tried to bar our way into the park.*

barbarian *n.* a rough, uncivilized person. (In the Ancient World a barbarian meant anyone who was neither Greek nor Roman). **barbaric** *adj.* cruel. **barbarity** *n.* savage cruelty.

barbecue *n.* a frame for roasting meat, etc.; an outdoor party at which such food is cooked and served. *vb.* roast food on a barbecue.

barber *n.* a person who cuts men's hair.

bare 1. *adj.* naked; not covered. 2. *vb.* expose. *The dog bared its teeth.* 3. *adj.* empty. *The room looked bare without its furniture.* **barely** *adv.* only just, scarcely.

bargain 1. *n.* something bought cheap. 2. *vb.* haggle; argue over the price.

barge 1. *n.* a flat-bottomed boat used on canals and rivers. 2. *vb.* knock into.

baritone *n.* & *adj.* male singing voice between tenor and bass.

bark 1. *n.* & *vb.* the sharp noise made by a dog. 2. *n.* outer covering of a tree.

barley *n.* a cereal plant.

bar mitzvah *n.* Jewish boy of 13; the religious ceremony for the boy.

barn *n.* a farm building for animals or for storing grain or hay.

barnacle *n.* a small sea creature with a soft body surrounded by hard, bony plates.

barometer *n.* an instrument for measuring air pressure.

baron *n.* a lord; a peer. (In Britain a baron is the lowest rank of the peerage.) **baroness** *n.* female peer in her own right or the wife of a baron.

baroque *n.* & *adj.* a heavily decorated European style of architecture about 1600 to 1750.

barrack *n.* a building where soldiers live.

barracuda *n* large West Indian fish.

barrage *n.* dam built across a river.

barrel *n.* 1. a container with curved sides. 2. the tube of a gun.

barren *adj.* bare, sterile; unable to bear offspring.

barricade *n.* a hastily built fortification across the road. *vb.* fortify in haste.

barrier *n.* a fence or rail; an obstacle.

barrister *n.* a lawyer who can plead in the English courts.

barrow *n.* 1. a small cart, usually with one wheel, used in gardening. 2. a prehistoric burial mound.

barter *vb.* exchange goods for other goods without using money; swap.

base 1. *n.* the part of an object on which it stands. 2. *n.* a headquarters. 3. *vb.* establish, found.

baseball *n.* an American game played with a ball and bat by two teams of nine players each, who compete to score the greatest number of runs in nine innings.

basement *n.* a floor of a building below the ground.

Bar mitzvah is a ceremony for Jewish boys who are thought old enough to obey the commandments of the Jewish religion.

B

bash *vb.* strike violently, smash.

bashful *adj.* shy.

basic *adj.* fundamental, forming the base.

basil *n.* an aromatic herb.

basilica *n.* a church in the form of a long oblong hall with apse at one end and two colonnades; a Roman Catholic church with special privileges.

basin *n.* 1. a container for holding water or other liquid; a bowl for washing one's hands. 2. (in geography) the land drained by a river.

basis *n.* (plural **bases**) foundation; principle.

basket *n.* a container, often made from cane. *Some baskets are used for carrying shopping, while others are used for wastepaper.*

basketball *n.* a game in which two teams of five players each attempt to score points by throwing a ball through one of two metal rings placed above each end of a rectangular court.

bas mitzvah *n.* Jewish girl of about 13; the religious ceremony for the girl.

bass 1. *n.* (rhymes with *case*) lowest male singing voice. 2. *n.* (rhymes with *mass*) a sea fish.

bassoon *n.* a large musical wind instrument that makes low notes.

bastard *n.* an illegitimate child.

baste *vb.* 1. pour fat over roasting meat. 2. to sew with long loose stitches.

bat 1. *n.* a small mouse-like flying animal. 2. *n.* a piece of wood for hitting a ball. *vb.* hit a ball with a bat.

batch *n.* a number of cakes or loaves baked together; a group of things that come together. *We must answer this batch of letters.*

bath *n.* a large basin for washing the whole body.

bathe *vb.* swim or wash. **bather** *n.*

bathroom *n.* a room containing a bath, for washing.

bathyscaphe *n.* an underwater vessel for exploring the ocean depths.

batik *n.* an Eastern method of producing designs on cloth with the use of wax and dyes.

baton *n.* the stick a conductor uses to beat time for an orchestra.

batter 1. *vb.* hit very hard. 2. *n.* a mixture of flour, eggs and milk cooked to make pancakes etc.

battery (plural **batteries**) *n.* 1. a container for storing electricity. 2. *n.* two to six guns which work together.

battle *n.* a fight between two armies. *vb.* fight, struggle. *The wind was so strong, we had to battle against it.*

battleship *n.* a large, heavily armored naval ship with batteries of guns.

bauxite *n.* a clay which is the chief source of the metal aluminum.

bay 1. *n.* part of the seashore that makes a wide curve inward. 2. *n.* a kind of laurel. 3. *n.* a recess, e.g. a bay window. 4. *vb.* cry made by hounds. 5. *n.* & *adj.* reddish-brown horse.

bayonet *n.* a blade which can be attached to the end of a rifle.

bazaar (*be-***zar**) *n.* 1. a market in Eastern countries. 2. a sale to raise money.

BC *abbr.* time before Jesus Christ was born.

be *vb.* have some quality; exist. *When will you be free?*

A noctule bat.

beach *n.* the shore between the high and low tide marks; the edge of the sea or lake.

beacon *n.* a warning or signal light or fire.

bead *n.* a small piece of wood, glass or other material with a hole through it. *Beads are threaded on string to make necklaces and other jewelry.*

beagle *n.* small hound used in hunting hares.

beak *n.* the hard outer part of a bird's mouth.

beaker *n.* a large cup with no handle; a glass vessel used in chemistry.

beam 1. *n.* a big heavy bar used as a support in a building or in a ship. 2. *n.* a ray of light, like *the beam of a torch*. 3. *vb.* smile widely.

bean *n.* the fruit or seed of certain plants, eaten as food, and related to peas. *Broad beans; green beans; French beans, etc.*

bear 1. *n.* a large kind of furry mammal. 2. *vb.* tolerate, support or put up with something. *I can't bear the thought of it.* 3. *vb.* give birth to.

beard *n.* hair that grows on the lower part of a man's face.

bearing *n.* 1. way a person acts or moves. 2. relative position. 3. part of a machine that supports moving parts and reduces friction.

beast *n.* an animal.

beat 1. *vb.* hit hard and often. *The cruel man beat the boy.* *n.* throb, pulse, rhythm. 2. *vb.* conquer or defeat. *John beat me at table tennis.*

beauty *n.* good looks, loveliness. *She was famous for her beauty.* **beautiful** *adj.* **beautify** *vb.*

beaver *n.* a furry, flat-tailed mammal that lives on land and in the water.

became *vb.* past of **become**.

because *conj.* as a result of; for the reason that. *Do it because I say so.*

beckon *vb.* call by signs, make a silent signal.

become *vb.* grow to be. *He has become a strong athlete.*

bed *n.* 1. something to sleep on. 2. a place where flowers are planted. 3. bottom of the sea or river.

bedding *n.* sheets, blankets, etc.; straw, etc., for cattle to lie on.

bedeck *vb.* decorate, adorn.

bedouin *n.* a wandering desert tribe of Arabs.

bedroom *n.* a room with a bed or beds.

bee *n.* an insect that makes honey. *People keep bees in a beehive.*

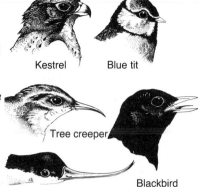

Kestrel — Blue tit — Tree creeper — Blackbird — Avocet

Birds' beaks have many shapes. Kestrels have hooked bills to tear flesh. Tits have small strong bills to hammer nuts. Blackbirds use their slim bills to feed on worms. The avocet skims the mud surface with its upturned bill.

beech *n.* a smooth, silvery-barked, glossy-leaved tree.

beef *n.* the meat of cattle. **beefy** *adj.* thickset, strong.

beehive *n.* a small box where bees are kept.

been *vb.* past participle of **be**.

beer *n.* alcoholic drink made from malted barley, flavored with hops. *Ale and lager are both kinds of beer.*

beet *n.* a plant with an edible root, a variety of which is used to make sugar.

A green tiger beetle.

beetle *n.* an insect with hard wing covers.

before 1. *prep.* in front of. *Age before beauty.* 2. *conj.* at an earlier time; previous to. *They ran away before I could stop them.*

beg *vb*. ask earnestly for help, especially for money. **beggar** *n*. someone who begs.

began *vb*. past of **begin**.

begin *vb*. (past **began**; past part. **begun**) start doing something; commence. **beginning** *n*. **beginner** *n*.

behave *vb*. act in a particular way. *Sue behaved very badly at the party*. act well. *Try to behave*. **behavior** *n*.

behead *vb*. cut someone's head off; execute someone in this way.

behind 1. *adv*. somewhere else; at the rear. *I left my book behind*. 2. *prep*. on the other side of something. *The burglar was hiding behind the curtain*.

beige *n. & adj*. a light brown color.

being 1. *n*. a person. *A human being*. 2. *vb. part*. in a certain state or situation. *Stop being so difficult*.

belch *vb*. let out wind from the stomach through the mouth; throw out smoke from a volcano.

belfry *n*. bell tower.

believe *vb*. feel sure about the truth of something. **belief** *n*.

bell *n*. a hollow object which makes a musical sound when struck.

bellow *vb*. shout or roar. *n*. the noise made by a bull.

bellows *pl. n*. hand instrument for pumping air into a fire, etc.

belly *n*. the stomach.

belong *vb*. be someone's property; be owned by someone. *Does this watch belong to you?*

belongings *pl.n*. possessions, one's property.

below *prep. & adv*. underneath; lower than; beneath.

belt *n*. a strap of leather or other material worn around the waist; strap connecting wheels of machinery. *vb*. thrash, beat with a belt.

bench *n*. a long wooden seat, often without a back.

bend 1. *n*. a curve; not straight. 2. *vb*. curve over; lean over from upright.

bene- *prefix* meaning well.

benefit *n*. advantage. *She speaks perfect French because she has the benefit of living in France*. profit; pension, allowance. *vb*. do good for.

bent *vb*. past of **bend**.

bequeath *vb*. leave in a will. **bequest** *n*. what has been bequeathed.

beret (*ber-ray*) *n*. a round flat hat, commonly worn in France and Spain.

berry *n*. a small fruit with lots of seeds.

berserk *adj*. in a violent frenzy.

berth *n*. 1. a bunk or bed in a ship or train. 2. the place where a ship docks. *The ship was tied up at her berth*.

beside *prep*. at the side of, close to.

besides *adv*. as well; in addition.

besiege (*bi-seej*) *vb*. to surround with armed forces.

best *adj*. of the finest quality; very good; excellent. *vb*. defeat; outwit.

bestial *adj*. like a beast; rude; cruel.

bet *vb. & n*. wager; put money on (a horse); assume something to be the case. *I bet you can't climb that garden wall*.

beta *n*. second letter of the Greek alphabet: β

betray *vb*. give someone up, or let them down; deceive. *The spy was betrayed to the enemy*. **betrayal** *n*.

better *adj*. improved; more suitable, recovering or having recovered health; *vb*. make better.

between *prep*. in the middle of. *The player kicked the ball straight between the goalposts*.

beverage *n*. any kind of drink. *Orangeade and beer are both beverages*.

beware *vb*. be warned. *The sign said: "Beware of the dog."*

bewilder *vb*. confuse, puzzle, mystify. **bewildering** *adj*.

beyond *prep*. on the far side of. *Julia's house is beyond the church*.

bi- *prefix* meaning twice or double; appearing or occurring once in every two, e.g. **bilateral** with two sides; **bilingual** speaking two languages; **biped** two-footed animal.

bias *n*. a leaning toward, inclination; prejudice.

B

bib *n.* cloth or plastic shield placed under a child's chin to protect clothing.

Bible *n.* the sacred book of the Christian religion.

bicycle *n.* a two-wheeled vehicle powered by its rider.

bicker *vb.* quarrel in a pointless way.

bid 1. *vb.* offer to pay a price at an auction. 2. *n.* call (in card games). 3. *vb.* command.

bidet (*bee-day*) *n.* a low basin on which one sits to wash the lower part of the body. The word is French for "pony."

big *adj.* large; important.

bigot *n.* a person who obstinately sticks to a belief or opinion.

bikini *n.* a scanty two-piece bathing suit.

bill *n.* 1. a paper showing how much you owe for something you have bought. 2. a bird's beak.

billboard *n.* 1. a flat surface on which bills are posted. 2. the spot on the bow of a ship where the anchor rests.

billiards *n.* a game in which balls are struck by a cue into pockets at the edge of a flat table.

billion *n.* one thousand million (1,000,000,000). Sometimes still used in Britain to mean one million million (1,000,000,000,000).

billow *n.* wave. *vb.* to rise or roll in waves, to bulge or swell out.

billygoat *n.* a male goat.

bin *n.* a storage container, such as a breadbin or dustbin.

binary *adj.* made up of two parts or units. In the binary arithmetic system only two numbers are used, 0 and 1.

bind *vb.* tie; make fast.

binding 1. *n.* book cover. 2. *adj.* obligatory.

bingo *n.* a numbers game, usually with many players.

binoculars *n.* field glasses; an instrument to make things far away look closer. *You look through a pair of binoculars with both eyes.*

bio- *prefix* meaning life or of life.

biography *n.* the written story of a person's life.

biology *n.* the study of living things. **biologist** *n.*

biplane *n.* an aircraft with two sets of wings.

birch *n.* a tree with a slim trunk and branches, and a smooth bark.

bird *n.* the only feathered member of the animal kingdom, with front limbs adapted as wings.

birth *n.* coming into life; emergence of a child or animal from the body of its mother.

birth control *n.* contraception, the prevention of pregnancy.

birthday *n.* the day or anniversary of a person's birth.

biscuit *n.* a small, flat, thin roll.

bisect *vb.* divide into two equal parts.

bishop *n.* 1. a priest in charge of a diocese, or group of parishes. 2. a piece in chess.

bison *n.* an American buffalo.

bit *n.* 1. a small piece. 2. a metal bar that goes in a horse's mouth: part of the bridle. 3. single unit of information expressed in binary numbers, especially for computers.

bitch *n.* a female dog, fox or wolf.

bite *n.* & *vb.* take a piece of something, usually food, with the teeth.

bitter *adj.* sharp, unpleasant taste; not sweet. **bitterness** *n.*

The bison is a large animal of the cattle family. There were once great herds of them in America, where they came to be called "buffalo."

black 1. *n.* the darkest of all colors; the opposite of white. 2. *adj. & n.* belonging to a dark-skinned race.

blackball *vb.* vote against, such as to exclude a candidate by putting a black ball in a ballot box.

blackberry *n.* the fruit of the bramble.

blackbird *n.* songbird related to the thrush.

blackboard *n.* a board, usually painted black, which can be written on with chalk and is used for teaching.

black box *n.* electronic equipment on an aircraft which records details of the flight.

blackcurrant *n.* the small black fruit of a garden plant, much used to make drinks.

black hole *n.* an area in space where the pull of gravity is so strong that nothing can escape, not even light.

blacklist *vb.* to boycott or punish someone.

black magic *n.* evil magic; witchcraft.

blackmail *n. & vb.* the crime of demanding money from someone in return for keeping something secret. *The man said that if I gave him $5 he would keep quiet about the window I broke. This was blackmail.* **blackmailer** *n.*

blackout *n.* temporary loss of consciousness or light.

black sheep *n.* scoundrel; member of a family who is a good-for-nothing.

blacksmith *n.* a person who works with iron and makes shoes for horses.

bladder *n.* the part of the body where liquid wastes gather before they are passed out.

blade *n.* the sharp cutting edge of a knife, razor, sword, etc.

blame *vb.* say that it was the fault of something or someone that something went wrong. *n.* responsibility for bad happening.

blanche *vb.* take the color out of.

bland *adj.* smooth; gentle; mild; dull.

blank *adj.* empty; with nothing written on it.

blanket *n.* a sheet of (usually thick) cloth used as a bed covering.

blare *vb.* make a loud noise; shout. *I can't hear what you are saying with that radio blaring.*

blaspheme *vb.* speak irreverently about God. **blasphemy** *n.*

blast *n.* a strong wind; the shock waves of an explosion.

blast furnace *n.* an enormous oven for producing iron from ore.

blast-off *n.* the moment when a rocket is launched into space.

blatant *adj.* noisy; obvious and obtrusive.

blaze *n.* a bright flame or fire.

blazer *n.* colored jacket, often part of a uniform.

bleach *n. & vb.* make white.

bleak *adj.* exposed, barren and often windswept.

bleat *vb. & n.* the cry of a sheep or goat.

bleed *vb.* lose blood.

blemish *vb.* mark, spoil. *n.* stain; fault.

blend *vb.* mix two or more substances together; go well with something.

bless *vb.* ask God to protect someone or something. **blessing** *n.*

blew *vb.* past of **blow.**

blight *n.* plant disease caused by fungus or insects.

blind 1. *adj.* not able to see. **blindness** *n.* 2. *n.* window cover.

blindfold *adj. & adv.* having the eyes covered with a handkerchief etc. *vb.* cover eyes.

blink *vb.* shut and open eyes rapidly.

blinker *n.* flap on a bridle to prevent a horse from seeing to the side.

bliss *n.* greatest happiness. **blissful** *adj.*

blister *n.* a swelling like a bubble on the skin, filled with a watery fluid.

blitz *n. & vb.* attack, usually sudden, from the air.

blizzard *n.* a snowstorm with very strong winds.

bloated *adj.* swollen, puffy.

B

blob *n.* a drop; small round mass.

block 1. *n.* a large, solid piece of something, e.g. wood or stone. 2. *n.* a large building divided into separate units. 3. *vb.* get in the way of. *A fallen tree can block a road.*

blockade *vb.* & *n.* cutting off of supplies to an enemy.

blood *n.* the red liquid that is pumped around our bodies by the heart.

bloom *n.* flower; first freshness or beauty. *In the bloom of youth.* *vb.* bear blooms; flourish.

blossom *n.* flower or mass of flowers, especially on fruit trees.

blot *n.* an inky stain; a smudge or mark. *vb.* make a blot on.

blouse *n.* a kind of loose shirt, usually worn by women.

blow 1. *n.* a hard knock. 2. *vb.* (past **blew**) make the air move. *The wind blows from the west.*

blubber 1. *n.* whale fat. 2. *vb.* weep excessively.

blue *n.* the color of the sky.

bluebell *n.* a name given to two different kinds of wild flowers: the wild hyacinth and the harebell.

bluebottle *n.* a name given to several species of large fly, having a blue abdomen, and particularly attracted to rotting meat.

bluff 1. *vb.* deceive, make pretense. 2. *adj.* outspoken, blunt.

blunder *n.* & *vb.* (make) a stupid mistake. *John made a blunder when he wrote 10 instead of 100.*

blunt *adj.* not sharp.

blur *n.* smudge; indistinct impression. *vb.* blot, obscure.

blurb *n.* publisher's description of a book usually printed on the jacket.

blush *vb.* become red in the face because you are ashamed or shy.

boa 1. *n.* a family of large snakes, mainly from South America, which kill their prey by crushing it to death. 2. *n.* a long, tube-shaped scarf, made of fur or feathers, once worn by women.

boar (rhymes with *sore*) *n.* a male pig; wild pig.

board 1. *n.* a long, flat piece of wood; a plank. 2. *n.* a flat piece of wood or card used for a special purpose. *A chess board is used for the game of chess.* 3. *n.* an authorized group of people, e.g. board of directors. 4. *vb.* get onto a ship, train or aircraft. *We must board the plane now.*

boast *vb.* talk about how good you think you are, brag.

boat *n.* a small or medium-sized vessel used for traveling on water. (The term "ship" is used for larger vessels such as liners and warships.)

boater *n.* hard, flat straw hat.

boatswain (**bo-***sun*) *n.* a senior seaman who controls the work of other seamen.

body *n.* 1. the visible part of a person or animal. 2. a group of people. 3. the main part of something. 4. an astronomical object. *A star is sometimes called a heavenly body.* **bodily** *adj.* of the body.

bodyguard *n.* person employed to protect someone.

bog *n.* spongy ground, a marsh.

bog down *vb.* overwhelm with work.

bogus *adj.* false, sham.

boil 1. *vb.* heat a liquid until it bubbles and steams. 2. *n.* painful, infected swelling on the body.

boisterous *adj.* noisy, lively.

bold *adj.* showing no fear.

Bolshevik *n.* a member of the Russian revolutionary party that seized power in 1917. **Bolshevism** *n.*

bolt 1. *n.* a metal fastening on a door or window. 2. *n.* a metal pin with a screw at one end that goes into a nut to fasten things. 3. *vb.* run away quickly. 4. *vb.* fasten with bolts.

bomb *n.* a container filled with explosive. *vb.* attack with bombs. **bomber** *n.* aircraft using bombs.

bombard *vb.* attack with gunfire; abuse.

bond *n.* 1. something that links or connects. *The close bond of friendship.* 2. a written promise to pay a sum or carry out a contract.

bone *n.* the hard framework that

supports the flesh and organs of all vertebrates (animals with backbones). *vb.* remove bones from. *She boned the fish.*

bonfire *n.* a big fire made in the open air.

bonnet 1. *n.* a woman's or baby's headdress tied on by strings.

bonny *adj.* pleasant, healthy-looking.

bonsai (*bon*-**sigh**) *n.* dwarf tree grown in a pot; an art which was developed in Japan.

bonus *n.* something extra; money paid in addition to wages or dividends.

book 1. *n.* pages of – usually – printed paper bound together in a cover. 2. *vb.* reserve a ticket or place.

bookkeeper *n.* a person who looks after business accounts and keeps them in order.

bookmaker *n.* someone who makes a living by taking bets on horse races, etc.

bookworm *n.* 1. an avid reader. 2. a grub that eats holes in books.

boom 1. *n.* & *vb.* deep, hollow sound. 2. *n.* period of great commercial activity. 3. *n.* a spar or pole attached at one end to a mast to stretch the foot of a sail.

boomerang *n.* a throwing stick used by Australian aborigines for hunting. *vb.* recoil like a boomerang.

boon *n.* benefit, blessing.

boost *vb.* help on (by shoving); raise voltage. **booster** *n.* auxiliary motor in a rocket.

boot *n.* a sort of shoe that also covers the ankle and sometimes the leg. *vb.* kick.

booty *n.* plunder, spoils.

border *n.* 1. the part near the edge of something. 2. the land near the line dividing two countries.

bore 1. *vb.* drill out; make a hole in. 2. *vb.* make someone weary with uninteresting conversation. *n.* a boring person; someone who does not know when he or she is not wanted. **boredom** *n.* 3. *n.* inside

diameter of a gun barrel.

borrow *vb.* get something from someone else which you use and then give back. The other person *lends* it to you.

bosom *n.* breast. **bosom friend**. intimate friend.

boss *n.* 1. the chief person in an organization; the person you work for. 2. a stud or ornament in the center of a shield.

botany *n.* the study of plants and how they grow. **botanist** *n.*

botch *vb.* patch badly, make a bungle of something.

both *adj.* & *pron.* the two together. *She invited both of us to her party.*

bother 1. *vb.* worry, annoy. *n.* a nuisance. 2. *vb.* take the trouble. *Why should I bother to telephone?*

bottle *n.* a container, usually made of glass, in which liquid is kept. *vb.* put in bottles.

bottom 1. *n.* the lowest part of something. *adj.* lowest, last. *Bottom drawer.* 2. *n.* a person's seat or backside.

The curved boomerang, shown here with an aborigine shield, is used for sport and hunting.

bough *n.* the branch of a tree.

bought *vb.* past of **buy**.

boulder *n.* a large rock rounded by action of water, etc.

bounce *vb.* spring up again like a ball that is dropped on the ground.

bound *vb.* past of **bind**.

B

boundary *n*. 1. the border or frontier of a country; a line separating one place from another. 2. the edge of a field.

bounty *n*. gift, bonus.

bout (*bowt*) *n*. turn, attack, fit (of illness).

bovine *adj*. oxlike; stupid.

bow (rhymes with *low*) *n*. 1. a piece of wood curved by a tight string. *A bow is used for shooting arrows.* 2. a knot with loops. 3. a stick with long hairs attached to it, which is used for playing musical instruments like violins.

bow (rhymes with *cow*) 1. *n*. the front of a ship. 2. *vb*. & *n*. bend at the waist to greet an important person.

bowels *pl*. *n*. the part of the body where solid wastes gather; intestines.

bower *n*. dwelling, retreat, shelter.

bowl 1. *n*. a deep dish or basin. 2. *vb*. roll a ball in the game of bowling.

bowler *n*. 1. person bowling. 2. hard hat with round crown.

bowling *n*. any of several games in which balls are rolled on a green or down an alley at an object or group of objects.

box 1. *n*. a hollow, container, often made of wood or cardboard. *vb*. put in a box. 2. *vb*. fight with the fists. 3. *n*. a small evergreen tree or shrub which has hard yellowish wood.

boxer *n*. 1. a person who fights with the fists; one who boxes. 2. a kind of dog related to the bulldog.

boxing *n*. sport of fighting with fists.

boy *n*. a young male person.

boycott *vb*. refuse to speak to someone; have nothing to do with. *n*. the act of boycotting someone or something.

boyhood *n*. time of being a boy.

brace 1. *n*. a carpenter's tool. 2. *n*. a pair or couple, especially of game. 3. *vb*. tighten, support, make firm.

bracelet *n*. a band worn around the arm or wrist.

bracing *adj*. invigorating.

bracken *n*. a kind of fern.

bracket *n*. 1. a support to hold a shelf. 2. one of a pair of marks [ ] used to enclose words or mathematical symbols. *vb*. enclose with brackets.

bradawl *n*. small tool used for boring.

brae (*Sc.*) *n*. a hill.

braid *vb*. plait, interlace.

braille (rhymes with *sail*) *n*. raised letters that a blind person can read by touching them.

brain *n*. the gray matter in the head which controls the work of the body, and with which you think; the intellect itself. **brainy** *adj*. clever.

braise *vb*. stew in a covered pan.

brake *n*. something that is pressed against a wheel to stop it turning. *vb*. apply the brake.

bramble *n*. a blackberry bush.

branch *n*. 1. one of the arm-like parts of a tree growing out of the trunk. 2. a division of a large business or service organization, family, etc.

brand 1. *vb*. to burn the owner's symbol on the hide of cattle with a hot iron. 2. *n*. a make of goods. 3. *n*. a poetic word for a sword.

brandish *vb*. wave about, especially a weapon.

brandy *n*. an alcoholic drink distilled from wine.

brass *n*. a bright, yellowish metal made by mixing copper and zinc.

brave 1. *adj*. fearless. *vb*. meet boldly without fear. **bravery** *n*. 2. *n*. an American Indian warrior.

brawl *n*. a rowdy quarrel. *vb*. quarrel noisily.

brawn *n*. muscular strength.

bread *n*. a food made from flour and baked in an oven.

breadth *n*. width, broadness, distance from side to side.

break 1. *vb*. smash. 2. *n*. a rest. *When she had finished her work, she took a break.* 3. *n*. in pool or billiards, a series of scoring strokes.

break down 1. *vb*. (of a piece of machinery) to stop working.

2. separate something into the parts it is made up of. *It's quite a big job, but if we break it down sensibly, we can do it.*

breaker *n.* heavy ocean wave which breaks on rocks or shore.

breakfast *n.* the first meal of the day, usually eaten in the early morning.

breakthrough *n.* major advance in science, etc.

breakwater *n.* a structure built in the sea, usually near a harbor, to break the force of the waves.

bream *n.* a freshwater or sea fish.

breast (rhymes with *rest*) *n.* the milk-secreting organ in mammals; the chest of a person or an animal.

breathalyser *n.* device for measuring the amount of alcohol in the blood.

breathe (*breeth*) *vb.* take air into the lungs and let it out again. **breath** (*breth*) *n.* air drawn in and expelled by lungs.

breed 1. *n.* animals that produce others of exactly the same kind. *The Labrador is a breed of dog.* 2. *vb.* produce young ones.

breeze *n.* a gentle wind.

brevity *n.* briefness, shortness in speech or writing. *Brevity is the soul of wit.*

brewery *n.* a place where beer is brewed, or made. **brew** *vb.* make beer.

bribe *n.* money or something else offered to obtain some services – usually dishonest or illegal. *vb.* offer a bribe.

brick *n.* a block of hardened clay used in building.

bride *n.* a woman who is about to be married or who has just been married. **bridal** *adj.* of a bride or wedding.

bridegroom *n.* a man who is about to be married or who has just been married.

bridesmaid *n.* a girl who helps a bride at her wedding.

bridge 1. *n.* a structure that enables people or vehicles to cross a road, river or other obstacle. *vb.* span a space with a bridge. 2. *n.* platform

suspension

arch

Different types of bridges.

cantilever   beam

on a ship for navigating, etc.
3. *n.* the name of a card game for four players.

bridle *n.* the harness that goes on a horse's head, including the reins.

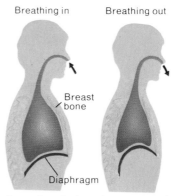

Breathing in   Breathing out

Breast bone

Diaphragm

As you breathe in and out, a muscular sheet – the diaphragm – contracts and relaxes, increasing and decreasing the volume of your lungs. Air is breathed in through the mouth and nose. It passes into the windpipe or trachea. This divides into two bronchi, *which enter the lungs and divide into a number of smaller tubes called* bronchioles.

31

B

brief 1. *adj*. lasting for a short time only. *The meeting was a brief one.* 2. *n*. an instruction, particularly to a lawyer.

brigand *n*. a robber.

bright (rhymes with *bite*) *adj*. 1. shiny, cheerful. 2. clever. **brightness** *n*.

brilliant 1. *adj*. very bright. *A brilliant star shone between the clouds.* 2. *adj*. very clever. **brilliance** *n*.

brim *n*. 1. the edge of a cup or container. *The bucket was full to the brim.* 2. the projecting edge of a hat.

bring *vb*. fetch or carry.

bring up *vb*. care for a child as it grows.

brink *n*. the edge of something, such as a river or precipice.

brisk *adj*. lively, alert.

bristle 1. *n*. a short stiff hair. 2. *vb*. become angry.

brittle *adj*. easily snapped or broken.

broad *adj*. wide, a long way across.

broadcast 1. *vb*. & *n*. send out in all directions, particularly by radio or television. 2. *vb*. scatter seed.

broaden *vb*. make or become broader.

broccoli *n*. hardy variety of cauliflower.

brochure *n*. pamphlet or booklet.

brock *n*. a badger.

broke, broken *vb*. past and past part. of **break**.

bronchitis *n*. inflammation of the windpipe, resulting in coughing, wheezing and shortness of breath.

brontosaurus *n*. a giant dinosaur which lived 150 million years ago.

bronze *n*. a reddish-brown metal made from mixing copper and tin.

Bronze Age the time between the Stone Age and the Iron Age when people made weapons and tools of bronze.

brooch (rhymes with *coach*) *n*. a piece of jewelry that is pinned onto clothing.

brood *n*. birds hatched at the same time. *vb*. sit on eggs; meditate deeply; worry about.

brook *n*. a small stream.

broom *n*. 1. a brush with a long handle. 2. yellow-flowered shrub.

broth *n*. a thin soup.

brother *n*. a son of the same parents as someone; member of a religious order, trade union, etc.

brought *vb*. past of **bring**.

brow *n*. the forehead; top of a hill in a road. **browbeat** *vb*. bully.

brown *n*. & *adj*. the name of a dark color between black and orange; the color of earth.

brownie *n*. 1. a small friendly elf. 2. a junior Girl Scout.

bruise (*brooze*) *n*. a blue-black mark on the skin caused by an injury, a fall, etc. *vb*. inflict bruises.

brush 1. *n*. implement with bristles for sweeping, smoothing hair, cleaning teeth, etc. *vb*. use a brush. 2. *n*. fox's tail.

brute *n*. an animal; unkind person. **brutal** *adj*. inhuman; unfeeling; merciless.

bubble *n*. a thin skin of liquid filled with a gas.

buccaneer *n*. a pirate who plundered Spanish ships in America in the 17th and 18th centuries.

buck 1. *n*. a male deer or rabbit. 2. *vb*. (of a horse) kick up the heels.

bucket *n*. an open container with a handle, often used for carrying water.

buckle *n*. & *vb*. a fastener, usually on a belt or strap; to fasten with a buckle.

bud *n*. a young flower or leaf before it opens. *vb*. sprout buds.

budge *vb*. move slightly; shift.

budgerigar *n*. a brightly colored Australian bird, similar to a small parrot.

budget *n*. financial statement or forecast of revenue and expenditure for a specific period. *vb*. (for) allow for in a budget.

buffalo *n*. in Asia, a kind of wild ox; in North America, a bison.

buffet (*buff*-**fay**) 1. *n*. refreshment bar; meal set out on a table from which people help themselves.

2. *vb.* & *n.* (**buff**-*ut*) strike, knock about.

bug *n.* one of a group of insects with a mouth that can prick and suck.

bugle *n.* a musical instrument, usually made of brass or copper, similar to a trumpet but without the stops, and mainly used for military calls or signals.

build (rhymes with *milled*) *vb.* make something by putting different parts together. *This bird builds its nest from twigs and feathers.* **building** *n.* a structure with roof and walls.

building site *n.* the place where a building is being built.

built *vb.* past of **build**.

bulb *n.* 1. an electric lamp. 2. the roundish underground stem of some plants, like onions.

bulky *adj.* large and clumsy.

bull *n.* a male of the cattle family or a male elephant.

bulldog *n.* a breed of muscular, short-haired English dog.

bulldozer *n.* a heavy tractor for clearing land.

bullet *n.* a piece of shaped metal made to be shot from a handgun.

bullion *n.* bars of gold or silver before being turned into coins, medals, etc.

bullock *n.* castrated bull.

bully *vb.* & *n.* a person who uses his or her strength to frighten other, weaker people.

bulrush *n.* a tall plant that grows near water.

bumblebee *n.* a large hairy bee that hums noisily.

bump 1. *vb.* knock into something. *n.* a collision, a jolt. 2. *n.* a lump or swelling.

bumper 1. *adj.* large or abundant. *A bumper crop of wheat.* 2. *n.* the bars or fenders that protect the front and back of a car.

bun *n.* a kind of small round cake or bread roll.

bunch *n.* a number of things of the same kind together, like a *bunch of grapes.* *vb.* make into a bunch.

bundle *n.* a number of things wrapped up together. *vb.* tie into a bundle.

bungalow *n.* a house with all its rooms on the ground floor.

bungle *vb.* blunder; do something awkwardly.

bunion *n.* a lump or inflamed swelling on the big toe.

bunk *n.* a narrow bed fixed to the wall, often one above the other.

buoy (**boo**-*ee*) *n.* an anchored float marking a channel or a reef for ships. **buoyant** *adj.* apt to float; cheerful.

burden *n.* & *vb.* a load; difficulty to bear.

burglar *n.* a person who breaks into a house to steal. **burglary** *n.* **burgle** *vb.*

burial *n.* burying of a dead body; a funeral.

buried *vb.* past of **bury**.

burly *adj.* large and sturdy.

A bulb is a very short stem with closely packed, fleshy food-storing leaves. New bulbs are formed in between the base of the leaves.

B

burn 1. *vb.* (past and past part. **burnt, burned**) destroy or damage something by fire. *n.* injury or mark caused by burning. 2. *n.* (*Sc.*) a brook; stream.

burrow *n.* a hole made in the ground by an animal as a home. *vb.* make or live in a burrow.

burst *vb.* break apart suddenly, or explode. *The balloon burst with a loud bang.*

burst in or **into** *vb.* rush in. *Jane burst into the room.*

bury *vb.* put something in the ground; hide away.

bus *n.* a motor vehicle for carrying large numbers of people (short for "omnibus" – a Latin word meaning "for all").

bush *n.* a shrub; a small thick tree.

bushman *n.* a native of the southern African deserts.

business (**biz-*ness***) 1. *n.* a shop or organization. 2. *n.* a person's work or occupation. *My father's business is running a bookshop.*

bust *n.* 1. a statue of a person's head and shoulders. 2. a woman's breast. 3. *adj.* (*slang*) bankrupt; penniless. *They all lost their jobs when their company went bust.*

bustle *vb.* hurry (or make others hurry) about. *n.* excited activity.

busy (*bizzy*) *adj.* having a lot to do.

but *conj.* however; on the other hand.

butcher *n.* a person who kills or cuts up animals to sell their meat.

butler *n.* head manservant in a household.

butt *vb.* to hit with the head.

butter *n.* a soft, yellow food made from fats contained in cream. *vb.* spread butter.

buttercup *n.* a small wild flower with yellow petals.

butterfly *n.* an insect with large colorful wings. Unlike the moth, it flies during the daytime.

buttock *n.* one of the two fleshy parts of the bottom or backside.

button *n.* a small round object, made of plastic, leather, horn, etc., which is used for fastening clothes.

buttress *n.* a prop, support built against a wall. *vb.* support, strengthen.

buy *vb.* (past **bought**) purchase something; obtain goods in exchange for money.

buzz *vb.* make a noise like a bee.

buzzard *n.* the name of a family of birds of prey related to the falcon.

by *prep.* along; through; during; as a result of. *Little by little. By the way. By force.*

by-election *n.* an election held to fill a vacancy caused by death or resignation.

bystander *n.* a spectator.

byre *n.* cow shed.

Right: The amazing change from a caterpillar into a butterfly. A caterpillar's life is spent feeding and growing. From time to time it sheds its skin, to show a larger skin underneath. When fully grown it attaches itself to a suitable place with silk threads. It sheds its skin once more. This time the skin hardens into the case of a chrysalis or pupa. Inside the pupa amazing changes take place until an adult butterfly appears and flies away.

cab *n*. 1. a taxi. 2. the part of a truck or locomotive in which the driver sits.

cabbage *n*. a vegetable with thick green leaves growing very close together.

cabin *n*. 1. a room in a ship or aircraft. 2. a hut; a simple house.

cabinet *n*. 1. a cupboard or similar piece of furniture. 2. the senior members of a government.

cable *n*. 1. a strong wire or rope; a bundle of telegraph wires. 2. an overseas telegram. *vb*. send a message by cable.

cackle *vb*. & *n*. noise made by a hen; silly talk; foolish laughter.

cactus *n*. (plural **cacti**) a prickly desert plant with a thick green stem.

caddie *n*. a person who carries clubs for a golfer.

caddy *n*. a small tea container.

cadet *n*. a young person studying to become a member of the armed forces or the police.

cadge *vb*. beg; take advantage of someone's generosity.

café (*caf*-**fay**) *n*. a place where food and drink is sold; a small restaurant.

cage *n*. a box with bars in which birds or animals are kept. *vb*. keep in a cage.

cake *n*. a sweet kind of food made from flour, butter, eggs, sugar, etc., and baked in an oven; a hard mass (of soap, etc.).

calamity *n*. a disaster, terrible misfortune.

calcium *n*. a metallic chemical element (symbol – Ca) present in many rocks and minerals such as limestone and gypsum. Calcium is also present in teeth and bones.

calculate *vb*. work out with math, reckon. **calculation** *n*. **calculator** *n*. an electronic machine for doing mathematics.

calendar *n*. a list of the days, weeks and months of the year.

calf (rhymes with *half*) (plural **calves**) *n*. 1. a young cow, seal, elephant or whale. 2. the fleshy back part of the leg below the knee.

call *n*. & *vb*. 1. shout, cry out; summon. 2. speak to on the telephone. 3. name. 4. pay a short

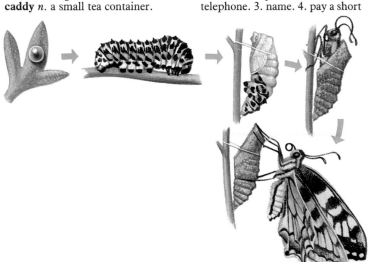

C

visit. **caller** *n.*

call for *vb.* 1. demand. *The committee called for reforms.* 2. go and fetch. *I shall call for you on my way to the match.*

calligraphy (*kal-ig-raf-ee*) *n.* handwriting as an art.

calling *n.* profession; occupation.

call off *vb.* decide not to do something that has been arranged. *The game was called off because the field was flooded.*

calm (rhymes with *palm*) *adj.* quiet, smooth. *vb.* soothe, make or become calm. *n.* stillness.

calorie *n.* a unit of heat. Calories are also used as a measure of the energy produced by food and drink. A person on a diet may need to count the calories in his or her food intake.

calve *vb.* give birth to a calf.

calypso *n.* West Indian song.

came *vb.* past of **come**.

camel *n.* an animal with a long neck and one hump or two on its back.

camellia *n.* evergreen shrub with beautiful rose-like flowers.

camera *n.* an instrument for taking photographs.

camouflage *vb. & n.* disguise of guns, ships, aircraft, and so on with paint, tree branches, or nets so that they cannot easily be seen.

camp *n.* a place where people stay in tents or huts. *vb.* to live in a tent.

campaign *vb. & n.* a series of military or political operations, an organized program.

campus *n.* grounds of a college or university.

can 1. *vb.* be able to. *Can you run faster than me?* 2. *vb.* be allowed to. *You can come and go as you like.* 3. *n.* a metal container; a tin.

canal *n.* a man-made waterway for barges or for taking water to fields.

canary *n.* a small yellow, singing bird which is often kept in a cage as a pet. *adj.* color of a canary.

canasta *n.* a card game of the rummy family.

cancel *vb.* cross out; bring to an end;

call off. *The football game was cancelled.* **cancellation** *n.*

cancer *n.* a name given to a variety of serious diseases; a disease of the bodily cells; a growth or tumor.

candid *adj.* outspoken, sincere, frank. **candor** *n.*

candidate *n.* a person who seeks election or appointment; a person who takes any examination.

candle *n.* a stick of wax with a string or wick through the middle.

candlestick *n.* a holder for a candle.

candy *n.* crystallized sugar; sweets.

cane *n.* the hollow, jointed stem of large reeds and grasses such as bamboo, used to make walking sticks and furniture; walking stick. *vb.* beat with a cane.

canine *n.* of or belonging to a dog.

canister *n.* small box for holding dry products such as tea.

cannibal *n.* a human being who eats human flesh.

canning *n.* a way of preserving food by heating and sealing it in airtight containers. The heat kills any germs in the food. The airtight containers keep out bacteria that make it spoil.

cannon *n.* a big, heavy gun.

canny *adj.* shrewd.

canoe (*can-oo*) *n.* a light boat that is paddled through the water.

canon *n.* 1. a church dignitary. 2. a church decree, rule.

canopy *n.* a covering over a throne, bed, etc.

canteen *n.* restaurant in factory or office.

canter *vb. & n.* an easy gallop on horseback.

cantor *n.* a choir leader, often of the Jewish faith.

canvas *n.* a coarse cloth used for tents and sails. Artists paint on it.

canvass *vb.* go to people and ask them to vote for your political party, etc. *We shall canvass for John Smith.*

canyon *n.* a deep gorge, usually cut through rock by a river.

cap *n.* 1. a soft hat with a peak at the front. 2. a lid.

capable *adj*. able; competent.

capacity *n*. ability; the amount that can be held in something.

cape *n*. 1. a coat with no sleeves, worn over the shoulders. 2. a piece of land that juts out into the sea.

capital *n*. 1. the city where the government of a country works. 2. letters written like this: A, M, R, Z. 3. money with which business is started; accumulated wealth in stocks or shares, etc.

capsize *vb*. overturn, especially in a boat.

capstan *n*. apparatus for winding in cables, etc.

capsule *n*. 1. a small cylindrical case containing medicine. 2. part of a spacecraft.

captain *n*. 1. the officer in charge of a ship. 2. an army officer below a major and above a lieutenant.

caption *n*. the words near a picture which explain what it is.

captivate *vb*. fascinate, charm.

captive *n*. a prisoner.

capture *vb*. take someone prisoner.

car *n*. a motor vehicle.

caramel *n*. burnt sugar used as a flavoring; a kind of toffee.

carat *n*. a measure of weight for precious stones; also used as a measure of the purity of gold.

caravan *n*. 1. a home on wheels, pulled by a car or horse. 2. a group of people traveling together across a desert.

carbon *n*. a nonmetallic element that is found in all living things, both plant and animal. (symbol – C).

carbon dioxide *n*. a gas (symbol – CO_2) that occurs in small quantities in the atmosphere. People and animals breathe in oxygen and breathe out mainly carbon dioxide.

carbon monoxide *n*. a very poisonous gas (symbol – CO) with no smell, which is present in car exhaust fumes.

carburetor *n*. apparatus in internal-combustion engines for mixing air with gas vapor for combustion.

carcass *n*. dead body of an animal.

cardboard *n*. extra-thick card or paper.

cardiac *adj*. of the heart.

cardigan *n*. a knitted woolen jacket.

cardinal *n*. 1. a senior priest in the Roman Catholic Church. 2. a red American songbird.

care *n*. anxiety, concern, serious attention. *vb*. feel concern, anxiety; affection for.

career 1. *vb*. go fast and perhaps dangerously. 2. *n*. the series of jobs or positions that people have during their working life. *He has spent his whole career as a teacher.*

care for *vb*. look after someone; love someone.

careless *adj*. not thinking about what one does.

caret *n*. mark (λ) showing where missing word should be placed in writing.

cargo *n*. (plural **cargoes**) goods carried by ship or aircraft.

caribou *n*. wild reindeer of North America.

caricature *n*. an exaggerated or distorted drawing of someone which makes them appear ridiculous or absurd. *Many political cartoons contain caricatures.*

caries (rhymes with **bear**-*ease*) *n*. decay of tooth.

carnation *n*. a large, brightly colored flower, related to the garden pink.

carnival *n*. a public occasion for making merry. *In New Orleans there is a famous carnival called Mardi Gras.*

carnivore *n*. an animal that eats meat.

carol *n*. a kind of song, usually religious, and sung at Christmas.

carp 1. *n*. large freshwater fish. 2. *vb*. find fault.

carpenter *n*. a person who makes things from wood.

carpet *n*. heavy floor covering of woven or knotted material.

carriage *n*. vehicle, usually with four wheels, pulled by horses; a coach for passengers on a train.

C

carrion n. the decaying flesh of a dead body.

carrot n. a plant with an orange-red root which is used as a vegetable.

carry on vb. continue doing something.

cart n. a two-wheeled vehicle pulled by a horse, ox or other animal.

cartilage (**car**-till-ij) n. a material in the body similar to bone but lighter and more flexible. *You have pads of cartilage in your knee joints.*

cartography n. art of making maps or charts.

carton n. cardboard box.

cartoon n. a funny drawing, often of people in politics. **cartoonist** n.

cartridge n. the case holding the explosive that fires a bullet.

carve vb. 1. shape a piece of wood or stone. 2. cut up meat to serve at a meal.

cascade n. waterfall. vb. fall like a cascade.

case n. 1. a box for carrying things or storing them. 2. an example; an instance. *There was a case of whooping cough in the class.* 3. a trial in a law court. *The man and woman in the case were found guilty.*

cash n. money in paper notes and coins. vb. exchange a check for money.

cashier n. the person who takes in and pays out money in a shop, hotel or other business.

cashmere n. wool from goats of Kashmir.

casino (ka-**seen**-o) n. public building for gambling.

cask n. a wooden barrel, often used for wines or spirits.

casket n. small case for jewels; coffin.

casserole n. vessel in which food is both cooked and served.

cassette n. a container for holding magnetic tape used for recording.

cassock n. long robe, usually black, worn by clergymen.

cassowary n. a large flightless bird of New Guinea and Australia related to the ostrich and emu.

cast 1. vb. throw or fling. 2. vb. give parts in a play. 3. n. an impression or mold, generally done in plaster. *The police made a cast of the footprint.* **casting** n.

castanets pl. n. small wooden instruments held in the hand and clicked as accompaniment to dance.

castaway n. a person left on a distant land, often after the ship has been wrecked.

castle n. a large building with thick walls, fortified against attack.

castrate vb. remove the testicles so that a mammal cannot mate and reproduce.

casual adj. accidental, by chance. *A casual meeting.* informal. *Casual manners.*

An early type of Norman castle known as a motte and bailey. It consisted of a wooden tower on an earth mound connected to a stockaded courtyard or bailey.

casualty *n.* a person who is ill or injured. In warfare, casualties are soldiers who have been killed or wounded.

cat *n.* a small furry domestic animal; any member of the cat family.

catacombs *pl. n.* underground cemeteries containing passageways and crypts for burial of the dead.

catalog (**cat**-*a-log*) *n.* a list of things, such as the pictures in an exhibition or the books in a library.

catalyst (**cat**-*a-list*) *n.* a substance that speeds up a chemical reaction but is left unchanged and so can be used several times for the process of catalysis.

catamaran *n.* a boat with two hulls joined together.

catapult *n.* 1. a Y-shaped stick with a piece of elastic fixed to it. *A catapult is used for throwing small stones.* 2. an ancient weapon for throwing large stones. 3. a device for launching aircraft from an aircraft carrier.

cataract *n.* 1. a waterfall. 2. a condition of the eye, affecting vision.

catarrh *n.* a runny nose; a cold in the head.

catastrophe *n.* a sudden and widespread disaster.

catch 1. *n.* the lock or fastening of a door. 2. *vb.* get hold of something or someone, perhaps after a chase. 3. *vb.* get a disease or illness. *I hope you don't catch my cold.*

category *n.* class or order of something.

caterpillar *n.* the larva stage in the growth of a butterfly or moth.

cathedral *n.* the main church of an area (diocese) in which a bishop or archbishop has his *cathedra* (Latin for "chair").

catkin *n.* the hanging, fluffy flower of the hazel, willow and some other trees.

cattle *pl. n.* heavily built grass-eating mammals which include all oxen and cows.

caught *vb.* past of **catch**.

cauliflower *n.* a kind of cabbage, whose tightly bunched flowers form whitish heads.

cause (rhymes with *saws*) 1. *vb.* make something happen. *My dog was the cause of the accident.* 2. *n.* a principle or ideal to which a person or group of persons is devoted. *Freedom is a noble cause.*

causeway *n.* a raised path through marshland or water.

caution 1. *n.* care; carefulness. *Proceed with caution.* 2. *vb.* warn (especially of the police).

cavalry *n.* soldiers who fight on horseback.

cave *n.* an open chamber in the side of a hill or under the ground.

caveman *n.* a prehistoric human who lived in caves.

caviar *n.* the eggs, or roe, of certain species of fish, especially the sturgeon, prized as a delicacy.

cavity *n.* hole, space within a solid body.

cease *vb.* stop.

cedar *n.* a large, spreading, evergreen coniferous tree.

cede (*seed*) *vb.* surrender, give up.

ceiling (*seeling*) *n.* the roof of a room.

celebrate *vb.* hold a party or other festivity in honor of an important event. **celebration** *n.*

celebrity *n.* famous, celebrated person.

celery *n.* a vegetable plant. It is the crisp stalk-like leaves that are eaten.

cell *n.* 1. a small room in a monastery, convent, or prison. 2. a very small unit of living matter in animals and plants.

cellar *n.* an underground room for storing things.

cello (*chello*) *n.* a stringed instrument like a large violin. **cellist** *n.*

cellulose *n.* the substance that gives plants their rigidity or stiffness.

Celsius *adj.* another name for centigrade scale on a thermometer, named after its inventor, Anders Celsius.

cement *n.* a gray powder that, when mixed with water, becomes hard.

cemetery n. a place (not a churchyard) where people are buried-

cenotaph n. monument to persons buried elsewhere.

census n. a counting of all the people in a country.

cent n. an American, Australian, Canadian or New Zealand coin. *There are 100 cents in a dollar.*

centaur n. an imaginary creature, half man and half horse.

centenary n. a hundredth anniversary. *It was the centenary of the great writer's birth.*

center (rhymes with *enter*) n. the middle part or point of something.

centi- *prefix* meaning 100 or one hundredth.

centigrade scale n. a temperature scale on which water freezes at 0° and boils at 100° (symbol – **C**).

centimeter n. a metric measure of length. *There are 100 centimeters in a meter.*

centipede n. a wormlike creature with a long body and many legs.

central adj. at or near the center. *Andy lives in central Birmingham.*

centrifugal force n. an outward force produced by a body rotating in a circle.

centurion n. a Roman soldier in command of a *century* (100 men).

century n. 1. 100 years. 2. a company of soldiers in ancient Roman army. 3. a group of 100 like things.

ceramic n. & adj. concerning pottery or **ceramics** pl.n.

cereal n. grain crops such as maize, rice or wheat used for food; breakfast food made from grain.

ceremony n. a dignified occasion; religious rite. *The wedding ceremony took place in an old church.*

ceremonial adj. with ceremony, formal.

certain adj. 1. sure. *I am certain they will come soon.* 2. some. *Certain people are color blind.* **certainty** n.

certificate n. a piece of paper that is proof of something. *Nicola was given a certificate to show she had swum five lengths of the pool.*

certify vb. declare officially.

chaff 1. n. husks of corn which need to be separated from the grain. 2. vb. make fun of someone (now slightly old-fashioned).

chaffinch n. small songbird.

chain n. a line of rings joined together. *The rings in a chain are called "links."*

chair n. a piece of furniture for sitting on.

chairman n. a person who presides over a meeting. Also **chairwoman** and **chairperson.**

chalet (*shall*-lay) n. Swiss house of wood with overhanging roof.

chalk n. a kind of soft white rock; white material used for writing on a blackboard.

challenge n. & vb. question, as a sentry; question truth of; invite to fight.

chameleon (*"ch"* spoken like *k*) n. type of tree lizard living mainly in tropical Africa.

champagne (*sham-*pain) n. sparkling white wine.

champion n. the overall winner. vb. defend, uphold.

championship n. a competition to find the best person or team.

chance n. a possibility of something happening. *Leroy has a good chance of becoming champion, but Eric has no chance at all.*

chancel n. part of church near the altar used by choir and clergy.

chancy adj. risky.

change 1. vb. make something different. *The girls changed their hairstyles.* 2. n. the money given back when you give too much money for something you are buying. *I bought a loaf of bread and the assistant gave me change for my dollar.*

channel n. 1. a narrow strip of water joining two seas. 2. a narrow passage, natural or artificial, for water to run through.

chant n. & vb. recite in a half-singing style; intone.

chaos (**kay**-*oss*) *n.* utter confusion. **chaotic** *adj.*

chapel *n.* a small church, or part of a large church.

chaperon (**shap**-*er-own*) *vb.* & *n.* an older person in charge of a child at parties, etc.

chaplain *n.* clergyman attached to an institution or the armed forces.

chapter *n.* one section of a book.

char 1. *vb.* to scorch. 2. *n.* a cleaning lady (short for charwoman). 3. *n.* a charred substance.

character *n.* 1. the things that make you the person you are. *Margaret's character was so pleasant that everyone liked her.* 2. one of the people in a book or play. *Little Red Riding Hood is a character in a children's story.*

charade (*sha*-**raid**) *n.* game in which syllables of a word are acted out separately, the whole word being guessed at by the audience.

charcoal *n.* a form of carbon made by heating wood with little air present.

charge 1. *vb.* rush forward and attack. 2. *vb.* ask a certain price for something. 3. *n.* manage, be responsible for. *Simon was left in charge of the department while the manager was out.*

chariot *n.* a horse-drawn vehicle used for fighting and racing long ago. **charioteer** *n.* driver of a chariot.

charity *n.* help and kindness given to others.

charm *n.* something that has magic power. *He carried a rabbit's foot charm.* **charming** *adj.* very attractive; delightful.

chart *n.* 1 a sea map for sailors, showing the sea depth, the position of buoys, rocks, etc. 2. information shown by a diagram or graph.

chase *vb.* run after and try to catch.

chasm ("*ch*" spoken like *k*) *n.* wide hollow, gap.

chat *vb.* & *n.* talk in a friendly way. **chatty** *adj.*

château (*sha*-**tow**) *n.* the French word for castle.

chatter *vb.* 1. talk nonstop about unimportant things. 2. (of teeth) rattling together from fear or cold.

chauffeur (*show*-**fur**) *n.* someone paid to drive an employer's car.

chauvinism *n.* exaggerated and blind patriotism; passionate support for a cause.

cheap *adj.* not expensive; low in price (and therefore with a suggestion of poor quality). **cheapen** *vb.* make or become cheap.

cheat *vb.* act dishonestly in order to help oneself. *n.* someone who cheats.

check *vb.* 1. make sure that something is right. *Did you check that all the windows were closed?* 2. stop or hold back for a short time. *He was checked in the goal area, but still managed to shoot. n.* 3. a piece of paper which, when filled in and signed, tells a bank to pay money to someone.

cheek *n.* 1. the fleshy part of your face on either side of your mouth. 2. impudence. **cheeky** *adj.*

cheer *vb.* 1. make happy; comfort. 2. shout joyfully.

cheerful *adj.* looking and feeling happy.

cheese *n.* a food made from milk.

cheetah *n.* a spotted, feline animal found mostly in East Africa. It is the world's fastest mammal.

chef (*sheff*) *n.* a head cook who is in charge of a large kitchen.

chemical (**kem**-*ical*) *n.* a substance used in chemistry.

chemist (**kem**-ist) *n.* a person who is trained in chemistry.

chemistry *n.* a branch of science that is about what substances are made of and how they work together.

cherish *vb.* value highly, treat with affection.

cherry *n.* the small round fruit of the cherry tree.

chess *n.* a game for two people, each with 16 pieces (chessmen), played on a board of 64 squares.

41

C

chest *n.* 1. a large, strong box with a lid. 2. the upper part of the front of one's body.

chestnut *n.* a large tree with prickly fruits containing shiny, red-brown nuts (chestnuts).

chew *vb.* crush food in your mouth with your teeth.

chic (*sheek*) *adj.* elegant, very smart.

chick *n.* a baby bird.

chicken *n.* a young hen. *adj.* (*slang*) cowardly.

chicken pox *n.* a disease that causes red itchy spots on the skin.

chief 1. *n.* a ruler or leader. 2. *adj.* most important; main. *Farming is the chief industry in many countries of the world.*

chilblain *n.* a painful swelling that sometimes forms on people's hands and feet in cold weather.

child *n.* young person (plural **children**).

chill 1. *vb.* cool. 2. *n.* a cold or fever. **chilly.** *adj.*

chime *vb.* & *n.* set of tuned bells.

chimney *n.* a structure in a building that allows the smoke from a fire to escape.

chimpanzee *n.* an African ape.

chin *n.* the lowest part of the face, below the mouth.

china *n.* fine clay baked and glazed, made into plates, cups and so on.

chink 1. *n.* narrow opening, gap. 2. *n.* & *vb.* sound of glasses or coins hitting together.

chintz *n.* glazed cotton cloth printed with flower patterns.

chip *n.* 1. a small piece broken off something. 2. a tiny electronic device, usually made of silicon, that holds a circuit with thousands of transistors.

chipmunk *n.* a small member of the squirrel family.

chips *pl. n.* slices of fried potato.

chiropodist (*ki-*rop*-o-dist*) *n.* person who treats feet, e.g corns and toenails.

chisel *n.* a sharp tool used for shaping wood, stone, etc. *vb.* cut or shape with a chisel.

chivalry (**shiv**-*al-ree*) *n.* medieval system of knighthood; gallantry, courage, etc.

chive *n.* herb related to the onion.

chlorine *n.* a yellow-green, poisonous, choking gas used in the manufacture of bleach, hydrochloric acid; small quantities are used to kill germs in drinking water (symbol – Cl).

chlorophyll ("*ch*" spoken as *k*) *n.* green coloring matter found in plant cells.

chocolate *n.* food or drink made from the ground and roasted beans from the cacao tree.

choice *n.* the act of choosing; the thing chosen.

choir (*kwire*) *n.* a group of people trained to sing together.

choke 1. *vb.* not able to breathe because of something in your throat or lungs. 2. *vb.* block something up. 3. *n.* a control on a car that helps it start when the engine is cold.

choose *vb.* decide between two or more possibilities; to come to a decision.

chop 1. *vb.* cut into pieces, often with an ax. 2. *n.* a thick slice of meat with a bit of bone in it.

chopsticks *pl. n.* a pair of sticks held in one hand and used in Oriental countries for eating.

chord (*kord*) *n.* group of musical notes sounded together.

chore *n.* job about the house; dull, unenjoyable work.

choreography (*ko-ree-*og*-rafee*) *n.* the art of arranging the steps and movements of a dance. **choreographer** *n.*

chorus (**kore**-*rus*) *n.* choir, band of singers; part of a song that everyone sings after a solo part. **choral** *adj.* of, sung by, a choir or chorus.

christen *vb.* give a name to and receive into the Christian Church; baptize. *Our baby was christened Angela by the priest.* **christening** *n.*

Christian *n.* a believer in and follower of the teachings of Jesus Christ.

Christianity *n.* the religion that was started by Jesus Christ.

Christmas *n.* the festival on December 25 celebrating the birth of Jesus.

chromium *n.* a hard white metal that does not rust (symbol – *Cr*).

chromosome *n.* a tiny threadlike structure, several of which occur in a cell nucleus and contain genes (hereditary instructions).

chronic *adj.* (of diseases) lasting, recurring; (*casual*) bad, boring.

chronicle (**kron**-*ic-al*) *n.* record of events in the order they happened. *vb.* write a chronicle.

chronometer *n.* a very accurate clock used as a navigational instrument to determine longitude at sea or in the air.

chrysalis *n.* a stage in the development of an insect between caterpillar and adult. *The caterpillar turned into a chrysalis, and then it became a butterfly.*

chunk *n.* thick lump or block.

church *n.* a building used by Christians for worship (from a Greek word meaning "belonging to the Lord").

churchyard *n.* the land surrounding a church, usually used as a burial ground.

churn *n.* vessel for making butter. *vb.* stir or agitate violently.

chutney *n.* flavoring for food, usually made from mangos, chillies, and other ingredients.

cider *n.* the juice of fruit; as in apple cider.

cigar *n.* tobacco rolled in a tobacco leaf for smoking.

cigarette *n.* a small roll of tobacco in thin paper for smoking.

cinder *n.* piece of partly burned coal or wood.

cinema *n.* a theater where moving pictures are shown.

cinnamon *n.* a spice from the bark of the Ceylon laurel tree; light yellow-brown color of cinnamon.

cipher see **code**.

circa *prep.* a Latin word meaning about and used mainly with dates. It is usually abbreviated to *c.*, e.g. *c.* 1782.

circle *n.* a round flat shape, the line about this shape.

circuit *n.* 1. a circular journey. 2. the path of electric current.

circular 1. *adj.* in the shape of a circle; round. 2. *n.* a letter or other document sent to a number of people.

circulate *vb.* move or send around.

circulation *n.* 1. movement of blood around the body. 2. number of copies of a newspaper sold.

circum- (*sur-come*) *prefix* meaning round, about, e.g. **circumnavigate** sail around; **circumstance** everything surrounding an act, event, etc.

circumcision *n.* the cutting away of the foreskin of the penis. This is practiced by many religions, but is especially important to the Jews.

circumference *n.* the distance around the outside of a circle.

circus *n.* a traveling show with clowns, animals and acrobats, usually held in a tent.

citadel *n.* fortress protecting a city.

citizen *n.* 1. a person who lives in a town or city. 2. a person who has every right to live in a particular country. *She was an American citizen.*

city *n.* a large or important town.

civil engineering *n.* the branch of engineering that deals with man-made structures.

civilian *adj.* & *n.* a person who is not in one of the fighting services.

civilization *n.* a group of people in an advanced stage of development.

civilize *vb.* make cultured, enlighten. **civilized** *adj.* living in a well-organized way.

claim *vb.* 1. say that something is yours. *You should claim your prize.* 2. say that something is a fact. *He claims that he can lift great weights.*

clammy *adj.* damp and sticky.

clamor *vb.* & *n.* (make) loud demand, noisy outcry.

clamp 1. *n.* a metal object for

holding things in place. 2. *vb.* fasten with a clamp.

clan *n.* a group of families who claim to share the same ancestor.

clap *vb.* applaud by smacking one's hands together.

clapper *n.* tongue or striker of bell.

claret *n.* a red wine from Bordeaux. Also its color.

clarify *vb.* make clear, explain.

clarinet *n.* a musical wind instrument with a single reed.

clarity *n.* clearness.

clash 1. *n.* a loud noise; the noise made by banging cymbals. 2. *vb.* (of colors) go badly together.

clasp 1. *n.* a fastening, such as a buckle or brooch. 2. *vb.* hold tightly. *They clasped hands.*

class *n.* a group of the same kind of people, e.g. children who are taught together. *I go to the class at the ballet school.*

classic *adj.* & *n.* 1. established quality of excellence, especially in art. 2. of ancient Greece and Rome and their cultures. **classical** *adj.* of ancient Greece or Rome.

clause (*klawz*) *n.* 1. part of a sentence. 2. section in a document.

claustrophobia (*klaws-tro-*foab*-ia*) *n.* fear of being in enclosed spaces.

claw *n.* a pointed nail on an animal's foot.

clay *n.* a soft kind of earth that gets hard when baked.

clean *adj.* not dirty; bright. *vb.* remove dirt from something.

clear *adj.* easy to see through. *The glass was clear.* easy to understand. *The meaning of the word was quite clear.* free from obstacles. *Before you cross, see that the road is clear. vb.* make or become clear.

clematis *n.* a climbing shrub.

clement *adj.* showing mercy; gentle, mild, soft. **clemency** *n.*

clerk (rhymes with *jerk*) *n.* a person who works in an office writing things down.

clever *adj.* bright; intelligent.

cliché (*klee-*shay) *n.* commonplace, unoriginal expression, idea, etc.

cliff *n.* a very steep, high bank, especially by the sea.

climate *n.* the usual weather of a place over a long period.

climax *n.* the high point of a piece of music, drama, expedition, holiday, etc. *The climb to the top of the castle walls formed the climax of the school visit.*

climb *n.* & *vb.* go up, sometimes using both hands and feet to hold on.

cling *vb.* hang on to something.

clinic *n.* a small hospital, for outpatients.

clip 1. *vb.* & *n.* a fastener or device for holding things together. 2. *vb.* cut with scissors, cut short.

clipper *n.* a fast sailing ship of the mid-1800s.

cloak (rhymes with *poke*) *n.* a loose coat with no sleeves; a long cape.

cloakroom *n.* a place to leave your coat.

clock *n.* a machine for telling the time.

clockwise *adj.* going around in the same direction as the hands of a clock. **counterclockwise** going around in the opposite direction to a clock.

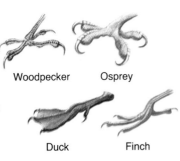

Woodpecker   Osprey

Duck   Finch

Birds' claws tell us about their way of life. The osprey's hooked claws, for example, are for grasping food.

Labels on image: Cirrus, Cirrostratus, Cirrocumulus, Altostratus, Altocumulus, Stratocumulus, Cumulus, Nimbostratus, Cumulonimbus, Stratus

Fluffy cumulus clouds usually mean fine weather, but layers of low stratus clouds bring rain.

clockwork *n.* worked by a spring that is wound up.

clod *n.* 1. lump of earth. 2. lout, blockhead.

clog 1. *vb.* choke, fill up or obstruct. 2. *n.* a wooden shoe, especially in the Netherlands.

cloister *n.* covered way (arcade) open on one side and overlooking a quadrangle.

close 1. *adj.* (rhymes with *dose*) nearby; narrow. 2. *vb.* (rhymes with *nose*) shut; bring to an end.

cloth *n.* a material made by weaving fibers such as wool, linen or nylon.

clothes *pl. n.* things to wear.

clotheshorse frame to dry clothes on.

cloud *n.* great clusters of tiny water droplets in the air.

cloudburst *n.* torrential rainstorm.

clout *n.* heavy swinging blow with the hand; to have power.

clove *n.* the dried bud of the clove tree, used as a spice.

cloven *adj.* divided.

clover *n.* a small green plant, usually with three leaves, which often grows in fields. The flowers are usually red or white. Widely cultivated as animal fodder.

clown *n.* a person who does funny things, especially in a circus.

club *n.* 1. a heavy stick with which to hit things. 2. a group that people can join to do things together. *We have a chess club in our school.*

cluck *vb. & n.* sound made by a hen.

clue *n.* something that helps you to solve a puzzle.

clumsy *adj.* heavy and awkward.

clung *vb.* past of **cling**.

cluster *vb. & n.* number of things growing closely together; a group or bunch.

clutch 1. *vb.* seize or grab eagerly. *n.* a firm hold. 2. *n.* device for engaging and disengaging gears, etc. 3. *n.* nest of eggs.

coach 1. *n.* a four-wheeled horse-

A stagecoach could travel at about 9 mph along well made roads.

drawn carriage; a single-decker bus. 2. *vb.* teach someone, especially a sport. *n.* someone who helps others to prepare for examinations.

coal *n.* a black mineral that burns slowly and gives out heat.

coarse *adj.* rough; not fine.

coast *n.* land along the edge of the sea.

coat *n.* 1. an article of clothing with sleeves that covers the top half of the body; an overcoat. 2. a covering. *That door needs another coat of paint.*

coax *vb.* persuade gently.

cobbler *n.* a person who mends shoes.

cobra *n.* a poisonous snake that can expand its neck into a hood.

cobweb *n.* a fine web made by a spider.

cock *n.* a male bird, especially a farmyard fowl.

cockatoo *n.* a crested parrot.

cockerel *n.* a young cock bird.

cockle *n.* a kind of shellfish.

cockney *n.* a person from the East End of London.

cockpit *n.* the area where the pilot sits in an aircraft; the driver's seat in a racing car. (Originally an enclosed space for contests between fighting cocks.)

cocoa *n.* chocolate powder made from the seeds, or beans, of the cacao tree of South America and West Africa.

coconut *n.* large oval, hard-shelled fruit of the coconut palm.

cocoon *n.* covering made by a caterpillar to protect itself during the chrysalis stage.

cod *n.* a large sea fish eaten as a food.

code *n.* 1. a secret system of writing; cipher. 2. a set of rules. *We should all learn the Highway Code.* 3. a signal system. *Bob learned the Morse code.*

coeducation *n.* education of boys and girls together.

coffee *n.* a drink made from the roasted and ground beans of the coffee plant.

coffer *n.* box or chest for storing money, etc.

coffin *n.* a box in which a dead person is buried or cremated.

cog *n.* one of the teeth around the rim of a gear wheel.

coil *vb. & n.* wind something in circles or spirals. *The old electric heater had two coils of wire that gave off heat.*

coin *n.* a piece of metal, usually of a uniform size and design, used as money.

coincide *vb.* happen at the same time; agree exactly. **coincidence** *n.* combination of events happening by chance at the same time.

coke *n.* what is left of coal after the gases have been removed by heating.

cold 1. *adj.* not hot. 2. *n.* a kind of illness which gives people a runny nose and causes sneezing and a sore throat.

collaborate *vb.* work together (with), cooperate. **collaboration** *n.*

collage (*koll*-adge) *n.* a picture made up of pieces of cloth, paper or other materials.

collapse *vb.* fall down; fall to pieces; *n.* breakdown. **collapsible** *adj.* folding.

collar *n.* part of a shirt or other clothing that goes around the neck; a leather band around an animal's neck.

collect *vb.* gather or bring together. *We collect coins.* gather from a number of people. *They went to the* *houses to collect money for charity.*

college *n.* a place where people go to study after secondary school; part of a university.

collide *vb.* bump into something by mistake. **collision** *n.*

collie *n.* a long-haired breed of sheepdog, originally from Scotland.

collier *n.* a coal miner; a ship that carries coal.

colon *n.* 1. the large intestine. 2. punctuation mark (:).

colonel (**kern**-el) *n.* a senior rank in the army, below that of brigadier, but above lieutenant-colonel.

colony *n.* 1. a group of settlers in a new country who are still governed by their mother country; the country where the settlers live. *Hong Kong is still a British colony.* 2. a group of people or animals that live together. *He came upon a large colony of bees.* **colonial** *adj.* **colonize** *vb.*

color *n.* red, blue, green, etc. *vb.* the act of applying color.

colt *n.* a young male horse.

column *n.* a tall round pillar composed of a base, a shaft and a capital top. The capital is often decorated.

comb *n. & vb.* a small object with "teeth" used by people for making their hair tidy.

combat *n. & vb.* fight; battle.

combine *vb.* join together.

combine harvester *n.* a large farm machine that cuts grain and threshes it.

combustion *n.* another word for burning, a chemical reaction that produces light and heat. **combustible** *adj.*

come *vb.* arrive; draw near. *"Come" is the opposite of "go.".*

come about *vb.* happen. *It came about that we all met at the beach.*

come across *vb.* find something when you do not expect to. *I came across your letter when I was tidying my desk.*

comedy *n.* a funny play. **comedian** *n.* a stage or TV entertainer who tells

jokes or plays comic roles.

comet *n.* a body of (probably) ice and gas, which looks like a star but moves around our sun.

come to *vb.* 1. total cost of several things. *When it is all added together it will come to $17.43.* 2. recover consciousness. *He has just come to after his operation.*

comfort *vb.* help someone who is unhappy. *Sandra comforted the little girl until her mother arrived.* **comfortable** *adj.*

comic 1. *adj.* funny. 2. *n.* humorous illustrated strip or cartoon.

comma *n.* a punctuation mark like this (,) that is used to show a pause or separation in writing.

command 1. *vb.* order someone to do something. 2. *n.* be in charge of. *Napoleon took command of the whole army.*

commence *vb.* begin. **commencement** *n.*

comment *n. & vb.* a remark made about someone or something; an observation. **commentary** *n.* continuous comments on some happening, especially when it is taking place, e.g. a football commentary.

commerce *n.* trade. **commercial** *adj.* concerned with trade. *n.* broadcast advertisement.

commit *vb.* 1. do, carry out. 2. hand over, entrust.

committee *n.* a small group of people who are appointed by a larger group of people to run the larger group's affairs. *Our club's committee meets once a month.*

common *adj.* usual, normal; often seen. *A thrush is a very common bird.*

common sense *n.* good, ordinary, sensible thinking.

communicate *vb.* pass on information or feelings to other people. **communication** *n.* the passing of information from one person to another.

communion *n.* 1. an act of sharing; fellowship; 2. Christian celebration of the Lord's supper.

C

communiqué (*kom-mune-ik-aye*) *n.* an official announcement.

Communism *n.* a political system which holds that all property should be held in common.

community *n.* all the people who live in a place.

commuter *n.* a person who travels some distance daily to and from work. **commute** *vb.*

compact (*kom-pact*) *adj.* packed closely together; easy to handle.

companion *n.* a friend; someone who goes with you.

company *n.* 1. an organization in business to make, buy or sell things. 2. visitors in your house.

compare *vb.* look at things to see how alike or unlike they are. *Roger compared the two chairs and decided to buy the larger one.* **comparison** *n.*

compartment *n.* marked off division of an enclosed space (box, railway carriage, etc).

compass *n.* 1. an instrument that shows direction, used for finding the way. 2. an instrument for drawing circles or for measuring.

compassion *n.* having pity or sorrow for the sufferings of another. **compassionate** *adj.*

compel *vb.* force, make or urge someone to do something.

compensate *vb.* make up for (the loss of). **compensation** *n.* something given to make up for.

compete *vb.* take part in a contest. *All the girls will compete in the race.*

competition *n.* a contest in which a number of people take part to see who is the best.

competent *adj.* able, efficient, qualified. **competence** *n.*

complain *vb.* say that you are not pleased with something. **complaint** *n.* a grievance, protest; bodily illness.

complement *n.* something that fills up, completes, or makes perfect.

complete 1. *adj.* whole; the full number. *When the party was complete, it numbered 16 boys.* 2. *vb.* finish. *It will take three months to complete the new school.*

complex *adj.* complicated, difficult to understand. **complexity** *n.*

complexion *n.* color and appearance of the skin, especially of the face.

complicated *adj.* made up of many different parts; difficult to understand. **complicate** *vb.* make complicated, entangle.

complication *n.* complicated state; new illness developing in the course of another.

compliment *n. & vb.* praise, flattery, formal greeting.

comply *vb.* do as asked or commanded.

compose *vb.* write a story or make up a piece of music. **composer** *n.* a person who makes up music.

compound *n.* something made up of separate parts or elements. *vb.* mix or combine into a whole.

comprehend *vb.* understand; include. **comprehensible** *adj.* intelligible. **comprehensive** *adj.* all-inclusive.

comprise *vb.* include, consist of.

compromise *vb. & n.* a settlement of differences by meeting halfway, each side giving up part of its claim.

computer *n.* an electronic calculating machine that stores information and works with enormous speed.

comrade *n.* a friend; a companion.

concave *adj.* a surface that curves inward, like the inside of a saucer.

conceal *vb.* hide.

concede (*con-seed*) *vb.* give up; grant; allow.

conceive (*con-seeve*) *vb.* become pregnant; think of.

concentrate *vb.* bring together, compress; focus attention on.

concentration *n.* the act of concentrating or giving one's attention to.

conception *n.* 1. becoming pregnant. 2. idea.

concern *vb.* have to do with; cause a feeling of responsibility. *I am concerned about your bad tooth.* *n.* what one is interested in; a business.

concerning *prep.* about, with regard to.

concert *n.* a musical entertainment.

concise *adj.* made shorter; abbreviated. *A concise encyclopedia.*

conclude *vb.* bring to an end; come to an opinion. *He concluded she was right.* **conclusion** *n.* ending; final opinion. **conclusive** *adj.* convincing.

concrete *n.* a hard building material made of cement, sand, gravel and water. see **cement**

condemn *vb.* pronounce someone or something guilty or unfit for use. *The judge condemned the criminal to five years in prison.*

condense *vb.* 1. make something more solid; shorten. *She condensed the story by cutting out some unnecessary sentences.* 2. change from a gas into a liquid. *The steam condensed into water.*

condition *n.* 1. state of being, health. *She is in no fit condition to go dancing.* 2. provision, specification. *You may go on condition you finish your homework first.*

conduct 1. *vb.* (*kon-duct*) lead, manage; direct a performance, orchestra, etc. 2. *n.* (*kon-duct*) direction, behavior. *His conduct was terrible.*

conductor *n.* 1. a person who leads a group of singers or musicians; a person who collects fares on a bus or train. 2. any material that allows electricity to pass through it is called a conductor. Metals are good conductors, the best being silver and copper. Substances that do not conduct electricity are called insulators.

cone *n.* 1. solid body with a round bottom and a pointed top. 2. the fruit of a fir or pine tree.

confess *vb.* admit to doing wrong; own up. **confession** *n.*

confetti *pl. n.* tiny pieces of colored paper tossed at gala events such as parties and weddings.

confidence *n.* 1. feeling of certainty; a trust in one's own abilities.

2. thing told as a secret. **confident** *adj.*

confidential *adj.* private, secret.

confine *vb.* shut up, imprison; keep within limits. **confinement** *n.*

confirm *vb.* 1. establish more firmly; ratify. 2. admit to full membership of the Christian church. **confirmation** *n.*

conflict 1. *n.* a war or fighting; an argument. 2. *vb.* differ; disagree.

conform *vb.* follow the accepted customs and rules, comply.

confront *vb.* face, oppose.

confuse *vb.* mix up, throw into disorder; mistake one thing for another. **confusion** *n.*

congratulate *vb.* tell someone you are glad that they have done well.

congregate *vb.* gather together in a crowd, or **congregation** *n.*

Congress *n.* the U.S. House of Representatives and Senate.

conifer *n.* an evergreen tree with cones for fruit.

conjuror *n.* a person who performs

Conifers all have leathery, needlelike or scale-like leaves and they produce cones.

Scotch pine   Spruce

Cedar

Larch   Cypress

C

tricks that look like magic. **conjure** *vb.*

connect *vb.* join things together. *This road connects our town to the main highway.* **connection** *n.*

connoisseur *n.* well-informed person in matters of taste, etc.

conquer (**con**-ker) *vb.* defeat an enemy, overcome. **conquest** *n.*

conquistador *n.* Spanish soldier-explorer of the 1500s.

conscience (**kon**-*shunz*) *n.* sense of right and wrong.

conscious (**kon**-*shuss*) *adj.* awake, alert, active.

consecrate *vb.* set apart; make holy; devote. *He consecrated all his time to music.*

consent *vb.* agree to. *n.* permission. *You took the book without my consent.*

consequence *n.* outcome, result of something. *The consequence of his actions.*

conserve *vb.* keep something as it was without changing it. **conservation** *n.* looking after things so they are not spoiled or destroyed.

conservative *adj.* opposed to great change; cautious.

consider *vb.* think about. *Did you consider buying a new belt?* **consideration** *n.* quality of being thoughtful esp. of other people. **considerate** *adj.*

consist *vb.* be composed of.

consonant *n.* any letter of the alphabet except A, E, I, O, U, which are vowels.

conspiracy *n.* a secret plot, often with an evil purpose. **conspire** *vb.* plot secretly for an evil purpose.

constant *adj.* all the time.

constellation *n.* a group of stars which make a recognizable shape in the sky.

constitution *n.* 1. laws or rules by which a country, society, etc., is governed. 2. a person's physical condition. *He has a strong constitution.*

constrict *vb.* make narrow, compress. **constriction** *n.*

construct *vb.* build, fit together.

A Spanish conquistador.

construction *n.* **constructive** *adj.* creative, helpful.

consult *vb.* try to get advice or help from someone or from a book. *When we do not know the meaning of a word we consult a dictionary.* **consultation** *n.*

consume *vb.* eat or drink; devour; destroy. *Fire consumed the building.*

contact *vb.* meet; join; get in touch with someone. *n.* a link; an electrical connection; a person you can get in touch with. *I have a good contact working in TV.*

contain *vb.* hold something. *This box contains my belongings.* **container** *n.*

contempt *n.* 1. the act of despising. 2. disobedience to or open disrespect of a court or judge.

contented *adj.* peaceful and satisfied.

contents 1. *n.* the things that are in something. *The contents of Rudolph's pockets were a penknife, a rubber band, and two candy bars.*

contest *n.* a competition; a fight.

continent *n.* one of the seven main land masses of the world: North America, South America, Asia, Africa, Europe, Australia and Antarctica.

continue *vb.* go on being or doing. *We will continue collecting stamps.* **continual** *adj.* unceasing. **continuous** *adj.* uninterrupted, unbroken.

contour *n.* an outline; line on a map joining points of equal height.

This lens is convex (thickest in the middle). It makes the pin look larger.

contraception *n.* birth control, **contraceptive** *n.* device or drug which prevents conception.

contract 1. *n.* an agreement. *The butcher had a contract to deliver meat to the school.* 2. *vb.* grow smaller. *A heated metal bar contracts as it becomes colder.* **contraction** *n.* tightening of the muscles.

contradict *vb.* go against a person in what he or she says; deny, oppose. **contradiction** *n.* denial, inconsistency.

contrast *vb.* compare different things and notice the differences. *n.* the difference shown by comparing things.

contribute *vb.* give (money etc.). *She's contributed to a number of charities.* **contribution** *n.*

control *vb.* 1. be in charge of. 2. operate machinery. *n.* a lever, wheel or knob which is used to control machinery.

controversy *n.* dispute, argument.

convalescent *n. & adj.* regaining health after illness. **convalesce** *vb.*

convene *vb.* call a meeting, meet. **convention** *n.* formal assembly to discuss business, etc.

convenient *adj.* suitable, handy. *Our new house is only two minutes from school. It is very convenient.*

convent *n.* a place where nuns live and work.

converge *vb.* come nearer together. *The two boats were converging rapidly and were in danger of colliding.*

conversation *n.* talk. **converse** *vb.*

convex *adj.* a surface that curves outward, like an upturned saucer.

convey *vb.* carry from one place to another; transmit sound, etc.; lead.

convict 1. *n.* (**kon**-*vikt*) a criminal who has been sent to prison. 2. *vb.* (kon-**vict**) prove someone guilty of a crime.

convoy *n.* a group of merchant ships sailing together under naval escort for protection.

cook *vb.* prepare food for table. *n.* a person who cooks.

cooking *n.* a way of making meals by heating food.

cool *adj.* rather cold; the opposite of warm.

cooperate *vb.* work with others to do something. *If we cooperate we will finish the job sooner.* **cooperation** *n.* **cooperative** *adj.* willing to help.

copper *n.* a reddish-brown metal (symbol – *Cu*).

copy *vb.* make something look exactly like something else. *n.* exact reproduction.

copyright *n.* the ownership of a piece of writing or other art form.

coral *n.* hard pink or white material made mainly in warm, shallow seas from the skeletons of tiny animals.

cord *n.* a thin rope or stout length of string.

corduroy *n.* a cotton velvet fabric with ridges or "wales" in the pile.

core *n.* the center of, the middle part. *Our dog likes to eat the core of my apple.*

corgi *n.* a small Welsh breed of dog.

cork *n.* the light tough bark of the cork-oak tree; a bottle stopper made from cork.

corkscrew *n.* a tool for taking corks out of bottles.

corm *n.* a bulblike underground swelling on the stem of a plant. *A crocus grows from a corm.*

C

cormorant n. a sea bird.

corn n. the seeds of wheat, oats, rye and barley; the ears or kernels of corncob corn.

corner n. a point where two sides meet. *The front door is near the corner of the building.*

cornet n. a brass instrument similar to the trumpet.

cornflour n. finely ground maize, rice, etc.

coronation n. the ceremony when a king or queen is crowned.

corpse n. dead human body.

correct adj. right; true; with no mistakes. *All my work was correct today.* vb. put right any mistakes. *Our teacher corrects our work every day.* **correction** n.

correspond vb. 1. be similar to. 2. exchange letters. **correspondence** n.

corridor n. a long passage in a building.

corroborate vb. support something with more evidence. *The witness will corroborate my story.*

corrode vb. wear away by the action of rust, etc. **corrosion** n.

corrupt vb. spoil, influence badly. adj. evil, rotten. **corruption** n.

cosmetics n. beauty preparations for hair, skin, etc. **cosmetic** adj.

cosmic rays pl. n. tiny particles that crash into the earth's atmosphere from outer space.

cosmonaut n. (usually) a Soviet astronaut.

cost 1. n. the amount one has to pay for something. 2. vb. cause the loss of. *His attempt to save the boy cost him his life.* **costly** adj. expensive.

costume n. clothes, especially the clothes worn by actors.

cot n. a small bed. (Formerly a naval officer's swinging bed).

cottage n. a small house usually in the country.

cotton n. fiber from the seeds of the cotton plant.

couch n. a long, soft seat.

cougar n. another name for the puma, or mountain lion, a large member of the cat family native to the Americas.

cough (**koff**) n. & vb. a sudden and noisy rush of air from the lungs.

council n. a group of people who meet to make decisions.

counsel vb. & n. advice. *He gave Tom some wise counsel;* an adviser in law.

count 1. vb. add up. *Have you started to count the money yet?* 2. n. a European nobleman.

counter 1. n. a table or flat surface in a shop. 2. n. a small piece used in a board game. 3. prefix meaning against, opposing, opposite, rival, e.g. **counteract** act in opposition to; **counterbalance** act against in equal strength; **counterattraction** rival attraction.

countess n. wife of an earl.

country n. the whole land where people live. *France is the country of the French.* the land outside towns. *We like to walk in the country on weekends.*

county n. a part of the country with its own local government.

couple n. two; a pair.

coupon n. detachable ticket which can be exchanged for something or used to apply for something.

courage n. bravery.

courier (**koo**-ree-er) n. messenger; often someone in the diplomatic service.

course n. 1. the direction in which something goes. *We followed the course of the river to its mouth.* 2. one of successive parts of a meal. *The dessert course.*

court n. 1. the place where trials are held. 2. the place where a king or queen lives, and the people who live there. 3. an area marked out for certain outdoor games, as a tennis court or squash court.

courteous (**kur**-tee-us) adj. polite, well-mannered. **courtesy** n.

cousin n. the child of your aunt or uncle.

cover vb. put something over something else.

covering *n.* something that covers something. *Bark is the covering of a tree trunk.*

cow *n.* 1. a farm animal kept for its milk. 2. a female of the ox family or a female elephant, whale or seal.

coward *n.* a person who cannot hide fear and who lacks courage.

cowardice *n.* cowardly conduct. **cowardly** *adj.*

cowboy *n.* a person who looks after cattle on the American prairies.

cowslip *n.* a plant of the primrose family.

coy *adj.* excessively shy.

coyote (*koy-oh-ti*) *n.* the wild dog of North America, resembling a small wolf.

coypu *n.* South American aquatic rodent whose fur is highly valued.

crab *n.* a marine animal with a hard shell and 10 legs, two of which have large claws.

crack 1. *vb.* split; break. *Jack cracked a nut.* **cracked** *adj.* split, broken. 2. *n.* a sharp noise. 3. *n.* a split or small opening. *There is a crack in the cup.*

cracker *n.* 1. a small party favor enclosed in a cylinder of colored paper which snaps when the ends are pulled. 2. a crisp biscuit or wafer.

cradle *n.* a bed for a small baby, usually on rockers.

craft *n.* 1. skilled work with the hands. 2. a boat; an aircraft.

craftsman *n.* a skilled person who works at a craft.

cram *vb.* stuff into a small space.

cramp *n.* 1. sudden painful contraction of the muscles. 2. restrict; write too small.

crane (bird) *n.* a large water bird with long legs.

crane (machine) *n.* a machine that lifts and moves heavy things.

crash *n.* & *vb.* 1. a loud noise. 2. a collision. *Several cars were involved in the crash.*

crass *adj.* ignorant and stupid.

crate *n.* a large box made from thin pieces of wood.

crater *n.* 1. mouth of a volcano. 2. a hole in the ground made by the explosion of a bomb or shell.

crave *vb.* have a great desire for. **craving** *n.*

crawl 1. *vb.* move on all fours like a baby. 2. *n.* an overarm stroke in swimming.

crayon *n.* a stick of colored chalk or wax for drawing.

craze *n.* a general but passing fashion.

crazy *adj.* foolish, mad; eager for.

creak *n.* & *vb.* (make) harsh, squeaky sound.

cream *n.* the fatty part of milk. *n* & *adj.* the color of cream (yellowish white).

crease *n.* 1. a mark or line made in folding cloth, paper, etc.

create *vb.* make something; bring something into existence. *Authors create characters for their stories.*

Crabs and lobsters belong to a group of animals known as crustaceans.

creation *n.* the thing made or created.

creator *n.* 1. a person who creates. 2. the God who created the universe.

creature *n.* any living being.

creek *n.* a small stream, often a tributary to a river.

creep *vb.* move along close to the ground; crawl; move stealthily.

creeper *n.* a plant that creeps along the ground or up a wall.

cremate *vb.* burn to ashes (especially dead bodies).

C

Creole *n. & adj.* person of European descent born in West Indies or Latin America; person of mixed French or Spanish and Negro descent.

crêpe paper (crêpe rhymes with *grape*) *n.* a special sort of crinkly paper.

crept *vb.* past of **creep**.

crescent *n.* the moon when less than one-quarter of it is visible; any object with one side concave and the other convex.

cress *n.* a family of plants, such as watercress, some of which are eaten in salads.

crest *n.* 1. tuft of hair or feathers on the head of certain birds and animals. 2. emblem on a coat of arms. 3. highest point.

crew *n.* workers on a ship or aircraft.

crib *n.* 1. a baby's bed. 2. rack for animal fodder. 3. a literal translation of something in a foreign language. 4. a note used for cheating in an examination.

cribbage *n.* a card game.

crick *n.* cramp or stiffness in the back of the neck.

cricket *n.* 1. a small insect like a grasshopper that leaps and makes a chirping noise. 2. an outdoor summer game played with bats and a ball by teams of 11 players.

cried *vb.* past of **cry**.

crime *n.* something done that is against the law.

criminal *n.* someone who is guilty of a crime.

crimson *n. & adj.* a deep red color.

cringe *vb.* shrink in fear.

cripple *n.* someone whose body is so badly hurt or deformed as to be lame or unable to do things easily. *vb.* disable, maim.

crisis *n.* a decisive point; a difficult time.

crisp *adj.* dry and hard, but easy to break.

criticize (**krit**-*is*-*ize*) *vb.* express judgment on (work of art, etc.); analyze; find fault with. **critic** *n.*

person who criticizes, reviews a work of art, etc. **critical** *adj.* fault-finding; concerning a crisis or risk. *A critical operation.*

croak *vb. & n.* (make) a harsh, hoarse sound of a frog, raven, etc.

crochet (*kro*-**shay**) *n.* kind of knitting done with a hooked needle.

crockery *n.* earthenware or china vessels, e.g. cups, plates, etc.

crocodile *n.* a fierce, long reptile that lives in rivers.

When a crocodile closes its jaws, the fourth tooth of the lower jaw can still be seen. In alligators and their relatives this tooth cannot be seen.

crocus *n.* a small garden flower of the iris family.

crook 1. *n.* stick with a hooked top, used by shepherds. 2. *n.* a cheat, swindler. *vb.* bend, cheat.

crooked *adj.* 1. not straight. 2. dishonest.

croon *vb.* sing softly. **crooner** *n.*

crop 1. *n.* the plants that are gathered each year from a farm. 2. *vb.* cut short.

croquet (*krow*-**kay**) *n.* game played on a lawn in which balls are hit with a mallet through a series of hoops.

cross *n.* 1. the mark (X). 2. the wooden frame on which Jesus was crucified; the sign of the cross (+)

as the symbol of the Christian faith.

crossbow *n.* spring-operated medieval weapon which fired an iron bolt.

crossing *n.* a place where people can go to the other side of the street. *It is safer to walk at the crossing.*

crossroads *n.* a place where two roads intersect.

crosswind *n.* blowing from the side.

crow 1. *n.* a large, black bird with a harsh cry. 2. *vb.* give a shrill cry like a cock. 3. *vb.* boast.

crowbar *n.* bar of iron used as a lever.

crowd *n.* a lot of people gathered together.

crown *n.* the headdress of a king or queen.

crucial *adj.* critical, decisive.

crucifix *n.* a figure or picture of Christ on the cross.

crude *adj.* rough, unfinished, raw in natural state. **crudeness**, *n.* **crudity** *n.*

cruel *adj.* liking to give pain to others. **cruelty** *n.*

cruise *vb.* sail about for pleasure. **cruiser** *n.* warship designed for speed.

crumb *n.* a small scrap of bread or other food.

crumble *vb.* fall or break into small pieces.

crumpet *n.* soft round cake which is toasted and buttered.

crumple *vb.* crease carelessly; crush into a ball.

crunch *vb.* crush, grind noisily with the teeth; tread underfoot making noise of grinding gravel.

crusade *n.* & *vb.* a campaign or movement or undertaking to further a cause.

crush *vb.* 1. press on and break into pieces. *If you sit on the crackers you will crush them.* 2. defeat. *Napoleon went on to crush all his enemies.*

crust *n.* a hard, outer layer, like a crust of bread. **crusty** *adj.* having much crust; irritable.

crustacean *n.* one of a group of animals, most of which have a hard,

chalky shell and live in the sea.

crutch *n.* something that helps a lame person to walk.

cry *vb.* make a loud noise; weep or sob.

crypt *n.* the basement of a church; an underground place of worship.

cryptogram *n.* a message written in code.

crystal 1. *n.* a hard glasslike mineral. 2. *adj.* the shape which tiny pieces

All the crystals that make up a substance are always the same shape.

of many chemicals, such as salt, always take. 3. *n.* a kind of good quality, very clear glass.

cub *n.* 1. a young bear, lion, fox, tiger, or some other animal. 2. a junior Boy Scout.

cube *n.* a solid object with six equal sides. **cubic** *adj.* cube shaped.

cuckoo *n.* a family of birds that lay their eggs in the nests of other birds.

cucumber *n.* the long, narrow, green fruit of a kind of vine, eaten in salads.

cud *n.* food that cows and other ruminants bring back from their first stomach to chew again.

cuddle *vb.* hug, **cuddly** *adj.* pleasant to hug, like soft toys.

cue *n.* 1. a long rod for playing billiards, pool, etc. 2. signal for an

c

actor to enter stage or start a speech; hint.

cuff 1. *n.* the end of the sleeve. 2. *n.* & *vb.* hit someone with the open hand.

culprit *n.* a guilty person.

cultivate *vb.* help plants to grow by preparing the soil well and looking after them.

culture *n.* type of civilization. **cultured** *adj.* well educated.

cunning *adj.* crafty; artful. *The fox is a cunning animal.*

cup *n.* an open, bowl-shaped vessel for drinking beverages.

cupboard (*cub-erd*) *n.* a closet with shelves for storing things.

curate *n.* assistant to a parish priest.

curb 1. *vb.* part of a bridle used to check or restrain a horse; a restraint. 2. *n.* the stone edge of a pavement.

cure *vb.* 1. make well. 2. preserve some substances such as leather, tobacco and some meats by drying, smoking or salting them.

curious *adj.* 1. odd; strange. *Jane was wearing a very curious hat.* 2. wanting to find out about something. *I am very curious as to why she is wearing that hat.*

curlew *n.* wading bird with a long curved bill.

curly *adj.* something that is twisted into shape like a spiral or coil, especially hair. **curl** *n.* & *vb.*

currant *n.* a small, seedless dried grape.

currency *n.* the money that is used in a country.

current *n.* air or water running in one direction.

current (electric) *n.* the movement or flow of electricity.

curry *n.* a hot, spicy food, originally made in India and Pakistan.

curse *n.* asking that evil or punishment fall on a person. *vb.* swear.

curtail *vb.* shorten, reduce.

curtain *n.* a piece of cloth used as a screen, particularly as a covering for windows. *The Iron Curtain is the name given to the frontier between the communist countries of Eastern Europe and the democratic countries of Western Europe.*

curtsy *vb.* & *n.* old-fashioned gesture of respect made by women by bending the knees.

curve *n.* & *vb.* bend; a line that is not straight.

cushion *n.* an object like a small pillow, used for making a chair more comfortable. *vb.* protect (as if with cushions).

custard *n.* sauce made with milk and eggs or cornflour.

custody *n.* the state of being detained, often in jail, while awaiting trial. **custodian** *n.* guardian, keeper.

custom *n.* the usual way of doing something. *It is the custom in some countries to kiss people on both cheeks when you meet them.* **customary** *adj.* usual.

customer *n.* a person who buys things from a shop or business, sometimes regularly.

cut *vb.* slice with a knife or other sharp objects. *Can I have a bandage? I've just cut my knee.*

cutlery *n.* knives, fork, spoons, etc., used at table.

cycle 1. *vb.* ride a bicycle. 2. *n.* a series of changes. *These pictures illustrate the life cycle of a frog.*

cyclone *n.* a violent storm with strong winds.

cygnet *n.* a young swan.

cylinder *n.* 1. a solid or hollow tube-shaped object. 2. the part of an engine in which the piston moves.

cymbals *n. pl.* a metal musical instrument consisting of two brass plates that are struck against each other to make a clashing sound.

cynic (*sin-ik*) *n.* a person who sees no good in anything. **cynical** *adj.* sneering; disbelieving good in anything.

cypress (*sigh-press*) *n.* tall, evergreen conifer with dark foliage.

czar (**tzar**) (*zar*) *n.* title of the former rulers of Russia.

damson *n*. a small, dark-red kind of plum.

dance *vb*. & *n*. move the feet and body in a rhythmical way, especially to music. **dancer** *n*. one who dances.

dandelion *n*. a wild flower with bright yellow petals.

dandruff *n*. scurf on skin of skull.

danger *n*. something that is likely to

dab 1. *vb*. press repeatedly. *She dabbed at her eyes with a handkerchief to dry them.* 2. *n*. a kind of flatfish.

dabble *vb*. 1. splash about. 2. undertake in an amateurish way.

dachshund *n*. a small dog with a long body and short legs once used in Germany for hunting badgers.

daddy *n*. a word for "father" used by children.

daffodil *n*. a tall yellow flowering bulb that grows in the spring.

daft *adj*. silly, foolish, crazy.

dagger *n*. a short, two-edged knife used as a weapon.

dahlia *n*. a brightly colored family of garden flowers related to the daisy.

daily 1. *adj*. something that happens every day. 2. *adv*. every day. 3. *n*. a newspaper that is published every weekday.

dainty *adj*. small, neat and elegant; fastidious.

dairy *n*. a place where milk is kept and butter and cheese are made.

daisy *n*. a small wild flower with a yellow center surrounded by white petals.

dale *n*. valley.

dam *n*. a thick wall of earth, rock or concrete for holding back water. *vb*. restrain with a dam.

damage *vb*. injure or do harm to something. *You will damage the gate if you swing on it. n*. harm, injury. *Little damage was done.*

damn *vb*. condemn.

damp *adj*. rather wet; soggy; not dry *n*. moisture. *vb*. moisten; smother.

Four different kinds of dam are shown here.

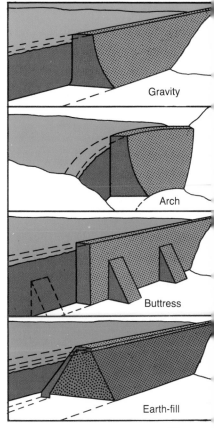

Gravity

Arch

Buttress

Earth-fill

do harm to you. *The ice on the step is a danger to everyone.* **dangerous** *adj*.

dare *vb*. 1. be brave enough to do something, venture. *I wouldn't dare cross that road at night.* 2. ask someone to show how brave they are, defy. *I dare you to jump over the stream.* **daring** *adj. & n.*

dark 1. *n. & adj.* without light; nighttime; gloomy. *I should go home before it gets dark.* 2. *adj.* not light in color. 3. *adj.* having black or brown hair or skin. **darken** *vb*. make or become dark. **darkness** *n*. absence of light.

darling *n. & adj.* a dearly loved person; a pet.

darn *n. & vb.* mend a hole in cloth by sewing threads across it.

dart 1. *vb*. move forward suddenly. 2. *n*. a small sharp-pointed arrow; a game in which darts are thrown.

dash 1. *vb*. rush; run quickly. 2. *n*. the punctuation mark (—). 3. *n*. a sprinkling. *A dash of sauce.*

dashing *adj*. showy.

data *n*. a fact or thing known used as basis for calculating, reasoning, etc. *There is little data to go on.*

date 1. *n*. the day, the month, the year, or all three together. *The date today is July 13. vb.* mark with a date; become out-of-date, old-fashioned. **dateless** *adj*. timeless. 2. *n*. the sweet, sticky fruit that grows on a date palm.

daub *vb*. smear, paint badly.

daughter *n*. a person's female child. **daughter-in-law** *n*. wife of a person's son.

daunt *vb*. lessen the courage of, intimidate.

dawdle *vb*. move slowly, waste time.

dawn *n*. sunrise, daybreak. *vb*. begin to grow light.

day *n*. the time from midnight to the next midnight; also the part of the day from sunrise to sunset.

daytime *n*. the time when it is light; the opposite of nighttime.

daze *vb*. bewilder; confuse.

dazzle *vb*. shine very brightly; blind for a moment with a bright light. *It*

can be difficult to drive a car when the sun dazzles you.*

de- *prefix* meaning down, away, off, from, not, e.g. **decode**, **deduce**, **deform**, **degrade**.

deacon *n*. minor priest. **deaconess** (fem).

dead *adj*. no longer alive.

dead heat *n*. a race in which two or more competitors finish at exactly the same time.

deadlock *n*. inaction, the result of two sides being equally powerful.

deadly *adj*. causing death. *Deadly nightshade is a fatally poisonous plant.*

deaf *adj*. not able to hear well or at all. **deafen** *vb*. **deafness** *n*.

deal *vb*. 1. tell about. *The book deals with butterflies and moths.* 2. give out. *It is your turn to deal the cards.*

deal in *vb*. buy and sell. *The butcher deals in meat.* **dealer** *n*. a person who buys and sells.

deal with *vb*. do whatever has to be done. *You tidy this room and I'll deal with the kitchen.*

dean *n*. head of a cathedral administration (chapter); head of a college or university. **deanery** *n*. dean's house; group of parishes under a dean.

dear *adj*. 1. greatly loved. 2. costing a lot of money; expensive.

dearth *n*. scarcity, lack of (especially of food).

death *n*. end of life; destruction. **deathly** *adj*. like death.

debase *vb*. lower the quality or value.

debate *vb*. discuss or argue in public. *n*. a formal discussion. **debatable** *adj*. something that can be disputed.

debris (*day*-**bree**) *n*. wreckage, broken pieces left after an accident.

debt (rhymes with *yet*) *n*. something that you owe someone.

decade *n*. a 10-year period.

decapitate *vb*. cut off the head.

decathlon *n*. an Olympic sport, consisting of 10 events.

decay *vb*. rot, go bad.

decease *vb.* die. **deceased** *n.* & *adj.* dead (person).

deceive (*de-***seeve**) *vb.* make someone believe something that you know is not true; cheat. **deceit** *n.* trick. **deceitful** *adj.*

December *n.* the twelfth month of the year.

decent *adj.* modest; fairly good; kindly and tolerant.

decibel *n.* a unit of measurement of the intensity of sound.

decide *vb.* make up your mind about something.

deciduous *adj.* trees such as maples and poplars, that lose all their leaves in winter.

decimal *adj.* & *n.* a way of writing fractions by using tens and tenths. Each place to the right of the decimal point stands for one tenth of the value of the place on its left; so 2.1 = 2 units + 1 tenth; 2.14 = 2 units + 1 tenth + 4 hundredths; 3.276 = 3 units + 2 tenths + 7 hundredths + 6 thousandths.

deck 1. *n.* the floor of a ship on which you walk. 2. *vb.* dress up; decorate.

declare *vb.* make known publicly. *When we have all made an attempt, the teacher will declare the winner.* **declaration** *n.* a formal announcement.

decline *vb.* get smaller. *Many theaters are suffering from declining audiences.* go down (in quality). *n.* gradual decrease.

decorate *vb.* 1. make more attractive by ornamenting. 2. give someone a medal.

decoy (**dee-***koy*) *n.* a model or other device to act as a trap for game birds, etc. *vb.* (di-**koy**) entice, snare.

decrease *vb.* make something grow less.

decree *n.* an official order. *vb.* order.

deduce *vb.* arrive at a conclusion from the facts given.

deed *n.* something which is done, usually good or bad or brave.

deep *adj.* 1. going a long way down.

The river is very deep near the bridge. 2. wide. *The shelf was not deep enough.* 3. dark. *The dress was a deep red.* **deepen** *vb.* make or to become deeper.

deer *n.* quick, graceful animals belonging to the cow or antelope families.

A red deer displays his antlers, which he uses to fight other deer at breeding time.

deface *vb.* spoil something by writing on it or in some other way disfigure.

defeat *vb.* beat someone at a game or in battle. *n.* a lost battle or contest.

defect 1. *n.* (**dee-***fekt*) fault, blemish. 2. *vb.* (*di-***fect**) desert. **defector** *n.*

defend *vb.* guard or make safe. **defense** *n.* resistance against attack; military fortifications, armaments. *A castle wall is a defense.* (in law) a defendant's case.

defer *vb.* 1. put off, postpone. 2. give in to another's opinion.

defiant *adj.* rebellious. **defy** *vb.* challenge. *I defy you to prove it.* **defiance** *n.* open rebellion.

deficient (*di-***fish**-*ent*) *adj.* incomplete, insufficient.

define *vb*. explain the meaning of words; mark out limits. **definition** *n*.

definite *adj*. certain, without doubt.

definitive *adj*. decisive, final.

deform *vb*. spoil the shape of.

defunct *adj*. dead, no longer existing.

defy *vb*. challenge, confront, resist.

degree *n*. 1. a unit of measurement for temperature or angles. It is often written like this: 10° means 10 degrees. 2. a title given by a university to someone who has passed an examination.

dehydrate (*dee-hi-drate*) *vb*. dry out the water from something. *Powdered milk is dehydrated.*

deity *n*. a god.

delay *vb*. make late or slow down; put off.

delegate *n*. a representative to a meeting, etc. *vb*. send as a representative or assign responsibility to someone.

delete *vb*. cross out, erase.

deliberate *adj*. something that is done on purpose. *That was a deliberate foul.*

delicacy *n*. choice kind of food.

delicate *adj*. soft and not strong; dainty.

delicious *adj*. delightful to eat.

delightful *adj*. very pleasant.

deliver *vb*. 1. take things to a place where they are needed. *The boy delivers our newspapers every morning.* 2. give a speech. 3. help at the birth of a baby. *The doctor arrived in time to deliver the baby.* **delivery** *n*.

delta *n*. the triangle of sand and soil deposited at the mouth of some rivers; fourth letter of Greek alphabet Δ.

deluge *n*. a heavy rainstorm; a downpour. *vb*. flood.

demand *vb*. ask for something that you think is due to you. *I shall demand payment of the money now.* *n*. a request, urgent claim.

democracy *n*. a country in which the government is chosen by all the adult electors; this kind of government. *Denmark is a democracy.*

demolish *vb*. tear down. *They are demolishing the office building at the end of our street.* **demolition** *n*.

demon *n*. devil or evil spirit.

demonstrate *vb*. 1. show or explain something to others. 2. take part in a protest march or similar political activity.

den *n*. the hidden home of an animal.

denarius (plural **denarii**) *n*. ancient Roman silver coin.

denied *vb*. past of **deny**.

denim *n*. durable twilled fabric.

denounce *vb*. speak critically or violently against.

dense *adj*. thick. **density** *n*.

dent *vb*. & *n*. a mark or hole. *He dented the side of his car. That car has a dent in its side.*

dental *adj*. of teeth or dentistry.

dentist *n*. a person who takes care of and treats teeth. **dentistry** *n*.

denture *n*. a set of false teeth.

deny (*den-eye*) *vb*. say that something is not true. **denial** *n*.

deodorant *n*. a substance that gets rid of smells.

depart *vb*. leave; go away. **departure** *n*.

department *n*. a separate part of a whole, e.g. a branch of government or business.

depend on *vb*. rely on someone for money or other things. *The child*

The delta of the Nile River forms many smaller rivers.

depends on us for all his or her needs.

depict *vb.* describe, draw.

deplore *vb.* regret greatly, grieve. **deplorable** *adj.* regrettable, shocking.

deport *vb.* send out of the country; exile.

deposit *n.* a sum of money put down in advance of a larger payment. *They have put down a deposit on the trip and will pay the rest before they go away. vb.* place, put a deposit down.

depot (**deep**-*owe*) *n.* a storehouse or railroad station.

depreciate *vb.* fall in value. *The car depreciated by 20 percent in three months.*

deprive *vb.* prevent from use or enjoyment; take away.

depth *n.* the distance from the top downward (how deep something is) or from the front to the back. *The depth of the shelf is just right.*

derrick *n.* 1. framework over a bore hole, e.g. an oil well. 2. a kind of crane, especially for unloading ships.

descend (*de*-**send**) *vb.* 1. go down. 2. come from, be derived from.

describe *vb.* say what something or somebody is like. *We can describe the man exactly.* **description** *n.* detailed account. **descriptive** *adj.*

desert (**dez**-*ert*) *n.* a large dry area of land where there is little water or rain.

desert (*dez*-**ert**) *vb.* abandon; leave behind. *Why did you desert us when we most needed you?*

deserve *vb.* be worthy of something. *You deserve the prize because of all your hard work.*

desiccate *vb.* dry up; preserve food by drying.

design (rhymes with *line*) *vb.* make a plan or pattern for something. *n.* plan. **designer** *n.*

designate *vb.* appoint; specify.

designedly *adv.* intentionally.

desire *vb.* want something very much. *n.* wish, longing. **desirable** *adj.* worth wanting; advisable.

desk *n.* a piece of furniture, like a table, for writing on.

despair *n. & vb.* give up hope.

despise *vb.* look down on; think oneself superior. **despicable** *adj.* contemptible, unworthy.

dessert (*dez*-**ert**) *n.* the last course of a meal, usually sweet.

destiny *n.* fate, predetermined future.

destitute *adj. & n.* absolute poverty.

destroy *vb.* break up; make something useless. **destruction** *n.* **destructive** *adj.*

detach *vb.* remove something that was previously attached to something else.

detail *n.* a very small part of something.

detain *n.* hold someone up; make a person late.

detect *vb.* discover, find out. **detection** *n.*

detective *n.* a person who follows clues to find a criminal. *adj.* concerned with detection or detectives.

deter (*di*-**ter**) discourage, hinder. **deterrent** *n.* something that deters, as, for example, bug spray.

detergent *n.* a substance which removes dirt; a kind of washing powder.

deteriorate *vb.* become worse in condition or quality. *Her health began to deteriorate after the accident.*

determined *vb.* past of **determine.** with your mind firmly made up.

This map shows the world's deserts, about a third of the world's surface.

D

detest *vb.* hate someone or something; loathe.

detonate *vb.* set off an explosion. **detonator** *n.* device for setting off an explosion.

detour *n.* roundabout way temporarily replacing a more direct route.

detract *vb.* (from) lessen the credit due to; belittle.

devastate *vb.* lay waste, destroy completely. **devastation** *n.*

develop *vb.* grow gradually. *A tadpole develops into a frog.* **development** *n.*

deviate *vb.* turn aside from main course.

device (*di-vise*) *n.* something made to do a particular thing.

devil *n.* an evil spirit; a demon. **devilish** *adj.* cruel; wicked.

devise (*di-vize*) *vb.* plan.

devote *vb.* set aside; give up. *Monks and nuns devote a large part of each day to prayer.* **devoted** *adj.* loyal, very affectionate. **devotion** *n.* great loyalty; love; (plural) prayers.

devour *vb.* eat something up whole. *The lions quickly devoured the antelope.*

devout *adj.* religious; pious; reverential.

dew *n.* the tiny drops of water that form on cool surfaces at night outdoors. **dewy** *adj.*

dexterity *n.* skill. **dextrous** *adj.*

diabetes *n.* a disorder in which too much glucose builds up in the blood.

diagnose *vb.* decide what illness someone is suffering from. *The doctor diagnosed measles.* **diagnosis** *n.*

diagonal *adj.* a straight line across a rectangular area from one corner to the opposite corner. *n.* an oblique line.

diagram *n.* a drawing that explains something. *The word "diagonal" is explained here with a diagram.*

dial *n.* the face of a clock, watch or instrument; the numbered part of a telephone. *vb.* use the dial of a telephone.

dialect *n.* a form of a language which

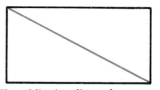

The red line is a diagonal.

is slightly different from the usual one.

dialogue *n.* conversation in speech; the spoken part of a play; argument and exchange of views. *The dialogue between America and the USSR continues.*

diameter *n.* a line right across a circle passing through the center.

diamond *n.* 1. a very hard, brilliant precious stone. 2. a four-sided figure with equal sides but no right angles.

diaper *n.* a baby's absorbent towel or underpants.

diary *n.* a book in which someone writes down what happens each day. **diarist.** *n.* a person who keeps a diary, or notes down future engagements.

dice *pl.n.* (singular **die**) small cubes with one to six dots on each side, used in games. *vb.* play with dice; cut into small cubes. *The cook diced the carrots.*

dictate *vb.* speak or read aloud something to be written down. *She dictated letters to her secretary.*

dictator *n.* absolute ruler; a tyrant.

diction *n.* correctness and clearness of speech.

dictionary *n.* a book containing an alphabetical list of words with an explanation of their meaning or a translation of the words into another language.

did *vb.* past of **do**.

didactic *adj.* meant to instruct.

die 1. *vb.* stop living; become dead. 2. *n.* the singular form of "dice."

diesel engine *n.* an internal combustion engine that burns a certain kind of oil to supply power.

diet (*di-et*) *vb. & n.* the food you usually eat; special meals that some people have to make them healthy, and others have to help them lose weight.

dif- *prefix* see **dis-**.

differ *vb.* be unlike; disagree. **difference** *n.* amount of unlikeness; a disagreement.

different *adj.* separate; not the same, unlike.

difficult *adj.* hard; not easy. **difficulty** *n.* hard to overcome; an obstacle.

diffidence *n.* shyness; disinterest.

diffuse (*di-***fyuze**) *vb.* disperse; spread around.

dig *vb.* (past **dug**) make a hole in the ground; turn over the earth, usually with a spade.

digest 1. *vb.* change the food you have eaten in such a way that your body can use it. **digestion** *n.* 2. *n.* summary.

digit *n.* 1. a finger or toe. 2. a figure or number. *The number 100 contains three digits.*

digital *adj.* having figures or numbers. *A digital watch does not*

have hands, but shows the time in figures.

digitalis *n.* a drug made from leaves of foxgloves, often used for heart problems.

dignity *n.* a quality of worthy, estimable behavior. **dignify** *vb.* do honor to.

dike *n.* a ditch; a wall to keep the sea out of the surrounding land (especially in the Netherlands).

dilate (**dye-***late*) *vb.* widen, expand, enlarge. *The pupils of the eyes dilate in the dark.*

dilemma *n.* a choice involving one of two unsatisfactory alternatives; having to choose the lesser of two evils.

dilute *vb.* water down, reduce strength of.

dim *adj.* not bright. *vb.* make or become darker.

dime *n.* a coin worth 10 cents.

dimension *n.* size, extent.

diminish *vb.* make or become less.

din *n.* a loud, ugly noise.

dinar *n.* currency of Yugoslavia.

dinghy *n.* a small, open boat.

dingo *n.* the wild dog of Australia.

dining room *n.* the room in which meals are eaten.

dinner *n.* the main meal of the day, usually eaten in the evening. **dine.** *vb.*

dinosaur *n.* one of a large group of prehistoric reptiles that became extinct millions of years ago.

diocese (**di-***oss-ese*) *n.* district under control of a bishop.

dip *vb.* put something into a liquid.

diphtheria *n.* dangerous infectious disease of the throat.

diplomacy *n.* the art of keeping good relations between countries; the use of charm or tact in relationships between people. **diplomat** *n.* official representative in diplomacy; skilled negotiator. **diplomatic** *adj.* tactful.

direct 1. *vb.* show or tell someone how to do something or go somewhere. 2. *adv.* the quickest way from one point to another. *This train goes direct to New York.*

There were many kinds of dinosaurs. Some were flesh-eaters; others were huge plant-eaters.

direction *n.* the way from one place to another.

directly *adv.* very soon; in a direct way.

dirty *adj.* not clean; covered by **dirt** *n.*

dis- *prefix* that turns the main word into its opposite, usually negative, e.g. **disband**, **disbelieve**, **discolor**, **disconnect**, **discontinue**, **discourage**.

disable (*diss-ay-ball*) *vb.* make incapable through injury, cripple.

disagree *vb.* 1. have different ideas about something. 2. have a bad effect. *I cannot eat onions; they disagree with me.* **disagreeable** *adj.* unpleasant.

disappear *vb.* vanish; be seen no more. **disappearance** *n.*

disappoint *vb.* make someone sad by not doing what was hoped for; fail to fulfill expectations.

disarray *n.* lack of order, confusion.

disaster *n.* a terrible accident. *Fifty people were killed in the disaster.* **disastrous** *adj.*

discern *vb.* see clearly with the mind. **discerning** *adj.*

disciple *n.* a follower. *Jesus left his disciples to carry on his work.*

discotheque (**disco**) *n.* a place where people dance to recorded music.

discover *vb.* find out something new.

discriminate *vb.* make or see differences between; make a distinction and single out, often for unfair treatment.

discus *n.* disk used in hurling competitions; a discus-throwing contest.

discuss *vb.* talk about something with other people. **discussion** *n.*

disease *n.* illness.

disgrace *n.* shame; downfall. *vb.* bring shame upon.

disguise *n.* & *vb.* change what someone or something looks like. *His disguise was a mask and black cloak. He disguised himself.*

disgust *n.* strong loathing for **disgusting** *adj.*

dish *n.* a plate; a particular kind of food.

dishonest *adj.* lying or cheating; not honest.

disinfect *vb.* make something free from germs and disease. **disinfectant** *n.*

disk *n.* a flat circle, like a stereo record.

dislike *vb.* unfavorable feeling.

dismal *adj.* gloomy; feeble. *The players gave a dismal performance of the piece.*

dismay *vb.* & *n.* upset; fill with fear, despair.

dismiss *vb.* send away; order someone to leave a job; disregard. **dismissal** *n.*

disobedient *adj.* refusing to obey. *The girl did not do what her teacher told her. She was disobedient.* **disobedience** *n.* **disobey** *vb.*

display *vb.* show something off. *n.* an exhibition; show.

dispute (*dis-pyoot*) *vb.* quarrel, argue; call in question.

disregard *vb.* pay no attention to.

dissect *vb.* cut up a plant or dead animal in order to examine it scientifically.

dissident *n.* a person who disagrees with or opposes authority.

dissolve *vb.* mix something in a liquid so that it becomes part of the liquid. *Salt dissolves easily in water.*

distance *n.* the length between two points.

distant *adj.* far away.

distill *vb.* turn into steam or other vapor and then condense back into a liquid. *Brandy is made by the distillation of wine.*

distinct *adj.* clear; separate; different in kind.

distinguish *vb.* see differences between; make a distinction between; separate into classes. **distinguished** *adj.* famous, eminent.

distract *vb.* draw attention away; bewilder. **distraction** *n.* relaxation, amusement; mental confusion.

distress *vb.* cause unhappiness. *n.* great trouble, grief.

distribute *vb.* give each of a number of people a share of something.

Please distribute these books to the class.

district *n*. part of a city or country.

disturb *vb*. interrupt or annoy someone; move something from its usual position. **disturbance** *n*.

ditch *n*. a narrow channel for water.

ditto *n*. the same; repeat statement.

dive *vb*. plunge into water headfirst.

diver *n*. someone who dives; someone who goes deep into water for long periods by carrying an air supply or having air pumped down from the surface.

divert *vb*. turn aside from; amuse.

divide *vb*. 1. separate, cut into parts; share. 2. find out how many times one number goes into another. *If you divide eight by two, the answer is four.*

divine *adj*. of or like God or a god; sacred.

divorce *n*. & *vb*. the legal ending of a marriage.

do *vb*. (past **did**) carry out an action.

docile *adj*. easily led, teachable.

dock 1. *n*. a place in a harbor where ships are loaded and unloaded. *vb*. bring ships into dock. 2. *n*. the place in a law court where the prisoner stands.

doctor *n*. a person who treats sick people; also a graduate holding a degree. *vb*. treat medically; falsify.

doctrine *n*. religious or political beliefs or dogma.

document *n*. written information.

dodge *vb*. get quickly out of the way; duck. *The little boy neatly dodged the snowball.*

dodo *n*. a now extinct, giant flightless bird with stumpy legs.

doe *n*. a female deer or rabbit.

dog *n*. one of a family of mammals which includes wolves, jackals and foxes.

dogma *n*. a system of beliefs; authoritative doctrine. **dogmatic** *adj*. intolerant.

dole *n*. money paid to unemployed people.

doll *n*. a small model of a person, usually for a child to play with.

The mosque called the Dome of the Rock in Jerusalem.

dollar *n*. a banknote or coin used in many countries, including Australia, Canada, Hong Kong, the USA and New Zealand.

dolphin *n*. a small type of whale.

dome *n*. a rounded roof like an upsidedown bowl.

domestic *adj*. to do with the home.

domesticated *adj*. word describing an animal that is used to living with people.

dominate *vb*. overshadow; exert control over.

domino *n*. (plural **dominoes**) one of 28 pieces marked with dots (or blank) used in a game of dominoes.

don *n*. fellow or tutor in a college or university.

donate *vb*. make a **donation**, e.g. gift of money.

done *vb*. past part. of **do**.

donkey *n*. an ass; an animal of the horse family with long ears.

don't *vb*. contraction of **do not**.

doodle *vb*. draw in an absent minded way. *n*. a drawing done in this way.

doom *n*. destiny or fate *vb*. condemn.

door *n*. a movable panel (usually of wood or glass) which opens or closes the entrance to a room or building.

dormitory *n*. a bedroom for several people, especially in a school or monastery.

D

dormouse *n*. a small gnawing rodent.

dose *n*. amount of medicine to be taken at regular times. *vb*. give medicine to.

dot *n*. small spot or point. *vb*. mark with a dot. *Dot the i's.*

double 1. *adj*. twice the amount. 2. *vb*. make twice as great. 3. *n*. a person exactly like someone else.

double-cross *vb*. betray.

doubt (rhymes with *out*) *vb*. feel unsure about something. *I doubt whether you are right. n.* feeling of uncertainty.

dough (rhymes with *go*) *n*. a mixture of flour and water for making bread or pastry.

doughnut *n*. a sweet doughy cake fried in fat. *Doughnuts are usually round and may be ring-shaped.*

dour (rhymes with *bower*) *adj*. stubborn, grim, stern.

dove *n*. a bird related to the pigeon.

dovecot *n*. a house or loft for pigeons.

dowager *n*. widow of a titled person.

dowdy *adj*. drab, badly dressed.

down 1. *prep*. toward somewhere lower. *She went down the hill.* 2. *n*. very soft feathers.

downward *adv*. toward a lower level.

doze *vb*. be half asleep.

dozen *n*. twelve.

drab *adj*. dull light brown; colorless.

drachma *n*. unit of Greek money.

draft (rhymes with *raft*) 1. *n*. a flow of air, especially coming through a narrow gap in a door or window. 2. *n*. the first plan or rough sketch of something. 3. *n. & vb.* call up for military service.

drag *vb*. pull roughly along the ground.

dragon *n*. a fierce legendary creature that breathed fire.

dragonfly *n*. a brightly colored insect with long wings that lives near water.

drain *n*. a pipe that takes waste water away. *vb*. to take water away through pipes and ditches; empty. *When he gives a toast, they will all drain their glasses.*

drake *n*. a male duck.

drama *n*. an acted story; a play; the art of the theater. **dramatic** *adj*. **dramatist** *n*. a person who writes plays.

drank *vb*. past of **drink**.

draper *n*. a person who deals in cloth.

drastic *adj*. severe.

draw *vb*. 1. make a picture or diagram with pen, pencil or crayon but not with paint. 2. the result of a game in which neither team nor player wins. 3. pull. *They draw water from the well.*

drawback *n*. a disadvantage.

drawbridge *n*. a bridge across a moat that could be pulled up when a castle was being attacked.

drawer *n*. a box-shaped part of a chest or cupboard that can be pulled open.

dread *vb*. fear terribly, especially before an event.

A demoiselle dragonfly. The male waves blue wings to attract a female who is browner.

dreadful *adj.* terrible; unpleasant. (originally "inspiring dread.")
dread *n.* fear.

dreadlocks *pl. n.* long ringlets of hair worn notably by Rastafarians.

dream *n.* something that you think is happening during sleep. *vb.* experience a dream.

dreary *adj.* gloomy, tedious.

dredge *vb.* clear away sand and mud from under water.

drench *vb.* soak, make entirely wet.

dress 1. *n.* a single piece of clothing covering the body from the shoulders to the legs, worn by women and girls. 2. *vb.* put on clothes. 3. *vb.* clean and trim wool, cloth, poultry, etc.

dresser *n.* a chest of drawers or bureau with a mirror.

drew *vb.* past of **draw**.

dribble *vb.* 1. let saliva (spit) fall from corner of the mouth. 2. in basketball, work ball forward with short bounces.

dried *vb.* past of **dry**.

drift *vb.* be carried slowly along by wind or water. *Without its engine, the ship will drift onto the rocks.*

drill *n.* 1. a pointed tool that is turned to bore holes. 2. exercises that are part of a soldier's training.

drink 1. *vb.* (past **drank**) swallow water or other liquid. 2. *n.* any liquid that is swallowed.

drip *vb.* fall in drops.

dripping *n.* fat melted from roasting meat.

drive 1. *vb.* (past **drove**) steer a car or other vehicle. 2. *vb.* strike a golf ball. 3. *n.* a road from the street to the front of a house (driveway).

drivel *n.* nonsensical talk. *vb.* talk foolishly.

driver *n.* the person who steers a car or other vehicle.

drizzle *n. & vb.* fine dense rain.

dromedary *n.* a fast camel with one hump.

drone *n.* a male bee or ant that does no work.

droop *vb.* hang down limply, wilt.

drop 1. *n.* a small amount of liquid, a

One type of drawbridge: the hinged bridge is attached by chains to a beam above that pulls it up quickly.

raindrop. 2. *vb.* let something fall.

drop in *vb.* visit someone without telling them you are coming.

drought (rhymes with *out*) *n.* a long period of dry weather.

drove *vb.* past of **drive**.

drown *vb.* die by suffocation in water; drench.

drowsy *adj.* sleepy, not fully awake.

drug *n.* a medicine; a substance that takes away anxiety or pain. *vb.* make stupid with drugs; add drugs to food etc.

drum *n.* a round, hollow musical instrument with a skin stretched over a frame. *vb.* play a drum.

drunk 1. *adj.* having drunk too much alcohol. *People who drive when they are drunk are responsible for too many accidents.* 2. *n.* a person who habitually drinks too much. 3. *vb.* past part. of **drink**.

drupe *n.* fruit such as a plum with a stone contained in fleshy pulp.

dry *adj.* not wet; without water.

dual *adj.* making a pair, double. *Dual exhausts.*

dubious (**dew**-*bius*) *adj.* doubtful, open to question.

duck 1. *n.* a web-footed water bird

D

with a broad beak. 2. *vb*. bend down quickly to get out of the way of something.

duckling *n*. a young duck.

due *adj*. owing; merited; expected. *The plane is due at ten o'clock.*

duet *n*. a piece of music for two performers.

dug *vb*. past of **dig**.

duke *n*. an important nobleman, next to a prince in rank. *A duke's wife is called a duchess.*

dull *adj*. not bright; not sharp; not interesting. *It is never dull when Mrs. Perfect teaches our class.*

dumb *adj*. 1. not able to speak. 2. (*slang*) stupid.

dummy *n*. model of a human figure.

dump *vb*. put in a heap. *n*. rubbish collection spot; (*casual*) a dull place.

dumpling *n*. small piece of steamed or boiled dough.

dunce *n*. a person slow at learning.

dune *n*. a low hill of sand.

dung *n*. farmyard manure.

dungeon (**dun**-*jun*) *n*. an underground prison.

duplicate *vb*. make exact copy of.

durable *adj*. strong and long lasting.

during *prep*. 1. throughout. *The old man slept during the entire speech.* 2. at some time in. *They arrived during the afternoon.*

dusk *n*. the time of evening when it is starting to get dark; twilight.

dust *n*. tiny grains of dirt.

dustbin *n*. a container for household rubbish.

dust bowl *n*. a dry area (especially in the western Great Plains of the USA) which has many dust storms.

duty *n*. something that you must do. *The policeman's duty is to arrest the burglar.*

dwarf *n*. a person, animal, or plant that does not grow to full size.

dwell *vb*. 1. live somewhere. 2. write or speak about at great length.

dwindle *vb*. steadily become smaller, grow less.

dye (rhymes with *lie*) *vb*. change color of something by putting in a special liquid called a **dye** (*n*.).

dyke see **dike**.

dynamic *adj*. very active; filled with energy.

dynamite *n*. a powerful explosive used for blasting.

dynasty *n*. a historical line of kings or queens.

dysentery (**dis**-*en-ter-ee*) *n*. serious disease of the bowels.

dyslexia *n*. word blindness, inability to read easily.

dyspepsia *n*. indigestion, especially when chronic. **dyspeptic** *adj*.

Because deserts are dry and do not have much vegetation, loose sand can be driven along by the wind.

A golden eagle.

each *adj.* every member of a group thought of separately. *He held a gun in each hand.*

eager *adj.* keen; enthusiastic. **eagerness** *n.*

eagle *n.* a large bird of prey.

ear *n.* 1. the organ, or part of the body, with which we hear. 2. the sense of hearing.

earache (**ear-***ayk*) *n.* a pain in the ear.

earl *n.* the middle rank of the British peerage, between marquis and viscount. *The wife of an earl is called a countess.* **earldom** *n.*

early *adv.* & *adj.* soon; at the beginning (of the day). *She is an early riser.*

earn *vb.* 1. get something by working for it. 2. deserve. *She earns everyone's respect.*

earnest *adj.* serious; keen, but lacking in humor.

earnings *pl. n.* money earned.

earrings *pl. n.* ornaments worn in the ears.

earshot *n.* within hearing distance.

earth 1. *n.* the planet on which we live. 2. *n.* soil. **earthy** *adj.* of earth or soil; coarse. 3. *n.* hole of a burrowing animal.

earthquake *n.* a shaking movement of the surface of the earth.

earthwork *n.* a mound of earth used as a fortification.

earwig *n.* insect with pincers at the end of its abdomen.

ease *n.* comfort; freedom from pain. *vb.* make easier; relieve from pain; relax.

easel *n.* a frame to hold up a picture or blackboard.

east *n.* & *adj.* the direction in which the sun rises. *East winds blow from the east.* **eastward** *adv.* **eastern** *adj.*

Easter *n.* the day on which Christians remember the Resurrection of Jesus Christ.

easy *adj.* simple; not difficult.

easygoing *adj.* tolerant, not fussy.

eat *vb.* (past **ate** past part. **eaten**) chew and swallow food.

eat away *vb.* destroy gradually.

ebb *vb.* & *n.* the tide flowing back from land to sea.

ebony *n.* the name of various kinds of hard, black wood. *adj.* the color of ebony; black.

eccentric *adj.* odd, peculiar. *n.* a person with unusual habits or behavior.

ecclesiastical *adj.* of or concerning the church and clergy.

echo (**ek-***o*) *n.* & *vb.* a sound that is heard again when it bounces back or is reflected off something.

eclipse *n.* & *vb.* a time when the sun's light is cut off because the moon passes between the earth and the sun (an eclipse of the sun); a

Earth's shadow

Earth

Moon's orbit

Eclipsed Moon

Sun's rays

The earth casts a long shadow into space, away from the sun. If the moon passes through this shadow, it grows dim.

time when the moon's light is cut off because the earth passes between the sun and the moon (an eclipse of the moon).

ecology *n.* the study of the habits of living things, the places where they live and how they depend on each other. **ecological** *adj.* **ecologist** *n.*

economy *n.* 1. the management of a country's wealth. 2. a saving. *He is always trying to make false economies in our housekeeping.* **economical** *adj.* thrifty **economize** *vb.* avoid expense.

eczema (ek-*suh-muh*) *n.* a disease of the skin.

edge *n.* the part along the side or end of something. *The path ran around the edge of the field.*

edible *adj.* fit to be eaten.

edifice *n.* large building such as a church, etc.

edify *vb.* teach and improve mentally.

edit *vb.* prepare a piece of writing for publication in a book, newspaper or magazine. **editor** *n.* a person who edits.

edition *n.* copies of a book or periodical printed at one time.

educate *vb.* teach or train. **education** *n.* **educational** *adj.*

Edwardian *adj.* belonging to the reign of Edward VII (1901–10).

eel *n.* a long slim fish with fins like narrow ribbons.

effect *n.* result or consequence of our action.

effeminate *adj.* womanish behavior in a man.

efficient *adj.* capable, competent.

effigy *n.* image or likeness of a person.

effort *n.* hard work.

e.g. stands for two Latin words, **exempli gratia**, meaning "for example."

egg *n.* one of the roundish objects that young birds, insects, fish and reptiles live inside before they are born; an important kind of food. **egg on** *vb.* encourage.

egocentric *adj.* concerned with oneself; self-centered.

egoism *n.* selfishness.

eider *n.* a large sea duck, the soft down of which is used in eiderdowns (quilts).

either *adj. & pron.* one or the other; one of two. *He can take either road to get there.*

eject *vb.* remove; send out, expel. **ejection** *n.* **ejector** *n.*

elaborate *adj.* done in great detail.

elastic *n. & adj.* a material that stretches out and then goes back to the same size. *A rubber band is made of elastic.*

elbow *n.* the joint between the upper and lower arm. *vb.* thrust, jostle.

elder 1. *adj.* older. *My elder brother was born before I was.* **elderly** *adj.* becoming old; past middle age. 2. *n.*

an official of certain churches.

eldest *adj.* child of the greatest age. *My eldest brother was born before my elder brother.*

election *n.* a time when people can choose, by voting, the men and women who will govern their town or country, society or club. **elect** *vb.* choose by voting. **elector** *n.* a person entitled to vote. **electorate** *n.* the mass or body of electors.

electric *adj.* worked by electricity.

electrician *n.* a person who works with electricity or electrical equipment.

electricity *n.* energy that is used to make heat and light and is used to drive some machines. Electricity moves along wires from generating stations to where it is needed. **electrify** *vb.* charge with electricity; change to working by electricity. *The railroads will be electrified.*

electrocute *vb.* execute by using a powerful electric current.

electrode *n.* metal rod or plate through which an electric current enters or leaves a battery, etc.

electron *n.* small negatively charged subatomic particle.

electronics *pl. n.* the science that deals with things like television, radio and other pieces of apparatus that have devices such as transistors.

elegance *n.* refinement in taste; grace. **elegant** *adj.* tasteful.

elegy *n.* sad poem or song written usually for the dead.

element *n.* a substance that cannot be divided into simpler substances.

elementary *adj.* simple; introductory.

elephant *n.* the world's largest land mammal, characterized by a long trunk and curved tusks made of ivory.

elevate *vb.* lift up, raise. **elevator** *n.* a conveyance in buildings.

elf *n.* (plural **elves**) in storybooks, a small fairy.

elite (*ay*-**leet**) *n.* a select, privileged group; the best.

Elizabethan *adj.* belonging to the reign of Elizabeth I (1533-1603).

elk *n.* the name for two large kinds of

Hide
Thick and wrinkled.

Eyes
The elephant has poor sight.

Tusks
Made of ivory and used for digging and fighting.

Ears
Their enormous surfaces act like radiators to give off heat and keep the elephant cool.

Trunk
A flexible extra limb, with two lips at the end which enable it to grasp small objects. The Asiatic elephant has only one lip (below).

Feet
Broad with thick padded soles.

E

deer. The European elk is known as a moose in North America. The second kind is the American elk.

elm *n*. a broad-leaved tree, the leaves having zigzag edges like the teeth of a saw.

elongate *vb*. stretch out, make longer.

elope *vb*. run away with a lover to get married without parental permission. *n*. **elopement**.

em- *prefix* see **en-**.

emancipate *vb*. set free from control of another, e.g. social restraint, slavery.

embankment *n*. the built-up bank of a river or lake; a bank so constructed to carry a road or a railway.

embargo *n*. a ban on trading for a time.

embark *vb*. get on board ship.

embarrass *vb*. make someone feel uncomfortable or ill at ease. **embarrassment** *n*.

embassy *n*. the building used by an ambassador and his staff.

embezzle *vb*. take property, money, etc., that is not one's own but which has been put in one's charge.

emblem *n*. a badge, symbol.

embrace *vb*. take into the arms; accept; adopt (a cause).

embroidery *n*. decoration of cloth made by sewing a pattern of colored stitches. **embroider** *vb*.

embryo (*em-bree-yo*) *n*. an animal in an early stage before it is born. **embryonic** *adj*.

emend *vb*. correct, remove errors. **emendation** *n*.

emerald *n*. a precious green stone.

emerge *vb*. come out; come to notice.

emergency *n*. a sudden happening that needs quick action.

emigrate *vb*. go away from your own country to live. **emigration** *n*.

eminent *adj*. distinguished; standing above others because of some special quality.

emit *vb*. give out, send out. **emission** *n*.

emotion *n*. strong feeling (of love, hate, etc.). **emotional** *adj*. agitated in feeling; easily moved by feelings.

emperor *n*. the male ruler of an empire. A female ruler is an **empress**.

emphasis (*em-fa-sis*) *n*. stress, e.g. on words, to show importance. **emphasize** *vb*. stress, underline; state strongly.

empire *n*. a group of countries under one ruler. *The Roman Empire spread all around the Mediterranean Sea.*

employ *vb*. 1. pay people to work. **employee** *n*. a person who works for wages. **employer** *n*. a person who employs others. **employment** *n*. 2. use. *I employ a fine pen to fill in the details.*

emporium *n*. a large shop (rather old-fashioned).

empty *adj*. having nothing inside; unoccupied. *vb*. remove contents of. **emptiness** *n*.

emu *n*. a large Australian flightless bird.

en- prefix meaning to put into, on, effect, e.g. **enrage, enclose**. Before B, P and M, **en-** becomes **em-**.

enable *vb*. make able.

enamel *n*. a very hard, shiny paint; a hard, glass-like coating on metal pots and pottery or glass.

enchant *vb*. 1. put a magic spell on someone. 2. be very attractive to someone.

enclose *vb*. shut in on all sides. **enclosure** *n*. enclosed land.

encore (*on-kor*) *inter*. & *n*. shout of applause meaning *Again!* repetition of a song etc.

encounter *vb*. meet someone. *n*. a casual meeting.

encourage *vb*. make someone feel able to do something; urge someone on. **encouragement** *n*.

encyclopedia *n*. a book or set of books that give you information about many subjects, usually alphabetically arranged.

end *n*. the place where something stops; the edge or side of something. *vb*. to put a stop to.

endless *adj.* without ending; incessant.

endeavor (*en-***dev**-*er*) *vb.* try hard to do. *n.* an attempt.

endure *vb.* continue unchanged; tolerate suffering. **endurance** *n.* permanence; ability to withstand hardship.

enemy *n.* the people that one fights in time of war.

energy *n.* the strength or power to do work; vigor; activity. *Machines have energy. The food we eat gives us energy.* **energetic** *adj.*

engage *vb.* 1. bind by promise. 2. hire. 3. (in) take part in. 4. begin fighting. 5. interlock. *He engaged the gear.*

engine *n.* a machine which changes energy into power or movement. *The train was pulled by its great engine.*

engineer *n.* 1. a person who plans and builds bridges, roads, machines and big buildings. 2. a person who looks after or works with engines.

engrave *vb.* cut a picture or writing into wood, steel or other hard substance. **engraving** *n.* a print made by this method.

enigma *n.* a mystery, a riddle. **enigmatic** (-al) *adj.*

enjoy *vb.* get pleasure from. *I always enjoy going to the ballet.* **enjoyable** *adj.* **enjoyment** *n.*

enlarge *vb.* make or become bigger. **enlargement** *n.*

enlist *vb.* engage, take on (especially as a soldier).

enormous *adj.* very big.

enough *adj.* sufficient. *Have you had enough to eat?*

ensign *n.* a flag or badge.

ensue *vb.* happen afterward.

ensure *vb.* make safe or certain. *Please ensure the door is locked at night.*

enter *vb.* go into a place; record something (in a book); take part in a competition.

enterprise *n.* project or undertaking; an aptitude for taking on a project. *She showed great enterprise.*

entertain *vb.* 1. amuse people with a show. 2. have people as guests in your home. **entertainment** *n.* hospitality; public performance, e.g. in a theater. **entertainer** *n.* professional singer, dancer, etc.

enthusiasm *n.* great interest, zeal. **enthusiast** *n.* someone who is full of enthusiasm; a keen person.

entire *adj.* whole; complete.

entrance *n.* the place through which one enters or goes in.

entreat *vb.* beg, plead.

entry *n.* entrance; something entered in a book, etc.; a competitor in a race, etc.

envelope *n.* a paper covering for a letter; a wrapper.

environment *n.* surroundings; the place or kind of life surrounding an animal.

envoy *n.* a diplomat lower in rank than an ambassador.

envy *n.* & *vb.* a feeling of wanting what someone else has; jealousy. **envious** *adj.* full of envy. **enviable** *adj.* exciting envy; desirable.

epic *n.* 1. a long poem that tells a story, such as Homer's *Odyssey*. 2. an historical film made at great expense with large numbers of actors.

epidemic *n.* a disease which a large number of people have at the same time.

epigram *n.* a short witty remark or poem.

epilepsy *n.* a nervous disease marked by repeated fits and loss of consciousness.

epiphany (*i-***pif**-*anee*) *n.* Christian feast (January 6) marking the visit of the Magi to Jesus.

episode *n.* one event in a series of events; one part of a film or other serial. **episodic** *adj.*

epistle *n.* a letter (especially in the New Testament).

epoch *n.* an era, period marked by historic events.

equal *adj.* the same in size or number, etc.; a person of same rank. **equality** *n.* being equal.

E

equalize *vb.* make even or equal.

equate *vb.* regard as equal.

equator *n.* an imaginary line around the middle of the earth that is drawn on maps. **equatorial** *adj.* of, at, or near the equator.

equine *n.* of or like a horse.

equinox *n.* the time of year in spring and autumn when the day and night are of equal length all over the world. The equinoxes happen about March 21 and September 23.

equipment *n.* things needed to do something. **equip** *vb.* provide with things necessary, e.g. for fighting, playing games, etc.

equivalent *adj.* the same or equal in force, value or meaning. *In 1984, British £1.00 was the equivalent of about U.S. $1.40.*

era *n.* period of time, particularly of history.

eradicate *vb.* uproot, destroy, wipe out, abolish.

erase *vb.* rub out; wipe off.

erect *vb.* raise up, build. *adj.* upright. **erection** *n.* building.

ermine *n.* the white winter fur of a species of weasel.

erosion *n.* the slow wearing away of the land by wind, water and other means. **erode** *vb.* gradually wear away.

erotic *adj.* arousing sexual desire, passion.

err *vb.* make a mistake; sin.

errand *n.* short journey to carry messages etc.

error *n.* mistake; something that is done wrongly.

erupt *vb.* burst out violently, shoot out suddenly (as lava etc.).

eruption *n.* volcanic outbreak etc.

escalate *vb.* go up, increase by degrees.

escalator *n.* a moving staircase.

escape 1. *vb.* get away from or get free. *The lion escaped from its cage in the zoo.* 2. *n.* a leakage. *There was an escape of gas.*

escapement *n.* part of the works of a watch or clock.

escort *vb.* accompany for protection.

Eskimo *n.* (plural **Eskimos**) native people of the Arctic Circle.

especially *adj.* chiefly; more than normally. *I like raspberries, especially with cream.*

Esperanto *n.* an artificial international language invented by L.L. Zamenhof in 1887.

espionage *n.* spying.

esquire (**es**-*kwire*) *n.* polite title added to a man's name when

Above: *Deposits of eroded material – silt – build up along river banks, creating* levees *(low embankments).*

Below: *Rivers often cut back at their sources and "capture" other rivers, which become tributaries.*

addressing a letter: *J.P. Jones, Esq.*

essay *n.* a short piece of writing. *You may have to write essays in school.*

essence *n.* the main quality of something.

essential *adj.* very important; cannot do without.

establish *vb.* settle or organize; set up. *The expedition established a camp at the foot of the mountains.* **establishment** *n.*

estate *n.* an area of land that someone owns.

estimate *vb.* guess the size, weight or cost of something. *Can you estimate how tall that giraffe is?*

estuary *n.* the mouth of a large river.

et cetera *n.* (abbrev. **etc.**) and so on; and other things. *Cats, cows, horses, etc., are domestic animals.*

etch *vb.* draw on metal or glass by cutting lines with acid.

eternal *adj.* having no beginning or end; lasting forever. **eternity** *n.* infinite time; the afterlife.

ether (ee-*ther*) *n.* a liquid chemical, formerly used as an anesthetic, whose industrial uses include refrigeration.

ethnic *adj.* of race (people).

eucalyptus *n.* an Australian gum tree.

Eucharist (yoo-*kar-ist*) *n.* Christian service of Holy Communion.

eulogize *vb.* praise highly.

euphemism (yoo-*fem-izm*) *n.* the use of a mild or indirect word or expression in place of a harder, correct or true one. *He would not say "dead" but always used the euphemism "passed away."*

evacuate *vb.* 1. empty. 2. withdraw from a dangerous place. **evacuee** *n.* a person who is removed.

evade *vb.* escape, get away; avoid something or someone on purpose. *She evaded the question.*

evangelist *n.* a writer of one of the Gospels (Matthew, Mark, Luke or John); a preacher. **evangelism** *n.* the preaching of the gospel.

evaporate *vb.* turn from a liquid into a vapor or gas, usually because of heat. **evaporation** *n.*

even 1. *adv.* a word used to strengthen a statement. *He hasn't even read the book.* 2. *adj.* smooth; equal. 3. *adj.* divisible by two. *Even numbers are the opposite of odd numbers.*

evening *n.* the time between afternoon and night.

event *n.* an important happening. **eventful** *adj.* full of incident.

eventually *adv.* in the end, at last.

ever *adv.* always; at all times. *They*

Galileo's escapement. An escapement is a device that controls the uncoiling of the spring or weight which drives a mechanical clock.

lived happily ever after.

evergreen *n.* & *adj.* a tree whose leaves are green all year.

every *adj.* each one, every individual member of a group thought of as making up the whole group.

everybody, everyone *pron.* each person; all the people.

everything *pron.* all things; each thing.

everywhere *adv.* in every place.

evict *vb.* turn out from, expel. **eviction** *n.*

evidence *n.* proof; particularly in a trial.

evil *n.* & *adj.* very bad, wicked.

evolution *n.* the process by which animals and plants develop and change over millions of years.

ewe (rhymes with *new*) *n.* a female sheep.

ex- *prefix* meaning out, from, beyond; formerly (**ef-** before F; e

E

before many consonants).

exact *adj.* just right, perfectly correct.

exaggerate *vb.* make something sound bigger or smaller, or more or less important than it really is. **exaggeration** *n.*

exalt *vb.* praise. **exalted** *adj.* highly placed. *She has an exalted position in the government.*

exam, examination *n.* 1. an important test to find out how much you know. 2. a close look at something.

examine *vb.* look at something very carefully; inquire into; interrogate. **examiner** *n.*

example *n.* 1. something which shows what something else is like or how it works. *This cake is a good example of my cooking.* 2. a model; a warning to others.

exasperate *vb.* irritate, annoy, rouse to anger. **exasperation** *n.*

excavate *vb.* uncover by digging, unearth. **excavation** *n.*

exceed *vb.* go beyond. *It is dangerous to exceed the stated dose of this medicine.*

excellent *adj.* very good.

except *prep.* not included, omitting. *Everyone is here except John.*

exceptional *adj.* out of the ordinary, outstanding.

exchange *vb.* change one thing for another; swap.

excite *vb.* make someone look forward to something; thrill. **excitement** *n.*

exclude *vb.* shut out, keep out from. *He was excluded from the meeting.*

excursion *n.* short journey, pleasure trip.

excuse 1. *n.* an apology; a reason for not doing something, or for doing wrong. 2. *vb.* let someone off. *She was excused from choir practice, as she has a cold.*

execute *vb.* put someone to death legally as a punishment.

exercise *vb.* & *n.* 1. work that helps to make the body strong and healthy. 2. drill.

exert *vb.* bring into action; apply. **exertion** *n.* effort.

exhale *vb.* breathe out.

exhaust (*ex-awst*) 1. *vb.* use up completely; make very tired. 2. *n.* the part of an engine that lets out burned gases; the burned gases.

exhaustive *adj.* thorough, complete. *The police made exhaustive inquiries.*

exhibit *vb.* show something in public. *n.* the thing that is shown.

exhibition (*eks-i-bish-un*) *n.* a place or event where things are shown to the public, such as an art exhibition.

exile *n.* & *vb.* a person who has been forbidden by law to live in his or her own country. *He spent 10 years in exile.*

exist *vb.* be or live. **existence** *n.*

exit *vb.* go out; leave. *n.* the place through which you go out; a direction in a play which tells an actor to leave the stage.

exodus *n.* the departure of a large group of people. *The Book of Exodus in the Bible deals with the departure of the Israelites from Egypt.*

exotic *adj.* brought in from abroad; unusual.

expand *vb.* get larger.

expanse *n.* a broad area. *An expanse of sky.*

expect *vb.* think that something will happen; look forward to. *I expect they will be here soon.*

expedition *n.* a journey for a specific purpose, such as climbing a mountain; a group making such a journey.

expel *vb.* drive out, compel to leave.

expensive *adj.* costing a lot of money.

experience 1. *n.* something that happens to you, and from which you may learn. *Going to camp is a great experience.* 2. *vb.* feel; meet with. *They will experience great heat in the center of Africa.* **experienced** *adj.*

experiment *n.* a test; a trial. *vb.* carry out a test.

expert *n.* someone who has special

knowledge about something.

expire *vb.* breathe out air; breathe one's last breath, die.

expiration *n.* coming to an end; close.

explain *vb.* show or make the meaning clear. **explanation** *n.* statement or fact that explains something, makes it clear. *So that is the explanation of the conjuring trick.*

explode *vb.* burst with a loud bang and, usually, great damage.

exploit 1. *n.* an adventure. 2. *vb.* develop or use profitably. *You must exploit your talent.*

explore *vb.* look carefully around a place where you have not been before; examine, discuss a possibility, etc. **exploration** *n.*

explorer *n.* a person who travels to find out about places where people have not been before.

explosion (*ex-***plo**-*shun*) *n.* a loud noise when something explodes.

explosive *n.* anything, such as dynamite, used to make things explode or blow up.

exponent *n.* someone who explains or interprets.

export (**eks**-*port*) *vb.* sell goods to another country.

exports (**eks**-*ports*) *pl. n.* the goods that are exported.

expose *vb.* uncover; leave unprotected. *The troops were exposed to gunfire.* make public a villainy.

exposure *n.* 1. the act of exposing, leaving unprotected. 2. period of time light is allowed to fall on a sensitive emulsion in photography.

express 1. *vb.* explain something in words. *He has difficulty in expressing his meaning.* 2. *adj.* fast. *An express train.*

expression *n.* 1. an often-used word or words. 2. the look on a person's face.

extant *adj.* still living, existing.

extend *vb.* stretch out, lengthen; prolong.

exterior *n.* the outside part or surface.

exterminate *vb.* destroy completely.

external *adj.* outside, outer.

extinct *adj.* a thing which was living is extinct when none of its kind is alive any more. *Dinosaurs have been extinct for millions of years.*

extinguish *vb.* put out, cause to stop. *The firemen extinguished the blaze.*

extra *adj.* more than usual. *You will need extra clothes because it's so cold.*

extraordinary *adj.* very unusual.

extravagant *adj.* exceeding limits of necessity; spending too much.

extreme *adj.* very great or very far.

extremist *n.* a person who holds strong, uncompromising (political) views.

eye *n.* the organ, or part of the body, we use for seeing.

eyebrow *n.* the curve of hair above the eye.

eyelashes *pl.n.* the fringes of hair on the eyelids.

eyelid *n.* the flap of skin that covers the eye when it is closed.

eye-opener *n.* something which suddenly surprises you or makes you suddenly understand.

eyesight *n.* the ability to see.

eyewitness *n.* someone who sees an event happening.

The light from an object we are looking at goes through the lens of the eye and throws an image onto the retina at the back of the eye.

fable *n.* a story that tries to teach us something. The characters are usually animals that talk.

fabric *n.* cloth.

fabulous *adj.* in a fable; marvelous, incredible.

façade (*fass-***sahd***) n.* the front of a building; appearance given to other people.

face *n.* the front part of the head. *vb.* meet confidently and without fear.

facet *n.* one side of a cut gem.

facility *n.* ease; no difficulty in doing, learning, etc.

facsimile (*fak-***sim***-ilee) n.* exact copy.

fact *n.* something that really happened, so people know that it is true. *It is a fact that William the Conqueror invaded England in 1066.*

factory *n.* a building where people and machines work together to make things.

factual *adj.* concerned with or containing fact.

fad *n.* a craze, passing enthusiasm.

fade *vb.* 1. lose color. *Our curtains have faded in the sun.* 2. wither. *The flowers faded.* 3. disappear slowly. *The ship faded from sight in the mist.*

Fahrenheit (*fa-***ren***-hite) n.* a thermometer scale in which the freezing point of water is 32° and the boiling point is 212°. It was invented by a German, Gabriel Daniel Fahrenheit (1686–1736).

fail *vb.* be unsuccessful.

failing *n.* weakness, defect, short-coming.

failure *n.* lack of success; omission. *Failure in duty.*

faint 1. *adj.* weak; not clear. *We could hear a faint sound when we listened carefully.* 2. *vb.* become dizzy, with everything going black, so you may fall down; become unconscious.

fair 1. *adj.* acting in a just way, that is seen to be right. *Everyone should have a fair share of the cake.* 2. *adj.* light colored. *Mary has fair hair and blue eyes.* 3. *adj.* (of weather) good. 4. *n.* a group of outdoor amusements, with sideshows and merry-go-rounds.

fairly *adv.* moderately. *I know him fairly well.*

fairy *n.* an imaginary small creature with magic powers.

faith *n.* 1. a strong belief; trust. *I have complete faith in her.* 2. religion.

faithful *adj.* honest; trustworthy.

fake *n. & adj.* something that looks real but is not.

A peregrine falcon.

falcon *n.* a bird of prey related to the eagle.

fall 1. *vb.* drop to the ground. *n.* drop. 2. *n.* autumn.

fall behind *vb.* fail to keep up with. *He has no money, so he will fall behind with his rent.*

fall out 1. *vb.* quarrel. 2. *n.* **fallout** radioactive dust settling after nuclear explosion.

fall through *vb.* fail to take place.

false *adj.* not true; not real.

falsetto *n* & *adj*. male voice which is made artificially high.

falter *vb*. hesitate, stumble; lose courage.

fame *n*. outstanding reputation. *Her fame is worldwide.*

familiar *adj*. well-known.

family *n*. a group of people who are all related to each other.

famine *n*. a time when there is very little food in an area and people go hungry.

famous *adj*. widely known. *He is a famous musician.*

fan *n*. 1. a device that circulates air to another area. 2. a person who greatly admires someone famous; a supporter.

fancy *vb*. imagine, picture to oneself; take a liking to, *have a fancy for*; be under a delusion. *He fancies he can fly.*

fanfare *n*. a flourish played on a trumpet, usually to introduce an important person.

fang *n*. a long, sharp tooth, especially the poisonous tooth of snakes such as vipers and cobras.

fantasy *n*. something, usually pleasant, that you imagine or dream about, but is not real.

far *adj*. a long way off.

farce *n*. an amusing kind of play, full of misunderstandings; an absurd situation.

fare *n*. 1. the price of traveling on a bus, train, etc. 2. food and drink (now old-fashioned).

farewell *inter.*, *n*. & *adj*. goodbye. *A farewell speech.*

farm *n*. land and buildings where crops are grown and animals reared. *vb*. use land to grow crops or rear animals. **farmer** *n*.

far-off *adj*. distant.

farrago (*fa-***rah**-*go*) *n*. a mixture.

farrow *n*. litter of pigs. *vb*. give birth to pigs.

farther *adj*. (**further**) more distant.

farthest *adj*. (**furthest**) the most distant.

farthing *n*. former British coin worth a quarter of the former penny.

fascinate *vb*. attract, charm. **fascination** *n*.

Fascism *n*. a political belief and form of government in which a country has only one political party, and is ruled by a dictator.

fashion *n*. a way of dressing or doing things that most people like to copy at a certain time. *Huge sweaters were in fashion last year.*

fast 1. *adj*. very quick. 2. *adv*. firmly fixed. *My boot was stuck fast in the mud.* 3. *vb*. eat no food for a time.

fasten *vb*. tie; fix firmly. **fastener** *n*. **fastening** *n*.

fat 1. *adj*. plump, fleshy and round. 2. *n*. the soft, oily part of the body of a person or an animal.

fatal *adj*. causing death or disaster. *A fatal accident.*

fate *n*. power which some believe determines events; destiny.

father *n*. a person's male parent.

fathom 1. *n*. a nautical term used to measure the depth of water. A fathom equals six feet. 2. *vb*. measure the depth of water with a sounding line; get to the bottom of, understand.

fatigue *n*. weariness; weakness in a metal. *vb*. tire.

fatty *adj*. containing fat.

fault (rhymes with *salt*) *n*. an imperfection; a mistake.

fauna (**fawn**-*a*) *n*. animal life of a district.

favor 1. *n*. an act of kindness or help. *Can you do me a favor by picking up my dress?* 2. *vb*. like one person or thing more than another.

favorite *adj*. & *n*. the best-liked person or thing.

fawn 1. *n*. a young deer. *adj*. fawn-colored, yellowish brown. 2. *vb*. grovel, cringe (like a dog).

fear *vb*. feel frightened. *n*. the feeling of being frightened.

fearless *adj*. brave; without fear.

feast *n*. 1. a very grand meal. 2. a religious festival.

feat (*feet*) *n*. act or deed, especially showing strength or courage.

feather *n*. one of the many light

coverings that grow on a bird's body.

feature n. 1. one of the parts of the face. *Your nose is one of your features.* 2. an important part of something.

February n. The second month of the year.

fed 1. vb. past tense and past part. of **feed**. 2. adj. **fed up** (casual) bored. *She was fed up with her job.*

fee n. a payment made to someone for a professional service.

feeble adj. weak; indistinct.

feed vb. give food to a person or animal.

feel vb. be aware of something by touch; be conscious of; experience.

feeler n. the antenna of an insect, with which it touches or feels things.

feeling n. a sensation; an emotion; something that you know inside yourself, like knowing that you dislike someone. *A feeling of pain.*

feet pl. n. more than one foot.

feline adj. of cats or the cat family.

fell vb. past of **fall**. *Jack fell down and broke his crown.*

fellow n. a male person; a member of a learned society. adj. of the same class or kind. *A fellow countryman.*

felony n. serious crime such as murder.

felt 1. vb. past of **feel** 2. n. a kind of cloth made from bits of wool pressed together rather than woven.

female n. a woman; a girl; any animal that is not a male.

feminine adj. belonging to or characteristic of women. **feminist** n. supporter of women's rights.

fen n. low-lying marshland or bog.

fence 1. n. a wooden or metal barrier. 2. vb. fight with special swords.

fender n. 1. protective frame around an open fireplace; fireguard. 2. a car's bumper.

fennec n. North American fox.

fennel n. a yellow-flowered herb.

ferment vb. 1. undergo fermentation. 2. be in a state of agitation.

fern n. a plant with feathery leaves

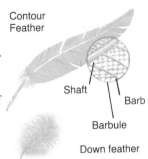

Contour Feather

Shaft

Barb

Barbule

Down feather

Birds have two kinds of feathers. Strong feathers cover the body and wings. Tiny hooks, or barbs, join the separate parts of the feather. Soft down feathers lie next to the skin.

which does not produce flowers.

ferocious adj. fierce, cruel, savage.

ferret n. a small animal that can be trained to hunt rabbits and rats. vb. hunt with ferrets; rummage.

ferry n. a boat that carries people for short distances. *We crossed the river by the ferry.*

fertile adj. able to produce a lot of good crops. *The Nile valley is very fertile.*

fertilize vb. make fruitful or

There are three fencing weapons: (from left) the foil, the epée, and saber.

F

productive.

fervent *adj*. ardent, intense. **fervor** *n*. zeal.

fester *vb*. become sore and filled with pus.

festival *n*. a time for celebration – dancing, music, and feasting.

fetch *vb*. collect something or bring it back.

fête (rhymes with *late*) *n*. a kind of open-air party where there are games and things to buy. *A fête is usually organized to collect money for charity.*

fetus (**feet-***us*) *n*. the developing offspring (baby) in its mother's womb.

fever *n*. body temperature that is above normal. **feverish** *adj*.

few *adj*. not many, a small number. *He has few friends.*

fez *n*. brimless red felt hat worn by Muslims.

fiancé (*fi-***on-***say*) *n*. person to whom a woman is engaged to be married. (feminine: **fiancée**).

fiasco (*fee-***ass-***koh*) *n*. complete breakdown; mess.

fib *n*. small lie.

fiber (**fie-***ber*) *n*. 1. a very fine thread. 2. material made from fibers.

fibula *n*. outer and smaller bone of the lower part of the leg.

fickle *adj*. changeable (especially in affections).

fiction *n*. a story that has been made up, that is not about real people or events.

fiddle 1. *n*. violin. *vb*. play a violin. 2. *n*. & *vb*. putter; meddle.

fidget *vb*. move about restlessly.

field *n*. a piece of ground, often used for growing crops or keeping animals, and usually surrounded by a hedge or fence.

fierce *adj*. cruel and angry.

fiery *adj*. like fire, flaming; quick-tempered.

fiesta *n*. Spanish word for "feast-day." All Latin American countries hold fiestas, celebrating either religious or political events.

fig *n*. the soft, sweet fruit of a small-sized tree of the same name, which has large leaves.

fight *n*. a violent contest, either in battle or in some kinds of sports, e.g. boxing. *vb*. take part in a fight.

fighter *n*. boxer; soldier. aircraft designed for combat.

figure *n*. 1. a sign for a number, such as 5 or 9. 2. a diagram in a book. 3. the shape of the body. *The athletes have good figures.*

figurehead *n*. statue on a ship's bow.

filament *n*. fine wire used in an electric light bulb.

file 1. *vb*. put papers in order. 2. *n*. holder for keeping papers in order. 3. *n*. a metal tool with roughened sides for smoothing surfaces.

fill *vb*. make something full. *Please fill the kettle.* occupy all the space.

filly *n*. a young female horse.

film 1. *n*. a thin covering. 2. *n*. a coated roll of plastic that can be placed in a camera and used to take photographs. 3. *n*. moving pictures. 4. *vb*. take moving pictures.

filter *vb*. strain a liquid through a fine mesh to remove impurities. *n*. a device for straining liquid.

filthy *adj*. offensively dirty.

fin *n*. part of a fish. *The fin helps the fish to swim and balance.*

final *adj*. the last.

finale (*fin-***ah-***lay*) *n*. final movement of instrumental musical composition or a public performance.

finally *adv*. at last.

finance *n*. the management of money matters. *vb*. provide money for. *He financed the play.*

finch *n*. a small bird belonging to a very large family of birds found almost everywhere except Australia.

find *vb*. discover or locate something.

find out *vb*. come to know something, discover. *Can you find out where he has gone?*

fine 1. *adj*. very thin or delicate. 2. *adj*. (of weather) good and clear. 3. *n*. money paid as a punishment.

finger *n*. one of the end parts, or digits, of the hand, including the thumb. *vb*. touch with the fingers.

fingerprint *n.* the mark left on something by the tip of your finger.

finish *vb. & n.* end something; complete a task.

fiord *n.* a long, narrow valley with steep sides along the coast, especially of Norway and Greenland.

fir *n.* an evergreen tree with flat needle-like leaves and erect cones.

fire 1. *n.* the bright light and heat that comes when something is burned. 2. *vb.* shoot a gun.

fire engine *n.* a vehicle used to carry hoses, ladders and equipment to put out fires.

fire escape *n.* a way out of a burning building.

fireman *n.* a person whose job it is to put out fires. *A fireman goes to a fire in a fire engine.*

fireplace *n.* an area in a room to hold an open fire.

fire station *n.* a fireman's headquarters, where fire engines are kept.

firewood *n.* small pieces of wood to fuel a fire.

fireworks *pl. n.* devices that burn with noise or striking colors, such as a rocket or a sparkler.

firm 1. *adj.* solid, hard, steady. 2. *n.* a business, company.

firmament *n.* the whole expanse of the sky with its stars and clouds.

first *adj. & adv.* number one in order; at the beginning.

first aid *n.* on-the-spot care of the victims of accidents or sudden illnesses.

fish 1. *n.* a cold-blooded vertebrate (backboned) animal that lives in water and breathes through gills. 2. *vb.* try to catch fish. **fishy** *adj.* of fish; smell of fish; suspicious.

fisherman *n.* a person who catches fish.

fishmonger *n.* a person who sells fish.

fission *n.* splitting or dividing into parts; the splitting of an atomic nucleus.

fist *n.* the tightly closed hand.

fit 1. *adj.* in good health or physical condition. 2. *vb.* be suitable, the right size. *Are you sure that shoe fits you?* 3. *n.* a sudden, violent convulsion.

fix 1. *vb.* mend something. 2. *vb.* decide. *We will fix a date for the match.* 3. *n.* a difficult position. *We are in a fix.*

fixture *n.* anything fixed firmly in position, within a house, store, building, etc.

flabbergast *vb.* astonish.

Color flags of the armed services are displayed at impressive ceremonial parades.

flabby *adj.* hanging loosely (especially of flesh); limp.

flaccid (**flak**-*sid*) *adj.* flabby, hanging loosely.

flag 1. *n.* a piece of colored cloth with a pattern on it as a symbol of the country or organization to which it belongs.

flagon *n.* a large, round, short-necked bottle (old-fashioned).

flagstone *n.* flat slab of stone for paving.

flair *n.* natural talent. *She has a flair for writing.*

flake *n.* a small, loose, flat piece of something, such as snow.

flamboyant *adj.* ornate, showy.

flame *n.* the burning gas from a fire.

flamingo *n.* a tropical bird, pink in color, with long legs and neck.

flan *n.* an open tart.

flange *n.* projecting rim that strengthens or guides.

flank *n.* the side of certain things, especially animals, or a formation. *vb.* stand at the side of.

flannel *n.* soft woolen cloth.

flap 1. *n.* a piece of material that hangs down over an opening. 2. *vb.* make something move up and down. *The wind flapped the clothes on the line.*

flare 1. *vb.* blaze up (of fire or light). *n.* bright light. 2. *vb.* spread outward, e.g. a skirt.

flash *n.* a sudden burst of light. *vb.* reflect light.

flask *n.* a stoppered bottle, particularly one for carrying liquor.

flat 1. *adj.* level and smooth. 2. *n.* a musical note one half step lower than the specified tone.

flatter *vb.* please someone by praising them more than they deserve.

flatulence *n.* gas in the stomach or bowels.

flaunt *vb.* show off, make a great display of.

flautist *n.* flute player; flutist.

flavor *n.* the taste and smell of food. *vb.* give flavor to; season.

flaw *n.* a defect or imperfection in something. *There is a flaw in your argument.*

flax *n.* a slender-stemmed plant with blue flowers. **flaxen** *adj.*

flea *n.* a small, jumping insect that feeds on blood.

fleck *n.* speck of color, light, etc. *vb.* mark with flecks.

fledgling *n.* a young bird that is just able to fly.

flee *vb.* run away from.

fleece *n.* a sheep's wooly covering.

fleet *n.* a number of ships under one leader.

fleeting *adj.* passing by quickly. *A fleeting moment.*

flesh *n.* the soft part of the body covering the bones.

flew *vb.* past of **fly**.

flex *v.* to bend, usually repeatedly.

flexible *adj.* easily bent this way and that.

flicker *vb.* shine or burn, now bright, now faint.

flight (rhymes with *bite*) *n.* 1. the act of flying. 2. a journey in an aircraft. 3. running away from danger.

flimsy *adj.* light and frail.

fling *n.* & *vb.* throw forcefully, hurl.

flint *n.* a glassy hard mineral that is a form of quartz.

flippant *adj.* to treat serious matters lightly.

flipper *n.* an arm like part used by seals and other water animals to swim.

flirt (*flurt*) *vb.* play at courting a person.

float 1. *vb.* be held up in air or in water. 2. *n.* a piece of cork or wood on a fishing line or net.

flock *n.* a large group of animals, particularly sheep or birds.

flog *vb.* whip, thrash with a stick, etc.

flood (*flud*) *n.* a lot of water that spreads over usually dry land. *vb.* cover with a flood.

floor *n.* 1. the part of the room on which one walks. 2. a level or story of a building. *Nick lives on the second floor.*

flop 1. *vb.* throw oneself down clumsily or loosely. 2. *n.* utter failure. *The musical flopped.*

flora *n.* plant life of a particular district.

florist *n.* a person or shop that sells flowers.

flounder 1. *n.* small flat fish. 2. *vb.* stumble, thrash about as if helpless in water; make a mess of things.

flour *n.* a powder made from grain and used in cooking. *Bread is made from flour.*

flourish *vb.* prosper, thrive, be healthy. *The shop is flourishing.*

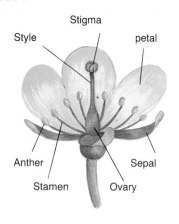

Stigma
Style
petal
Anther
Sepal
Stamen
Ovary

Section through a flower.

flow *vb.* move along as water does in a river. *n.* process of flowing.

flower *n.* the colored part of a plant that produces seeds. *vb.* blossom.

flown *vb.* past part. of **fly**.

flu abbreviation of influenza.

flue *n.* smoke channel in a chimney.

fluff *n.* soft down, hair, etc.

fluid *n.* any liquid or gas that can flow easily.

flung *vb.* past of **fling**.

flush *vb.* 1. blush. 2. clear out with sudden rush of water.

fluster *vb.* make confused or nervous; agitate.

flute *n.* a wind instrument with holes in the side. **flutist** *n.* flute player.

flutter *vb.* flap wings quickly and irregularly without flying.

fly 1. *vb.* move through the air; travel in an aircraft; depart suddenly. 2. *n.* one of a large group of winged insects.

foal *n.* a young horse.

foam *n.* a white mass of small bubbles; froth.

focus *vb.* adjust the lens of a camera, telescope, etc., in order to get a clear picture or view. *n.* distance from a lens at which the image is clear.

fodder *n.* food for cattle.

foe *n.* an enemy.

fog *n.* a thick mist that it is difficult to see through.

foil 1. *n.* metal sheet rolled or beaten very thin. 2. *vb.* defeat; beat off attacks.

fold 1. *vb.* bend part of a thing back over itself. 2. *n.* part of material that is folded; a crease.

folder *n.* file, holder for papers.

foliage *n.* the leaves of plants.

folk (rhymes with *smoke*) *n.* people.

folklore *n.* popular beliefs, legends and customs.

follow *vb.* go after a person or thing; pursue. **follower** *n.*

folly *n.* foolishness, a stupid action.

fondle *vb.* caress, pet.

font *n.* a (usually stone) basin for holding baptismal water.

food *n.* what is eaten. **feed** *vb.*

foolish *adj.* without much sense; silly.

foot 1. *n.* the part of the leg on which we stand, below the ankle. 2. *n.* the bottom of something. *The foot of the page.* 3. *n.* a measurement of length (12 inches).

football *n.* a game played between two teams; the ball used to play football.

footlights *pl. n.* lights along the front of a theater stage.

footnote *n.* note at the bottom of a printed page.

footprint *n.* the mark left by a foot on a surface.

footsteps *pl. n.* the sound of someone walking; footfalls. *I can hear footsteps on the stairs.*

for *prep.* 1. showing goal or direction. *He left for home.* 2. length of time or space. *She waited for an hour.* 3. showing preparation, purpose. *You must get ready for school.* 4. showing cause or reason. *He couldn't eat for laughing.*

forbid *vb.* (past **forbade**) prevent; prohibit. *I forbid you to tell lies.*

force 1. *vb.* make people do something they do not want to. 2. *n.* power; strength. 3. *n.* a group of people who work together, such as the *police force*.

ford *n.* a shallow place where a river can be crossed by walking across it.

fore- *prefix* meaning in front, beforehand, earlier, e.g. **foreleg, forefather, foreshadow.**

forecast *vb.* say what is likely to happen before it does. *n.* what is forecast. *Every morning we listen to the weather forecast on the radio.*

forehead *n.* the part of the face above the eyebrows.

foreign (for-*rin*) *adj.* from or of another country. **foreigner** *n.* a person from another country.

forest *n.* a large area of land covered thickly with trees.

forfeit (for-*fit*) *n., adj.* & *vb.* thing lost through crime; penalty for crime or neglect.

forge *vb.* work metals by heating them, then hammering and rolling.

forgave *vb.* past of **forgive.**

forgery *n.* writing or a picture that is made to look as if someone else has done it; a false copy.

forget *vb.* (past **forgot**) fail to remember something.

forgive *vb.* (past **forgave**) stop being angry with someone for something they have done to you; pardon. **forgiveness** *n.*

fork *n.* 1. a tool with two or more points for lifting food to the mouth. 2. a large pronged tool for digging earth. 3. a place where something divides. *Go on until you reach the fork in the road, and then keep to the left.*

form 1. *n.* the shape something has. 2. *n.* a printed paper with spaces where answers have to be filled in. 3. *vb.* make or turn into. *Water forms ice when it freezes.*

formal *adj.* following the rules, stiff, conventional.

format *n.* shape, size and style of a book, etc.

formerly *adv.* in past times.

formidable *adj.* hard to cope with; to be dreaded.

formula *n.* 1. a rule or fact in sciences written in signs or numbers. *The chemical formula for water is* H_2O. 2. set of instructions for making up medicines etc.

forsake *vb.* desert, give up, abandon.

fort *n.* a strong building that can be defended.

forte (for-*tay*) *n.* a person's strong point. *Common sense is his forte.*

fortify *vb.* make something strong or enduring.

fortnight *n.* a period of two weeks.

fortress *n.* a stronghold, fort.

fortunate *adj.* lucky, having or bringing good luck.

fortune *n.* 1. luck, fate. 2. a lot of money. *James inherited a fortune from his great-uncle.*

forward 1. *adj.* in front of; at the front. 2. *n.* a player position in football and other games.

fossil *n.* the remains of a prehistoric animal or plant that have turned to stone.

foster *vb.* bring up; encourage, promote.

foster-mother *n.* a woman who takes a child into her own home when the real parents cannot look after it. also **foster-father, foster-parent.**

fought *vb.* past of **fight.**

foul *adj.* dirty, disgusting, bad. *He has a foul temper.*

found *vb.* 1. past of **find.** 2. establish, originate. **founder** *n.* person who starts a firm, institution, etc.

foundation *n.* the strong base of a building, usually below ground.

foundry *n.* a place where metals or glass are melted and molded.

fountain *n.* an artificial structure with jets and basins of water; a spring of water.

fowl *n.* any bird, but particularly those kept for their eggs or meat.

fox *n.* a wild animal of the dog family with red-brown fur and a bushy tail. *vb.* deceive by outwitting.

foxglove *n.* a tall plant with purple or white flowers; source of the drug digitalis.

foyer (foi-*er*) *n.* entrance hall of a hotel, theater, etc.; lobby.

fraction (**frack**-*shun*). *n*. 1. a number that is less than a whole number. *½* (*one half*) *and ¼* (*one quarter*) *are fractions*. 2. a small part of something. *We only got a fraction of what we expected.*

fracture *vb*. & *n*. break; crack.

fragile *adj*. delicate; easily damaged.

fragment *n*. a small piece.

fragrant *adj*. sweet-smelling. **fragrance** *n*.

frail *adj*. feeble; weak, fragile. **frailty** *n*.

frame *n*. 1. a number of pieces that fit together to give something its shape. *The frame of our tent is made up of two posts with a pole going across between them.* 2. structure that holds a picture, window, etc.

franc *n*. unit of currency in France, Belgium, Switzerland, etc.

franchise *n*. right to vote.

frank *adj*. open and honest. **frankly** *adv*. **frankness** *n*.

frankincense *n*. sweet-smelling resin burnt as incense.

frantic *adj*. frenzied; excited with grief, pain, worry, etc.

fraud *n*. 1. a confidence trick or other crime that involves taking money by deceit. 2. a person who is not what he seems; a swindler.

freckle *n*. a small brown mark on the skin.

free 1. *adj*. costing no money. 2. *adj*. able to do what you want. *vb*. set at liberty, release.

freedom *n*. the state of being free, liberty; independence.

freeze *vb*. turn from a liquid to a solid by lowering the liquid's temperature to below its freezing point. *As water freezes it turns into ice.* **frozen** *adj*.

freezer *n*. a box or compartment kept very cold. *Food can be kept in a freezer for a long time.*

freight (rhymes with *late*) *n*. cargo, goods that are carried from one place to another.

freighter (rhymes with *later*) *n*. a ship or aircraft that carries freight.

frenzy *n*. violent rage, excitement.

frequency *n*. 1. repeated occurrence. 2. number of vibrations, waves, cycles per second.

frequent (**free**-*kwent*) *adj*. happening often. *vb*. (free-**kwent**) visit often.

fresco *n*. a painting made on freshly laid, still wet plaster. The greatest time of fresco painting was during the Renaissance in Italy.

fresh *adj*. new. *Start on a fresh page.* not stale; not preserved. *Fresh fruit and vegetables.*

fret 1. *n*. cut or sawn ornamental pattern in wood. 2. *n*. bar across fingerboard on a guitar etc. 3. *vb*. worry, grieve.

friction *n*. rubbing of two things together; the resistance something meets with when it rubs against something else.

Friday *n*. the name of the sixth day of the week, between Thursday and Saturday; named after Frigg, Norse goddess.

fridge *n*. abbreviation for refrigerator.

friend *n*. a person you know well and like. **friendship** *n*.

frieze *n*. ornamental band along the top of a wall.

frigate *n*. originally a sailing warship of the mid-18th century, today, large guided-missile destroyer.

frighten *vb*. make afraid.

frill *n*. pleated edging on clothing; unnecessary extravagance.

fringe 1. *n*. ornamental border of loose threads. 2. *n*. hair brushed down on forehead and cut straight, bangs. 3. *adj*. not central, so less important.

fritter *vb*. waste time, money, etc.

frivolous *adj*. silly, not serious. **frivolity** *n*.

frock *n*. a woman's or girl's dress (now rather old-fashioned).

frog *n*. a small, tailless, web-footed amphibian.

from *prep*. showing place or person where something starts. *That letter's from my sister.*

front *n*. the part of something that faces forward.

frontier *n.* part of a country touching another country.

frost *n.* the powdery ice that covers everything when it is very cold.

froth *n.* foam; a collection of bubbles on the top of a liquid.

frown *vb. & n.* pull the eyebrows together when you are cross or thinking hard.

froze *vb.* past of **freeze**.

fruit (rhymes with *boot*) *n.* that part of a plant which has seeds in it and which is often eaten.

fry *vb.* cook food in hot fat or oil.

fudge (*fuj*) *n.* a soft creamy candy.

fuel *n.* anything that is burned to make heat or to give energy, such as coal, oil, gas or wood.

fulcrum *n.* the support on which a lever moves.

full *adj.* without space for more; the opposite of "empty."

fulmar *n.* a gull-like arctic sea bird.

fumble *vb.* grope, use hands clumsily.

fumes *pl. n.* strong-smelling smoke.

fun *n.* amusement; a good time.

function (**funk**-*shun*) 1. *n.* the special work of a person or thing. *A hammer's function is to knock in nails.* 2. *vb.* do something. *This tool functions as a drill and as a screwdriver.*

fund *n.* sum of money used for a charity or other purpose.

fundamental *adj.* basic, essential.

funeral *n.* the ceremony when someone who has died is buried.

fungus (plural **fungi**) *n.* a small plant with no leaves, flowers or green coloring (chlorophyll), such as a mushroom.

funk *n.* paralyzing fear; coward. *vb.* try to get out of because of fear.

funnel *n.* a tube with a wide top and narrow bottom. *A funnel is used to pour liquid into a container with a narrow opening.* *vb.* use a funnel.

funny *adj.* 1. amusing; comical. *She read me a funny story.* 2. peculiar; odd. *He gave me a funny look.*

fur *n.* the soft, thick, hairy covering on some mammals. **furry** *adj.*

furious *adj.* raging, very angry.

furnace *n.* an enclosed fireplace producing great heat.

furniture *n.* chairs, tables, beds, desks and other similar things. **furnish** *vb.*

furrow *n.* a straight, narrow cut made in the ground by a plow.

fury *n.* violent anger.

fuse 1. *n.* a safety device in an electric circuit. 2. *n.* a device that sets off explosions. 3. *vb.* join together by heat.

fuselage (**fyoo**-*se-lazh*) *n.* the body of an aircraft.

fuss *n.* nervous excitement, bustle, bother. *vb.* worry, complain.

future *n.* the time yet to come.

A frog's life story. The jelly-covered eggs, called spawn, produce fishlike tadpoles which swim in the water. These gradually grow legs and lose their tails as they turn into frogs.

G

gabardine *n.* a fine durable cloth used for clothes.

gable *n.* triangular part of outer house wall between the sloping sides of the roof.

gadget *n.* a small thing made to do a particular job. *A can opener is a gadget.*

Gaelic *n.* one of the ancient languages of the Celts. It reached Ireland from Europe, and spread to Scotland and the Isle of Man. In Eire (Ireland) it is an official language, but only five percent of the people still use it regularly. "Clan" and "loch" are Gaelic words.

gag 1. *n.* something tied around someone's mouth to stop speech. 2. *n.* a joke, funny story. *vb.* make gags. 3. *vb.* retch, choke.

gaga *adj.* crazy or foolish.

gaggle *n.* a flock of geese.

gaiety *n.* cheerfulness, merrymaking.

gain (rhymes with *lane*) *vb.* win or reach. *Eric is sure to gain the prize. n.* addition, increase. *A gain in weight.*

gainsay *vb.* contradict, deny.

gala *n.* festivity.

galaxy *n.* a very large group of stars in outer space. *The Milky Way is a galaxy.*

gale *n.* a very strong wind.

gallant *adj.* brave, daring, courteous – especially to women.

galleon *n.* a large ancient Spanish sailing ship with a high stern.

gallery *n.* 1. a building where pictures or other works of art are shown. 2. the highest part of a theater or church where people sit.

galley *n.* 1. an open, seagoing vessel powered mainly by oars and used by Mediterranean nations from ancient times until the 1700s. 2. a ship's kitchen.

Gallic *adj.* relating to the Gauls; French.

gallon *n.* a liquid measure. *There are eight pints in a gallon.*

A cross-section of a galleon with three gun-decks. Hammocks were slung from the ceilings of the gun-decks. These heavy wooden fighting ships of the 1500s had square sails on their two front masts and three-cornered lateen sails on rear masts. Lateen sails helped galleons to sail against the wind.

A galaxy and (arrowed) a supernova. A supernova is an exploding star whose brilliant light lasts a few days.

gallop *n*. & *vb*. the fastest pace of a horse.

gallows *n*. wooden framework on which criminals used to be hanged.

galore *adv*. plenty. *At the party there was food and drink galore.*

galvanize *vb*. 1. reduce the corrosion (rust) of iron and steel by coating it with a thin layer of zinc. 2. shock someone into doing something.

gambit *n*. opening moves in a game of chess.

gamble *vb*. risk money in the hope of gaining more. **gambler** *n*. a person who gambles. **gambling** *n*.

game 1. *n*. a form of indoor or outdoor play, usually with rules. 2. *n*. wild animals that are hunted for food or for sport. 3. *adj*. ready; spirited.

gamma *n*. third letter of the Greek alphabet: γ.

gamma rays *adj*. & *pl.n*. high-frequency electromagnetic rays similar to, but more powerful than, X-rays. They can pass through iron one foot thick and are used in medicine against cancer.

gander *n*. a male goose.

gang *n*. a group of people working together.

gangster *n*. a member of a gang of criminals.

gangway *n*. 1. a movable bridge between a ship and the shore. 2. an opening for boarding a ship.

gannet *n*. large white seabird.

gap *n*. 1. an opening; a space. 2. a space of time. *There was a long gap in the conversation.*

gape *vb*. stare, open mouth wide, be wide open.

garage *n*. a place where cars are kept or repaired. *vb*. put or keep in a garage.

garbage *n*. rubbish, refuse, trash.

garden *n*. a piece of land for growing flowers, fruit or vegetables. *vb*. to work in a garden. **gardener** *n*. a person who looks after a garden.

gardenia *n*. one of a large group of tropical plants with fragrant white or yellow flowers.

gargle *vb*. wash the throat by bubbling liquid about in it. *n*. liquid used to gargle with.

gargoyle *n*. rainspout of a gutter carved with grotesque figures.

garish *adj*. too bright, over-colored, gaudy.

garlic *n*. plant grown for its strong-tasting bulb, used as flavoring in cooking.

garment *n*. a piece of clothing.

garret *n*. room immediately below the roof of a house; an attic.

garrison *n*. body of troops stationed in a town or fortress. *vb*. occupy as a garrison.

garter *n*. 1. strap or band used to support a stocking. 2. the highest order of knighthood in the United Kingdom.

G

G

Oil   Oil
        Natural gas

Natural gas is often found near oil, trapped between layers of rock beneath the Earth's surface.

gas *n.* 1. any substance like air. *They filled balloons with helium gas because it is lighter than air.* 2. various mixtures used for fuel. *We cook with gas in our house.* 3. gasoline.

gash *vb. & n.* a deep cut.

gasoline *n.* a liquid fuel made from oil and used to power motor vehicles.

gasp *n. & vb.* struggle to breathe; breathe in short, quick breaths.

gastric *adj.* concerning the stomach.

gastronomy *n.* the art of good eating and cooking.

gate *n.* an outside door, often in a wall or fence.

gate-crasher *n.* one who attends a party etc. without having been invited.

gather *vb.* bring or come together, collect, pick. *Marian gathered a bunch of roses.*

gaucho *n.* the South American cowboy of the pampas.

gauge (rhymes with *rage*) 1. *n.* an instrument for measuring. 2. *n.* the distance between a pair of railway lines; a standard measure. 3. *vb.* measure exactly; judge, reckon.

gaunt *adj.* lean, haggard.

gauze *n.* thin fabric of open texture.

gave *vb.* past of **give**

gay *adj.* cheerful and full of fun.

gaze *vb.* look at something for a long time. *n.* a fixed look.

gazelle *n.* slender, graceful, swift antelope found on dry grasslands in Africa and parts of Asia. Most species have a white streak on either side of the face, and the male gazelle has tall sweeping horns.

gazette *n.* a newspaper.

gear *n.* 1. a set of toothed wheels working together in a machine. 2. tackle; apparatus. 3. (*casual*) clothes.

Gears are used to increase or decrease the speed at which wheels turn. They are also used to increase or decrease the turning power of wheels.

geese *pl. n.* more than one goose.

geisha *n.* Japanese girl trained to entertain men.

gelatin (**jell-***a-tin*) *n.* substance obtained from animal skins and bones. Gelatin is hard, transparent and tasteless, and consists mostly of protein; it forms a stiff jelly when dissolved in water. It is used in cooking, medicine, and photography.

gelignite *n.* explosive used for blasting.

gem (*jem*) *n.* a jewel or precious stone.

gender *n.* sex.

gene *n.* basic part of each cell that transmits heredity characteristics.

genealogy *n.* a history of descent of persons and families from ancestors; pedigree.

general 1. *adj.* to do with most people or things. *There is a general feeling that dogs should be kept on leashes in the street.* 2. *n.* a senior officer in the army.

generate *vb.* make, produce, especially electricity.

generation *n.* all the people of about the same age. *I get along well with people of my mother's generation.*

generator *n.* a machine that produces electricity.

generous *adj.* ready to give freely and happily.

genesis *n.* origin, formation; the first book of the Old Testament.

genius (**jean-***ius*) *n.* a particularly clever, intelligent person.

gentile *n.* a person who is not a Jew.

gentle *adj.* quiet, mild or kind.

genuflect *vb.* bend the knee, especially in worship. **genuflexion** *n.*

genuine *adj.* real and true; authentic, not a sham.

genus *n.* (plural **genera**) a biological grouping of similar plants or animals. In the Latin name of a species, the first word is the name of the genus. For example, the dingo of Australia is called *Canis dingo. Canis* is the name of the

genus (the dog family). *Dingo* is the name of the species.

geo- *prefix* meaning earth, e.g. **geography**.

geography *n.* the study of the earth and what happens on it.

geology *n.* the study of the earth's history as shown in the rocks. **geological** *adj.* **geologist** *n.*

geometry *n.* the mathematical study of lines, surfaces, angles and solids. **geometric** *adj.*

Georgian *adj.* belonging to the reigns of King George I-VI.

geranium *n.* popular name for two groups of plants. One group, found wild in woodlands and also cultivated in gardens, has pink, purple or blue flowers. The other group, with scarlet, pink or white flowers, is often grown indoors or in greenhouses.

gerbil *n.* a small rodent (gnawing animal), also known as a desert rat, and popular as a pet.

geriatrics *n.* branch of medicine concerned with the health of the aged.

germ *n.* a microbe, especially one that makes people ill.

germinate *vb.* start to grow, especially of plants.

gesture *vb.* move the hand or head to show someone something. *She gestured toward the gate and everyone ran out. n.* an expressive movement.

get (past **got**, past part. **gotten**). *vb.* 1. gain, become or achieve something. *What will you do if you get rich?* 2. go. *Get out of my sight.*

get away with *vb.* avoid the result of something you have done or not done. *I did my work badly, but I will get away with it.*

get on *vb.* make progress.

get one's back up *vb.* to become angry.

get over *vb.* recover. *Penny was getting over the loss of her cat.*

get rid of *vb.* throw away, shake off, discard.

get-together *n.* a meeting, especially for special reasons.

Geysers occur in volcanic areas where water deep underground is superheated; bubbles of steam rise, expand and push water to the surface.

geyser (*guy-zer*) *n*. a natural hot spring from which hot water and steam erupt, often at regular intervals.

ghastly *adj*. horrible, terrifying.

ghetto *n*. once the Jewish quarter of a city; part of a city – especially slums – lived in by a particular group of people.

ghost *n*. the spirit of a dead person that some people believe walks at night.

giant *n*. a huge animal or plant.

gibbon *n*. a long-armed, tailless ape.

giblets *pl. n*. liver, gizzard, etc., of poultry.

giddy *adj*. dizzy; thoughtless.

gift *n*. a present, something that is given to someone. **gifted** *adj*. talented.

gig ("g" as in *give*) *n*. 1. light, two wheeled horse-drawn carriage. 2. public jazz, pop or rock performance.

gigantic (*jye-gan-tic*) *adj*. very large indeed.

giggle *n*. & *vb*. laugh in a silly way.

gill ("g" as in *give*) *n*. a part on each side of a fish through which it breathes.

gild *v*. put on a thin coating of gold.

gimmick *n*. new and showy device. *Her kitchen was fitted with all the latest gimmicks*. method of attracting attention, especially for publicity purposes.

gin *n*. 1. snare, trap (for animals). 2. colorless alcoholic beverage made from grain flavored with juniper.

ginger 1. *adj*. & *n*. a reddish-brown color. *She has ginger hair*. 2. *n*. the hot-tasting root of a plant, used as flavoring for ginger ale, gingerbread, etc.

gingerly *adj*. delicately, timidly.

gingham ("g" as in *give*) *n*. cotton cloth with checked or striped pattern.

giraffe *n*. an African animal with very long legs and neck.

girder *n*. beam, usually of steel.

girl *n*. a female child; a young woman. **girlish** *adj*.

gist (*jist*) *n*. general meaning of a subject.

give *vb*. hand something over to someone else without payment.

give back *vb*. return something to someone.

give in *vb*. agree to something unwillingly. *Bill kept asking for another ice cream, and at last his father gave in*.

give out *vb*. announce, distribute. *Can you give out the programs?*

give up *vb*. stop doing something. *My uncle will give up smoking on New Year's Day*.

gizzard *n*. a bird's second stomach used for grinding food.

glacier *n.* body of ice that moves down valleys under the force of gravity. (Ice sheets are even larger bodies of ice). *Glaciers have carved much of the world's most impressive mountain scenery.*

glad *adj.* pleased, happy.

gladiator *n.* a man who fought, often to the death, for the entertainment of spectators in ancient Rome.

glamour *n.* alluring charm, often of a false kind.

glance *vb.* look briefly at something. *He glanced at the newspaper and then put it aside. n.* a brief look.

gland *n.* an organ in the body which makes and secretes substances needed by the body.

glare 1. *vb.* look angrily at someone. 2. *n.* a strong continuous light.

glass *n.* 1. a hard, brittle material which can usually be seen through. 2. anything made of glass, such as a tumbler. 3. a mirror.

glasses *pl. n.* spectacles; lenses in frames to help you see better.

glaze 1. *n.* a mixture coated on pottery to give it a shiny surface. 2. *vb.* fit with glass or windows; coat pottery with glaze. **glazier** *n.* a person who glazes windows.

glean *vb.* gather corn left by harvesters; pick up facts here and there.

glen *n.* (*Sc*) valley.

glide *vb.* move very smoothly.

glider *n.* an aircraft that flies without an engine.

glimmer *vb. & n.* faint flickering light.

glitter *vb.* shine brightly and reflect light. *The Christmas tree decorations glitter in the candlelight.*

global *adj.* worldwide; general.

globe *n.* an object shaped like a ball, especially a map of the world shaped that way.

gloom *n.* dark, dismal; depression of the spirits. *The news filled him with gloom.* **gloomy** *adj.* dark, sullen.

glory *n.* splendor, fame; happiness of heaven. **glorious** *adj.* majestic; delightful.

gloss *n.* 1. smooth shining coating. *Gloss paint.* **glossy** *adj.* 2. *vb.* to cover up (an error, fault, etc.).

glossary *n.* a list, like a short dictionary, of special words used in a book.

glove *n.* a covering for the hand.

glow *vb.* shine with a bright, steady light.

glowworm *n.* a beetle whose wingless female emits a greenish light.

glucose *n.* a sweet substance that occurs widely in nature.

glue *n. & vb.* a sticky substance used for joining (gluing) things together.

glum *adj.* gloomy, morose.

glut *n.* too great a supply.

glutton *n.* a very greedy person. **gluttony** *n*

glycerine *n.* colorless, odorless, liquid alcohol, used in the making of perfume, cosmetics, explosives, antifreeze mixtures, and in medicine.

gnat (*nat*) *n.* a general name for any small, thin, two-winged insect with long delicate legs, such as the mosquito.

gnaw(*naw*) *vb.* chew at. *Dogs love to gnaw bones.*

gnome (*nome*) *n.* a small goblin that lives under the ground.

gnu (*new*) *n.* a large African oxlike antelope.

go (past **went**) *vb.* move from one place to another, travel, depart, turn, work, function, etc.

goal (rhymes with *hole*) *n.* 1. the posts between which a ball must be sent in some games; points scored by doing this. 2. something you are trying to achieve or some place you are trying to reach.

goat *n.* an animal with horns, related to sheep.

gobble *n. & vb.* 1. eat rapidly and greedily. 2. make the noise of a turkey.

goblin *n.* a legendary ugly and usually evil spirit or fairy.

god *n.* a supreme being that is worshipped because people believe that it has control over their lives.

godchild (**goddaughter, godson**). *n.* one for whom one acts as sponsor at a baptism, the sponsor being a **godparent** (**godmother** or **god-father**).

goddess *n.* a female god.

godly *adj.* pious.

go for *vb.* attack (usually animals).

goggles *pl. n.* large glasses that protect the eyes from water, wind or at work.

gold *n.* a precious, shiny yellow metal used for coinage, jewelry, etc. (symbol – *Au*). **golden** *adj.*

golden *adj.* the color of gold.

golden wedding *n.* 50th wedding anniversary.

goldfish *n.* an ornamental fish descended from a type of carp in China.

golf *n.* a game in which a small ball is driven by a club (stick) from hole to hole. **golfer** *n.*

gondola *n.* a narrow boat, with curved prow and stern, used on the canals in Venice. **gondolier** *n.*

gone *vb.* past part. of **go**.

gong *n.* metal disk giving a ringing note when struck.

good (**better, best**) *adj.* 1. of high quality. *I'm reading a very good book.* 2. well-behaved. *Be a good girl.*

good-bye *interj.* farewell; an expression of good wishes on parting.

Good Friday *n.* the Friday before Easter, observed as the anniversary of the Crucifixion of Jesus.

goodness *n.* being good, virtue, excellence.

goods *pl. n.* 1. things that are bought and sold. 2. things that are carried on trains or trucks. *They took the goods off the truck and put them on the train.*

goose *n.* (plural **geese**) a large, web-footed water bird of the duck family.

gooseberry *n.* the edible fruit of the gooseberry bush.

gopher *n.* burrowing rodent (gnawing animal) of North America.

The mask of Tutankhamen was made of solid gold. He was a pharaoh of Egypt in the 1350s BC.

gore *vb.* pierce or wound with horns.

gorge 1. *n.* deep narrow valley. 2. *vb.* eat greedily; stuff to capacity.

gorgeous *adj.* magnificent, splendid; marvelous. *Gorgeous gown.*

gorilla *n.* the largest of the apes.

gosling *n.* a young goose.

gospel *n.* one of the four books of the New Testament containing accounts of the life and teachings of Jesus.

gossip *vb.* chatter about other people and what they are doing. *n.* idle talk.

got *vb.* past and past part. of **get**.

go through *vb.* examine carefully.

gotten *vb.* past part. of **get**.

goulash *n.* highly seasoned Hungarian stew.

gourd *n.* large fleshy fruit of the cucumber family.

govern *vb.* rule, control people or a country.

government *n.* the people who rule or govern a country.

gown *n.* a woman's dress; a long flowing garment.

grab *vb.* seize quickly and roughly. *n.* an attempt to seize.

graceful *adj.* pleasing movement or shape.

grade *vb.* arrange according to quality etc. *n.* rank, class, division.

gradient *n.* slope of a road, railway, etc.

gradual *adj.* happening slowly. *The change was so gradual we hardly noticed it.*

graduate *vb.* get a degree or diploma. *n.* holder of a degree.

graffito *n.* (plural **graffiti** *graf-***fee**-*tee*) words or drawings scribbled on a wall.

graft *vb.* cut part of one plant and join it to another so that it grows. *n.* (surgical) transplant.

grain *n.* 1. the small, hard seeds of all plants like wheat, rice and maize. 2. the natural pattern in wood.

gram (or **gramme**) *n.* a small unit for measuring weight. *There are 1000 grams in a kilogram.*

grammar *n.* the rules for using words and putting them together.

granary *n.* a building where grain is stored.

grand *adj.* important, splendid.

grandchild (**grand-daughter son**) *n.* the child of one's own child.

grandfather *n.* the father of a mother or father. also **granddad, grandpa**.

grandmother *n.* the mother of a mother or father. also **grandma, granny**.

grandstand *n.* rows of seats at a sports ground, usually roofed.

granite *n.* a hard rock made largely of crystals of quartz and feldspar.

grant *vb.* allow, give. *He was granted a pension.* *n.* something granted, especially money.

grape *n.* a green or purple berry that grows in bunches on a vine.

grapefruit *n.* a large yellow citrus fruit, often eaten at breakfast.

graph (rhymes with **laugh**) *n.* a diagram used to show how numbers and amounts compare.

grapple 1. *n.* a clutching instrument. 2. *vb.* seize, grip, fight.

grasp *vb.* hold tightly; understand. **grasping** *adj.* greedy.

grass *n.* a plant with thin green leaves grown on lawns and in fields.

grasshopper *n.* a small jumping insect which chirps.

grass roots *n.* (in politics) at the local level. *States often pass new tax laws*

Male grasshoppers chirp by rubbing their back legs on their wings.

A gorilla is a huge, heavily built ape which lives in the forests of equatorial Africa.

that start at the grass roots.

grate 1. *n.* iron frame in a fireplace. 2. *vb.* produce harsh noise by rubbing something on a rough surface.

grateful *adj.* feeling of thanks for something. *She was very grateful to* *the nurses who looked after her in the hospital.*

grave 1. *n.* a hole in the ground in which a dead body is buried. 2. *adj.* serious, solemn.

gravel *n.* small stones used in the making of roads and paths.

graveyard *n.* a place where people are buried, near a church.

gravity *n.* 1. solemnity. 2. the force that pulls things together. *Gravity makes things fall.*

gravy *n.* hot sauce made with meat juices.

gray *n.* & *adj.* color midway between black and white.

graze 1. *vb.* eat growing grass; put out to pasture. 2. *n.* & *vb.* scrape lightly in passing.

grease *n.* any thick oil substance. *vb.* lubricate.

great *adj.* 1. large or heavy. *That's a great deal of money.* 2. important or famous. *He was a truly great man.*

Great Bear *n.* a constellation (*Ursa Major*) in the northern sky, made up of seven stars, "the Plough."

Great Dane *n.* large, strong dog of German origin, despite its name. It is quiet and good-tempered but can be very fierce and so makes a good guard dog.

Grecian *adj.* & *n.* Greek.

greedy *adj.* selfishly fond of food, money or other things. **greed** *n.*

green 1. *n.* & *adj.* a color like that of grass or leaves. 2. *n.* an open, grassy area.

greenbelt *n.* area of countryside around a town where building is restricted.

greenhorn *n.* someone without much experience.

greenhouse *n.* a building with a glass roof and glass walls in which plants are grown.

greet *vb.* welcome. *She always greets me with a kiss.* **greeting** *n.*

grenade *n.* small explosive shell thrown by hand.

grew *vb.* past of **grow**.

greyhound *n.* fast-running dog with a slender body and long powerful legs. Greyhounds are used for hunting game and for racing. In a greyhound race, the dogs chase a mechanical hare around an oval track.

grief (rhymes with *reef*) *n.* great sadness. **grieve** *vb.*

grim *adj.* severe, without joy.

grime *n.* dirt; squalor.

grin *n.* & *vb.* wide smile.

grind *vb.* 1. crush to a powder. *They grind wheat into flour at the mill.* 2. sharpen.

grip *vb.* & *n.* hold firmly.

grit *n.* 1. tiny pieces of stone or sand. 2. courage; staying power.

grizzly bear *n.* large bear from North America.

groan *vb.* make a deep sound of pain or sorrow. *n.* groaning sound.

grocer *n.* a person who sells meats, produce, household supplies, etc.

groom 1. *vb.* & *n.* brush and clean a horse; a person who looks after a horse for someone else. 2. *n.* a bridegroom.

groove *n.* a long, narrow cut in a surface.

grope *vb.* feel one's way by touch, fumble.

Greenhouses are warm inside because heat rays from the sun warm up everything inside. The heat is then trapped in the greenhouse.

gross 1. *adj.* large; fat; disgusting. 2. *adj.* (of prices, weights, etc.) including all items. 3. *n.* 12 dozen (144).

grotesque *adj.* distorted style of decorative art using fantastic human and animal shapes.

grotto *n.* cave, often artificial.

ground 1. *n.* the surface of the earth. 2. *vb.* past of **grind**.

group *n.* a number of people or things gathered together or belonging together. *vb.* form or fall into a group.

grouse 1. *n.* large game bird from the Northern Hemisphere which usually nests on the ground. There are about 30 species, mostly gray, brown or black in color. 2. *vb.* grumble.

grow (past **grew** past part. **grown**) *vb.* 1. become larger or taller. 2. live (of plants). 3. become. *They are growing old gracefully.*

growl *n.* & *vb.* a low, angry noise, as made by a dog.

grown-up *n.* any person who is an adult.

growth *n.* 1. the act of growing. 2. an abnormal tumor in the body.

grow up *vb.* stop being a child, attain maturity, become adult.

grub *n.* 1. the larva stage of an insect. 2. (*slang*) food. **grubby** *adj.* dirty.

grudge *vb.* envy, agree to do something unwillingly. *She grudged paying for it.*

grumble *vb.* complain in a cross way, protest. *n.* murmur, complaint.

grunt *vb.* & *n.* (make) a low noise like a pig.

guano *n.* rich manure composed of the dung of seabirds.

guarantee *n.* a promise to do something, especially to mend or replace something which goes wrong after it has been bought. *vb.* promise, answer for, secure.

guard *vb.* protect someone or something. *The police will guard the exhibition of jewels.* *n.* a person who guards things.

guerrilla *n.* a fighter who does not belong to a country's organized army.

guess *vb.* & *n.* form an opinion without really knowing the facts. *He didn't know how to spell the word, so he made a guess.*

guest *n.* a person who is visiting another person's house or who stays in a hotel.

guide *vb.* show someone the way. *n.* a person who guides other people.

guided missile *n.* a rocket- or jet-propelled missile with an explosive warhead.

guilder *n.* the main unit of Dutch currency.

guillotine *n.* an instrument for beheading people, named after a Dr. Guillotin, first used in the French Revolution. *vb.* execute with a guillotine.

A guillotine by which many were executed in the French Revolution.

guilty *adj.* having done something wrong. *The dog looked very guilty when we found the meat was gone.* **guilt** *n.*

guinea pig *n.* small tailless animal belonging to a family of South American rodents called cavies.

guitar *n.* a musical instrument with six strings which are plucked with the fingers. **guitarist** *n.* a guitar player.

gulf *n*. a large area of the sea almost surrounded by land.

gull *n*. a kind of large seabird.

gullet *n*. food passage through the throat.

gulp *vb*. & *n*. swallow noisily and quickly.

gum *n*. 1. the pink flesh in which the teeth are set. 2. glue. 3. chewing gum.

gun *n*. a weapon that fires bullets or some other missile from a long tube open at one end; a firearm.

gunpowder *n*. an explosive made by mixing special amounts of charcoal, sulphur and saltpeter.

gunsmith *n*. maker of guns.

gurgle *vb*. & *n*. bubbling sound.

guru *n*. religious teacher, especially in the Hindu religion.

gush *vb*. flow out suddenly. *Water gushed through the door.*

gust *n*. sudden rush of wind.

gusto *n*. zest.

guts *pl*. *n*. 1. the intestines. 2. (*casual*) courage.

gutter *n*. a small channel for carrying off rainwater.

guttural *adj*. & *n*. sound formed in the throat; harsh, grating.

guy (rhymes with *lie*) *n*. 1. (*casual*) a man or boy. 2. a rope or chain used to secure a tent, sail, etc.

guzzle *vb*. drink greedily.

gym or **gymnasium** *n*. a room for sports and training.

gymkhana *n*. a competition for horses and ponies and their riders.

gymnast *n*. a person who does exercises as a sport.

gymnastics *pl*. *n*. special exercises that develop fitness and coordination.

gynecology (guy-na-**kol**-*ojee*) *n*. branch of medicine treating diseases of women.

gypsy *n*. a member of a dark-haired group of wandering people.

gyroscope ("g" as in *giant*) *n*. a rapidly spinning wheel set in a frame which only touches another surface at one point.

habit *n*. 1. something that a person or animal does so often as to not think about it. 2. a monk's robe.

habitat *n*. the place where an animal or plant normally lives.

hacienda *n*. large estate or farm in Spanish-speaking countries.

hack 1. *vb*. chop roughly. 2. *vb*. cough harshly. 3. *n*. hired riding horse. 4. *n*. dull tedious work or person.

had *vb*. past of **have**.

haddock *n*. a fish, related to the cod, and important as food.

hag *n*. a witch, ugly old woman.

haggard *adj*. gaunt and hollow-eyed.

ha-ha 1. *inter*. expressing laughter or derision. 2. *n*. boundary fence sunk in ditch.

haiku (hye-*koo*) *n*. three-line Japanese poem of 17 syllables.

hail 1. *n*. frozen rain. *vb*. fall as hail. 2. *vb*. greet someone by calling out to him or her.

hair *n*. a thread-like substance growing out of the skin of mammals.

hairdresser *n*. someone who cuts and looks after other people's hair.

hairy *adj*. covered in hair; similar to hair.

hake *n*. a fish, related to the cod, and eaten as food.

half *n*. (plural **halves**) one of the two equal parts of something.

half time *n*. the intermission that takes place after completing half of a game, e.g. football.

halibut *n*. a large flatfish of the North Atlantic and North Pacific.

halitosis *n*. foul-smelling breath.

hall *n*. 1. the entrance room of a house. 2. a large room for meetings,

Hairstyles.

plays and other activities.

hallmark *n.* mark on gold or silver showing place of origin.

Halloween *n.* a festival held on October 31, the day before All Saints' Day. (Halloween roughly means "holy evening.") People once believed that ghosts, demons and witches roamed about on Halloween night.

halo (**hay**-*low*) *n.* a circle of light around something.

halt *vb.* & *n.* stop.

halter *n.* 1. rope with headstall for leading a horse. 2. a blouse with bare arms, shoulder, and midriff.

halve *vb.* divide into two equal parts.

ham *n.* 1. salted or smoked meat from a pig's thigh. 2. (*slang*) inexpert but showy performer.

hamburger *n.* a round cake of chopped beef, eaten hot, inside a bun.

hamlet *n.* small village, usually without a church.

hammer *n.* a tool for driving in nails or breaking things. *vb.* strike with a hammer.

hammock *n.* a kind of bed, made of canvas or other cloth, and hung from cords at both ends. *In the days of sailing ships, sailors usually slept in hammocks.*

hamster *n.* a small, roundish rodent, often kept as a pet.

hand 1. *n.* the part of the arm beyond the wrist with five fingers (one of which is the thumb). 2. *vb.* give something with the hand. *Please hand me a glass of milk.*

handbag *n.* a small bag or purse, usually carried by women; pocketbook.

handcuffs *pl. n.* a pair of bracelets for locking a prisoner's hands together.

handicap *n.* anything that makes it more difficult to do things. *In golf, good players have low handicaps.*

handicapped *adj.* having a physical, mental, or learning disability. *Blind people and deaf people are handicapped.*

handicraft *n.* a craft, skill or trade; a piece of work made by a craftsman or craftswoman.

handkerchief (**hang**-*ker-chief*) *n.* (plural **-chieves**) a piece of cloth or paper, carried in a pocket or handbag, used for wiping the nose.

handle 1. *n.* part of an object designed to be grasped. 2. *vb.* feel something with the hands.

handlebar *n.* the bar with which a bicycle or motorcycle is steered.

hand over *vb.* give something to someone else, often when you do not want to. *The thief made us hand over the money.*

handsome *adj.* good looking, usually applied to men.

handwriting *n.* writing done with a pen or pencil, not typed or printed. *She has very clear handwriting.*
handwritten *adj.*

hang *vb.* 1. hold from above so that the lower part is free. *Ripe cherries hang from that tree.* 2. execute a

H

person by hanging from the neck. past **hanged**

hang around *vb.* wait.

hangar *n.* a large building where aircraft are kept.

hang-glider *n.* frame on which a person can glide through the air.

happen *vb.* take place. *The sales happen every year in January.* take place by chance. *My friend and I happen to share the same birthday.*
happening *n.* something that happens; an event.

happiness *n.* the state of being happy or contented.

happy *adj.* contented; cheerful; pleased.

harangue *vb. & n.* a ranting, rousing speech.

harass *vb.* worry, trouble by repeated attacks. **harassment** *n.*

harbor *n.* a shelter for ships. *vb.* give shelter.

hard 1. *adj.* solid or firm; not soft. *The ground was too hard to dig.* 2. *adj.* difficult. *This problem is too hard for me to do.* 3. *adv.* with great effort. *She tried hard to win the match.* 4. *adj.* tough. *You're a hard man.*

hardback *n.* book bound in a hard, long-lasting cover.

hardly *adv.* only just. *She had hardly reached home when the telephone rang.*

hardware *n.* electronic parts of a computer.

hardy *adj.* strong, able to face difficulties.

hare *n.* an animal like a large rabbit with long ears and a short tail.

harm *vb. & n.* hurt, damage.

harmless *adj.* safe; not dangerous.

harmonica *n.* a mouth organ.

harmony *n.* 1. agreeable arrangement of parts. 2. a secondary tune that blends with the main melody.
harmonize *vb.*

harness *n.* all the leather straps and other equipment by which a horse is controlled.

harp *n.* a large musical instrument played by plucking strings with the fingers of both hands.

harpoon *n.* a spear on a rope for catching whales and large fish. *A harpoon is thrown or fired and can then be pulled back.* *vb.* strike with a harpoon.

harpsichord *n.* a stringed instrument with a keyboard similar to a piano.

harrow *n.* a device to break up the soil after plowing. Disk harrows contain sharp rotating disks mounted on a shaft. *vb.* 1. draw a harrow over. 2. distress.

harsh *adj.* rough, unkind; hard to the feelings; coarse to touch.

harvest *n.* the time for cutting and bringing in grain and other crops; the crops brought in at harvest time. *vb.* gather in the harvest.

hassle 1. *n.* heated disagreement 2. *vb.* harass.

haste *n.* hurry, quickness of movement. **hasten** *vb.*

hat *n.* a covering worn on the head.

hatch 1. *vb.* come out of an egg. 2. *n.* movable covering over an opening.

hatchback *n.* car with a back door hinged at the top.

hatchet *n.* a chopper; a small ax. *"To bury the hatchet" was an American Indian expression meaning "to make peace."*

Hares, unlike rabbits, raise their young in the open. Hares include the brown hare and Alpine hare of Europe, and the snowshoe rabbit and jackrabbit of North America.

hate *vb.* & *n.* loathe; dislike someone or something very much. **hatred** *n.* active dislike, intense loathing.

haul (rhymes with *ball*) *vb.* pull a heavy load.

haunt *vb.* (of a ghost) to visit a place often.

have *vb.* own or possess something.

havoc *n.* ruin, chaos, destruction.

hawk *n.* 1. a bird of prey. 2. someone who supports a warlike policy.

hawthorn *n.* a spiny shrub related to the rose and often found in hedges.

hay *n.* dried grass used to feed animals.

hay fever *n.* an allergy; people who suffer from hay fever react to the pollen in the air by sneezing.

haystack *n.* a large pile of hay.

hazard *vb.* risk, venture on. *Hazard a guess.*

hazel 1. *n.* a small nut tree. 2. *n.* & *adj.* the brownish-green color of some people's eyes.

H-bomb *n.* hydrogen bomb.

head *n.* 1. the top part of the body, above the neck. 2. the chief person, e.g. the head teacher in a school. *vb.* lead (a strike, etc.).

headache (rhymes with **bake**) *n.* a pain in the head.

headlight *n.* one of the main lights at the front of a vehicle.

headline *n.* a very brief summary in larger print at the top of a story in a newspaper.

headquarters *n.* the main office of an organization; an army base.

headway *n.* progress.

headwind *n.* blowing directly from in front.

heal *vb.* make better, particularly of a wound.

health (*helth*) *n.* how well or ill the body and mind are.

healthy *adj.* well and strong.

heap *n.* a pile of things. *vb.* pile things on, load.

hear *vb.* listen; notice a sound or noise. **hearing** *n.*

hearing aid *n.* a device worn by a person with impaired hearing to

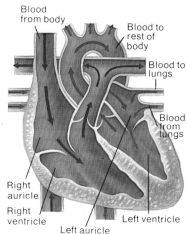

The heart is a muscular pump which is divided into two parts. One part pumps blood to the lungs. The other part pumps blood to the rest of the body.

amplify sounds.

hearse *n.* vehicle for carrying a coffin to the grave.

heart *n.* the organ or part of the body which pumps blood around the body.

heartless *adj.* without feeling or pity.

heartbreak *n.* great sorrow. **heartbreaking** *adj.*

hearth *n.* the floor or surroundings of a fireplace.

heat 1. *n.* hotness. 2. *vb.* make hot. *We heated the milk.*

heater *n.* something that produces heat. *The heater in my car takes a long time to warm up.*

heath *n.* a piece of unused land, usually with poor soil and drainage.

heave *vb.* shift, raise up with effort.

heaven (**heh-***ven*) *n.* the home of God. **heavens** *pl.n.* firmament.

heavy *adj.* having considerable weight; dull, boring.

Hebrew *n.* an ancient language now in common use in Israel.

H

hedge *n.* a row of bushes making a fence around a field or garden. *vb.* surround with a fence; give an evasive answer.

hedgehog *n.* a small animal that is covered by prickles. It defends itself by rolling into a ball.

heel *n.* the back part of the foot; part of sock etc. that covers or supports the heel.

hegira *n.* the flight of Muhammed from Mecca to Medina in 522 AD.

heifer (rhymes with *deafer*) *n.* a young cow that has not had a calf.

height (rhymes with *bite*) *n.* the measurement from the bottom to the top of something. **heighten** *vb.* raise, make higher.

heir/heiress (*air/air-ess*) *n.* the person who will inherit somebody's property or position. *Prince Charles is heir to the British throne.*

helicopter *n.* an aircraft with a horizontal rotor which acts as both propeller and wings.

helium *n.* a very light gas (symbol – He).

hell *n.* the home of the devil, place of punishment.

helm *n.* tiller, wheel, steering gear of a ship.

helmet *n.* a strong covering that protects the head. *The motorcyclist wore a crash helmet.*

help *vb.* & *n.* aid someone; come to

The hedgehog belongs to a group of mammals called insectivores, which means insect-eating. In fact, hedgehogs eat almost anything.

someone's assistance.

helpful *adj.* useful; providing help. *Thank you for being so helpful.*

helping 1. *adj.* giving help or assistance. *Can I give you a helping hand with the cleaning?* 2. *n.* a portion of food.

helpless *adj.* not able to look after yourself. *A baby bird is helpless if it falls out of the nest.*

hem *n.* the edge of cloth or clothing that is turned under and sewn.

hemisphere *n.* half a sphere; half the earth. *America is in the Western Hemisphere.*

hemlock *n.* poisonous herb.

Helicopters can fly in any direction, and even hover. The rotor blade controls the direction.

hen *n.* any female bird, but especially a farmyard chicken.

her *pron.* the female possessive pronoun. *It is her birthday today.*

heraldry *n.* the study of coats of arms.

herb *n.* a plant whose leaves are used for flavoring, medicine, or scent.

herbivore *n.* an animal that eats plants, especially grass. **herbivorous** *adj.*

herd *n.* a group of animals grazing or moving together.

here *adv.* in or at this place. *Come here.*

heredity *n.* the physical characteristics passed on from parents to offspring.

heresy *n.* opinion against what is generally accepted or officially declared. **heretic** *n.* person who supports heresy.

hermit *n.* a person who chooses to live alone, especially for religious reasons.

hero (plural **heroes**) *n.* 1. a man admired for his bravery. 2. the most important male character in a play, film or story. **heroic** *adj.* **heroism** *n.* heroic conduct, behavior worthy of a hero or heroine.

heroin *n.* a powerful, pain-killing but highly addictive drug made from morphine.

heroine *n.* 1. a woman admired for her bravery. 2. the most important female character in a play, film or story.

heron *n.* a long-legged wading bird.

herring *n.* a small sea fish. When smoked it is called a kipper.

hesitate *vb.* stop briefly; show indecision. **hesitation** *n.* **hesitant** *adj.*

hexagon *n.* a figure with six equal sides.

heyday *n.* peak, bloom (of youth, success, etc).

hibernate *vb.* spend the winter asleep. **hibernation** *n.*

hidden *vb.* past of **hide.**

hide 1. *vb.* put something where others cannot find it; go into a place

Sage
Mint
Thyme
Garlic
Parsley

Some of the common herbs used in cooking.

where you cannot be seen. 2. *n.* the skin of a large animal.

hideous *adj.* dreadfully ugly.

hieroglyphics *pl.n.* an ancient form of picture writing.

hi-fi *n. & adj.* short for high fidelity; apparatus to give good quality reproduction of recorded sound.

high *adj.* tall. *The mountain is two miles high.*

highbrow *n. & adj.* (person) of very intellectual interests.

highway *n.* a main road.

highwayman *n.* a robber on horseback.

hijack *vb.* (seize) control of a vehicle or aircraft during a journey by threat of violence.

A hexagon.

H

hike vb. & n. go for a long country walk. **hitchhike** vb. get free rides from passing motorists.

hill n. a steep place; a slope; a small mountain. **hilly** adj.

hilt n. the handle of a sword.

hinder vb. prevent, delay.

Hindu n. follower of the Hindu religion; someone from India.

hinge n. a joint on which a door or gate swings when it is opened or shut.

hint vb. suggest something without really saying it. *Carol hinted that she would like a new dress for her birthday.* n. disguised suggestion.

hip n. the joint where the leg joins the trunk of the body.

hippodrome n. oval arena for horse races and chariot races in ancient Greece.

hippopotamus n. a large African animal that lives in and near lakes and rivers.

hire vb. rent; pay for the use of something. *We hired a car for a week when we went to Florida.*

hiss vb. & n. (make) a long S sound like a snake to express anger, disapproval, etc.

history n. the study and written account of past events. **historian** n. a person who studies and writes about the past. **historic** adj. famous in history. *The battle of Gettysburg was an historic event.*

hit 1. vb. & n. strike or knock something; a blow. 2. n. a success, especially a record or show.

hitch 1. n. a setback, hold-up. 2. vb. fasten with a loop. 3. vb. thumb a ride (**hitchhike**).

hive n. 1. colony of bees. (or **beehive**) 2. a place for bees to live in.

hoard (*hord*) n. & vb. store away secretly; especially money.

hoarding n. temporary fence of boards around a building and often covered with posters.

hoarse adj. of the voice, rough or croaking.

hoax vb. & n. a trick or practical joke.

hobble vb. limp, stumble along.

hobby n. something a person likes doing when not working. *Nick's hobby is collecting stamps.*

hock 1. n. joint in hind leg of horse, dog, etc. 2. vb. pawn something.

hockey n. a game played with curved wooden sticks and a puck between two teams of players. also **ice hockey**.

hoe n. a tool for loosening the earth and digging out weeds. vb. use a hoe.

hog n. large pig.

hold 1. vb. keep firmly in the hand. 2. n. part of the hull of a ship where cargo is stored. 3. vb. contain. *This can hold a gallon.*

hold on vb. wait (especially on the telephone).

hold up vb. 1. delay. *I hope I haven't held you up.* 2. rob with a gun.

hole n. a hollow place; a pit, space or burrow.

holiday n. a day off work or school; a vacation. *We're going to France for our holiday this year.*

hollow 1. adj. not solid; empty inside. *The squirrels lived in a hollow tree.* 2. vb. to make hollow. 3. n. a hollow place or small valley.

holly n. an evergreen tree with glossy prickly leaves and red berries.

hollyhock n. tall flowering plant.

holography n. a way of producing three-dimensional images.

holy adj. having religious significance; connected with God. *The Bible is the holy book of Christianity.*

home n. the place where you live.

homesick adj. sad at being away from your home.

homework n. schoolwork that is done at home.

homicide (**hahm**-*mi-side*) n. killing of a human being.

honest (**on**-*est*) adj. truthful, not likely to cheat. **honesty** n.

honey n. the sweet substance made by bees from the nectar of flowers.

honeycomb n. the wax container

made by bees in which to store their honey.

honeymoon *n.* a holiday for a newly married couple. *vb.* go on a honeymoon.

honeysuckle *n.* climbing plant with sweet-smelling flowers; woodbine.

honor *n.* respect, high regard, esteem.

hood *n.* a covering for the head and neck; a covering for the motor of a car.

hoodwink *vb.* trick or mislead.

hoof (plural **hoofs** or **hooves**) *n.* the hard part of the foot of a horse, and of some other animals.

hook *n.* a bent piece of metal, such as a fishhook. *vb.* catch or fasten with a hook. **hooked** *adj.*

hooligan *n.* ruffian, member of a gang of hoodlums.

hoop *n.* ring of metal or wood for binding casks; a child's plaything; a metal arch used in the game of croquet.

hoot *vb.* & *n.* (make) a sound of mockery; sound of a car's horn, etc.; sound of an owl.

hop 1. *vb.* & *n.* jump on one leg, or (of a bird) with both feet together. 2. *n.* a plant belonging to the mulberry family used to make beer.

hope *vb.* & *n.* wish for something pleasant to happen. *I hope I pass the exam.*

hopeful *adj.* having hope.

hopefully 1. *adv.* in a hopeful way. 2. (*casual*) it is hoped. *Hopefully the weather will be warm.*

hopeless *adj.* without hope.

horizon *n.* the line where the land and the sky seem to meet.

horizontal *adj.* flat; level with the horizon.

hormone (**hoar**-*moan*) *n.* chemical substance which regulates the body's activities.

horn 1. *n.* one of the long, pointed growths on the head of some animals. 2. *n.* a brass musical instrument that is blown.

hornet *n.* large insect of wasp family.

horoscope *n.* a prediction about someone's future, based on the sign of the zodiac under which one was born; fortune-telling.

horrible *adj.* unpleasant, frightening or ugly.

horror *n.* fright. *He watched in horror as his boat drifted out to sea.*

horse *n.* a four-legged animal with hooves, long mane and tail, used for riding, or carrying a load.

horsepower *n.* a unit for measuring the power of engines.

horseshoe *n.* a U-shaped piece of iron used to protect a horse's hoof.

horticulture *n.* the art of gardening.

hose *n.* a long, flexible tube through which water and other liquids can pass. *vb.* wash down with a hose.

The Eohippus, in the foreground, was the ancestor of the horse. It lived about 50 million years ago. Its descendant, the Mesohippus, in the background, was slightly larger and had three toes on each foot.

H

hospital *n.* a building where sick or injured people are taken care of. **hospitalize** *vb.*

hospitality *n.* generous, friendly entertainment of guests.

host *n.* 1. a person who has guests in his house. 2. a huge crowd. 3. bread used in the Holy Communion or mass.

hostage (**hoss**-*tij*) *n.* a person who is held prisoner and threatened until certain demands are agreed to.

hostel *n.* lodging for students, etc.

Above right: *A reconstruction of a Mesopotamian farmhouse of about 5000 BC.*

Right: *A Chinese peasant home of about AD 25. It has a thatched roof, dirt floor and no furniture.*

A North American Indian shelter made of birch poles with a covering of birch bark.

106

hostess *n*. 1. a woman who has guests in her house. 2. a woman who looks after travelers on an aircraft (stewardess).

hostile *adj*. unfriendly.

hot *adj*. having high temperature. *It was so hot you could fry an egg on the sidewalk.*

hot dog *n*. a heated frankfurter in a roll.

hotel *n*. a building where travelers pay to sleep and have meals.

hotfoot *adv*. in great haste.

hound *n*. a name for various kinds of dogs, especially those used in hunting. *vb*. hunt with hounds.

hour *n*. a period of 60 minutes. *There are 24 hours in a day.* **hourly** *adj*. & *adv*. occurring once every hour.

house *n*. a building in which people live, a home.

houseboat *n*. a boat on which people live.

household *n*. all the people who live together in a house. *Our household consists of my mother, my brother and me.* **householder** *n*. head of a household.

housekeeper *n*. a person who is paid to look after a home.

housewife *n*. a married women who looks after the home.

housework *n*. work such as cleaning and washing done in the house.

hovel *n*. a small, very poor house or cottage.

hover *n*. stay in the air in one place. *A dragonfly hovers over the water.*

hovercraft *n*. an air-cushion vehicle designed to skim over the surface of water or land.

how *adv*. in what way. *How do you spell this word?*

however *adv*. & *conj*. by whatever means. *However hard you try.* but. *I'd like to go; however, I can't afford it.*

howl *vb*. & *n*. (make) a long, sad noise like a dog makes when it is hurt.

hub *n*. central part of a wheel from which the spokes radiate.

hue *n*. color, tint.

huff 1. *n*. fit of crossness. *He walked off in a huff.*

hug *vb*. embrace someone by clasping them tightly with your arms. *n*. a tight embrace.

huge *adj*. vast; enormous.

Huguenot (**hew**-*ge-no*) *n*. French Protestant in the 1700s.

hull *n*. the body of a ship.

hum 1. *n*. a low murmuring noise. 2. *vb*. sing with the mouth closed. *He always hums while he is working.*

human *adj*. & *n*. behaving or looking like people. *n*. human being.

humane *adj*. kind, gentle; merciful.

humanity *n*. the human race as a whole.

humble *adj*. 1. not vain or proud. *He was always very humble.* 2. of poor quality or little importance. *Be it ever so humble, there's no place like home.*

humbug *n*. 1. fraud; nonsense. *The speech was a lot of humbug.*

humdrum *adj*. dull, uneventful.

humidity *n*. the amount of moisture in the atmosphere. This moisture consists of tiny water particles moving about freely in the air. **humid** *adj*.

humiliate *vb*. offend, make a person look ridiculous or ashamed.

hummingbird *n*. a small brightly colored bird whose wings flap so quickly that they make a humming sound.

humor *n*. a mood. *She is in a bad humor.* an ability to be amused by or to laugh at funny sayings, drawings or stories. *Dominic has a very good sense of humor.* **humorous** *adj*.

hump *n*. a round lump like that on a camel's back.

hundred *n*. the figure 100; 10 times 10.

hung *vb*. past of **hang**.

hunger *n*. the feeling of needing food. **hungry** *adj*.

hunk *n*. a large slice (of bread, etc.).

hunt 1. *vb*. go after, and often kill, animals for sport or food. *n*. people hunting with a pack. 2. *vb*. look for something.

H

As the hydrofoil moves forward, the underwater wings lift it clear of the water.

hunter *n.* a person who hunts animals.

hurdling *n.* a foot race in which barriers called hurdles have to be jumped.

hurl *vb.* throw with great force. *n.* a violent throw.

hurricane *n.* a windy violent storm.

hurry *vb.* move quickly. *You'll be late if you don't hurry. n.* great haste; eagerness or urgency.

hurt *vb.* cause pain. *He's hurt his leg.*

husband *n.* a married man.

hush *vb.* make or become silent.
  hush up *vb.* keep secret. **hush-hush** *adj.* very secret.

husky 1. *adj.* having a hoarse, whispering voice. 2. *n.* a heavy-coated dog, bred to pull sleds in the far north of America.

hut *n.* a small building, often made of wood and used as a temporary shelter. *The children made a hut out of branches.*

hutch *n.* a cage or box for rabbits or other small animals.

hyacinth *n.* a garden flower, often blue or purple in color.

hybrid *n.* plant or animal produced by parents of different species, e.g.

a mule (male donkey and female horse).

hydrant *n.* above-ground pipe that supplies water for firefighting.

hydraulic power *n.* a form of power based on the pressure of water or other liquids which are forced through pipes.

hydro- *prefix* meaning water.

hydroelectric *adj.* producing electricity from the power of falling water.

hydrofoil *n.* a boat which, at speed, rises out of the water supported on wing-like struts, or *foils*, that project from the lower hull.

hydrogen *n.* a colorless, odorless, tasteless gas that is lighter than air (symbol – H).

hyena *n.* a savage, doglike creature that hunts in packs at night and feeds mostly on dead animals. Found mostly in India and parts of Africa.

hygiene *n.* the science of health and cleanliness. **hygienic** *adj.*

hymn (rhymes with *rim*) *n.* a religious song praising and glorifying God.

hyphen *n.* a mark like this (-) showing where a word has been divided at the end of a line, or where two words have been joined to make one, e.g. self-respect. **hyphenate** *vb.*

hypnosis *n.* a condition like deep sleep in which someone's actions can be controlled by another person. **hypnotize** *vb.*

hypochondria (*high-po-*kon-*dree-a*) *n.* a fear of becoming ill. **hypochondriac** *n.* & *adj.*

hypocrisy (*hip-*pok-*kra-see*) *n.* pretending to be good.

hypodermic syringe (*high-po-*dur-*mik*) *n.* an instrument with a hollow needle for injecting drugs under the skin.

hypotenuse (*high-*pot-*i-noose*) *n.* side of right-angled triangle opposite the right angle.

hysterical *adj.* in a state of wild excitement. **hysteria** *n.*

identical *adj.* exactly the same.
identify *vb.* establish identity of. *He identified the star at once.*
identity *n.* individuality; distinguishing character.
idiot *n.* a person who is so weak-minded that others have to look after him or her. **idiotic** *adj.* foolish.

I *pron.* first person singular; the speaker or writer.
ibex (plural **ibexes**) a species of wild goat living in the mountains of Europe, Asia and Africa. It has broader horns than the true wild goat.
ibis *n.* storklike bird with a long curved beak, found worldwide in warm regions, usually near water.
ice *n.* frozen water. *vb.* freeze; cover with icing (frosting).
iceberg *n.* a floating mass of ice.
ice cream *n.* a kind of soft, frozen sweet, sometimes eaten in wafer biscuits (cones).
ice hockey *n.* a game played on ice between two teams, using hockey sticks to hit a rubber puck with the aim of scoring goals. Each team has six players and a goalkeeper.
ice skate *n.* a boot with a blade underneath for skating (sliding rapidly) on ice. **ice-skate** *vb.*
icicle *n.* a hanging pointed piece of ice. *An icicle is made of dripping water that freezes.*
icing 1. *n.* a sweet covering for cakes, frosting. 2. *vb.* (**up**) formation of ice on an aircraft's wings.
icon *n.* the name in the Eastern Orthodox Church for any picture or image of Christ, the Virgin Mary, an angel or a saint. Usually it is a painting on wood showing the human form in a flat, stylized way.
idea *n.* a thought, a plan in the mind.
ideal *adj.* perfection, just what you want. *We thought that the plans for the holiday were ideal.* *n.* perfection.

If a sealed bottle of water is frozen, it will burst. This shows that when water becomes ice, it expands.

idle 1. *adj.* lazy; unoccupied. 2. *vb.* turn around slowly (of a car engine).
idol *n.* object of worship; fake god. **idolize** *vb.* worship, love greatly.
if *conj.* in the event that; on condition that; whether.
igloo *n.* an Eskimo hut made of blocks of snow.
igneous *adj.* formed by great heat or volcanic action.
ignite *vb.* set fire to.
ignorant *adj.* knowing very little; uneducated. **ignorance** *n.*
ignore *vb.* take no notice of something or somebody. *The man ignored us and walked straight past.*
iguana *n.* large lizard found in tropical America, Madagascar and Polynesia.
il- *prefix* before L indicates negation, against, e.g. **illegal** *adj.* against the law. **illogical** *adj.* not logical.
ill *adj.* unwell, sick. **illness** *n.*

illegal *adj.* against the law.

illiterate *adj.* unable to read. **illiteracy** *n.*

illuminate *vb.* light up; make clear. **illumination** *n.*

illustrate *vb.* explain with pictures. **illustration** *n.* a picture in a book or magazine.

im- *prefix* form of **in-** used before words beginning with b, m, and p meaning against, without, or not, e.g. **immature** *adj.* not mature. **impaired** *adj.* made worse. **immoral** *adj.* without morals.

imaginary *adj.* not real; existing only in a person's mind. *David has made up an imaginary friend called Little David.*

imagine *vb.* make up a picture in the mind. **imaginative** *adj.* using imagination. **imagination** *n.* fancy; creative power of the mind.

imitate *vb.* copy another person or thing. **imitation** *n.*

immediately *adv.* now; without losing time. *I must run down to the shops immediately before they close.*

immense *adj.* vast, huge, enormous.

immigrate *vb.* come to a country to live.

immigrant *n.* someone who comes to live in a country that is not his or her own.

imminent *adj.* about to happen. *Disaster is imminent.*

immunize *vb.* make safe from an illness. **immunization** *n.*

imp *n.* (in stories) a little devil.

impair *vb.* weaken. *The climate impaired his health.*

impala *n.* reddish-brown African antelope that lives in great herds.

impatient *adj.* not patient; not wanting to wait for others. **impatience.** *n.*

impede *vb.* get in the way of, hinder.

impersonate *vb.* pretend to be someone else.

impertinent *adj.* irrelevant; insolent.

implement 1. *n.* a tool or instrument. 2. *vb.* carry out, do.

import *vb.* (*im-***port**) bring goods into your country.

important *adj.* something that matters a great deal. *I have to go to a very important meeting this evening.* **importance** *n.*

impose *vb.* inflict on.

impossible *adj.* not possible; something that cannot be.

impresario *n.* manager of a musical company, etc.

impress *vb.* fix firmly in the mind; affect strongly. *His work impressed me.* **impressive** *adj.* creating a deep impression on the mind.

impromptu *adv.* & *adj.* without preparation.

improve *vb.* make or become better. **improvement** *n.*

in- *prefix* meaning negation, e.g. **inaccurate** *adj.* not accurate. **inactive** *adj.* not active. In most cases words beginning with this are the exact opposite of the main word, so it is generally only necessary to look up that definition to discover the contrary meaning, e.g. **adequate, inadequate**.

incense *n.* a substance, sometimes used in religious ceremonies, that gives off a sweet smell when burned.

incentive *n.* & *adj.* stimulus, something that encourages. *A raise can be an incentive to work harder.*

incessant *adj.* continual, unceasing.

inch *n.* a unit of measurement equal to 2.54 cm. *There are 12 inches in one foot.*

incident *n.* an event, a minor happening. *It was only an incident in the story.*

incite *vb.* stir up, rouse, urge on.

incline *vb.* lean, slope toward. **inclination** *n.* leaning; preference.

include *vb.* contain as part of the whole; take into account.

incognito *adj.*, *n.* & *adv.* (passing under) an assumed or false identity. *Traveling incognito.*

income *n.* pay; money received for work and from other sources during a period. *Income tax.*

incorporate *vb.* include and make part of.

increase (*in*-**crease**) *vb*. make greater in size or amount. *The number of pupils in our class has greatly increased.* (**in**-crease) *n*. growth, enlargement.

incredible *adj*. something that cannot be believed.

incubate *vb*. keep eggs warm in order to hatch them.

incur *vb*. (past **incurred**) bring upon oneself.

indeed *adv*. really; in truth. *It was a very big dog indeed.*

independent *adj*. free; not controlled by others. **independence** *n*.

index *n*. a list at the end of a book, giving all the subjects in the book in alphabetical order and the pages on which they appear.

Indian *n*. a person from India; one of the original people of the Americas.

indicate *vb*. point to; be a sign of. **indication** *n*.

indifference *n*. lack of concern, absence of feeling. **indifferent** *adj*. *He was indifferent to her feelings.*

indigenous (*in*-**dij**-e-*nus*) *adj*. native, belonging from the beginning. *Kangaroos are indigenous to Australia.*

indigestion *n*. difficulty in digesting food. **indigestible** *adj*.

indignant *adj*. angry, scornful, especially at injustices, cruelty, etc.

individual 1. *adj*. of or for one person only. *We each had an individual parcel of food.* 2. *n*. a person. *He's a strange individual.*

indoors *adv*. inside a building.

indulge *vb*. take pleasure in, gratify, desire. **indulgent** *adj*. too lenient.

industry *n*. 1. work done in factories. 2. a trade or business. *Steel-making is an important industry.* **industrial** *adj*. to do with manufacturing. **industrious** *adj*. hard-working.

inertia *n*. lack of energy; (in physics) property of an object that makes it resist being moved or changing its motion.

infant *n*. a baby or child under about two years of age. **infantile** *adj*. childish.

infantry *n*. soldiers who fight on foot, the main combat forces in most armies.

infection *n*. an illness that can be spread by harmful germs.

inferior *adj*. lower in rank or quality.

infinity *n*. a time or space without end; too big to be imagined.

infirmary *n*. a hospital (especially in schools).

inhabitant *n*. a person who lives in or **inhabits** (*vb*.) a place or country. *The Indians were the first inhabitants of America.*

inhale *vb*. breathe in.

inherit *vb*. receive money or property from someone who has died. **inheritance** *n*.

initial (*in*-**ish**-al) 1. *adj*. at the beginning. 2. *n*. the first letter in a name. *Simon Powell's initials are S.P.* *vb*. sign with initials.

injection *n*. medicine given with a hypodermic syringe. **inject** *vb*.

injure *vb*. hurt or damage. **injury** *n*. damage or harm, particularly to the body. *The unfortunate man died of his injuries.*

ink *n*. a colored fluid used for writing, drawing or printing.

inkling *n*. hint, suspicion. *She had no inkling I would turn up today.*

inland *adj*. away from the sea. *Chicago is an inland city.*

inn *n*. a public house where food and drink are sold and people can stay.

innate *adj*. inborn, natural.

innings *n*. a team's turn at bat in baseball.

innocent *adj*. not guilty; doing no harm. **innocence** *n*.

inoculate *vb*. give a mild form of a disease in order to protect a person from the disease. **inoculation** *n*.

inquest *n*. (**in**-*kwest*) official inquiry, especially into cause of death.

inquire *vb*. ask about something or someone. **inquiry** *n*. investigation. also **enquire, enquiry**.

inquisitive *adj*. wanting to find out about things, curious.

insanity *n*. madness; utter foolishness. **insane** *adj*.

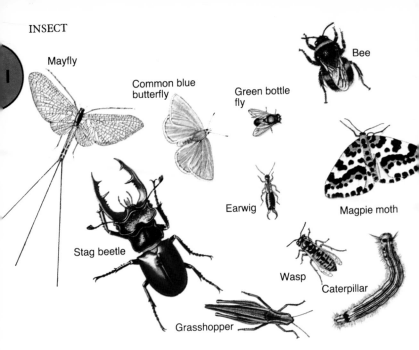

Mayfly

Common blue butterfly

Bee

Green bottle fly

Earwig

Magpie moth

Stag beetle

Wasp

Caterpillar

Grasshopper

insect *n.* a small creature with six legs and no backbone.

insecticide *n.* a poisonous mixture used to kill insects.

insert *vb.* put in, place in between. *n.* thing inserted.

inside *adj.* within. *The heart is inside the body.*

insignia *n.* badge of office, authority, etc.

insipid *adj.* without flavor; dull.

insist *vb.* press for, speak emphatically, demand.

insomnia *adj.* inability to sleep.

inspect *vb.* examine carefully. **inspection** *n.*

inspire *vb.* encourage someone to do something, influence. **inspiration** *n.* creative influence, a sudden idea.

installment *n.* a part of something, especially a story or payment.

instant *n.* a moment; a very short time. **instantly** *adv.* at once.

instead *adv.* in place of. *She is teaching the class instead of our usual teacher, who is ill.*

Insects of different kinds are found all over the world. They range from tiny fleas to beetles as big as your hand.

instinct *n.* something that makes animals do things that they have not learned to do, inborn behavior.

insult (*in-sult*) *vb.* be rude to someone. (*in-sult*) *n.* a rude remark. *It was an insult to call Bill a stupid, lazy fellow.*

institute *vb.* set up, establish. *n.* organization or establishment for a special purpose.

instruct *vb.* teach, direct. **instruction** *n.* teaching, orders.

instrument *n.* 1. a delicate tool or implement for a special purpose. 2. something used for making musical sounds. *A musical instrument.*

insulate *vb.* isolate, prevent passage of electricity etc. **insulator** *n.*

insulin *n.* a hormone secreted by the pancreas used in treating diabetes.

insurance *n.* a method of protecting against loss through such risks as fire or theft, accident or death. **insure** *vb.*

integrate *vb.* combine into one.

integrity *n.* honesty, purity, soundness.

intelligent *adj.* clever and able to understand easily.

intelligence *n.* the ability to reason and understand.

intend *vb.* mean to, have in mind to. *I intend to finish the weeding.* **intention** *n.* purpose, object.

intense *adj.* earnest; very strong. **intensity** *n.* **intensive** *adj.* concentrated. *The intensive care unit.*

inter- *prefix* meaning among, between, etc., e.g. **intercontinental**.

interest *n.* 1. enthusiasm, being keen on something. *He takes a great interest in my work.* 2. money paid (by or to a bank, etc.) on a loan. *I have just been paid the interest on my savings account.*

interested *adj.* wanting to know and learn about. *Robert is very interested in ships and borrowed three books about them.*

interfere *vb.* 1. meddle in other people's affairs. 2. get in the way of something.

interior *adj.* inside, inland. *n.* the inside of anything.

internal *adj.* belonging to the inside.

internal combustion engine *n.* type of engine that works by the combustion (burning) of a fuel-and-air mixture within the cylinders of the engine.

The cylinder action of a gas internal combustion engine. Induction: *The piston moves downward and the gas–air mixture is drawn into the cylinder.* Compression: *The piston rises, compressing the mixture.* Power: *The spark plug ignites the compressed mixture. The gases produced force the piston downward.* Exhaust: *As the piston moves upward again the burned gases are forced out.*

international *adj.* affecting or involving two or more nations. *The UN is an international organization.*

interpret *vb.* 1. judge the meaning to be. *He interpreted the signs as meaning that it would rain.* 2. translate from one language to another.

interrupt *vb.* disturb someone who is doing something. **interruption** *n.*

interview *n.* & *vb.* question someone to find information or to discover suitability for a job, etc.

intestines *pl. n.* the tubes through which our food passes after it has been through the stomach.

intimate *adj.* close, familiar. *An intimate friend.*

Induction

Compression

Ignition

Exhaust

into *prep.* put or go inside something. *Come into the kitchen.*

intricate *adj.* complicated and involved.

introduce *vb.* 1. make people known to each other. *Edward introduced me to his mother.* 2. bring into use.

introduction *n.* introducing; the first part of a book, which tells you what the book is about.

invade *vb.* go into another country or place to fight against the people. **invasion** *n.*

invalid *n.* an ill or disabled person.

invent *vb.* make something for the first time, devise, fabricate (a false story). **invention** (*in-ven-shun*) *n.* something that has been invented or made after study or experiment.

inventor *n.* someone who invents.

invertebrate *n.* an animal with no backbone, such as an insect, a worm, or snail. *adj.* without a backbone.

invisible *adj.* unseen; cannot be seen. *The hem was sewn so neatly that it was invisible.* **invisibility** *n.*

invite *vb.* ask someone to come somewhere. *Susan's aunt may invite her to go to India next year.*

invitation *n.* spoken or written words that ask you or invite you to come.

invoice *n.* a list of goods sent, with their prices.

iodine *n.* a gray-black crystal element which when heated gives off a violet vapor. Iodine is found in seaweed and is essential for the proper working of the thyroid gland.

ion *n.* an atom or group of atoms that is electrically charged because it has gained or lost electrons.

ionosphere *n.* a layer of the Earth's atmosphere starting at about 50 miles up and ending about 300 miles above sea level.

IOU (I owe you) *n.* a piece of paper signed by a borrower of money and given to the lender to acknowledge the debt.

iris *n.* 1. rainbow. 2. a perennial flower with pointed leaves. 3. the colored part of the eye.

irk *vb.* trouble, bother.

iron 1. *n.* a heavy, common metal (symbol – Fe). 2. *n.* a tool for pressing clothes. 3. *vb.* press wrinkles out of clothes.

iron lung *n.* a respirator or machine to aid breathing, used when the chest muscles are paralyzed.

irregular *n.* merchandise that is not regular, often costing less to buy. *My mom bought an irregular coat and saved $50.*

irrigate *vb.* bring water to dry land in order to help crops to grow. **irrigation** *n.*

irritate *vb.* make angry, annoy. **irritable** *adj.* easily annoyed.

Islam *n.* the religion revealed through the prophet Muhammed. **Islamic** *adj.*

island *n.* land area surrounded by water. **islander** *n.* someone who lives on an island.

isobar *n.* line on a weather map which connects places that have the same atmospheric pressure.

isolate *vb.* place alone, set apart.

isotope *n.* the form of an element that has neutrons added to or taken away from the nucleus of its atoms.

issue *vb. & n.* going or flowing out; offspring (children); putting into circulation money, books, etc.

isthmus *n.* a strip of land joining two larger areas of land.

italics *pl. n.* words that are printed at a slope *like this.*

itch *n.* an uncomfortable feeling in the skin which makes you want to scratch. **itchy** *adj.*

item *n.* a single unit on a list. *How many items of furniture should there be?*

itinerary *n.* plan or record of a journey.

it's short for it is. *It's late.*

its *pron.* the possessive form of it. *The cat was washing its face.*

ivory *n.* the white, bone-like material of which elephants' tusks are made.

ivy *n.* a climbing evergreen vine with shiny, dark-green leaves.

jab *vb. & n.* poke, stab. *In his anger, he jabbed at me with the end of his umbrella.*

jack *n.* 1. a tool for raising heavy weights off the ground. 2. a knave in a pack of cards.

jackal *n.* a kind of wild dog.

jackboot *n.* long boot reaching above the knee, worn in the 17th and 18th centuries.

jackdaw *n.* a bird of the crow family.

jacket *n.* a short long-sleeved coat, which may be part of a suit.

jackpot *n.* top prize in a slot machine.

jackrabbit *n.* a large hare found in western North America with long ears and long hind legs.

jade *n.* a hard green, blackish-green, or white stone.

jagged *adj.* rough or having sharply uneven edges. *The ship was wrecked on the jagged rocks.*

jaguar *n.* a large American yellow wildcat with black spots like a leopard.

jail *n.* prison. *vb.* put in prison.

jam 1. *vb.* push things together tightly. *He jammed his clothes into his suitcase.* 2. *vb.* cause interference on the radio. 3. *n.* food made by boiling fruit and sugar together.

jamboree (*jam-bu-ree*) *n.* rally of scouts; a large festive gathering.

jangle *n. & vb.* sound harshly; out of tune.

January *n.* the first month of the year.

jar 1. *n.* pot, often made of glass, for jam and other things. 2. *vb.* make a harsh, grating noise. **jarring** *adj.*

jargon *n.* the special or technical language of a group of people.

jasmine *n.* a shrub with white or yellow flowers and which yields oils that are used in perfume.

jaundice *n.* a disease in which there is a yellowing of the skin caused by too much yellow bile pigment in the blood.

jaunt *n.* short trip, especially for pleasure.

javelin *n.* a short, light throwing spear.

jaw *n.* the bones of the mouth. *Your teeth are set in your jaw.*

jay *n.* a bird belonging to the crow family.

jazz *n.* a type of popular American folk music.

jealous (*jel*-us) *adj.* being unhappy because you want what others have. **jealousy** *n.*

jeans *pl. n.* tight-fitting, casual trousers made of a tough, blue material called denim.

jeep *n.* a kind of car originally used by the U.S. Army for going over rough ground.

jeer *n. & vb.* mock, make fun of, scoff. *n.*

jelly *n.* a soft, wobbly kind of food, usually brightly colored and flavored with fruit.

jellyfish *n.* an invertebrate sea animal with a round, semitransparent soft body fringed with stinging tentacles.

The tentacles of a jellyfish catch food and carry it to the jellyfish's mouth, located under the body.

jenny *n.* female donkey.

jeopardy (*jep-ur-dee*) *n.* danger, peril. **jeopardize** *vb.* put in danger.

jerboa *n.* jumping rodent of Africa with long back legs.

jerk 1. *n.* a sudden rush or movement. 2. *vb.* move abruptly.

Jet engines burn a mixture of compressed air and fuel. The exhaust gases stream out of the back of the engine and provide thrust to move the plane.

jersey (plural **jerseys**) *n.* a knitted woolen upper garment.

jet *n.* 1. a fast stream of liquid or gas. 2. an aircraft with an engine that sucks in air at the front and expels it at the back, pushing the aircraft forward. 3. a hard, black mineral often used in jewelry.

jetsam *n.* cargo from a ship thrown overboard and then washed ashore.

jettison *vb.* throw overboard to lighten load in a time of disaster.

jetty *n.* a pier; a landing stage.

Jew *n.* a person of the Hebrew race or religion (Judaism). **Jewish** *adj.* **Jewry** *n.* Jews collectively.

jewel *n.* a precious stone.

jeweler *n.* a person who makes or sells jewelry.

jewelry *n.* objects with jewels or other decorations worn as adornment.

jiffy *n.* a moment. *I'll be there in a jiffy.*

jig *n.* & *vb.* a lively dance.

jigsaw *n.* & *vb.* a special kind of saw for cutting small pieces of wood very accurately. *A jigsaw puzzle is a mounted picture which has been jigsawed into pieces that fit back together.*

jingle *vb.* & *n.* (make) a tinkling noise; a clinking sound; a catchy tune or rhyme. *Many TV ads have clever jingles.*

jittery *adj.* nervous.

job *n.* a person's work.

jockey *n.* a person who rides in horse races, usually for wages.

jodhpurs (*jod-purrs*) *pl. n.* riding breeches that are loose-fitting around the hips but close-fitting from knee to ankle.

jog 1. *vb.* run at a slow, steady pace. 2. *n.* nudge (memory).

John Bull *n.* a character who is a personification or caricature of the English nation.

John Doe *n.* someone involved in a legal action whose real name is not known.

join *vb.* put together, unite; take part in; become a member of.

joiner *n.* a person who works with wood; a carpenter; someone who joins.

joint 1. *n.* a point where two parts join. *The knee is the joint between the upper and lower bones of the leg.* 2. *adj.* shared, common. *They have a joint bank account.*

join up *vb.* enlist in the army, navy or air force.

joist *n.* a beam supporting a floor or ceiling in a building.

joke *n.* a funny story or remark. *vb.* tell a joke or do something to amuse.

joker *n.* 1. a person who jokes. 2. a fifty-third card in a pack of cards, used in some games.

jolly *adj.* cheerful; merry. *Santa Claus is usually pictured as a jolly old gentleman with a white beard.*

jolt *vb.* move or shake with sudden jerks. *n.* a shock or sudden jerk. *The train came to a stop with a jolt.*

jostle *vb.* shove; push against.

jot *vb.* make a note; write down briefly. *Let me jot down your telephone number.*

journalist *n.* a person who writes about or edits the news in magazines and newspapers.

journey *n.* a distance traveled. *vb.* travel.

joust *n. & vb.* a combat between mounted knights in a tournament; to fight in a tournament.

joy *n.* happiness.

jubilee *n.* a festival or celebration, usually of an anniversary. *Queen Victoria celebrated her Diamond Jubilee after she had reigned for 60 years.*

judge 1. *vb.* decide what is right or best out of a number of people or things. 2. *n.* a person who judges, particularly in a law court or a

This is the ball and socket joint of the hip. It allows movement in any direction.

competition. **judgment** *n.* decision of a court; opinion; estimate.

judo *n.* a fighting sport, developed in Japan as a form of self-defense.

jug *n.* an object for holding liquids, with a handle and a narrow mouth.

juggler *n.* an entertainer who tosses things in the air, catches and throws them up again. **juggle** *vb.*

juice (rhymes with *loose*) *n.* the liquid part of fruit or other food. **juicy** *adj.*

July *n.* the seventh month of the year.

jumble *vb. & n.* a muddle; a disorder. *She jumbled the papers together.*

jumbo *adj.* (originally the name of a circus elephant) a massive person, animal or thing, e.g. jumbo jet.

jump *vb. & n.* leap, spring. **jumpy** *adj.* nervous.

jump at *vb.* accept enthusiastically. *Jane jumped at the chance for a ride to the horse show.*

jumper *n.* a sleeveless one-piece dress often worn with a blouse.

junction *n.* a join or place or meetings, especially where several roads or railway lines meet.

June *n.* the sixth month of the year.

jungle *n.* thick vegetation in tropical countries.

junior *adj.* younger; lower in rank.

juniper *n.* evergreen shrub or tree with purple leaves.

junk *n.* 1. rubbish. 2. a Chinese sailing boat.

jury *n.* people who are chosen to decide whether an accused person is guilty or not guilty in a law court.

just 1. *adv.* exactly. *That color is just right.* 2. *adv.* a moment ago. *I have only just arrived.* 3. *adj.* fair, honest. *That is a just law.*

justice *n.* 1. the law; fairness. 2. a judge. *A justice of the peace is a local magistrate.*

justify *vb.* show or prove to be right.

jut *vb.* stick out, project.

jute *n.* a coarse fiber used to make sacking, burlap, and twine.

juvenile *n.* a young person.

kaleidoscope *n.* a device made with mirrors which creates repeated colors and patterns.

kangaroo *n.* an Australian animal with strong back legs. The female has a pouch in which she carries her baby, called a joey.

karate (*ka*-**raht**-*tay*) *n.* an oriental style of unarmed combat, using kicks and punches. As a sport, it involves both mock fights and formal examinations for the various grades of skill.

kayak (**kye**-*ack*) *n.* an Eskimo canoe made of skins.

keel *n.* the heavy strip of metal or wood running along the bottom of a ship. *vb.* (over) capsize.

keen *adj.* eager; enthusiastic.

keep 1. *vb.* have something and not give it to anyone else. 2. *vb.* look after something for somebody. *Keep the book until I see you again.* 3. *n.* a strong tower in a castle.

keeper *n.* one who looks after people or things, particularly animals in a zoo. *He had been the elephant keeper for 20 years.*

keep on *vb.* continue doing something. *Stan keeps on talking, even when the teacher tells him not to.*

keepsake *n.* memento; something treasured because of the giver.

keep up with *vb.* not to lag behind. *He managed to keep up with the others in the race.*

keg *n.* a small barrel.

kelp *n.* kind of large brown seaweed.

kennel *n.* a shelter for a dog. *vb.* keep a dog in a kennel.

kept *vb.* past of **keep**.

kernel *n.* the soft inner part of a nut, seed, or cereal, which can be eaten.

kerosene *n.* an oil used for burning in heaters and lamps.

kestrel *n.* a kind of small hawk.

ketchup *n.* a sauce made from tomatoes and spices. also called catsup.

kettle *n.* a kind of pot with a lid, handle and spout, used for boiling liquids.

key (rhymes with *me*). 1. *n.* a metal device to turn a lock or wind a clock. 2. *n.* solution, explanation, code. 3. *n.* part of a machine or instrument pressed with the fingers. *The piano keys were made of ivory.* 4. one of the systems of notes in music. 5. *adj.* of vital importance.

keystone *n.* central stone supporting an arch.

khaki *adj.* a dull, yellow-green color.

kibbutz *n.* (plural **kibbutzim**) agricultural center in Israel.

kick *vb.* hit something, such as a ball, with your foot. **kickoff** *n.* kick of a ball which starts a game.

kid 1. *n.* a young goat. 2. *n.* a child. 3. *vb.* tease, hoax.

kidnap *vb.* steal someone, often to get money as a ransom. **kidnapper** *n.*

kidney *n.* (plural **kidneys**) one of a pair of bean-shaped organs of the body that remove waste matter from the blood.

kill *vb.* put to death; take the life of someone or something.

kiln *n.* an oven or furnace for baking bricks or pottery to make them hard.

kilo- *prefix* a Greek word for 1000. **kilowatt. kilogram.**

kilogram *n.* a measure of weight, often shortened to kg. *There are 1000 grams in one kilogram.*

kilometer *n.* a measure of length, often shortened to km. *There are 1000 meters in a kilometer.*

kilt *n.* a skirt often made of tartan cloth. *Kilts are worn by men and women in Scotland and some other countries.*

kimono (*ki-***moan**-*oh*) *n.* a loose gown with wide sleeves worn in Japan.

kin *n.* relatives.

kind 1. *adj.* pleasant or gentle. 2. *n.* type or sort. *What kind of tree is that?*

kindness *n.* the act of being kind, or treating someone well. *Thank you for all your kindness to me.*

kindergarten *n.* a school for very young children.

king *n.* a male ruler; a monarch.

kingdom *n.* a country ruled by a king or a queen.

kingfisher *n.* a small, brightly colored bird with a large head and a beak like a dagger.

kiosk (**key**-*ossk*) *n.* a small hut or stall, used for selling newspapers, candy, etc.

kipper *n.* a smoked herring, sometimes eaten for breakfast in Britain.

kiss *vb.* & *n.* touch with the lips as a sign of love or friendship.

kitchen *n.* a room in a house where the cooking is done. **kitchenette** *n.* a small kitchen.

kite *n.* 1. a bird of prey related to the falcon family, noted for its long wings, deeply forked tail and graceful flight. 2. a frame of wood covered with light material which can be made to fly.

kitten *n.* a young cat. **kittenish** *adj.*

kittiwake *n.* kind of seagull.

kiwi (**kee**-*wee*) *n.* a New Zealand bird that cannot fly.

knack (*nack*) *n.* skill or ability.

knave (*nave*) *n.* 1. rascal, cheat. 2. the jack in a pack of cards.

knead (*need*) *vb.* work dough or clay with the hands.

knee (*nee*) *n.* the hinged joint in the middle of the leg. **kneecap** *n.* the bone at the front of the knee; the patella.

kneel (*neel*) *vb.* go down on your knees, especially in prayer.

knew (*new*) *vb.* past of **know**.

knickers (*nickers*) *pl. n.* short pants that are loose-fitting but gathered around the knees.

knife (*nife*) *n.* a sharp-bladed cutting tool with a handle. *vb.* (past **knifed**) stab with knife.

knight (*nite*) *n.* in the Middle Ages a mounted nobleman who served his king; today, the lowest British rank of a titled person with the title "Sir"; a chess piece.

knit (*nit*) *vb.* make clothing out of wool or other fiber, using knitting needles.

knob (*nob*) *n.* a round handle.

knock (*nock*) *n.* & *vb.* hit or strike something. *Was that a knock at the door?*

knock down *vb.* force to the ground with a blow.

knocker *n.* an ornamental hammer on a door.

knock off *vb.* stop work for the day.

knot (*not*) 1. *n.* string or rope tied in such a way that it cannot come undone. *vb.* form knots. 2. *n.* hard mass in wood where a branch joins the trunk. 3. *n.* a unit of speed (nautical miles per hour) used for ships. A nautical mile is 6000 feet. **knotty** *adj.* full of knots; puzzling.

know (past **knew**) *vb.* 1. be sure of something; be in possession of the facts. *Do you know which is the longest river in the world?* 2. be familiar with, or recognize someone or something. *I'll know him when I see him.*

know-how *n.* practical knowledge.

knowledge (**noll**-*edge*) *n.* understanding; information in the mind. **knowledgeable** *adj.*

knuckle (*nuckle*) *n.* the bones at the finger joint, especially at the root of the finger.

koala *n.* a small, furry Australian animal that lives in trees.

kookaburra *n.* an Australian bird related to the kingfisher. It is also known as the "laughing jackass" because of its loud, laughter-like call.

Koran *n.* the sacred book of Islam.

kosher *adj.* food that has been prepared in accordance with Jewish law.

label *n*. a piece of paper or card with writing on it attached to something. The label may say what the thing is or where it is going. *vb*. attach a label.

labor *n*. work; people who work. *vb*. work hard.

laboratory *n*. a place equipped for scientific experiments.

Labrador retriever *n*. a sporting dog originally from Newfoundland with a short black or golden coat.

labyrinth *n*. a maze, a tangle of intricate ways and connections.

lace 1. *n*. a delicate fabric made with patterns of thread. 2. *n*. cord for fastening a shoe, dress, etc. *vb*. fasten with laces. 3. *vb*. add alcohol to other drinks.

laceration *n*. a cut that is torn and ragged. *It took 10 stitches to close the laceration.*

lack *n*. & *vb*. need, be without, be missing. **lacking** *adj*.

lacquer *n*. a hard, shiny varnish; a substance sprayed on the hair to keep it in place. *vb*. coat with lacquer.

lacrosse *n*. a team game played with a racket that has a net to catch and throw the ball with.

lad *n*. a boy.

ladder *n*. two lengths of wood or other material fastened with cross-bars (called rungs). *A ladder is used for climbing up and down walls.*

ladle *n*. a large deep spoon used for serving soup. *vb*. transfer with a ladle.

lady *n*. 1. a female person. 2. a woman's title. *Lady Smith is the wife of Sir John Smith.*

ladybug *n*. a small flying beetle with bright spots.

lager (**lah**-*gur*) *n*. a light-colored beer.

lagoon *n*. a shallow saltwater lake separated from the sea by a sand bank.

laid *vb*. past and past part. of **lay**.

lair *n*. a wild animal's den.

lake *n*. a large area of water surrounded by land.

lamb *n*. a young sheep; the meat of a young sheep. *vb*. give birth (to lambs).

lame *adj*. not able to walk properly.

lament *vb*. mourn. *n*. elegy, sorrowful song. **lamentable** *adj*. sad; pitiful; deplorable.

lamp *n*. a light, often portable.

lamplighter *n*. someone who lights a lamp.

lance 1. *n*. a kind of spear that was used by knights and cavalry. 2. *vb*. (in surgery) to pierce or cut open.

land 1. *n*. all those parts of the earth's surface which are not sea. 2. *n*. the area owned by someone. *Farmer Green's land goes as far as the river.* 3. *vb*. come to land from the sea or the air. *Our plane should land early.*

landing *n*. 1. bringing in to ground; bringing in to shore. 2. level part at the top of a flight of stairs.

landlady, landlord *n*. a person who owns a house or other property and rents it out to others; keeper of an inn. *I must pay the rent to my landlady tomorrow.*

landmark *n*. something that can be seen from a distance and which helps you find the way. *A church steeple is often used as a landmark.*

landscape *n*. what you see when you look across a large area of land; a picture of a landscape.

lane *n*. 1. a narrow road, or pathway. 2. one of the divisions of a highway. *He drove all the way in the inside lane.*

language *n.* the words we use to talk or write to each other. *Many different languages are spoken in Africa.*

lank *adj.* drooping, limp, thin. **lanky** *adj.*

lantern *n.* a case with glass sides for holding a light so that it does not blow out.

lap 1. *n.* your upper legs when you are sitting. 2. *vb.* drink with the tongue like an animal. 3. *n.* one circuit of a racetrack.

lapel *n.* folded-back part of the front of a coat.

lapse *vb.* & *n.* falling back, fall into disuse; a mistake.

lapwing *n.* bird of the plover family.

larch *n.* a cone-bearing tree that loses its leaves in winter.

lard *n.* fat of a pig prepared for cooking.

larder *n.* a room where food is kept cool; pantry.

large *adj.* big, broad, or great.

lark 1. *n.* a small brown bird famous for its beautiful song. 2. *n.* & *vb.* a frolic, mischief.

larva (plural **larvae**) *n.* an insect in the first stage when it comes from its egg.

larynx *n.* the cavity in the upper windpipe (air passage in the throat) where sounds are produced, also called the voice box.

laser *n.* a device for sending out enormously strong light waves.

lash *vb.* make rapid movements (of tail etc.); thrash or fasten with a rope. *n.* whip.

lass *n.* a girl.

lasso (**lass**-*oo*) *n.* a long rope with a loop used by cowboys to catch cattle and horses. *vb.* (*lass*-**oo**) use a lasso.

last 1. *adj.* coming at the end. *I came last in the race.* 2. *vb.* stay or continue. *Have we enough food to last the week?* 3. *n.* a model of a foot used by shoemakers.

late *adj.* 1. tardy; past the correct time. *They were late for the class.* 2. previous; no longer alive. *He knew the late king.*

lately *adv.* not long ago.

latex *n.* milky juice of some trees, especially rubber trees.

lathe *n.* a machine for holding and turning wood or metal while it is being shaped.

lather (rhymes with *rather*) *n.* froth that is formed by mixing soap with water. *vb.* to spread lather.

Latin *n.* language of ancient Rome. *adj.* concerning countries where languages are descended from Latin.

latitude *n.* 1. a distance measured in degrees north or south of the equator. 2. freedom of movement, scope.

latter *adj.* & *n.* the more recent, the second one mentioned of two. *Romulus and Remus were brothers: the latter (Remus) was younger than the former (Romulus).*

laugh *vb.* the sound you make when you think something is funny. **laughter** *n.*

launch (*lawnch*) 1. *n.* a sort of power-boat. 2. *vb.* put a boat into water. 3. *vb.* send something off. *The rocket was launched from Cape Canaveral.*

launderette *n.* a shop with washing machines and dryers where people pay to do their laundry.

laundry *n.* a place where clothes are washed; the clothes that have to be washed.

laurel *n.* sweet bay tree, whose leaves the ancient Greeks and Romans made into wreaths, emblems of victory.

lava *n.* hot liquid rock that is expelled from an active volcano.

lavatory *n.* a wash basin; a room with a sink and toilet in it.

lavender *n.* a small Mediterranean shrub with fragrant narrow leaves and pale purple flowers, cultivated on a large scale for use in the perfume industry.

law *n.* (a set of) rules, usually made by a government, that people have to obey. **lawful** *adj.* permitted by law.

121

L

lawn *n*. 1. an area of short cut grass. 2. a fine sheer cloth used for nightgowns, blouses and other clothes.

lawn mower *n*. a machine for cutting grass.

lawyer *n*. a person who works in the law; a solicitor, barrister or advocate; an attorney.

lax *adj*. careless, not strict.

lay 1. *vb*. past of **lie**. *We lay down on the lawn*. 2. *vb*. (past **laid**) of a bird, lay (produce) eggs. 3. *vb*. (past **laid**) put down; prepare a table. 4. *n*. as distinct from clergy, laity; non-professional.

lay away *vb*. to put something away that you will use or buy at a later time.

layer *n*. something that is spread over a surface of something else. *A thick layer of clay had washed over the river bank*.

lazy *adj*. not wanting to do much work; idle. **laze** *vb*. relax.

lead (rhymes with *bed*) *n*. a soft, heavy, blue-gray metal.

lead (rhymes with *reed*). 1. *vb*. go in front to guide others. 2. *n*. the first place. *Chris had the lead in the school play last year*. 3. *n*. a leather strap. for leading a dog (also called a leash).

leader *n*. a person who leads.

leaf (plural **leaves**) *n*. 1. one of the flat green parts of a plant growing from the stems of a branch. 2. a sheet of paper or metal foil.

league (*leeg*) *n*. 1. a group of sports clubs that play matches against each other. 2. an alliance; nations that agree to help each other.

leak *vb*. & *n*. a hole through which liquid or gas can escape.

lean 1. *vb*. be or put in a sloping position. *The ladder is leaning against the house*. 2. *adj*. thin, having little fat.

leap *vb*. & *n*. jump high or far. **leapt** *vb*. past of **leap**.

learn *vb*. (past **learned**) get knowledge or information, find out. *Did you learn French at school?*

learned (**lern**-*id*) *adj*. having much knowledge. **learner** *n*. a person learning.

lease *n*. legal document renting land, a house, etc., for a stated period and on certain conditions. *vb*. grant or take on a lease. **leaseholder** *n*.

least *adj*. the smallest in size or quantity.

leather (**leth**-*er*) *n*. material made from the skin or hide of animals. *Shoes are made of leather*.

leave 1. *vb*. (past **left**) go away. *I leave for Paris tomorrow*. 2. *vb*. part with something; to lose it. *Did you leave your case at home?* 3. *vb*. not to use something. *Do you always leave so much of your food?* 4. *n*. permission to be absent; a holiday. *He was given a month's leave from his job*.

leaves *pl. n*. more than one **leaf**.

lecture *n*. a lesson or period of instruction. *vb*. deliver a lecture; tell off, reprimand. **lecturer** *n*.

led *vb*. past of **lead**.

ledge *n*. a narrow shelf on a wall or cliff.

ledger *n*. a (large) book, particularly one used for keeping accounts.

leek *n*. a vegetable with a thick, white stem and broad, flat leaves; it is related to the onion.

left 1. *vb*. past of **leave**. 2. *n*. & *adj*. the side opposite to right. *In Britain, people drive on the left*.

leg *n*. one of the two lower limbs of the human body. *Most animals have four or more legs*.

legal (**lee**-*gal*) *adj*. to do with the law; correct by the law. *Is it legal to ride a bicycle on the pavement?* **legalize** *vb*. make lawful.

legend (**ledge**-*end*) *n*. an old story. **legendary** *adj*. told about in old stories.

legion *n*. a division of the Roman army of between 3000 and 6000 men; any large force; an association.

legislate *vb*. make laws.

leisure (**lee**-*sure*) *adj*. & *n*. rest, time free from work.

lemming *n*. a small Arctic rodent.

lemon *n.* a small oval citrus fruit with a yellow skin and acid juice. Lemon trees are widely cultivated in southern Europe and the Middle East.

lemonade *n.* a lemon-flavored drink.

lend *vb.* give something to someone for a time, expecting to get it back. The other person borrows it.

length *n.* from one end to the other in distance or time. **lengthen** *vb.* make or become longer.

lens *n.* (plural **lenses**) a piece of glass with one or two curved surfaces, used in cameras, glasses, telescopes and microscopes.

causing loss of feeling and a gradual eating away of the skin.

less *adj.* a smaller amount. **lessen** *vb.* make less; reduce.

lesser *adj.* not so great as, smaller of two. *The lesser of two evils.*

lesson *n.* an exercise or assignment to be studied by a pupil; a warning, an example.

lest *conj.* for fear that, in order to avoid.

let *vb.* allow someone to do something. *Bob let us see his scar.*

let down *vb.* fail to do something that somebody expected you to do. *The workers promised to repair our*

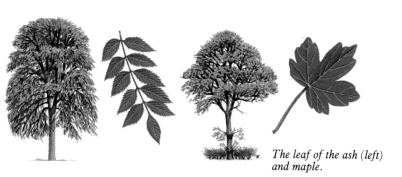

The leaf of the ash (left) and maple.

Lent *n.* the 40 days that Christians observe as a preparation for Easter. It begins on Ash Wednesday.

lent *vb.* past of **lend**.

lentil *n.* the seed of a food plant of the pea family that grows in hot countries.

leopard (**lep**-*ard*) *n.* large African animal belonging to the cat family with black spots on a yellowish coat. In India leopards are called panthers.

leotard (**lee**-*o-tard*) *n.* a close-fitting one-piece garment worn for gymnastics, dance, and other sports.

leprechaun (**lep**-*ri-cawn*) *n.* a mischievous Irish elf.

leprosy *n.* a disease of the skin

roof, but they let us down, and the rain came in.

let off *vb.* 1. free someone who has done wrong. *Our teacher let us off the hook when she saw all the extra work we had done.* 2. cause a firework to explode.

lethal *adj.* causing death.

letter *n.* 1. a part of the alphabet. *Our alphabet contains 26 letters.* 2. a written message, usually sent by mail.

letter carrier *n.* another word for a mail carrier.

lettering *n.* (the style) of letters used in an inscription, etc.

lettuce *n.* a salad vegetable that grows close to the ground on a very short stem; it has large green leaves.

level 1. *adj.* horizontal; even. *The surface of the table is perfectly level.* *vb.* make flat. 2. *n.* the base from which a height is measured. *The height of mountains is measured from sea level.*
3. *n.* the height to which a liquid rises in a container. *Please check the water level in the radiator.*

lever *n.* a tool used to lift something heavy or force it open. *vb.* use a lever; raise with a lever.

leveret *n.* a young hare.

levy *vb.* raise or collect taxes. *n.* the tax raised.

lexicon *n.* a dictionary.

liar *n.* someone who does not tell the truth.

liberal *adj.* abundant, free, generous; tolerant.

liberate *vb.* set free, release.

liberty *n.* freedom; the right to do what one wants.

library *n.* a building or room where books are kept and, usually, borrowed from. **librarian** *n.* a person trained to work in a library.

lice *n.* plural of **louse.**

license *n.* a permit to do something. *He has a license to drive a car.* *vb.* to give a license; authorize.

lichen (*lie-ken*) *n.* a small dry-looking plant that grows on rocks or trees.

lick *vb.* & *n.* touch something with the tongue.

lid *n.* the top covering of something, such as a pot.

lie 1. *vb.* & *n.* (say) something that is not true. 2. *vb.* put yourself down flat. *If you lie on the floor, you can see the crack.* 3. *vb.* (of places) be in a certain place. *The small islands lie just off the coast.*

life *n.* (plural **lives**) 1. all living things. *When did life begin on earth?* 2. the time between birth and death. 3. liveliness; energy. *The young children were full of life.*

lifeboat *n.* a boat for rescuing people at sea.

lift 1. *vb.* raise up; take up. 2. *n.* a ride in a vehicle given to a walker.

lift-off *n.* the takeoff of a rocket.

light 1. *n.* something that shines brightly so that we can see things; illumination. 2. *vb.* set on fire. 3. *adj.* not heavy. 4. *adj.* not dark in color. *A light-blue suit.*

lighten *vb.* 1. make or become lighter; make easier to bear. 2. make or grow bright.

lighter 1. *n.* device for lighting cigarettes. 2. *n.* flat-bottomed boat used for unloading goods from a ship. 3. *adj.* comparative of "light:" not so heavy; not so dark.

lighthouse *n.* a tower with a flashing light in it that warns ships away from dangerous rocks.

lighting *n.* artificial light such as candles or lamps.

lightning *n.* a flash of light in the sky during a thunderstorm.

like 1. *vb.* think well of someone or something. 2. *vb.* enjoy doing something. 3. *adj.* similar to. *She looks like her sister.*

likely *adv.* expected to happen, probable. *It is likely to rain this afternoon.*

lilac *n.* a shrub grown in many parts of the world for its fragrant white or purple flowers.

lilt *vb.* sing rhythmically.

lily *n.* a plant growing from a bulb, with showy flowers. The lily family includes onions, asparagus and tulips.

limb *n.* a leg or an arm.

lime *n.* 1. a substance obtained from heating limestone, and used in making cement. 2. the small, green, lemon-like fruit of a tropical tree. 3. a deciduous tree also called the linden.

limerick *n.* a funny five-line poem with this form:

> *There was a young man from Nepal*
> *Who went to a fancy dress ball;*
> *He thought he would risk it*
> *And go as a biscuit,*
> *But a dog ate him up in the hall.*

limestone *n.* a rock containing the chemical substance calcium carbonate.

limit 1. *n.* a line or point that you

cannot or should not go beyond.
*The speed limit in the town is 30 miles
an hour.* 2. *vb.* restrict something.
*You should limit her to three candies
before dinner.*

limp 1. *adj.* not stiff. *The skirt became
very limp after she washed it.* 2. *vb.*
walk unevenly.

limpet *n.* a kind of shellfish that
clings to rocks.

line 1. *n.* a long, thin mark. 2. *n.* a
piece of rope or string. 3. *n.* a row
of people or things. *We stand in line
for dinner.* 4. *n.* a transport system.
There goes a green line bus. 5. *vb.* put
a lining into something.

linen *n.* cloth made from the fibers of
the flax plant.

liner *n.* a big passenger ship.

linger *vb.* wait about, be slow to go,
delay.

linguist *n.* 1. a person who speaks
several languages. 2. a person who
makes a scientific study of how
language works.

lining *n.* a layer of material inside
something. *Her coat has a purple silk
lining.*

link 1. *n.* one loop of a chain. 2. *vb.*
connect things together.

linoleum *n.* a floor covering.

linseed *n.* seed of flax.

lion *n.* a large member of the cat
family.

lioness *n.* a female lion. **lionize** *vb.*
treat as a celebrity.

lip *n.* 1. one of the top or bottom
edges of the mouth. 2. the specially
shaped part of a jug from which the
liquid is poured.

liquid *n.* a substance like water that
flows. *A liquid is not a gas or a solid.*
adj. in a fluid state. **liquefy** *vb.*
make or become liquid.

lisp *vb.* speak using a "th" sound for
"s" and "z."

list 1. *n.* a number of names or things
written down one above the other.
*Did you put bread on the shopping
list?* *vb.* enter on list. 2. *n.* & *vb.*
leaning of ship to one side.

listen *vb.* pay attention to sound.
Listen to this.

listless *adj.* without much desire to
be active. *Mary felt listless after her
illness.*

lit *vb.* past and past part. of **light.**

literate *adj.* able to read and write;
educated.

literature *n.* books and writing, in
general of a high quality and valued
for their form and style.

liter (rhymes with *heater*) *n.* a liquid
measure (about one quart).

litter 1. *n.* rubbish thrown away in a
public place. 2. *vb.* all the newly
born offspring of an animal. *Our cat
had a litter of four kittens.*

little *adj.* not much; small or tiny.

liturgy *n.* the form of service or ritual
of a church.

live (rhymes with *hive*) *adj.* living.
*There are no live animals in the
museum.* **lively** *adj.* full of life and
energy.

live (rhymes with *give*) *vb.* 1. exist;
be alive. *He lived 100 years ago.*
2. inhabit. *They live in the center of
London.*

liver *n.* an organ of the body that
does many jobs, including getting
rid of things the body does not want
and making things it needs.

livery *n.* 1. distinctive uniform worn
by servants of a great household or
city company. 2. a stable for
boarding or hiring horses.

livestock *n.* farm animals.

living *adj.* alive.

living room *n.* a sitting room; the
main room in a house. *They kept the
TV set in the living room.*

lizard *n.* a four-legged reptile with a
tail.

llama *n.* an animal of South America
related to the camel family, but
without a hump.

load (rhymes with *code*) 1. *n.*
something that has to be carried.
*She took a load of washing to the
launderette.* 2. *vb.* fill or cover
something. *They loaded the car with
luggage.*

loaf 1. *n.* a complete piece of bread.
I bought two loaves from the baker.
2. *vb.* laze about.

loan *n.* something that has been lent to you, usually money.

loathe (rhymes with *clothe*) *vb.* detest, dislike very much.

lobby *n.* entrance hall to hotel, theater, etc.

lobster *n.* a shellfish with a hard shell and 10 legs, two of which carry large claws.

local *adj.* belonging to a fairly small area. *This local newspaper gives news about our town.*

localize *vb.* restrict to a particular place.

locate *vb.* find exact position; establish in a particular place.

loch *n.* a Scottish lake.

lock 1. *vb.* fasten something. *n.* a fastening for a door or a box that needs a key to open it. 2. *n.* a piece of hair. 3. *n.* a section of a canal or river where the water levels can be changed by opening and shutting large gates.

locker *n.* a cupboard that can be locked.

locket *n.* a small case worn on a chain around the neck. *A locket may contain a picture.*

someone's house and pay to stay there. 3. *n.* a beaver's home.

loft *n.* a room at the top of a house used for storing things; an attic.

log *n.* 1. a length of tree that has been cut down. 2. a written record of happenings, especially in a ship.

logic *n.* the science of or particular method of reasoning. **logical** *adj.* in accordance with the principles of logic.

loiter *vb.* go along very slowly; dawdle.

lollipop *n.* a candy on a stick.

lonely *adj.* 1. without friends. 2. away from other people. *They had a lonely house in the woods.*

long 1. *adj.* having a specified length. *How long is that table?* 2. *adj.* of unusually great length. *He has very long legs.* 3. *vb.* wish for very much. *I long to see you.*

longitude *n.* a distance measured in degrees east or west from a line on the map joining Greenwich, England, and the North and South Poles.

look *vb.* use one's eyes to see something.

Lock gates

A lock raises or lowers barges on a canal from one level to another.

Sluices

Lock chamber

Water level rises as sluices let water in.

locomotive *n.* a machine on wheels that pulls trains.

locust *n.* an insect like a grasshopper.

lodge 1. *n.* a small house at the gates of a large house. 2. *vb.* stay in

look after *vb.* take care of. *Can you look after our cat while we are away?*

look forward to *vb.* think with pleasure about something that is going to happen.

looking glass *n.* a mirror.

look into *vb*. investigate.

look out 1. *vb*. watch to see whether anyone is coming, or whether something will happen. 2. *n*. **lookout** a sentry.

look up *vb*. search for an item as if in a dictionary, encyclopedia or other book. 2. improve. *The weather is looking up.*

look up to *vb*. admire someone. *I always looked up to my brother because he was so good at football.*

loom 1. *n*. a machine for weaving cloth. 2. *vb*. appear in a vague or misty way; get larger. *The house loomed through the fog.*

loop *n*. a circle or part circle of wire, string or other material.

loose *adj*. not tight or firm. *One of my teeth is loose.* **loosen** *vb*. make or become loose.

loot *n*. & *vb*. plunder.

lop *vb*. cut off the ends of (especially a tree).

lord *n*. a nobleman.

lorry *n*. a big, open vehicle that carries heavy loads.

lose *vb*. (past **lost**) 1. no longer possess. 2. go astray. 3. be beaten in a game.

lost *vb*. past part. of **lose**.

lotion (**low**-*shun*) *n*. a liquid applied to the skin for cosmetic or medicinal reasons.

loud *adj*. noisy; not quiet.

loudspeaker *n*. part of a radio or record player that changes electric waves into sound.

lounge 1. *vb*. sit or stand in a lazy way. 2. *n*. a sitting room.

louse *n*. (plural **lice**) a small bloodsucking insect that feeds on animals or humans.

love *vb*. & *n*. be very fond of someone or something.

lovely *adj*. attractive; pretty. *What a lovely room.*

low *adj*. not high; near the ground. *A low table.*

lower 1. *adj*. not as high as. 2. *vb*. make something less high.

loyal *adj*. faithful to others. *We trust him as a loyal friend.*

lubricate *vb*. use oil or grease to make a machine work smoothly by cutting down the friction between two surfaces.

lucid *adj*. clear, easy to understand.

luck *n*. chance; good fortune. *Wish me luck.*

lucky *adj*. fortunate. *How lucky you were passing by.*

ludicrous *adj*. ridiculous, absurd. *That is a ludicrous suit you are wearing.*

luggage *n*. the cases, bags and other containers that are taken on a journey.

lukewarm *adj*. tepid; slightly warm; halfhearted.

lullaby *n*. a song that is sung to send a baby to sleep. **lull** *vb*. cause to sleep; soothe.

lumbago *n*. inflammation of the muscles of the lower back.

lumber *n*. timber prepared for use.

lumberjack *n*. a person who cuts down trees, especially in North America.

lump *n*. a bump, a swelling.

lunacy *n*. foolishness; insanity.

lunar *adj*. of or about the moon. *There will be a lunar eclipse this week.*

lunatic *n*. person who is insane.

lunch *n*. the midday meal (from **luncheon**, now rare) *vb*. eat lunch.

lung *n*. your body has two lungs inside your chest, forming a single organ by which you breathe.

lunge *vb*. & *n*. thrust at or attack suddenly.

lupin *n*. plant with flowers on a long spike.

lurk *vb*. wait unseen. *Strange creatures lurk in these woods.*

lust *n*. great desire.

lute *n*. pear-shaped plucked string instrument similar to a guitar.

luxury *n*. an expensive thing that is not really needed. *Most people think that a fur coat is a luxury.* **luxurious** *adj*. very comfortable.

lynx *n*. a wildcat with a short tail and tufted ears.

lyre *n*. a harplike instrument.

L

maggot *n*. larva, grub of a fly.

magic *adj. & n*. the belief that by doing or saying certain things, nature can be controlled and people can be influenced supernaturally.

magician (*ma-ji-shun*) *n*. a person who does magic tricks.

magistrate *n*. a minor judge; a person who has the power to put the law into force.

If the north pole of one magnet comes near the south pole of another, the two are pulled together. But two south poles repel each other. So do two north poles.

macabre *adj*. horrifying, gruesome.

macaroni *n*. long tubes of flour paste that are cooked and eaten. *Macaroni and spaghetti are Italian dishes.*

macaroon *n*. sweet biscuit made with coconut or almonds.

macaw *n*. a large brightly colored parrot found in the tropical rainforests of Central and South America. Many species have gaudy green, blue, red or yellow feathers.

mace *n*. 1. symbolic staff of authority. 2. spice made from outer skin of nutmeg.

machete (*ma-chet-ee*) *n*. heavy knife used for cutting vegetation and as a weapon in Central America.

machine *n*. a tool that has movable parts working together to do something.

machine gun *n*. a gun that can fire many bullets very quickly without being reloaded.

machinery *n*. machines; the moving parts of machines.

mackerel *n*. slender, streamlined fish with a wide-forked tail, found in all the world's seas.

mackintosh *n*. a waterproof coat, raincoat.

mad *adj*. insane, crazy; angry.
  madden *vb*. irritate; make mad.

madam (*mad-um*) *n*. polite form of addressing a woman.

made *vb*. past of **make**.

magazine *n*. 1. a soft-covered book of text and advertisements that comes out weekly or monthly. 2. the part of a gun that holds the bullets.

magma *n*. molten rock which, when it solidifies, becomes igneous rock.

magnet *n*. a piece of iron or steel that can pull other pieces of iron and steel toward it. **magnetic** *adj*. acting like a magnet.

magnesium *n*. a light, silver-white metallic element (symbol – *Mg*).

magnificent *adj*. marvelous; very impressive.

magnify *vb*. make something appear bigger. *If you look through a drop of water, it will magnify things.* **magnification** *n*.

magnifying glass *n*. a lens that magnifies things.

magnolia *n.* a tree or shrub famous for its large, pale, fragrant flowers which bloom early in spring.

magpie *n.* black-and-white bird related to the crow.

Magyar *n.* & *adj.* language and people of Hungary.

mahogany *n.* a tall tree growing in tropical Africa and America whose hard, red wood is used for making furniture.

maid *n.* a girl; a female servant.

mail 1. *n.* letters and parcels sent by post. *vb.* send by post. 2. *n.* armor made of metal rings.

mailbox *n.* a receptacle for letters.

maim *n.* injure, cripple.

main *adj.* the most important; the largest. *The main road runs near our house.*

mainland *n.* principal or larger land mass, without the nearby islands.

mainly *adv.* for the most part, chiefly.

maintain *vb.* 1. keep in good order. 2. support. 3. assert as true. 4. carry on.

maize *n.* a cereal crop. also called sweetcorn and Indian corn.

majesty *n.* having impressive or royal appearance; a title given to kings and queens, who are addressed as "Your Majesty." **majestic** *adj.*

major 1. *n.* an army officer between captain and lieutenant colonel. 2. *adj.* important. *The scientist made a major new discovery.*

majority *n.* greater part of a number; more than half. *The majority of the class went swimming.*

make 1. *vb.* (past **made**) create or invent something; prepare; gain. 2. *n.* the maker's name. *What make is your car?*

makeshift *adj.* temporary substitute.

makeup *n.* the cosmetics (paints and powders) people put on their faces.

make up for *vb.* do something good after you have done something bad. *I was nasty to my sister, but I made up for it by helping her this afternoon.*

mal- *prefix* meaning bad or inadequate, e.g. **malformed** *adj.*

badly formed. **maltreat** *vb.* treat badly.

malaria *n.* a disease which occurs mostly in tropical and subtropical areas. It is transmitted from infected to healthy people by the female Anopheles mosquito.

male 1. *n.* & *adj.* (of) a boy or man. 2. *n.* any creature of the sex that does not lay eggs or give birth.

mallet *n.* wooden hammer; implement for hitting croquet ball.

malt *n.* barley prepared for brewing.

mammal *n.* any of the animals of which the females feed their young with milk from their bodies.

mammoth *n.* a large animal like an elephant, but now extinct.

man *n.* (plural **men**) a grown-up male human; sometimes also used to mean all people, men and women (**mankind**). *vb.* supply with men; guard.

manage *vb.* 1. take charge of something. *She manages a supermarket.* 2. succeed in doing something even if it is not easy. *I can just manage to keep up with you.*

manager *n.* a person whose job is to take charge of other people at work.

mane *n.* the long hair on the neck of a horse or lion.

maneuver (*man*-**oo**-*ver*) *n.* planned movement of troops; skillful plan. *vb.* guide, manipulate.

manger *n.* a box for horses or cattle to eat from in a stable.

mania *n.* a mental illness; a craze.

manicure *n.* & *vb.* care of the hands and nails. **manicurist** *n.*

manifesto *n.* statement of policy.

mankind *n.* all people – men, women and children – everywhere.

man-made *adj.* artificial; made by humans. *A canal is a man-made river.*

manner *n.* the way a thing is done or happens. **manners** *pl. n.* how you behave toward others. *She has very good manners.*

manor *n.* in the Middle Ages, a lord's house and the land he owned.

M

mansion (**man-***shun*) *n*. a large, grand house.

manslaughter *n*. killing a person without planning to do so.

manu- *prefix* meaning hand, e.g. **manuscript** written by hand.

manual 1. *adj*. of or done with the hands. *Has your car got a manual or automatic shift?* 2. *n*. handbook, textbook.

manufacture *vb*. make things in a factory.

many *adj*. a lot; several; a large number. *A millipede has many legs*.

map *n*. a drawing of the earth's surface or part of it, often showing things such as rivers, mountains, countries and towns. *vb*. to make a map.

maple *n*. a deciduous tree native to the Northern Hemisphere. In autumn, its leaves turn spectacular shades of yellow, orange and red. One species, the sugar maple, is tapped for its sweet syrup. The maple leaf is the emblem of Canada.

marathon *n*. a very hard long-distance race of 26 miles 385 yards. It has been run in the Olympic Games since 1896.

marble *n*. 1. a hard stone that can be carved and polished. 2. a small glass or china ball used in games.

march *vb*. walk with a regular pace like a soldier. *n*. a piece of music to which people can march.

March *n*. the third month of the year.

mare *n*. a female horse.

margarine *n*. a fat used instead of butter.

margin *n*. the blank space around the edge of a page of printing or writing; border.

marigold *n*. a garden plant belonging to the daisy family, with bright yellow or orange flowers.

marina *n*. a dock for yachts with every facility for a yachting vacation.

marine (*mu-reen*) *adj*. to do with the sea. *A whale is a marine animal*. *n*. a soldier serving on board ship.

mariner *n*. an old-fashioned word for a sailor.

marionette *n*. a puppet moved by strings.

mark 1. *n*. & *vb*. a spot or pattern on something. *There is a dirty mark on your shirt*. 2. *vb*. judge quality of and correct. *The teacher will mark our homework*. 3. *n*. unit of money in Germany.

market *n*. a group of open-air shops or stalls; anywhere that goods are sold. *vb*. sell goods in a market.

marmalade *n*. a jam made from oranges and lemons.

marquis, marquess (**mar-***kwiss*) *n*. nobleman ranking below a duke but above an earl.

marriage *n*. wedlock.

marrow *n*. 1. soft tissue containing blood vessels in the cavities of bones. 2. large fleshy vegetable of the gourd family.

marry *vb*. become husband and wife, unite in **marriage** *n*.

marsh *n*. low-lying, wet land.

marsupial *n*. one of a group of mammals in which the females carry their young in a pouch on their bodies, like a kangaroo.

martial *adj*. warlike.

martin *n*. small bird related to the swallow.

martyr *n*. someone who suffers or dies for beliefs. *There were many martyrs among the early Christians*.

marvelous *adj*. splendid; excellent. *What a marvelous view*. **marvel** *n*. wonderful happening. *vb*. be astonished.

Marxist *n*. & *adj*. of or a supporter of the thinking of Karl Marx (1818–83). **Marxism** *n*.

marzipan *n*. sweet paste made from almonds.

mascara *n*. coloring used on eye-lashes.

mascot *n*. a person, animal or thing thought to bring good luck. *The regiment's mascot is a goat*.

masculine *adj*. male, manly; vigorous.

mash *vb*. & *n*. (to make) pulp.

mask *n.* a covering for the face; a disguise; face of a fox, dog, etc. *vb.* cover with a mask; disguise.

mason *n.* a person who works in stone; a builder.

mass *n.* 1. a large amount. 2. the amount of material in something. 3. Eucharist or Holy Communion service.

massacre *vb.* & *n.* brutal killing of large numbers of people.

massage *vb.* & *n.* treatment of body by rubbing and pressing with the hands.

massive *adj.* huge and solid.

mast *n.* 1. the pole that holds a ship's sails. 2. fruit of beech and oak used as pig fodder.

master *n.* a man who has other people working for him; the captain of a merchant ship; a male schoolteacher. **masterly** *adj.* skilful. **mastery** *n.* control, authority.

masterpiece *n.* a work of art done with great skill.

mastiff *n.* large thickset dog.

mat *n.* a floor or table covering.

match 1. *n.* a game or contest. *A football match.* 2. *n.* a small thin piece of wood, with the end coated with an inflammable substance, used for lighting fires, etc. 3. *n.* equal to. *The champion boxer was more than a match for the challenger.* 4. *vb.* go with something. *Does this handbag match my shoes?*

mate 1. *n.* a companion; (usually of animals) each parent of a young one is the mate of the other parent. 2. *vb.* produce young. 3. *n.* an officer of a merchant ship, under a captain.

material *n.* any substance from which something is or can be made. *Bricks, wood and cement are all building materials.*

maternal *adj.* of or concerning a mother; motherly.

mathematics *pl. n.* (*abbrev.* **math**) the science of numbers and shapes.

matinée (*mat-n-*ay) *n.* afternoon performance in a theater.

matrimony *n.* marriage.

A comic mask – as worn by actors in ancient Greece.

matron *n.* a woman attendant, guard or superintendent in an institution; a married woman of mature age (now old-fashioned).

matt *adj.* dull, without shine. *Matt paint.*

matter 1. *n.* the stuff of which things are made. 2. *vb.* be important. *We think it matters that you are late.*

mattress *n.* a cloth case stuffed with hair, feathers, or other material, often supported with springs, and placed on top of a bed for lying on.

mature *vb.* & *adj.* ripe, completely developed. **maturity** *n.*

mauve (rhymes with *rove*) *n.* & *adj.* a pale purple color.

maximum *adj.* & *n.* the greatest possible. *The maximum speed limit in the U.S.A. is 55 miles per hour.*

may *vb.* something that could possibly happen. *I may be able to help you.*

May *n.* the fifth month of the year.

maybe *adv.* perhaps.

mayonnaise *n.* a cold sauce made with oil, vinegar and eggs.

mayor (rhymes with *mare*) *n.* the head of a town or city.

maze *n.* a network of winding paths from which it is difficult to find a way out.

meadow *n.* a grassy field, particularly near a river.

meager (*me-*gur) *adj.* lean, poor.

meal *n.* 1. food eaten at a particular time, e.g. breakfast, lunch and dinner. *When do you have your main meal?* 2. grain ground to powder; flour.

mean 1. *vb*. stand for; show. *A red flag means danger*. 2. *vb*. intend to do something. *We always mean to be good, but often we aren't*. 3. *adj*. miserly; unwilling to share with others. 4. *adj*. average.

meander *vb*. wander about.

meaning *n*. what something means. *The English meaning of the French word "chat" is "cat"*.

means *pl. n*. 1. method by which something is done. 2. money.

meant *vb*. past of **mean**.

meanwhile *adv*. (or **meantime**) during the same time. *We were in the garden. Meanwhile the thieves entered the house by a front window*.

measles *n*. an infectious disease which causes red spots on the body and a fever.

measure *vb*. find the size or amount of a thing. *n*. something in which size, weight, length, etc., can be stated. *A foot is a measure of length*.

meat *n*. the flesh of cows, sheep and other animals eaten as food.

mechanic *n*. a person who works with machines.

mechanical *adj*. to do with machines; worked by machinery.

mechanics *pl. n*. the branch of physics that deals with the effect of force acting on bodies.

medal *n*. a flat piece of metal, often like a coin, with words or a picture on it, given as recognition for excellence or achievement.

meddle *vb*. interfere in.

medicine (*med-u-sin*) *n*. 1. the science of healing. 2. something taken to make you better when you are ill.

medieval (*med-ee-val*) *adj*. of the Middle Ages.

mediocre (*meed-ee-oh-kur*) *adj*. average quality, second-rate.

meditate *vb*. think deeply about. **meditation** *n*.

medium (*mee-de-um*) *adj*. middle size. *The robber was of medium height with fair hair*.

meet *vb*. (past **met**) join or come face to face with someone. *When shall we meet again?*

meeting *n*. a coming together of two or more people.

megalith *n*. large prehistoric stone.

melancholy (*mel-an-co-lee*) *adj*. sad, gloomy.

mellow *adj*. soft and ripe. *vb*. soften (with age or experience).

melody *n*. tune; principal part in harmonized music. **melodic** *adj*.

melon *n*. a creeping or climbing plant grown in warm climates for its large juicy fruit.

melt *vb*. turn a solid into a liquid by heating it. *The ice cream melted in the sun*.

member *n*. 1. a person who belongs to a group or team of people. *Winston is a member of the football team*. 2. a limb, an arm or leg.

memory *n*. the ability to remember things; what is remembered. *I have a very clear memory of being in the hospital*. **memorize** *vb*. learn by heart. **memorable** *adj*.

men *n*. plural of **man**.

menace *n*. & *vb*. threat(en).

menagerie *n*. collection of wild animals.

mend *vb*. & *n*. repair. *On the mend* getting better.

menorah *n*. the seven-branched candlestick used in Jewish worship. The seven branches are supposed to represent the sun, moon and five planets known to antiquity.

mental *adj*. concerning the mind.

mention *vb*. refer to, remark. *n*. brief note.

menu *n*. a list of the food you can have at a meal in a restaurant.

merchant *n*. a person who makes a living by buying and selling things.

mercury *n*. a heavy, silver-colored liquid metal; quicksilver.

mercy *n*. readiness to forgive, compassion; a fortunate happening.

merge *vb*. blend, combine with. **merger** *n*.

meridian *n*. any line of longitude. *The prime meridian (0° longitude) passes through Greenwich Observatory in England*.

M

merit *vb.* deserve, be worthy of. *You merit praise for your work.*

mermaid *n.* a legendary creature with a woman's body and a fish's tail.

merry *adj.* happy and cheerful.

merry-go-round *n.* a fairground machine with toy animals and vehicles that you ride on as it goes around.

mesmerize *vb.* hypnotize.

mess *n.* 1. untidiness and dirt. 2. a place where soldiers and sailors take their meals.

message *n.* a piece of information sent to somebody.

messenger *n.* a person who carries a message.

Messrs. (mess-*erz*) abbreviated plural of Mr. used in the title of a company (*Messrs. Jones, Smith & Sons*) or in a list of men's names.

met *vb.* past of **meet**.

metal *n.* any sort of material like iron, steel, tin or copper.

metaphor *n.* word or phrase taken from one field of experience and used to say something in another field, e.g. *"All the world's a stage." "Did you land a job today?" "No, not a bite".*

meteor *n.* a small solid body that rushes from outer space into the earth's atmosphere.

meteorite *n.* a meteor that reaches the earth without burning up.

meteorology *n.* the study of the changing conditions in the atmosphere and the causes of weather.

meter *n.* 1. a measure of length. *There are 100 centimeters in a meter.* 2. an instrument for measuring or recording quantities, speed, etc. *The gas meter shows how much gas we use in our house.* 3. the rhythm of a line of verse.

method *n.* a way of doing something; a system.

metric *adj.* the system of measuring based on the meter, the kilogram and the liter.

mice *n.* plural of **mouse**.

micro- *prefix* meaning small, minute; a millionth part of, e.g. **microfilm, microwave**.

microbe *n.* a tiny creature that can be seen only through a microscope.

microphone *n.* an instrument that picks up sound waves and turns them into electric waves for broadcasting or recording.

microscope *n.* an instrument for making very small things big enough to see; it magnifies them.

middle *n.* the center part of something; a person's waist.

midge *n.* small insect; gnat.

midget *n.* a very small person.

midnight *n.* twelve o'clock at night.

midwife *n.* a woman who helps at the birth of a child. **midwifery** *n.*

might 1. *vb.* past of **may**. *You might have told me earlier.* 2. *n.* power; strength.

mighty *adj.* very strong.

migraine *n.* a throbbing headache accompanied by nausea.

migrate *vb.* move from one place to another to live, as birds do in the autumn. **migration** *n.*

mild *adj.* moderate; gentle; (of weather) temperate.

mildew *n.* tiny fungus on plants or on growing decaying matter.

mile *n.* a measure of distance; 1760 yards.

militant *adj.* aggressive, warlike.

military *adj.* to do with soldiers and war.

milk *n.* a food that all baby mammals live on. It comes from the breasts, or mammaries, of the baby's mother. The baby sucks the milk from its mother's nipple. *vb.* draw milk from.

millennium *n.* a thousand years.

millet *n.* important cereal crop, cultivated as a basic food in the drier regions of Africa and Asia – especially in India and China.

milligram *n.* a very small measure of weight; one thousandth of a gram.

millimeter *n.* a small measure of length, shortened to *mm* (10 mm=1 centimeter).

M

milliner n. person who designs, makes, sells women's hats.

million n. one thousand thousand (1,000,000).

millionaire n. a person who has a million dollars.

millipede n. small wormlike animal with a tough outer skeleton, segmented body and two pairs of legs on almost every segment.

mime vb. & n. act without using words.

mimic vb. imitate someone. n. a person who mimics.

minaret n. a tall tower attached to a mosque from the top of which Muslims are called to prayer.

mince vb. cut into tiny pieces. n. meat that is chopped up finely.

mincemeat n. a mixture of dried fruits and fat that is cooked in pies and tarts, especially at Christmas.

mind 1. n. that part of a person which thinks, has ideas, and remembers; the brain. 2. vb. look after. *Our dog minds the house when we are out.* 3. vb. object to something. *I do mind being left alone.*

mine 1. pron. belonging to me. 2. n. a deep hole in the ground from which coal or other minerals are taken. vb. take minerals from the ground. **miner** n. a mine worker.

mineral n. a crystalline material that comes from the ground. *Coal, salt, and diamonds are all minerals.* adj. of or belonging to minerals.

mingle vb. blend, mix (with).

miniature adj. very small in scale.

minimize vb. reduce to smallest possible amount.

minimum adj. the least possible amount. *The minimum price of a seat was $2.*

minister n. 1. a clergyman; a parson. **ministry** n.

mink n. cat-sized semiaquatic mammal with a brown coat and bushy tail.

minnow n. small freshwater fish belonging to the carp family. Most species are under six inches long.

minor adj. lesser or smaller, unimportant. *His car was involved in a minor accident, and was only slightly damaged.*

mint n. 1. a green, leafy herb used for flavoring food. 2. a place where coins are made.

minus prep. the mathematical sign ($-$) meaning take away or less than ($6-4=2$).

minute (min-*it*) n. a short period of time. *There are 60 minutes in one hour.*

minute (*my*-nute) adj. very tiny.

miracle n. a remarkable event that cannot be explained.

mirage n. an image of something caused by atmospheric conditions; a visual illusion.

mirror n. a shiny surface that reflects things; a looking glass. vb. reflect as a mirror.

mis- prefix meaning bad or wrongly. The meaning of such words can be found by referring to the main word, e.g. **misbehave, misprint, mispronounce.**

mischief n. naughtiness. **mischievous** adj.

miser n. a person who loves money for itself; a mean person.

miserable adj. very unhappy.

misery n. great unhappiness.

miss vb. 1. fail to hit, catch or see something that you want to. *If Sally does not hurry she will miss the train.* 2. be sad because someone is not with you. *When mother was in the hospital, we all missed her very much.*

Miss n. the title that goes before the name of an unmarried woman. *Miss Moody is the head teacher of our school.*

missile n. an object or weapon that is thrown or sent through the air, often by a rocket.

missing adj. not present; not found.

mission (mi-*shun*) n. team sent to do some special work; specific task.

missionary adj. & n. a person who goes to another country to tell people about his or her religion or to do helpful work.

missive n. a letter to be sent.

mist *n.* a thin fog; water vapor in the air.

mistake *vb.* & *n.* (past **mistook** past part. **mistaken**) something you do without intending to; an error. *I made a mistake in my arithmetic.*

mister *n.* (written as Mr.) the title that goes before a man's surname. *Our teacher is called Mr. Todd.*

mistletoe *n.* an evergreen plant with shiny white berries which grows as a parasite on trees, especially apple trees; widely used as a Christmas decoration.

miter *n.* 1. headdress worn by a bishop. 2. special joint at corner of picture frame, etc.

mitten *n.* a kind of glove with one place for four fingers together and another for the thumb separately.

mix *vb.* mingle or join together. **mixer** *n.* a machine for mixing ingredients.

mixture *n.* anything made by mixing things together.

moan *n.* & *vb.* groan, especially with pain or unhappiness; grumble.

moat *n.* a deep ditch around a castle.

mob *n.* noisy crowd, gang. *vb.* crowd around.

mobile *adj.* moving, movable. **mobility** *n.*

moccasin *n.* shoe made of deerskin or soft leather.

mock *vb.* make fun of, scoff at. **mockery** *n.*

model *n.* 1. a copy of something, usually smaller. *The architect showed us the model he had made of the new building. vb.* make a model. 2. someone who sits while an artist or photographer paints or photographs; someone whose job is to wear and show new clothes.

moderate (*mod-er-at*) *adj.* not extreme; of average quality.

modern *adj.* of present or recent times. *My mother likes living in a modern house, but my father would like to move to an older one.* **modernize** *vb.* (make modern) bring up to date.

modest *adj.* not boastful, not excessive. **modesty**. *n.*

mohair *n.* hair of the Angora goat.

moist *adj.* slightly wet. **moisten** *vb.* to make moist. **moisture** *n.*

mold (rhymes with *sold*) 1. *n.* a hollow container. When a hot substance is poured into a mold it cools into the shape of the container. 2. *vb.* to shape. 3. *n.* a small fungus that grows on damp decaying things.

mole *n.* 1. a small furry animal that lives in a tunnel underground. 2. a small dark mark on the skin. 3. a secret spy.

molt (rhymes with *colt*) *vb.* shed old feathers, hair, shell, or skin periodically. *Snakes molt and have new skin under the old one.*

molecule *n.* a number of atoms joined together to form a stable and definite structure.

molest (*mo-lest*) *vb.* annoy, pester.

mollusk *n.* one of a group of animals with soft bodies and no backbone. Most mollusks, like snails, limpets and oysters, have hard shells.

moment *n.* a very short period of time. *Wait a moment.*

monarch ("ch" like "k") *n.* a king or queen.

monastery *n.* a place where monks live and work. **monastic** *adj.*

Monday *n.* the second day of the week, between Sunday and Tuesday; named after the moon.

money *n.* coins or bank notes used to buy things.

mongoose *n.* (plural **mongooses**) a small mammal of Africa and southern Asia, a relative of the weasel. It has a low body, a bushy tail and short legs. An adult mongoose is about 1½ feet long.

mongrel *adj.* & *n.* a dog that is a mixture of different types of dogs.

monk (rhymes with *bunk*) *n.* a member of a religious group of men who live, work and pray together in a monastery.

monkey (*mun-kee*) *n.* a furry animal that belongs to the same group as apes and people.

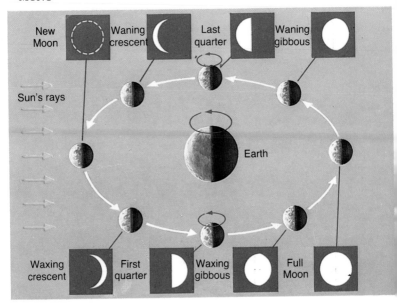

New Moon
Waning crescent
Last quarter
Waning gibbous
Sun's rays
Earth
Waxing crescent
First quarter
Waxing gibbous
Full Moon

mono- *prefix* meaning one, alone, e.g. **monochrome** painting in one color. **monosyllable** word with one syllable, e.g. me.

monopoly *n*. sole control of something.

monorail *n*. a railway which runs on one rail.

monsieur (*mus-***yer**) *n*. (plural **messieurs** pronounced **may**-*s*-**yer**) the French for mister or sir.

monsoon *n*. a wind system in which prevailing winds blow in opposite directions in winter and summer. *In India, the well-known summer monsoon brings heavy rainfall.*

monster *n*. a large and frightening creature. **monstrous** *adj*. very large.

month *n*. one of the 12 parts into which the year is divided. **monthly** *adv*. once a month.

monument *n*. something that reminds us of a person or event. *The Tomb of the Unknown Soldiers is a monument to soldiers who died in American wars.*

mood *n*. the way you feel. **moody**

The phases of the moon. The time from New to Full is called "waxing" – an old word meaning to grow. After Full, the moon "wanes" or shrinks to invisibility once more.

adj. subject to changes of mood; gloomy.

moon *n*. the Earth's only natural satellite and our nearest neighbor in space.

moonlight *n*. the light from the moon.

moor 1. *n*. an open boggy wasteland often covered with grasses. 2. *vb*. tie up a boat.

moose *n*. (plural **moose**) a large, dark brown deer found in the cold northern forests of Alaska and Canada. The male carries huge, flattened antlers. *Moose are similar to the European and Asian elk.*

mop *n*. a bundle of fibers on the end of a stick, used for cleaning floors.

136

moped (**mo**-*ped*) *n.* a kind of small motorized bicycle.

morale (*more*-**ahl**) *n.* condition of the state of mind and confidence of people. *Morale is high! We're going to win!*

morals 1. *pl. n.* rules or system of good behavior. **moral** *adj.* concerned with what is right or wrong.

moral *n.* a practical lesson. *He's in the hospital. The moral of that is, don't ride on the wrong side of the road.*

more *adj.* a greater amount or number. *May I have some more pudding?*

morning *n.* the early part of the day, between night and afternoon.

Morse code *n.* a system of sending messages by a series of dots and dashes for letters.

mortal *adj.* that which must die; causing death. *A mortal wound. n.* a human being.

mortar *n.* 1. a mixture of cement, lime, sand and water. *Mortar is used to hold bricks together.* 2. a vessel for grinding substances in (with a **pestle**).

mortgage *n.* transfer of property as security for a sum of money borrowed. *vb.* give over by mortgage.

mosaic *adj. & n.* a picture made from little bits of colored stone or glass set into cement.

Moslem see **Muslim**.

mosque (*mosk*) *n.* a building in which Muslims worship.

mosquito (*mos*-**kee**-*to*) *n.* (plural **mosquitoes**) small insect that sucks blood. *Some mosquitoes carry malaria and other diseases.*

moss *n.* small green or yellow plants that grow on damp surfaces in low, closely packed clusters.

most *adj., pron. & adv.* the greatest; the largest number.

motel *n.* a roadside hotel for people who arrive by car.

moth *n.* a winged insect, like a butterfly, that usually flies at night.

mother *n.* a female parent; a woman who has children. *vb.* care for or protect.

motion *n.* 1. moving. 2. gesture. 3. formal proposition.

motive *n.* something that causes a person to take action.

motor *n.* an engine that uses electricity, gas or oil to produce a movement.

The first car made by Gottlieb Daimler in 1886.

motorcycle *n.* a two-wheeled vehicle propelled by an internal combustion engine.

motorist *n.* someone who drives a car.

motorize *vb.* to put a motor on something. *We motorized our boat.*

mottled *adj.* marked with spots of different colors.

mount 1. *vb.* go up something; get onto a horse to ride it; rise sharply. *The cost of candy mounted after the sugar shortage.* 2. *n.* a saddle horse; small hill.

mountain *n.* a very high hill.

mountaineer *n.* a person who climbs mountains.

mourning *n.* grief, great sadness after someone dies. **mourn** *vb.*

A muezzin calling faithful Muslims to prayer from a minaret.

mouse *n.* (plural **mice**) a very small rodent.

moustache *n.* hair grown on the upper lip.

mouth *n.* the opening in the face into which you put food and through which your voice comes; that part of a river where it flows into the sea.

mouth organ *n.* a small musical instrument played by blowing and sucking.

move *vb.* change position of something; change residence, location, etc.; stir, affect with emotion. *n.* e.g. a chess move. **movable** *adj.* that can be moved.

movement *n.* 1. activity; the act of moving. 2. section of a piece of music.

movie *n.* motion picture.

mow (rhymes with *toe*) *vb.* cut grass or hay. **mower** *n.* mowing machine.

Mr. *abbrev.* the polite title given to a man (short for Mister), e.g. *Mr. Smith.*

Mrs. *abbrev.* the polite title that goes before the surname of a married woman.

Ms. (*miz*) *n.* a polite title used before the surname of a woman. It does not show whether or not she is married.

much *adj & adv.* a great deal; a considerable amount. *You are making too much noise.*

muck *n.* manure, filth.

mud *n.* wet, soft earth. **muddy** *adj.* covered with mud.

muddle *n.* a confused mess. *vb.* muddy up; confuse.

muezzin *n.* Muslim who calls people to daily prayer from atop a minaret.

mug 1. *n.* a tall kind of cup without a saucer. 2. *n.* person's face or mouth. 3. *vb.* assault someone, usually in order to rob. *n.* mugger.

mule *n.* 1. a horselike animal that is the foal of a male ass and a female horse or pony (a mare). 2. kind of slipper without a back.

multi- *prefix* meaning many, e.g. **multilateral** many sided.

multiply *vb.* make something a given number of times bigger. *When you multiply by three, the answer is three times greater.* **multiplication** *n.*

mumble *vb.* mutter; talk indistinctly.

mummy *n.* the preserved body of a human or animal. *v.* **mummify**.

mumps *n.* an illness that makes the neck and sides of the face swell.

mural *n.* a picture painted on a wall.

murder *n. & vb.* criminal killing of someone. **murderer** *n.* **murderess** *n.*

murmur *vb. n.* make a low sound; mutter. *All he could hear was the gentle murmur of the river.*

muscle (**mus**-*sel*) *n.* one of the fleshy parts of the body that make you move. *You make movement by tightening the right muscles.* **muscular** *adj.*

museum (*mu-zee-um*) *n.* a building where interesting things from other times and places are kept and shown to the public.

mushroom *n.* a kind of fungus that is safe to eat.

music *n.* the sound made by someone who sings or who plays a musical instrument. **musical** *adj.*

musical *n.* a play or film in which music is an essential part.

musician (*mu-***zish**-*un*) *n.* a person who makes music.

musket *n.* a firearm, in use from about 1540 to about 1840. It was muzzle-loading and smooth-bored. Matchlocks, wheellocks and flintlocks were all different versions of it, as the firing mechanism was improved.

Muslim *n.* a follower of the Islamic religion.

mussel *n.* a small mollusk found mainly in the sea.

must *auxiliary verb* (a verb which goes with and helps another verb). expressing command. *You must not walk on the grass.* expressing obligation. *I must finish this letter today.* expressing a result or deduction. *She left two hours ago. She must be nearly home by now.* expressing the obvious. *You must have heard of Henry VIII.*

mustard *n.* a hot-tasting condiment made from the mustard plant and used to flavor food; dark yellow color.

mutilate *vb.* injure, damage, disfigure.

mutiny *n.* uprising, revolt, especially by members of armed forces.

mutter *vb.* speak in a low tone, under your breath; murmur.

mutton *n.* the meat of a sheep.

muzzle 1. *n.* open end of a gun barrel. 2. *n.* animal's snout 3. *vb.* to restrain from expression.

mystery *n.* something that is difficult to explain or understand. **mysterious** *adj.*

myth *n.* an old story about imaginary people.

nag 1. *n.* a horse, usually small and of poor quality. 2. *vb.* worry and find fault with constantly; scold. **nagging** *adj.*

nail 1. *n.* thin piece of metal with a point at one end and a flat head at the other, used to fasten things together. *vb.* fasten with nails. 2. *n.* the hard layer over the outer tip of a finger or toe.

naked *adj.* bare, without any clothes on; unprotected (eye).

name *n.* the word which we use for a person, animal or thing. *vb.* give a name to.

namely *adv.* that is to say.

namesake *n.* a person of the same name.

nanny *n.* a child's nurse.

nanny goat *n.* a female goat.

nap *n.* & *vb.* (take) a short sleep.

naphtha *n.* a highly flammable oil.

napkin *n.* a cloth for wiping fingers and lips and for protecting clothes at meals.

narcissus *n.* plant similar to a daffodil; name of a mythological Greek youth who fell in love with his own reflected image and was turned into a flower.

narrate (**nare**-*rate*) *vb.* relate, give an account of. **narrative** *n.* story.

narrator *n.* person who tells a story.

narrow *adj.* not wide, small in width; intolerant (**narrow-minded**).

narwhal *n.* a small whale, about 17 feet long, found in the Arctic Ocean. Narwhals swim together in great schools and feed mainly on cuttlefish and squid.

nasal *adj.* of the nose.

N

nasturtium (na-**stir**-*shum*) *n.* garden climbing plant with orange, red, or yellow flowers.

nasty *adj.* unpleasant; not nice; spiteful.

nation (**nay**-*shun*) *n.* a country and the people who live in it.

national (**nash**-*u*-*nal*) *adj.* belonging to one country. *The national flag of the United States is the Stars and Stripes.* **nationality** *n.* *He has British nationality.*

national anthem *n.* official hymn or song of a nation.

nationalist *n.* a person who wants independence for his or her country or province.

nationalize *vb.* transfer industry etc. from private ownership to control by the state.

national parks *pl. n.* special areas of land that are set aside and protected by governments.

native *n.* a person who was born in a particular place. *Angus is a native of Scotland.*

nativity *n.* being born; a birthday. *A nativity play is about the birth of Jesus.*

natural *adj.* made by nature, not by people or machines.

natural gas *n.* a gas which occurs naturally underground and does not have to be manufactured.

naturalist *n.* student of nature.

naturally *adv.* of course; as might be expected; without putting on airs; plain.

nature *n.* 1. the whole universe and all its life. *Nature includes everything that is not made by people or machines.* 2. essential character or quality of a person or thing. *It was not in her nature to be unkind.*

naughty *adj.* badly-behaved, wicked (usually used of children).

nausea (**naw**-*zee*-*ah*) *n.* urge to vomit; extreme disgust. **nauseous** *adj.* disgusting.

nautical *adj.* concerned with ships, sailors and navigation.

nautilus *n.* a sea animal with a soft body inside a hard, spiral shell. The shell is lined with a shiny substance called mother-of-pearl.

nave *n.* the main part of the church from the front porch to the altar.

navel *n.* the "belly button," a depression in the stomach left after the umbilical cord is cut.

navigate *vb.* find the way for a ship or aircraft.

navigation *n.* working out the correct route for a ship, aircraft, etc.

navy *n.* a country's warships and all the people who sail in them. **naval** *adj.* concerning the navy and ships.

near *adv. & prep.* not far in time or distance. *Tom stood near the door.*

nearly *adv.* almost. *You nearly missed the bus.*

neat *adj.* tidy, having everything in the right place.

necessary *adv.* that which has to be done. *It is necessary to have a license to drive a car.* **necessity** *n.* something that is needed, indispensable thing.

neck *n.* the narrow part of the body between the head and the shoulders.

necklace (**neck**-*lus*) *n.* a string of beads or other ornaments worn around the neck.

nectar *n.* a sweet liquid in flowers that is collected by bees.

nectarine *n.* a type of peach. Nectarines taste like peaches but they are smaller and have a smooth skin instead of a fuzzy one.

need *vb.* require; want something urgently. *She's been working very hard and needs a vacation.* *n.* a want or requirement.

needle *n.* 1. a pointed instrument used for sewing or knitting. 2. a pointer in a meter or a compass. 3. leaf of fir or pine.

needlework *n.* sewing, embroidery, etc.

negative 1. *adj.* expressing denial or refusal. *He gave a negative answer by which he means no.* the opposite of positive. 2. *n.* photographic image in which light areas are dark and dark areas are light.

neglect *vb.* give little care to. *If you

neglect *your garden, it will become full of weeds.* **negligence** *n.*

negotiate *vb.* discuss so as to reach an agreement. *The union is negotiating with the management over working hours.* deal with, manage. **negotiation** *n.*

Negress *n.* a Negro woman or girl.

Negro *n.* a person who belongs to the black-skinned race, especially one (originating) from Africa.

neigh *n. & vb.* a noise made by a horse.

neighbor (**nay**-*ber*) *n.* someone who lives near you.

neighborhood *n.* the area around the place where you live. **neighborly** *adj.* like a good neighbor, friendly.

neither *adj. & pron.* not one nor the other.

neon *n.* a colorless gas used in light tubes (symbol – *Ne*).

nephew *n.* the son of your brother or sister.

nerve *n.* 1. a fiber that carries sensations and messages between the body and the brain. 2. boldness and self-assurance.

nervous *adj.* easily frightened, excitable, tense; also **nervy**.

nest *n.* a home that a bird or other animal makes out of twigs, grass, feathers, etc., generally as a shelter for its eggs and its young. *vb.* make or have a nest.

nestling *n.* a bird too young to leave the nest.

net 1. *n.* a material made of loosely woven string, thread or wire, so there are many holes between the threads. *vb.* catch or cover with a net. 2. *adj.* the price of something after discount, postal charges, etc. have been taken off. Similarly for **net weight**.

nettle 1. *n.* a common weed with stinging hairs on its leaves. 2. *vb.* irritate, provoke.

neuter (**new**-*ter*) *adj.* neither male nor female.

neutral *adj.* 1. not taking sides, especially in a war or dispute. 2. having no electrical charge.

neutron *n.* an electrically neutral atomic particle.

never *adv.* not ever; at no time. *I've never seen him before.*

new *adj.* made or used for the first time; not old.

news *n.* recent or up-to-date information; a program about recent events on TV or radio; the contents of a newspaper.

newspaper *n.* a set of printed sheets of paper containing news, and usually published either daily or weekly.

newt *n.* a lizardlike amphibian.

next 1. *adj.* nearby. *They live next to us.* 2. *adv.* following. *What would you like to do next?*

nib *n.* the point of a pen.

nibble *vb.* eat in very small bites. *n.* a small bite.

nice *adj.* good or pleasant. *Have a nice time.*

Some birds' nests. The golden oriole (1) makes a hanging nest; the tailor bird weaves a nest between leaves (2); the tit's mossy nest is almost enclosed (3); and the American robin's nest is a cup of mud and twigs (4).

nick 1. *n.* notch. 2. *n.* final critical moment. *In the nick of time.* 3. *v.* notch, cut.

nickel 1. *n.* a tough, hard, silvery-white metal element widely used in the form of plating and in alloys. It is electroplated onto metals such as steel to protect them from corrosion, and is added, with chromium, to steel to make it stainless. 2. *n.* a U.S. coin worth five cents.

nickname *n.* an extra name given to a person or place. *We call Mr. Baker by his nickname, Floury.*

niece (rhymes with *fleece*) *n.* the daughter of your brother or sister.

night *n.* the time between evening and morning, when it is dark.

nightly *adj.* happening or recurring every night.

nightingale *n.* a bird famous for its beautiful song which is usually heard in the late evening or early morning. Nightingales live in damp shady woodlands and feed on insects.

nightmare *n.* a frightening dream.

nil *n.* nothing, zero.

nimble *adj.* quick-moving; agile.

nip *vb.* pinch like a crab.

nit *n.* the egg of the louse found in the hair.

nitrogen *n.* a colorless, tasteless gas. It is an element (symbol – N).

noble *adj.* (or **nobleman** *n.*) a man of high rank, such as a duke.

nobody *n.* no one; no person. *There's nobody here.*

nocturnal *adj.* belonging to, or active in, the night.

nod *vb.* & *n.* bow the head slightly; be drowsy.

noise *n.* a sound (usually disagreeable or loud). *Don't make so much noise.* **noisy** *adj.* making a lot of noise.

nomad *n.* a member of a group of people who wander from place to place.

non- *prefix* meaning not. The sense of words with the prefix should be clear when the meaning of the main word is known, e.g. **nonsmoker** a person who does not smoke. **nonstop** without stopping.

nonsense *n.* foolish talk or behavior.

noon *n.* midday; twelve o'clock in the daytime.

noose *n.* a loop of rope. *The noose becomes tighter when one end of the rope is pulled.* *vb.* catch with a noose, make a noose in.

nor *conj.* and not, not either.

Nordic *adj.* of or relating to tall, blond Germanic people of northern Europe.

norm *n.* standard of quality, etc.

normal *adj.* regular, as expected. *The normal temperature of the human body is 98.6°F..*

Norse *n.* & *adj.* (language) of ancient Scandinavia, especially Norway.

north *n.* one of the points of the compass. *When you face the sunrise, north is on your left.*

nose *n.* the organ in the middle of the face used by people and many animals for breathing and smelling.

nostalgia *n.* homesickness; a wish to return to some past period.

nostril *n.* either of the openings in the nose through which you breathe and smell.

nosy *adj.* inquisitive.

not *adv.* a word that makes a statement negative. *I do not know what you are talking about.*

note 1. *vb.* write down a few words to remind yourself or someone else about something. **notebook** 2. *n.* a short letter. 3. *n.* a single musical sound. *Catherine played one note on the piano.* 4. *n.* paper money.

noted *adj.* famous, well-known (for).

nothing *n.* not anything. *Have you nothing to say?*

notice (*no-tiss*) 1. *n.* something written down or shown to people to tell them something. *The notice on the door said, "KEEP OUT."* 2. *vb.* see something. *I noticed that she had a new hat.*

notify *vb.* inform, make known. **notification** *n.*

● Electron

● Proton

● Neutron

A carbon atom is made up of six electrons orbiting a nucleus of six protons and six neutrons.

nougat (**noo**-*gut*) *n.* candy made from nuts, sugar and egg whites.

noun *n.* the name of a person, place or thing. *John, Paris and cat are all nouns.*

novel 1. *n.* a long written story. **novelist** *n.* writer of novels. 2. *adj.* new, strange, unknown.

November *n.* the eleventh month of the year.

novice (**nov**-*iss*) *n.* beginner; a person who enters a convent or monastery on a trial basis.

now *adv.* at the present moment. *You may go home now.*

nowadays *adv.* at the present time.

nowhere *adv.* not anywhere.

nozzle *n.* spout of a waterhose, etc.

nuclear *adj.* 1. to do with atomic energy. *When the nucleus of an atom is split, it produces nuclear energy.* 2. (in other sciences) to do with the central parts of larger things.

nucleus *n.* a central part of something, such as an atom or a cell (in biology).

nude *adj.* naked; bare; having no clothes.

nudge *vb.* & *n.* (a) push gently with the elbow to attract attention.

nugget *n.* solid lump, especially of precious metal, e.g. gold.

nuisance *n.* something or somebody that causes trouble.

numb (rhymes with *gum*) *adj.* not able to feel. *vb.* make numb.

number *n.* 1. a word or figure showing how many. *5, 37 and 6 are all numbers.* 2. a quantity or amount. *There were a large number of books left on the shelf.*

numerous *adj.* great numbers of, many.

numismatic *adj.* to do with coins and medals.

nun *n.* a woman who has taken vows to live a religious life.

nurse 1. *n.* a person who is trained to look after people who are ill, very young or very old. 2. *vb.* act as a nurse; cherish. 3. suckle.

nursery *n.* 1. a room for a baby or small child. *A nursery school is for very young children.* 2. a place where young plants are grown for sale.

nut *n.* 1. the fruit of certain plants with a hard shell. 2. a piece of metal with a hole in the center that screws on to a bolt to fasten it.

nutmeg *n.* the hard seed of a tropical fruit used as a spice; another spice, **mace**, comes from the outer part of the nutmeg fruit.

nylon *n.* a strong, elastic, artificial (man-made) fiber.

nymph *n.* 1. minor goddess of nature in ancient mythology. 2. larva of certain insects such as dragonflies.

oak *n.* a large tree on which acorns grow.

oar (rhymes with *sore*) *n.* a pole with a flat end for making a rowboat move through water. *Most rowboats have two oars.*

oasis (*o-ay-sis*) *n.* a fertile place in the desert.

oath *n.* a solemn promise.

oats *pl. n.* grain from a cereal. *Ground oats are called oatmeal and are used to make porridge.*

obedient *adj.* doing what you are told. *Our dog was very naughty as a puppy, but now he is quite obedient.*

obelisk *n.* a stone monument, in the shape of a tall pillar: four-sided, narrowing upward, and topped by a small pyramid shape. *The Washington Monument is an example of an obelisk.*

obey (*o-bay*) *vb.* do what you are told.

obituary *n.* an announcement of a person's death.

object (**ob**-*ject*) 1. *n.* anything that can be touched or seen.

object *vb* (*ob*-**ject**) say that you do not agree with something. *She objected to the way the people were chosen.* **objection** *n.* expression of disapproval. **objectionable** *adj.* disagreeable.

oblige *vb.* 1. make someone do something. 2. do a favor. 3. bind someone by gratitude. **obligation** *n.* duty.

oblique *adj.* slanting; roundabout; indirect.

obliterate *vb.* destroy completely. *The bombs obliterated the center of the city.* **obliteration** *n.*

oblong *n.* a rectangle; a flat figure with two parallel pairs of straight sides, two longer than the others, and four right angles.

oboe *n.* a musical instrument made of wood and played by blowing.

obscure *adj.* dim, vague, indistinct. *vb.* hide.

observe *vb.* notice; watch carefully; follow orders, instructions. **observation** *n.* observing; comment.

observatory *n.* a place from which observations are made, usually of heavenly bodies.

obsolete *adj.* no longer used, discarded.

obstacle *n.* something that gets in the way; a hindrance.

obstinate *adj.* not easily made to agree to do something. *A donkey can be very obstinate if it does not want to work.*

obstruct *vb.* block; get in the way. **obstruction** *n.*

obtain *vb.* get possession of something.

obverse *n.* front surface of a coin or medal bearing the head or main design.

obvious *adj.* easily seen or understood.

occasion *n.* a special time or event. **occasional** *adj.*

occident *n.* the West or western part of the world. **occidental** *adj.*

occupation *n.* what you do or are doing; your job.

occupy *vb.* live in or be in. *Sam will occupy the second floor of the building.* **occupant** *n.* person living in a property.

occur *vb.* (past **occurred**) happen; take place. **occurrence** *n.* happening; incident.

ocean (*o-shun*) *n.* one of the great bodies of sea water that surround the continents.

o'clock *n.* the hour of the day. *We start school at nine o'clock.*

octagon *n.* a flat figure with eight equal sides. **octagonal** *adj.*

octave *n.* (in music) eight notes of a scale, e.g., C, D, E, F, G, A, B, C.

October *n.* the tenth month of the year.

octopus *n.* a sea animal with a soft body and eight arms.

odd *adj.* 1. peculiar, strange. 2. a number that cannot be divided exactly by two. *3, 27, and 101 are odd numbers.*

oddments *n. pl.* odds and ends; scraps; bits and pieces.

odor *n.* smell.

off *prep.* from; away from. *Stephen fell off his bicycle.*

offend *vb.* cause dislike, anger, etc. *I am sorry if I have offended you.* **offense** *n.*

offer *vb.* 1. say that you will do something for someone. *I thanked him for offering to help me clean the room.* 2. hold out something to someone. *Sean offered me a bag of candy.* *n.* a price proposed, usually by a buyer.

office *n.* a place where people work whose business needs writing and recording.

officer *n.* a senior person in the army, air force or navy; president or treasurer, etc., of a society.

offspring *n.* the child or children of a family; plants or young animals.

often *adv.* many times; frequently.

ogre (**o**-*ger*) *n.* a cruel giant in stories.

oil *n.* kinds of liquid that do not mix with water and usually burn easily. *vb.* apply oil; lubricate.

ointment *n.* a medicine made in a paste or cream.

old *adj.* having lived for a long time; out-of-date.

old-fashioned *adj.* out-of-date, not worn or used nowadays.

olive *n.* a small oval fruit with a hard stone and bitter, oily flesh. *adj.* dullish green color (color of an olive).

omelet, omelette *n.* a kind of pancake made of fried beaten eggs, often with a meat, vegetable or cheese filling.

Gases

Distillation tower.

Gasoline

Kerosene

Gas oil

Heavy oil

Gasoline, kerosene and lubricating oil are among the products that are distilled from the oil that is drilled from under the ground or under the sea. Each product has a different boiling point and so vaporizes at a different level.

omen *n.* sign of good or evil to come. **ominous** *adj.* threatening.

omit *vb.* leave out; fail to put in. **omission** *n.*

omni- *prefix* meaning all, e.g. **omnipotent** all powerful. **omnivorous** feeding on all kinds of food.

once *adv.* 1. at one time only. *I have only been to Venice once.* 2. at a time in the past. *She once lived in Africa.*

onion *n.* a strong-tasting bulb eaten as a vegetable or used to add flavor to other foods.

onlooker *n.* spectator.

only *adv. & adj.* a single one; no one or nothing else. *He was the only person to give the right answer.*

onyx (**on**-*iks*) *n.* semiprecious stone with layers of different colors.

opal *n.* a precious stone, a form of quartz much prized for its rainbow play of colors.

opaque (*o-pake*) *adj.* not letting the light through; unintelligible.

open *adj. & adv.* not closed. *Leave the door open. vb.* make or become open.

openly *adv.* in public; frankly.

opera *n.* a play in which the words are sung.

operate *vb.* 1. work. *Do you know how to operate the machine?* 2. carry out a surgical operation.

operation (*op-per-ay-shun*) *n.* 1. a treatment by a doctor in which the patient's body is cut. 2. a carefully planned action.

operator *n.* a person who works a machine, e.g. a telephone switchboard.

opinion *n.* what someone thinks; an idea with which not everyone agrees. **opinionated** *adj.* stubborn in one's opinions.

opossum *n.* a marsupial mammal that lives in North and South America.

opponent *n.* someone who opposes something; a foe.

opportune *adj.* suitable, convenient.

opportunity *n.* a good chance to do something. *While the children were out, their mother took the opportunity to clean their rooms.*

oppose *vb.* resist; be against. *I oppose the plan to rebuild the bus station.*

opposite 1. *n.* the reverse of something. *Fat is the opposite of thin.* 2. *adj.* on the other side. *The house on the opposite side of the road is painted blue.*

opt *vb.* make a choice.

optician (*op-tish-un*) *n.* a person who makes or sells glasses. **optic** *adj.* concerning the eyes or sight.

optimism *n.* belief that the best will happen. **optimist** *n.*

or *conj.* a connecting word introducing the second of two choices. *Coffee or tea?*

oral *adj.* spoken; concerning the mouth.

orange 1. *n.* round juicy fruit with a thick skin. 2. *n. & adj.* a color like an orange.

orangutan *n.* a reddish-brown ape that lives in the forests of Indonesia.

orator *n.* an eloquent public speaker.

oratorio *n.* musical work for choir and orchestra often on a religious subject and without action or scenery.

orb *n.* sphere or globe.

orbit *n.* the path followed by any body in space around another body. *vb.* travel in an orbit.

orchard *n.* a piece of ground where fruit trees are grown.

orchestra (*ork-estra*) *n.* a group of musicians who play together. **orchestral** *adj.*

orchid *n.* one of a family of showy perennial flowering plants.

order 1. *vb.* command somebody to do something. *The officer ordered the troops to advance.* 2. *n.* a list of things that you want. *The waiter took our order for lunch.* 3. *n.* a succession of events. 4. *n.* tidiness. 5. *n.* a religious community. *These monks belong to the Order of Saint Benedict.*

orderly 1. *adj.* tidy. 2. *n.* a soldier who looks after an officer; hospital employee who does routine work.

ordinary *adj.* normal; usual; not strange or interesting.

ore *n.* rock or earth from which metal can be taken.

organ *n.* 1. any part of an animal's body that has a particular job to do. *The heart is the organ that pumps blood around the body.* 2. a musical instrument with a keyboard and pipes. **organist** *n.* organ player.

organism *n.* a living animal or plant.

organization *n.* an organized group.

organize *vb.* make arrangements for something to happen; give orderly structure to.

orient *n.* the East or eastern part of the world. **oriental** *adj.*

origami *n.* Japanese art of folding paper into intricate shapes.

origin *n.* beginning, source; starting

point. **originate** *vb.* create, come into being; spring from.

original *adj.* the earliest or first; new, not copied. *n.* thing from which another is copied.

ornament *n.* something which is used as a decoration. *vb.* adorn. **ornamental** *adj.*

ornithology *n.* study of birds. **ornithologist** *n.*

orphan *n.* a person whose parents are dead. *adj.* **orphanage** *n.* an institution for orphans.

orthodox *adj.* holding correct or acceptable opinion; not heretical; conventional. **orthodoxy** *n.*

osmosis *n.* the process by which liquids pass through a porous membrane (skin) until the fluids on both sides of the membrane have been equalized in some way.

osprey *n.* a large fish-eating bird of prey found in most parts of the world. It is brown with a white head and underparts.

ostrich *n.* a very large bird that lives in southern Africa. Ostriches cannot fly, but are very fast runners.

other *adj.* one of two; different; alternative.

otherwise *adv.* 1. in another way. 2. if not, or else. *You'd better hurry, otherwise we'll go without you.*

otter *n.* a flesh-eating water animal that lives in many parts of the world.

ought auxiliary or helping *vb.* expressing duty, probability, etc. *We ought to help those in need. She ought to have been home by now.*

ounce *n.* small measure of weight. *There are 16 ounces in one pound.*

our *pron. & adj.* belonging to us. *Come to our house.*

oust *vb.* drive away, get rid of.

out- *prefix* meaning more, longer, outside, beyond.

out *adv.* not in; away from somewhere or something. *I'm afraid Mr. Jones is out this afternoon.*

outback *n.* the interior of Australia; the bush.

outboard motor *n.* a motor for driving a small boat. It is hung over the stern (back) of the craft.

outbreak *n.* a start; a breaking out; an epidemic.

outdoors *adv.* outside a house or other building.

outfit *n.* all the clothes needed for a special purpose.

outgrew past of **outgrow**.

outgrow *vb.* become too large for something. *Robert will soon outgrow his gray pants.*

outing *n.* a day's holiday.

outlaw *n.* a person who has broken the law; a bandit. *vb.* declare a person an outlaw.

outlay *n.* money spent on something.

outline *n.* the outside shape of something, a drawing that shows only the shape of something; the main facts about something.

outright *adv.* on the spot; completely.

outside *n. & adv.* the opposite of inside; the outer surface of something; the outdoors.

outskirts *n.* the edges of a town.

outspoken *adj.* frank, plain, factual.

outwit *vb.* be too clever for.

oval *n. & adj.* an egg-shaped figure.

ovation *n.* warm applause.

oven *n.* the enclosed part of a stove where food is baked or roasted.

over 1. *adj.* above. 2. *adv.* finished. 3. *prefix* (**over-**) excessive, beyond, further than. Words prefixed with **over-** are usually self-explanatory, if the main word is known.

overalls *n.* a piece of clothing worn over others to keep them clean.

overboard *adv.* having fallen into the water from a ship or boat. *"Man overboard."*

overcome *vb.* conquer.

overdraft *n.* a bank loan in which a customer's account shows that there are insufficient funds to meet checks. The bank charges interest on the amount outstanding.

overflow *vb.* flood, spill out. *I left my bath running and it overflowed all over the floor.*

overhang *n. & vb.* hang out over something.

overhaul *vb.* 1. examine thoroughly and repair if necessary. 2. overtake.

overhead *n.* the running costs of a business such as administrative and advertising costs not directly related to production.

overlap *vb.* cover one thing partly with another; partly coincide.

oversee *vb.* supervise, superintend.

overtake *vb.* pass another moving thing, particularly a vehicle.

overtime *n.* time spent working after the usual hours; extra wages paid for such work.

overture *n.* 1. musical introduction. 2. opening of negotiations.

owe (rhymes with *low*) *vb.* need to pay money back to someone.

owl *n.* a bird of prey that usually hunts by night.

own *vb.* possess or have. *Father owns that field.* **owner** *n.* someone who owns something. *My father is the owner of that field.*

ox *n.* (plural **oxen**) a domestic animal of the cattle family.

oxygen *n.* one of the gases of the air.

oyster *n.* a shellfish that is highly prized as a table delicacy.

ozone *n.* a form of oxygen in which each molecule contains three atoms instead of the usual two.

pace *n.* a single step; speed or way of walking. *vb.* walk slowly and regularly. *He paced up and down the room.*

pacify *vb.* make calm, peaceful.

pack 1. *vb.* put things into a bag or other container ready for a journey. *n.* a holder for carrying things on a journey. 2. *n.* a group of animals that hunt together.

package *n.* a parcel or bundle of things packed together.

packet *n.* a small parcel.

pack ice *n.* large pieces of floating ice in the ocean.

pact *n.* a solemn agreement.

pad 1. *vb.* walk along softly. 2. *n.* a kind of small cushion used to protect something from rubbing. 3. *n.* sheets of paper joined together at one edge.

paddle *n.* a short oar for making a canoe move through water. *vb.* propel with paddle; move hands or feet about in shallow water.

paddock *n.* small enclosed field for horses.

paddy *n.* 1. wet field where rice is grown. 2. the growing rice itself.

padlock *n.* a removable lock.

pagan *n. & adj.* a person who is not a member of one of the world's major religions; a heathen; a person of no religion.

page *n.* 1. a leaf or sheet of paper, particularly in a book. 2. a boy working as messenger in a hotel, attending the bride at a wedding, etc.

pageant *n.* an open-air show or display, often celebrating an historical event.

pagoda *n.* an Asian temple, usually in the form of a tower with many stories and several roofs.

paid *vb.* past of **pay**.

pail *n.* another word for bucket.

pain *n.* an unpleasant feeling in the body; suffering.

painful *adj.* feeling or causing pain. **painstaking** *adj.* careful.

paint *n.* colored liquid, which can be used for decorating and protecting walls or other surfaces, or for making pictures. *vb.* cover with paint; create a picture with paint.

painting *n.* a painted picture.

pair *n.* two of the same kind. *Look at that pair of doves sitting on my windowsill.*

pajamas *n.* a loose jacket and pants worn in bed.

pal *n.* a close friend.

palace *n.* the home of a ruler, such as a king, queen, or bishop.

palate *n.* the roof of the mouth.

pale *adj.* not having much color. **pallor** *n.* lack of color.

palette *n.* board with a thumbhole on which an artist mixes paints.

palindrome *n.* word or sentence, etc., that can be read the same backward or forward. *Able was I ere I saw Elba.*

palisade *n.* a fence made of stakes.

palm *n.* 1. the inner surface of the hand. 2. a tree with no branches but many large leaves near the top.

pampas *n.* vast grass-covered plain of South America.

pamper *vb.* spoil.

pamphlet (*pamf-let*) *n.* a leaflet.

pan 1. *n.* a wide, flat vessel or saucepan, especially one used for frying food. 2. *prefix* meaning of or all. *Pan-American means all states of North and South America.*

pancake *n.* a flat cake made from batter cooked in a frying pan.

pancreas *n.* a gland near the stomach which helps the digestion.

panda *n.* a bear-like animal from Asia.

pane *n.* a single sheet of glass in a window.

panel *n.* 1. a division of a surface such as in a door. 2. a group of experts, entertainers, etc.

panic *n.* a sudden fear or terror which may lead people to act unthinkingly. *vb.* be affected by panic. **panicky** *adj.*

panorama *n.* a wide, all around view. **panoramic** *adj.*

pansy *n.* a garden flower of the violet family, usually purple, yellow or white in color.

pant *vb.* breathe in and out quickly.

panther *n.* a leopard.

pantomime *n.* a kind of play with music and dancing; a performance that uses only facial and bodily gestures.

pantry *n.* a room or large cupboard where food, cutlery, crockery, etc. are kept.

pants *pl. n.* trousers.

papal *adj.* of or relating to the Pope.

paper *n.* thin, flat sheets of material for writing or printing on. *vb.* stick paper on walls.

paperback *n.* book bound in a paper cover.

papier-mâché (*pa-per-mu-shay*) *n.* pulped paper used for modeling.

papoose *n.* North American Indian baby.

paprika *n.* a mild, sweet red pepper.

papyrus (*pap-i-rus*) *n.* a kind of paper made from the papyrus reed in ancient Egypt.

par *n.* equality, normal amount.

parable *n.* a story that teaches a simple lesson.

parachute *n.* an umbrellalike apparatus used for floating down from an aircraft. *vb.* descend by parachute.

parade 1. *n.* a procession. 2. *n.* soldiers gathered for inspection. *vb.* assemble; display.

paradox *n.* a statement which seems contradictory but is nonetheless true.

paraffin *n.* an oil used for burning in jet engines, heaters and lamps.

paragraph *n.* several sentences grouped together because they deal with one main idea.

P

parakeet *n.* small, long-tailed parrot.

parallel *vb. & adj.* lines that are the same distance from each other along their entire length. *The tracks of a railway are parallel.*

paralysis *n.* **paralyze** *vb.* (make) helpless.

paralyzed *adj.* unable to move or feel.

paramount *adj.* supreme.

parapet *n.* low wall along edge of roof etc.

paraplegia *n.* paralysis of the legs and lower part of the body.

parasite *n.* an animal or plant that lives in or on another living animal or plant. **parasitic** *adj.*

parasol *n.* a sunshade similar to an umbrella.

parcel *n.* a package that has been wrapped up in paper, usually for sending through the mail.

parchment *n.* the skin of a sheep or goat, specially dried and prepared, and used in former times for writing on. *Parchment was used for books and documents before the introduction of paper.*

pardon *vb.* forgive someone. *n.* forgiveness.

parent *n.* a mother or father.

parental *adj.* of parents.

parish *n.* 1. the district that surrounds and belongs to a church. 2. a local Protestant church community.

park 1. *n.* a public garden. 2. *vb.* stop one's car in a parking place. **parking lot** *n.* a place where people can leave their cars.

parliament *n.* the group of people who are elected to make the laws of a country.

parody *n.* piece of music or literature in which an artist's style is imitated in order to amuse or ridicule; satirical imitation.

parole *n & vb.* a release of a prisoner before his or her prison sentence is finished.

parrot *n.* a brightly colored tropical bird with a hooked beak.

parsley *n.* an herb grown in temperate lands. Its fine, curly leaves are used either fresh to decorate foods, or fresh or dried as a flavoring.

parsnip *n.* a sweet root vegetable.

part 1. *n.* a piece of something; not the whole thing; a role in a play. 2. *vb.* divide into parts; leave one another's company.

participate *vb.* take part in; share.

participle *n.* an adjective formed from a verb, e.g. a going concern.

particle *n.* a very small part of something.

particular *adj.* one rather than another. *This particular book is very interesting.* **particularly** *adv. I particularly like this book.*

partition 1. *n.* a temporary wall or screen. 2. *vb.* separate into parts. *India was partitioned into two countries – India and Pakistan.*

partly *adj.* to some extent; not all. *The pedestrian was partly to blame for the accident.*

partner *n. & vb.* a person who does something with someone else. *Alice is my tennis partner.* **partnership** *n.*

partridge *n.* common game bird, related to the pheasant, found in Europe, Africa and Asia. Most species live on the ground.

party *n.* a group of people who come together to enjoy themselves; an organized group that tries to get certain people elected.

pass 1. *vb.* go by. *You have to pass the school to reach the park.* 2. *vb.* give something to someone who cannot reach it. *Please will you pass me the butter.* 3. *vb.* satisfy examiners. *I passed all my exams.* 4. *n.* a piece of paper that allows you to go somewhere or do something. *My grandma has a pass that allows her to go free on the buses.* 5. *n.* a narrow passage through mountains.

passage *n.* a narrow way between buildings or through a building.

passenger *n.* a person being taken in a motor vehicle, ship or aircraft.

passerine *n. & adj.* (in zoology) a very large order of perching birds.

passion *n.* strong emotion; enthusiasm.

Passover *n.* an important Jewish religious festival, lasting eight days and held in springtime. It commemorates the escape from Egypt under Moses. There is a ritual meal in the home on the first evening.

passport *n.* a document that travelers show when going from one country to another.

password *n.* a secret word that helps one to be recognized by a sentry.

past 1. *n.* the time before the present time. *The Sumerians lived in the distant past.* 2. *adv.* up to and farther than something. *You go past the school to get to the hospital.*

pasta *n.* Italian dish made from cooked flour paste in various shapes, e.g. macaroni, spaghetti, etc.

paste *n.* any thick, semi-liquid substance, such as toothpaste; a kind of glue used for sticking paper. *vb.* stick things together with paste.

pastel *n.* a crayon. *adj.* soft, pale (color).

pastern *n.* the part of a horse's foot between fetlock and hoof – the "ankle."

pasteurize *vb.* kill germs by heating, especially milk. The way to do this was discovered by Louis Pasteur.

pastime *n.* a game, a hobby; anything done to pass the time in a pleasant way.

pastor *n.* a clergyman.

pastry *n.* baked goods made of a mixture of flour, fat, and water.

pasture *n.* a field or piece of land for grazing livestock.

pat *vb.* & *n.* tap with the flat of the hand. *She patted the dog, which wagged its tail.*

patch 1. *n.* a small piece of ground or color. *There was a small patch of grass in the playground.* 2. *n.* a small piece of material sewn on to clothing to cover a hole. 3. *vb.* mend with a patch.

patchwork *n.* bits of material sewn together in a pattern.

patella *n.* the kneecap.

patent 1. *n.* document giving an inventor the exclusive right to make and profit from his invention for a certain number of years. 2. *adj.* obvious; unconcealed.

paternal *adj.* of or relating to a father, fatherly.

path *n.* a narrow track or footway.

pathetic *adj.* moving one to pity or contempt.

patience (**pay**-*shunce*) *n.* be able to wait calmly without complaining.

patient (**pay**-*shent*) 1. *n.* someone who is looked after by a doctor. 2. *adj.* able to wait a long time without getting cross.

patio *n.* courtyard near a house.

patriarch *n.* father or founder of a tribe. *Abraham was a patriarch of Old Testament times.*

patriot *n.* a person who loves his country and all it stands for.

patriotism. *n.*

patrol 1. *vb.* & *n.* go around a place to see that everything is correct. *His job is to patrol the factory at night.* 2. *n.* a small group of soldiers, aircraft or ships carrying out a special task in wartime. 3. *n.* a small group in the Scout movement.

pattern *n.* 1. a design that is repeated on something to decorate it. *I have a dress with a pattern of flowers on it.* 2. anything that is copied to make something else. *Mother used my dress as a pattern to make a dress for my sister.* 3. a repeating feature in mathematics.

pause (*paws*) *n.* stopping for a short time. *vb.* stop temporarily; hesitate.

pave *vb.* cover the ground with flat stones or concrete.

pavement *n.* an artificially covered path at the side of a road.

paw *n.* the foot of some kinds of animal, such as dogs and cats.

pawn 1. *n.* a chessman of least value. 2. *vb.* hand over something of value as security for money borrowed.

pay 1. *n.* money for doing a job, particularly when given weekly or monthly. 2. *vb.* hand over money in exchange for something.

pea *n.* climbing plant cultivated for its seeds which are eaten as a vegetable. The round seeds – peas – are contained in a long pod and picked when they are unripe and green.

peace *n.* freedom from war or violence; calm.

peach *n.* a sweet, roundish, juicy kind of fruit with a hard stone and yellow-red, fuzzy skin.

peacock *n.* a large ornamental kind of pheasant, the male peafowl.

peak *n.* the top of a mountain; highest point, (on a graph etc.).

peal *n.* a loud ringing of bells.

peanut *n.* a groundnut; a nut that grows in a pod under the ground.

pear *n.* a sweet, juicy fruit that is narrow at one end.

pearl *n.* a silver-white gem found in some oysters (a kind of shellfish).

peasant *n.* (obsolete) a person who works on the land.

peat *n.* a kind of turf which can be used as a fuel instead of coal.

pebble *n.* a small, rounded stone.

peccary *n.* a wild pig of Central and South America.

peck *vb.* strike or pierce repeatedly with the bill or beak.

peculiar *adj.* very strange or unusual. *The man was wearing a peculiar hat with green feathers all over it.*

pedal *n.* a part that is pressed by the foot to make something work. *The pedals of a bicycle turn the wheel. vb.* press pedals.

pedestal *n.* base of a column.

pedestrian *n.* a person walking. *adj.* of walking; dull, uninspired, commonplace.

pedigree *n. & adj.* a record of the members of a family who have lived up to now. *Our dog has a pedigree that shows even her great-grandparents.*

peel *vb.* remove the skin of a fruit or vegetable. *n.* a piece of fruit or vegetable skin. *Don't throw orange peel onto the pavement.*

peep *vb.* look at something quickly, or through a small hole or space. *n.* a glance.

peer 1. *vb.* look at closely, as if unable to see properly. 2. *n.* an equal. 3. *n.* a lord (fem. **peeress**).

peg 1. *n.* a small piece of wood or other material, used for hanging things on. *Hang your coat on that peg.* 2. *n. & vb.* (place in) a definite category.

Pekinese *vb.* small breed of dog with a snub-nose and long, silky hair.

pelican *n.* a large, brown or white water bird.

pelt 1. *vb.* hurl or strike repeatedly. 2. *n.* an animal's skin or fur.

pen *n.* 1. a small fenced place for animals. 2. a tool for writing that uses ink. 3. a female swan.

penalize *vb.* give a penalty to, or put at a disadvantage.

penalty *n.* fine or punishment.

pencil *n.* a writing instrument consisting of graphite ("lead") encased in wood. *You can usually rub out marks made with a pencil.*

pendant *n.* an ornament that hangs down on a chain.

pendulum *n.* a weighted rod that is hung so that it can swing back and forth, as on some clocks.

penetrate *vb.* pierce, pass into.

penetrating *adj.* discerning.

penguin *n.* a flightless, fish-eating sea bird, found in the Southern Hemisphere, especially the Antarctic.

penicillin *n.* a substance used in medicine to kill bacteria.

A king penguin – a flightless bird found in the colder parts of the Southern Hemisphere. It uses its wings as flippers to swim.

peninsula *n.* a piece of land almost surrounded by sea. *Italy is a peninsula.* **peninsular** *adj.*

penis *n.* male organ of reproduction in humans and mammals.

penknife (**pen**-*nife*) *n.* a small knife that shuts into itself.

pen pal *n.* someone who writes to you and to whom you write although you have not met.

pension (**pen**-*shun*) *n.* money paid regularly to someone who has retired from work. *vb.* give a pension.

penta- *prefix* meaning five, e.g. **pentagon** *n.* a five-sided figure.

Pentecost *n.* Jewish harvest festival. Christian Whitsun.

penultimate *adj.* next to last.

people (**pee**-*pl*) *n.* men, women and children; human beings; race. *All the people on our street came to the party.* *vb.* populate.

pepper *n.* a hot-tasting powder made from dried berries of various tropical plants. *Pepper is used to flavor food.*

peppermint *n.* kind of mint grown for its oils.

per *prep.* by, through, by means of, for each, e.g. **percent** for each hundred, a fraction written as part of 100. *50 percent is 50 parts in 100, or ½; 10 percent is 10 parts in 100, or 1/10. Percent is usually written %*

perceive (*pur*-**seeve**) *vb.* become aware of. **perception** *n.* understanding; acute awareness.

perch 1. *n.* a resting place for a bird. *vb.* rest on a perch. 2. *n.* a common freshwater fish.

percussion instrument *n.* a musical instrument that is struck or shaken. *Drums, tambourines and triangles are percussion instruments.*

perennial *n.* & *adj.* lasting for a long time; for more than a year. *Roses and lilies-of-the-valley are perennial flowers.*

perfect *adj.* so good that it cannot be made better. *vb.* make perfect.

perforate *vb.* make holes in.

perform *vb.* do something in front of other people. *We performed our play in front of the whole school.* do something; carry out. *I am sure that he will perform the task perfectly.* **performer** *n.*

performance *n.* something that is done so that other people can see or hear it.

perfume (**purr**-*fyoom*) 1. *n.* a scent, a sweet-smelling liquid. (*purr*-**fyoom**) 2. *vb.* spread a sweet scent around.

perhaps *adv.* maybe; possibly. *Perhaps they have forgotten to come.*

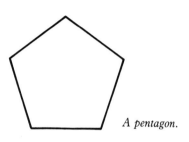

A pentagon.

peril *n.* danger, risk of danger.

perimeter (*per*-**rim**-*e*-*ter*) *n.* the distance around the outside of an area.

period *n.* 1. a length of time. 2. occurrence of menstruation. **periodic** *adj.*

periodical *n.* publication which appears at regular intervals.

periscope *n.* an instrument like a tube with mirrors in it that lets someone see over something. *We used a periscope to see over the heads of the crowd.*

perish *vb.* become destroyed, come to an end, die. **perishable** *adj.* not long-lasting. *Salads are highly perishable.*

permafrost *n.* a term used for layers of soil or rock that are permanently frozen.

permanent *adj.* unchanging; not expected to change. *This is now our permanent address.* **permanence** *n.*

P

permission *n.* being allowed to do something. *The teacher gave us permission to go home early.*

permit (**purr**-*mit*) *n.* writing license stating that something is allowed. (*pur*-**mit**) *vb.* allow.

perpendicular *adj.* upright, at right angles to the horizon.

perpetual *adj.* lasting forever.

persist *vb.* go on resolutely, stubbornly; take a firm stand.

person *n.* any man, woman or child. *Did a person in a brown hat come in here?*

personality *n.* special characteristics that distinguish a person; a character; a well-known personality.

perspective *n.* a method of representing in two dimensions the optical effect of distance in three dimensions.

persuade (*per*-**swade**) *vb.* make or try to make someone change his or her mind; influence, convince. **persuasion** *n.*

pessimism *n.* a belief that everything will turn out badly; the opposite of optimism. **pessimist** *n.*

pest *n.* plant or animal that is harmful or causes trouble. *Rats are pests on a farm because they eat grain.*

pester *vb.* annoy continually; keep asking questions.

pestle *n.* implement for pounding substances (in a mortar).

pet *n.* a tame animal kept for fun. *vb.* treat as a pet; fondle.

petal *n.* one of the leaflike parts of the flower of a plant.

peter out *vb.* come gradually to an end.

petrify *vb.* (literally) turn into stone; terrify.

petticoat *n.* a kind of underskirt worn by girls and women, usually a little shorter than the outer clothes.

petty *adj.* small, unimportant, trivial. **petty cash** *n.* cash kept for small items.

pew (rhymes with *few*) *n.* a bench in a church.

pewter (**pyou**-*ter*) a dull gray metal which is an alloy (mixture) of lead and tin.

pharaoh (**fair**-*oh*) *n.* a king of ancient Egypt.

phase *n.* a stage in the development of something; one of the various stages of the moon's monthly journey around the earth. *vb.* carry out by phases.

pheasant *n.* a long-tailed game bird common in many parts of the world.

phenomenon (*fe*-**nom**-*enon*) *n.* a remarkable person, happening or thing. **phenomenal** *adj.* amazing.

phi (*fie*) *n.* the 21st letter of the Greek alphabet (φ) which is shown in English spelling as *ph.* All words beginning with *ph* in English come from Greek words and are pronounced with the sound of **f**, e.g. **phone** (*fone*).

philharmonic *n.* symphony orchestra.

philosophy *n.* the search for understanding; the study of ideas. **philosopher** *n.*

phobia *n.* strong fear, dislike of.

phoenix *n.* a mythical Arabian bird which was supposed to burn itself to death every 500 years and then be miraculously reborn from its own ashes.

phone *n.* & *vb.* short for **telephone**.

phonetics *pl. n.* the branch of the study of languages that deals with pronunciation and which uses special **phonetic alphabets** to cover all the different sounds that languages use. **phonetic** *adj.*

phoney (**fo**-*ney*) *adj.* sham, not genuine.

phosphorus *n.* a nonmetallic element that occurs in various physical forms (symbol – *P.*)

photography *n.* the process or art of taking pictures with a camera.

photostat *vb.* & *n.* a copy of writing or pictures made by a special machine.

photosynthesis *n.* a process by which green plants turn carbon dioxide and water into carbohydrates.

phrase *n.* a group of words linked together to form part of a sentence. *"Part of a sentence" is a phrase in the last sentence.*

physical *adj.* 1. having to do with the body. 2. (of a map), showing features like high and low ground and rivers.

physics *n.* the study of light, heat, sound and energy.

piano *n.* a musical stringed instrument with a keyboard. **pianist** *n.* a person who plays the piano.

piccolo *n.* a small musical wind instrument which produces very high notes.

pick 1. *vb.* select or choose something. 2. *vb.* dig at something (with your fingers). 3. *n.* a sharp tool for digging.

picket *n. & vb.* 1. a person posted by a union during a strike, who may try to prevent from working those who want to work. 2. a pointed stake driven into the ground.

pickle *vb.* preserve vegetables or other food in vinegar, brine, etc. **pickle** *n.*

pick up *vb.* 1. lift something up with your hand. *Pick up your pencils when I say now.* 2. give someone a ride in your car. *I picked up old Mr. Brown and took him to the library.*

picnic *n. & vb.* a meal eaten out of doors in the countryside. *This field will be just right for our picnic.* (past **picknicked**).

picture *n.* a drawing, painting, photograph or other illustration. *vb.* describe; imagine.

pie *n.* food in a pastry crust.

piebald *adj. & n.* (color of) horse with patches of black and white.

piece *n.* a part of something; a fragment; a musical or literary composition. *vb.* put together, mend.

pier (*peer*) *n.* a structure built out over water. *A pier is a place for ships to stop at.*

pierce *vb.* bore through, make a hole in, perforate.

pig *n.* swine; a farm animal whose meat provides pork and bacon.

pigeon (*pid-jun*) *n.* a medium-sized bird found all over the world. *Many pigeons live in towns and cities.*

piglet *n.* a young pig.

pigment *n.* substance that gives color, e.g. to paints, plastics, etc.

pigmy see **pygmy**.

pigsty *n.* a building for pigs.

pigtail *n.* a tight braid or plait of hair.

pike *n.* 1. a kind of spear used in former times. 2. a fierce freshwater fish.

pilchard *n.* small fish of the herring family.

pile 1. *n.* a heap of things on top of each other. *vb.* throw in a pile. 2. *n.* (atomic pile) nuclear reactor.

pilgrim *n.* a person who travels to visit a holy place. **pilgrimage** *n.* a pilgrim's journey.

pill *n.* a small ball of medicine.

pillar *n.* a post, often made of stone, for supporting a building.

pillbox *n.* a box to keep pills in.

pillion *n.* a saddle for a passenger on a motorcycle or bicycle.

pillow *n.* a kind of cushion on a bed for supporting the head.

pillowcase *n.* removable washable cover for a pillow.

pilot *n.* a person qualified to fly an aircraft; a person who is trained to take a ship through difficult waters. *vb.* guide, act as pilot of. *adj.* experimental.

pimple *n.* small inflamed swelling on the skin.

pin *n.* a small, thin piece of metal like a tiny nail, sharp at one end, and used for fastening things together. *vb.* fasten with pins.

pinafore *n.* a kind of apron worn over a dress. *She wears a pinafore to keep her dress clean.*

pincer *n.* 1. claw of a crab, lobster, etc. 2. **pincers**. *pl.* a tool for gripping things, especially for pulling out nails.

pinch *vb.* 1. grip between a finger and a thumb; hurt by squeezing. 2. (*slang*) steal.

155

pine *n.* an evergreen coniferous (cone-bearing) tree with needlelike leaves. **pine cone** *n.* fruit of the pine.

pineapple *n.* a large, sweet, juicy tropical fruit with a prickly covering.

pinion *n.* bird's wing, especially the outer joint.

pink 1. *n. & adj.* a pale red color. 2. *n.* a kind of garden flower.

pint *n.* a measure for liquids, etc. *There are eight pints in one gallon.*

pioneer *n.* a person who goes to a new place or country to settle; someone who is the first to do something.

pious *adj.* holy, devout.

pip *n.* the seed of a fruit.

pipe *n.* 1. a tube along which water etc. can flow. 2. a device, usually wooden, for smoking tobacco.

pipedream *n.* a fantastic plan or hope.

pipeline *n.* pipe with pumps for conveying gases, liquids, etc.

piper *n.* person who plays pipes.

piranha *n.* savage freshwater fish from tropical South America.

pirate *n.* a sea robber.

pirouette *n. & vb.* (in ballet) a spin on one leg.

pistil *n.* the seed-producing part of a flower.

pistol *n.* a small gun that is held in one hand.

pit *n.* 1. a deep hole with steep sides. 2. a mine.

pitch 1. *n.* a distillation of tars, resin. 2. *vb.* throw something. 3. *n.* a sticky black material like tar. 4. *vb.* put up a tent. *They will pitch the tent out of the wind.* 5. *n.* the sound of a musical note, i.e. whether it is higher or lower than another.

pitcher *n.* 1. container for holding and pouring liquids. 2. a person who throws (**pitches**) the ball to the batter in baseball.

pitchfork *n.* a long-handled fork used for lifting hay.

pitfall *n.* a covered pit acting as an animal trap; an unknown danger.

pity *vb. & n.* a feeling of sadness for

Mercury   Venus   Earth   Ma

Our sun's family of planets.

someone's troubles.

placard *n.* a notice or poster in a public place.

place *n.* a particular area or location. *vb.* put something in position.

placid *adj.* calm; not easily upset.

plagiarize *vb.* use someone else's ideas or writings and pass them off as one's own.

plague (*playg*) *n.* a dangerous illness which is very quick to spread. *vb.* pester, bother.

plain 1. *adj.* simple; ordinary; with no pattern on it. *Her dress was plain blue with a lace collar.* 2. *n.* a large flat area of country, usually treeless.

plaintiff *n.* person who brings a suit or action in a court of law.

plait (rhymes with *ate*) *n. & vb.* weave three or more strips together.

plan 1. *n.* a drawing that shows where things are. 2. *vb.* decide what you are going to do. *Shall we plan a hike this weekend?*

plane 1. *n.* short for airplane. 2. *n. & vb.* a tool for making wood smooth. 3. *n.* a tall tree with large leaves and bark that peels.

piter   Saturn   Uranus   Neptune   Pluto

planet *n*. one of the bodies that move around a star.

planetarium *n*. a big room or building, with a domed ceiling, for reproducing the movement of planets and other heavenly bodies.

plank *n*. a long flat piece of wood.

plankton *n*. tiny plants and animals that drift in the sea.

plant 1. *n*. any living thing (particularly a flower) that is not an animal. *vb*. put a plant in the ground. *We have just planted several trees.* 2. *n*. a factory or any other industrial building or machinery.

plaster *n*. a coating put on walls and ceilings, to give a surface for decoration. It is made from certain cement powders, mixed with water and sand. *vb*. smear with plaster.

plastic 1. *n*. a light, strong material that is manufactured. 2. *adj*. pliable, malleable; made of plastic.

plate *n*. a flat, round piece of crockery from which food is eaten.

plateau (*plat-***oh**) *n*. (plural **plateaus**, **plateaux**) level land higher than the land around it.

platform *n*. a small raised stage; the raised place beside the railway lines where people wait at a station.

platinum *n*. silvery, valuable metal.

platitude *n*. a dull, stale, commonplace remark, e.g. *Long time no see.*

platypus *n*. an odd-looking, dark-brown furry aquatic mammal with a bill (beak).

play 1. *vb*. have fun and not work; perform on a musical instrument; take part in or play a game. 2. *n*. a story that is told by people acting and talking to each other, usually on a stage; a dramatic piece.

playground *n*. an area for children to play in.

playtime *n*. a period when children can stop working and amuse themselves; break time.

playwright *n*. a person who writes plays; a dramatist.

plead *vb*. present a case in a law court; urge.

pleasant *adj*. nice; good or agreeable.

please 1. *vb*. make someone happy. 2. *adv*. a word to show politeness or emphasis in a request. *Please shut the door.*

pleasure *n*. feeling of being happy.

pleat *n*. a fold in cloth or paper. *vb*. make a pleat.

plebiscite (**pleb**-*iss-ite*) *n*. direct voting by all electors on a particular question or issue.

plectrum *n*. an implement made of horn, plastic, or metal for plucking the strings of a guitar, zither, etc.

pledge *n*. security; something pawned; word of honor. *vb*. promise, give one's word.

P

plenty n. much; a lot. *We have plenty of time.* **plentiful** adj. in large numbers or quantities.

pleurisy n. painful inflammation of the delicate surface lining (pleura) of the lung.

plod vb. trudge; walk or work with effort.

plot 1. n. a secret agreement to do something, usually bad. *The police discovered a plot to rob the bank.* vb. scheme. 2. n. a small piece of ground. 3. n. the main things that happen in a story.

plow (rhymes with *how*) n. & vb. a machine used to cut and turn over land to prepare it for planting.

pluck 1. vb. pull feathers off a bird; gather; pick at strings on a guitar, violin, etc. 2. n. courage. **plucky** adj.

plug 1. n. a piece of wood, rubber or other material used to fill a hole. 2. n. a device for joining electrical equipment to the electricity supply. 3. vb. stop up with a plug.

plum n. a sweet round fruit with juicy flesh and a hard central stone.

plumage n. the entire clothing of feathers of a bird.

plumber (**plum**-*mer*) n. a person who fits and repairs water pipes in a building.

plump adj. rounded. vb. make plump. *She plumped up the cushions.*

plunder vb. rob violently, especially in war. n. things stolen by force; loot.

plunge vb. jump or fall into. *The man plunged into the canal after the drowning child.*

plural adj. a word which shows that there are more than one. *Cats, kittens and children are all plural nouns.*

plus prep. & adj. and, added to. *Four plus six equals ten.*

p.m. abbr. after midday, from the Latin words *post meridiem.*

pneumatic (*new*-**matt**-*ik*) adj. worked by air under pressure; filled with air.

pneumonia (*new-moan-ya*) n. a serious illness of the lungs.

poach vb. 1. cook by simmering in water, e.g. poached eggs. 2. take game or fish illegally. **poacher** n.

pocket n. a bag sewn into a garment for carrying things; receptacle for balls in billiards, etc.; a cavity or deposit (of gold, etc.). vb. put into one's pocket; take illegally.

pod n. a long seed holder on some plants. *Peas grow in a pod.*

poem (**po**-*em*) n. a piece of writing with a special rhythm. *Poems are often written in short lines with the last word in one line rhyming with the last word of another line.*

poet (**po**-*et*) n. a person who writes poems.

poetry (**po**-*etry*) n. poems; verse.

point 1. n. the sharp end of something, such as a needle or pencil. 2. vb. stick out a finger in the direction of something. 3. n. the main idea. *Do you see the point of what has just been said?*

poison n. & vb. a substance that makes people become ill or die. **poisonous** adj.

poke vb. push with a stick, finger, etc. **poker** n. instrument for stirring a fire.

poker n. a card game in which the player bets that the value of his hand is higher than those of the other players.

polar adj. of or near the North or South Poles. *Polar bears live near the North Pole.*

pole n. 1. either the most northerly point of the earth (the North Pole) or the most southerly point (the South Pole). 2. one of the ends of a magnet. 3. a long, thin piece of wood or metal; a post.

police n. the people who help to keep the law and catch criminals. vb. control, provide with police.

policy n. a considered method of action carried out by a government, etc.

polish vb. make something smooth and glossy. n. smoothness; substance used to polish a surface.

polite adj. well-mannered.

politics *pl. n.* the science or art of government. **politician** *n.* a person taking part in politics.

poll (rhymes with *coal*) *n.* voting, number of votes. *Opinion poll.*

pollen *n.* a fine powder on flowers which fertilizes other flowers. **pollinate** *vb.* fertilize with pollen.

pollution *n.* the spoiling of air, soil, water or the environment by poisonous wastes. **pollute** *vb.*

polo *n.* a game similar to hockey and played on horseback.

poltergeist *n.* a noisy ghost. *The poltergeist made strange noises in the attic at night.*

poly- *prefix* meaning many, e.g. **polyandry** having more than one husband. **polysyllable** a word with more than one syllable.

polytechnic (*poll-i-***tek***-nik*) *n.* a school giving instruction in many technical subjects.

pomegranate *n.* a fruit with a red rind whose flesh is full of seeds.

The Earth acts like a giant compass, with its poles near the north and south poles. The needle of a compass is magnetized, so it swings until one end points to the north magnetic pole.

A porcupine.

pomp *n.* splendor and ceremony.

pond *n.* a small area of water; a tiny lake which may be natural or artificial.

pony *n.* (plural **ponies**) a small horse.

poodle *n.* small lively dog with a black or white curly coat; the coat is often clipped. Poodles were originally Russian gundogs.

pool *n.* 1. a small, deep area of water; a pond. 2. a game like billiards.

poor 1. *adj. & n.* having little or no money. 2. *adj.* deserving pity. *The poor old lady has been ill for many years.* 3. *adj.* not good. *Tom's exam results were very poor.*

pop 1. *n.* a small bang. 2. *abbr.* short for popular, as in pop music and pop art.

pope *n.* the head of the Roman Catholic Church.

poplar *n.* slender, quick-growing tree of the willow family.

pop music *n.* short for popular music.

popular *adj.* liked by a lot of people. *I think Andrew is the most popular boy in our class.* **popularity** *n.* being generally liked. **popularize** *vb.* make popular.

population *n.* all the people living in a place, city, country or the world. **populate** *vb.* fill with people.

porcelain *n.* fine china.

porch *n.* a covered entrance to a building.

porcupine *n.* a large rodent covered with pointed spines.

pore *n.* a tiny opening in the skin. **porous** *adj.* having pores and so allowing liquid through.

pork *n.* the flesh of a pig.

porpoise *n.* a small sea animal of the whale family.

P

porridge *n.* soft food made of grains boiled in milk or water.

port 1. *n.* a harbor; a town by the sea with a harbor. 2. *n. & adj.* the left side of the ship or aircraft as you are facing forward. 3. *n.* airport: buildings, runways, etc., for airplanes and passengers. 4. *n.* the name of a Portuguese wine.

portable *adj.* capable of being carried, especially by hand. *A portable typewriter.*

portcullis *n.* a grating lowered to protect a gateway in a castle.

porter *n.* a person who is employed to carry things; doorkeeper, especially of large buildings.

porthole *n.* a round window in a ship.

portray *vb.* make a picture of. **portrait** *n.* a picture of a person.

Portuguese man-of-war *n.* a kind of jellyfish.

pose *vb.* 1. arrange or place. 2. behave in an affected way; show off. 3. put (a question or problem).

position *n.* the place taken by somebody or something. *When you are all in position, the race will begin.* *vb.* place in position.

positive 1. *adj.* not negative; clear, confident, undoubted. 2. *n.* photographic print.

possess *vb.* have or own. *Do you possess any money?* **possession** *n.* thing owned. **possessive** *adj.* unwilling to share.

possible *adj. & n.* that which can happen, exist or be achieved.

possum *n.* (phalanger) the name given to a group of Australian marsupials.

post- *prefix* meaning behind or after, e.g. **postmortem** examination after death.

post 1. *n.* the mail. *vb.* send a letter. 2. *n.* a thick upright pole, such as a goalpost. 3. *n.* a job or position.

postcard *n.* a card, often with a picture on one side, which you can write a message on and send through the post. *A postcard does not need an envelope.*

poster *n.* a picture, usually with writing, which goes on a wall to advertise something.

post office *n.* a building or room in which postal business is carried out.

postpone *vb.* put off until a later time, defer. **postponement** *n.*

pot *n.* round vessel for holding liquids, etc. *vb.* plant in a flowerpot.

potassium *n.* an extremely reactive metallic element (symbol – K).

potato *n.* (plural **potatoes**) the edible tuber of the potato plant, widely eaten as a vegetable.

potter *n.* a person who makes pottery.

pottery *n.* pots and other things made of baked clay; a place where pottery is made.

An ancient Greek pot.

pouch *n.* small bag; the receptacle in which marsupials – kangaroos, etc. – carry their young.

poultry *n.* hens, ducks, geese, turkeys and any other domestic fowl.

pounce *vb.* make a sudden attack. *The cat pounced on the mouse.*

pound 1. *n.* a measure of weight. *There are 16 ounces in one pound.* 2. *n.* a British unit of money. *There are 100 pence in a pound.* 3. *vb.* hit heavily and often.

pour *vb.* cause liquid to flow in a continuous stream, e.g. from a bottle.

poverty *n.* the lack of money.

powder *n.* fine dry particles; cosmetics or medicine in this form. *vb.* sprinkle with powder.

power *n.* the strength or ability to do something; a country with great influence.

powerful *adj.* very strong or important or influential.

power station *n.* a building for generating and distributing electricity.

practicable *adj.* capable of being done or used.

practical *adj.* able to do useful things.

practice *n.* something you do often to get better at it. *My piano practice lasts for an hour every day.* action not theory; professional business of doctor, lawyer, etc.

practice *vb.* do something often so that you can do it well. *I practice the piano every day.*

prairie *n.* a wide plain with very few trees, especially in North America.

praise *n.* & *vb.* say good things about someone or something.

prank *n.* practical or mischievous joke.

prawn *n.* a small sea animal with a thin shell and five pairs of legs. *Prawns look like large shrimps and can be eaten as food.*

pray *vb.* talk to God.

prayer *n.* what is said when talking to God.

pre- *prefix* meaning beforehand, e.g. **prehistoric** before history was written.

preach *vb.* give a sermon; give advice. **preacher** *n.*

prearrange *vb.* arrange ahead of time.

precaution *n.* care or action taken beforehand to prevent harm or bring about good results.

precious (**press**-*shuss*) *adj.* very valuable, costly.

precipice *n.* the steep side of a mountain or high cliff.

précis (**pray**-*see*) *n.* summary of essential facts.

precise *adj.* exact, very accurate. *Give me the precise details of what happened.*

predator *n.* an animal that hunts other animals. *A tiger is a predator in the jungle.*

predict *vb.* say what is likely to happen in the future; forecast.

preen *vb.* (of birds) cleaning feathers with the beak; groom oneself.

preface *n.* an introduction to a book.

prefer *vb.* like one thing rather than another. *I prefer skiing to jogging.*

pregnant *adj.* to be going to have a baby.

prehistoric *adj.* things that happened before written history.

prejudice *n.* biased or one-sided opinion-

preliminary *adj.* introductory; before the main business.

première (*prem-yair*) *n.* first showing of a film or performance of a play.

premium *n.* the regular payment for an insurance policy; a bonus.

prepare *vb.* get ready. **preparation** *n.*

Presbyterian *n.* a member of the Presbyterian church.

prescription *n.* a doctor's order for medicine. **prescribe** *vb.* advise use of.

presence *n.* being in a place; the bearing or appearance of a person.

present (*prez-ent*) 1. *n.* something that is given to somebody, a gift. 2. *n.* this time; now. *At present there are 20 children in my class.* 3. *adv.* being in the place spoken about. *Who was present at the meeting last night?*

present (*pree-zent*) *vb.* 1. give someone something in public. *The mayor presented prizes at our school assembly.* 2. show or perform. *Our class presented a play for our parents.* **presentable** *adj.* fit to be shown.

presently *adv.* soon; now.

preserve *vb.* keep safe from harm; make something last a long time. *The ancient Egyptians preserved their dead pharaohs as mummies.*

president *n.* the (usually) elected head of a country or organization.

P

press 1. *vb.* push on something. *The boys pressed their noses against the window of the cake shop.* 2. *vb.* press something flat by pushing hard on it. *Father presses his trousers.* 3. *n.* a printing machine. 4. *n.* newspapers.

pressure (rhymes with *thresher*) *n.* how much one thing is pressing on another or against the walls of a container; urgency.

prestige *n.* having a good reputation; having influence.

presume *vb.* take for granted; suppose to be true. **presumption** *n.* 1. having reason to think something probable. 2. impudence.

pretend *vb.* give the impression that something is the case when it is not. *Let's pretend we're asleep.*

pretext *n.* false excuse.

pretty *adj.* attractive; nice-looking. *Victoria wore a pretty dress to the party.* *adv.* fairly, moderately.

prevail *vb.* triumph over; get one's own way.

prevalent *adj.* common, widespread.

prevent *vb.* stop something from happening. *The rain prevented us from going out.* **prevention** *n.*

preview *n.* an advance showing or performance of a film, play, etc., before it is seen by the public.

previous *adj.* former, coming before. **previously** *adv.*

prey (rhymes with *ray*) *n.* an animal that is hunted by another animal as food. *Rabbits and mice are the prey of owls.*

price *n.* the sum of money that is paid for something. *vb.* fix a price; find out the price of. *I priced the ring.*

priceless *adj.* 1. too valuable to have a price. 2. funny.

prick *vb.* make a mark with a small sharp point.

prickle *n.* a sharp point in the stem of a plant, a fine thorn.

pride *n.* the feeling of being proud; sense of one's own worth. *vb.* be proud of; flatter oneself.

priest (rhymes with *least*) *n.* a person who is trained to perform religious rites.

prim *adj.* neat; prudish, stiff.

primary *adj.* first in time or importance. *The primary colors are blue, red and yellow.*

prima donna *n.* principal female singer in an opera; a vain person.

primate *n.* 1. (biology) member of the highest order of mammals that includes lemurs, monkeys, apes and humans. 2. (ecclesiastical) an archbishop.

prime minister *n.* a head of government (especially in the British Commonwealth).

primitive *adj.* undeveloped, simple, rough; old-fashioned.

primrose *n.* a spring flower with usually yellow petals.

prince *n.* the son of a king or queen.

princess *n.* the daughter of a king or queen.

principal *adj.* the most important. *n.* head of a school.

principle *n.* an important rule; law of nature. *Always telling the truth is a good principle to follow.*

print 1. *n.* letters that you do not join together. 2. *vb.* use a machine to put letters or pictures onto paper. *This book has been printed on a hand press.*

printer *n.* a person or company that prints books, magazines, newspapers, etc.

printing *n.* a way of reproducing words and pictures by pressing an inked pattern on paper, fabric or metal.

printout *n.* printed sheets produced by a computer.

prior 1. *adj.* earlier. *A prior engagement.* 2. *adv.* before. *Prior to your arrival.* 3. *n.* head of a religious house called a **priory** (*n.*).

prism *n.* a solid block of transparent material used in various instruments to disperse (split up) or reflect light or other rays.

prison *n.* a secure building in which people who break the law may be kept.

prisoner *n.* a person who is kept in prison.

P

private *adj.* not open to the public; belonging to only one person or to a few people.

privilege *n.* a right given as a special advantage or favor.

prize *n.* something that is given to someone as a reward. *I won a prize in the competition. vb.* value highly.

probably *adv.* likely to happen, but not certain. *We will probably go to the country next week.*

probation *n.* 1. period of testing a person's suitability. 2. suspending a prisoner's sentence and allowing him or her freedom under supervision.

probe *vb.* explore or examine closely.

problem *n.* a question for which an answer is needed; a difficulty that needs to be solved. *We are having a problem with our roof.*

procedure *n.* method of doing things.

process *n.* a way of making something. *The process of making paper is a complicated one.*

procession *n.* a number of people and vehicles moving along together; a parade. **proceed** *vb.* go forward; continue; resume.

proclaim *vb.* announce publicly; declare. **proclamation** *n.*

procrastinate *vb.* delay, put off.

prodigal *adj.* wasteful, extravagant *n.* person who spends recklessly. *Jesus told the parable of the prodigal son.*

produce (**prod**-*yous*) *n.* things that are made or grown. (*pro*-**dyous**) *vb.* 1. make. 2. bring something out to show it. *The magician produced a rabbit from his hat.*

producer *n.* 1. someone who makes or grows something. 2. person who directs production of a play, etc.

product *n.* something that is produced. *The product of that factory is ice cream.*

profess *vb.* declare, admit openly (beliefs, etc.); have as a **profession** or occupation. **professional** *n.* & *adj.*

profit *n.* the difference between the cost of making something and the price it is sold at.

profound *adj.* deep; having great depth of knowledge; difficult to understand.

program *n.* 1. a set of instructions to a computer. 2. a list of events or things that are going to happen.

progress (**proh**-*gress*) *n.* advance, improvement. *vb.* (*proh*-**gress**) improve; move on.

progressive *adj.* moving forward, advancing. *n.* a person who favors social advances and reforms.

prohibit *vb.* forbid.

project (**proj**-*ekt*) *n.* a plan to be worked on. *Our class is working on a project to start a vegetable garden. vb.* (*proh*-**jekt**) make plans for; throw, jut out.

projectile *n.* a rocket.

projector *n.* machine for showing (projecting) motion or still pictures on a screen.

If you pass white light through a glass prism, it splits up into a band of colors – the same as the colors of a rainbow.

P

prolong vb. cause to continue, make longer.

promenade n. (place made for) leisurely walking in public.

prominent adj. outstanding, noticeable, distinguished. *He is a prominent member of the club.*

promise vb. pledge that you will do something. n. What you have promised to do. *I promised to tidy my room, but I did not keep my promise.*

promising adj. likely to turn out well.

promote vb. raise to a higher position or office; encourage. *We should like to promote a good atmosphere in the school.* **promotion** n. **promotional** adj.

prompt 1. adj. on time; without delay. 2. vb. urge; incite; help actor by saying words he or she has forgotten.

prone adj. 1. lying face down. 2. liable, disposed to. *He was prone to lie.*

prong n. one of the sharp ends of a fork.

pronghorn n. shy antelopelike animal of North America. It is about three feet tall.

pronoun n. a word used for a noun, like he, she, it, they, him, our.

pronounce vb. make the sound of a word. **pronunciation** n.

proof n. 1. something that shows that what is said is true, evidence. *I need some proof before I will believe it.* 2. impression of type that can be corrected before final printing. **proofreader** n. a person who corrects printers' proofs.

prop n. & vb. support, lean against something. *The ladder was propped against the wall.*

propaganda n. spreading of ideas or information and the information so spread.

propel vb. send forward.

propeller n. two or more blades that spin around.

proper adj. right, suitable. *She was not wearing the proper clothes for a party.*

properly adv. factually correct. *We were not properly informed.*

property n. things owned.

prophet n. 1. a person who tells what is going to happen in the future. 2. in the Bible, a person who speaks for God. **prophesy** vb. speak as a prophet; foretell.

proportion n. part of; a ratio. *The proportion of people who use hearing aids has increased.*

propose vb. suggest, put forward an idea; intend to; offer marriage. **proposal** n.

proprietor n. owner of a business.

prosaic adj. ordinary, not very interesting.

prose n. written language without meter; not poetry.

prosecute vb. take to court; start legal action. **prosecution** n.

prosper vb. flourish, grow rich, be successful. **prosperity** n. **prosperous** adj.

protect vb. keep safe from danger, guard. **protection** n. that which protects.

protein (pro-*teen*) n. a body-building material in some foods, like eggs, meat and milk.

protest (*proh*-test) vb. say or show how you think something is wrong; object to. *We had to protest about the new school rules.* (proh-*test*) n. an objection.

Protestant n. a member of any Christian church which resulted from the protest against and separation from the Roman Catholic church.

proto- *prefix* meaning first, e.g. **prototype** the first model of something before general production.

proud adj. 1. thinking that you are better than others. 2. pleased that someone else has done well. *Mother was very proud when I won a prize.*

prove vb. show that something is true. *Can you prove that you saw a ghost?*

proverb n. a short saying that gives a warning or advice.

provide *vb*. give sustenance or support; supply for use. *Our teacher provided us with new pencils.*

province 1. *n*. a large area of a country with its own government; 2. *pl. n*. the whole country outside the capital. **provincial** *adj*.

provision *n*. what is provided.
provisions *pl. n*. food and drink.
provisional *adj*. temporary.

provoke *vb*. stir up feeling; irritate.
provocation *n*.

prow *n*. the bow of a ship; the forepart.

prowl *vb*. go about silently and secretly.

prudish *adj*. prim, affected modesty.
prude *n*.

prune 1. *n*. a dried plum. 2. *vb*. cut away parts of a plant to control the way it grows.

pry *vb*. look into; interfere inquisitively.

psalm (*sahm*) *n*. a sacred song in the Book of Psalms in the Old Testament in the Bible.

psycho- (**sye**-*co*) *prefix* meaning of the mind.

psychology (*sye*-**koll**-*o-jee*) *n*. the study of the mind and how it works.

psychopath (**sye**-*kuh-path*) *n*. mentally ill or unstable person.

ptarmigan (**tar**-*mig-an*) *n*. a bird of the grouse family whose plumage changes from brown and white in summer to grey and white in winter.

pterodactyl (*tero*-**dack**-*til*) *n*. prehistoric flying reptile.

pub *n*. saloon, bar.

puberty *n*. period when boys and girls mature and become men and women capable of producing children.

public 1. *adj*. known to everyone; belonging to everyone. 2. *n*. the people; the community as a whole.

publication *n*. a work that is published.

publicity *n*. making known publicly by means of advertisements, etc.

publish *vb*. have a book, newspaper or magazine printed for sale or to be given away; make known generally.
publisher *n*.

pudding *n*. a food made of flour and other ingredients, often boiled; a soft, thick, creamy dessert.

puddle *n*. a very small pool of water, usually dirty and temporary.

puffin *n*. a bird of the auk family.

pug *n*. small breed of dog with a snub-nose and tightly curled tail.

pull *vb*. heave something toward yourself.

pull down *vb*. (of buildings) take them down, destroy.

pulley *n*. a wheel with a rope around it, used to lift or move heavy things more easily.

pull off *vb*. succeed with something.

pullover *n*. a jersey or sweater.

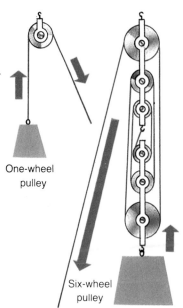

One-wheel pulley

Six-wheel pulley

With a six-wheel pulley you can lift a load six times greater than you could without it.

P

165

pulp 1. *n.* soft part of a fruit. 2. *n.* soft mass of dried vegetable matter, especially wood, for making paper. *vb.* destroy shape and hardness by beating something, often with water.

pulpit *n.* a raised structure in a church from which the priest or minister talks.

pulse *n.* the throbbing of your heart that you can feel in your wrist; rhythmical beat. **pulsate** *vb.*

puma *n.* large member of the cat family from America; cougar.

pump *vb.* push liquid or air through pipes. *The heart pumps blood around our bodies by contracting.* *n.* a machine or apparatus that does this.

pumpkin *n.* a large, usually round, orange-colored vegetable which grows on the ground in many warm parts of the world.

punch 1. *vb.* hit someone with the fist. *n.* a blow with the fist. 2. *n.* a tool for cutting holes. 3. *n.* a mixture of wine, lemon, hot water, spices, etc.

punctual *adj.* on time.

punctuation *n.* the marks used in writing like the period (.) the comma (,) the semicolon (;) the colon (:) the question mark (?) and exclamation mark (!) **punctuate** *vb.*

puncture *vb. & n.* pierce; make a hole in something; a hole.

punish *vb.* do something to someone who has done wrong so that he or she will not want to do it again. **punishment** *n.*

punt 1. *n.* long flat-bottomed boat propelled by a pole. 2. *n. & vb.* kick a ball.

puny *adj.* small.

pupa *n.* (plural **pupae**) the chrysalis stage in an insect's development.

pupil *n.* 1. a person who is learning from a teacher; a student. 2. the round dark opening in the colored part (the **iris**) of the eye.

puppet *n.* a kind of doll that can be made to move by pulling strings, fitting it onto the hand, etc.

puppy *n.* a young dog.

purchase *vb. & n.* buy; something that is bought.

pure *adj.* not mixed with anything; clean.

purple *adj. & n.* a dark, red-blue color.

purpose *n.* intention, object.

purr *vb.* the low vibrating sound made by a contented cat.

purse 1. *n.* an object used for carrying money. 2. *vb.* pucker your lips.

pursue *vb.* chase after. *The crowd pursued the thief.* **pursuit** *n.*

pus *n.* yellowish fluid around an inflamed part of the skin.

push *vb.* press against forcefully; shove something away without striking it.

put *vb.* place something somewhere.

put aside *vb.* keep something to use it later; save. *I put aside some of my money every week for my vacation.*

put off *vb.* 1. decide to do something later than planned. *We had the flu so we put off the party until next week.* 2. feel badly about something you dislike. *I was quite put off by the way she spoke to me.*

putty *n.* a grayish paste which hardens when dry and is used for fixing glass into window frames.

put up *vb.* accommodate for a short time. *I can put you up for the night.*

put up with *vb.* not to complain about something even though you do not like it; tolerate. *It's not a very nice place, but my brother likes it, so I will just have to put up with it.*

puzzle *n.* a difficult problem. *vb.* perplex.

Pygmy *n.* small, dark-skinned people who live in the hot equatorial forests of Africa. The men are seldom taller than five feet and the women are even smaller.

pyjamas see **pajamas**.

pylon *n.* tall metal tower supporting electric cables.

pyramid *n.* a structure with a square (or other) base and sloping sides that meet at the top.

python *n.* a large kind of snake.

quack 1. *vb.* make a noise like a duck. 2. *n.* a person who pretends to be a doctor, but is not properly qualified.

quadrangle *n.* a four-sided courtyard.

quadrant *n.* 1. an instrument for measuring vertical angles. 2. one-quarter of a circle.

quadruped *n.* a four-footed animal. *A horse is a quadruped.*

quadruplet *n.* one of four babies born at the same time to the same mother.

quail *n.* a small game bird, related to the partridge and found in most parts of the world.

quaint *adj.* odd but pleasant; old-fashioned. *We spent our holiday in a quaint little fishing village in New England.*

quake *vb.* tremble, e.g. with fear.

qualification *n.* 1. knowledge or skill making person fit for a post. 2. modification.

Inside the Great Pyramid, showing the burial chambers, air shafts and gallery.

qualify *vb.* 1. become fit for a post. 2. limit the meaning of a statement so that it is less general.

quality *n.* how good or bad a thing is. *We want the best quality of carpet.*

quantity *n.* how much; the size, weight, or number of anything. *What quantity of cement do you need?*

quarantine (**kwar**-*ant*-*een*) *n.* a period when someone who has a disease is kept away from other people so that they cannot catch it.

quarrel *vb.* & *n.* argue angrily. **quarrelsome** *adj.*

quarry *n.* 1. a place where stone for building and other purposes is taken out of the ground. 2. an animal that is hunted, prey.

quart (*kwort*) *n.* a measure of liquids (1.14 liters). *There are two pints in a quart.*

quarter *n.* 1. one of four equal parts of a whole; ¼. 2. a district. *The Latin Quarter of Paris.*

quarterly *adj.* due every quarter of the year, i.e., every three months. *n.* publication issued every quarter.

quartet *n.* four people doing something together, especially making music.

quartz *n.* a common, hard mineral.

quasar *n.* small brilliant object that emits radio waves far out in space.

quash *vb.* suppress, declare as not valid.

quasi- *prefix* meaning seemingly or almost.

quaver 1. *vb.* tremble; trill (of singing voice). 2. *n.* a very short note in music.

quay (*key*) *n.* a landing place for ships.

queen *n.* 1. the female ruler of a country or the wife of a king. 2. the most powerful piece at chess.

queer *adj.* strange and peculiar. *This soup tastes very queer.*

quell *vb.* overcome, subdue, crush.

quench *vb.* satisfy thirst; put out fire.

query *n.* a question. *vb.* ask a question.

quest *n.* a search.

167

Q

question *n. & vb.* something that you ask when you want to find out something and get an answer. *n.* subject being discussed.

question mark *n.* a punctuation mark, like this (?). It goes at the end of written questions.

queue (rhymes with *dew*) *n.* a line of people waiting for something.

quiche (*keesh*) *n.* a pastry shell filled with beaten egg and milk and savory ingredients.

quick *adj.* fast; speedy.

quickly *adv.* to do something fast and without delay. *Come quickly.*

quicksand *n.* a kind of swampy ground consisting of sand and water which will suck down a person or animal that tries to walk on it.

quicksilver *n.* another name for mercury (metal).

quiet *adj.* not noisy; calm.

quill *n.* large feather used as a pen or plectrum.

quilt *n.* padded bed covering.

quince *n.* a tree and its acid pear-shaped fruit.

quinine *n.* a strong, bitter-tasting substance made from the bark of the cinchona tree, used as a medicine to treat malaria.

quintet *n.* a group of five, usually musicians.

quintuplet *n.* one of five babies born at the same time to the same mother.

quit *vb.* leave; give up.

quite *adv.* 1. completely, wholly, entirely. *You are quite right.* 2. to a considerable extent. *He dives quite well, but he's a poor swimmer.*

quiver 1. *vb.* tremble slightly and rapidly; 2. *n.* a case for holding arrows.

quiz *n.* a set of questions asked to find out how much people know, usually as a competition.

quotation marks *pl. n.* punctuation marks like this ("......") or this ('......'). They are used in writing mainly to show spoken words.

quote *vb.* repeat someone else's words.

R

rabbi *n.* a teacher of Jewish law; the leader of a synagogue.

rabbit *n.* a small mammal with long ears and a very short tail.

Rabbits raise their young in burrows.

rabble *n.* a mob, disorganized crowd of people.

rabid *adj.* infected with rabies; mad.

rabies *n.* a usually fatal disease of the nervous system which is caught by being bitten by a rabid animal.

raccoon *n.* a tree-dwelling American mammal with long, grayish fur.

race 1. *n.* a group of people of common ancestry who are alike and have the same skin color. 2. *vb.* compete with others to find out who is fastest. *n.* a contest of speed.

racial *adj.*

racialist *n.* 1. a person who believes that the races are fundamentally different. 2. someone who supports or stirs up racist conflicts.

rack *n.* 1. framework or stand for holding objects. 2. a medieval instrument of torture.

racket *n*. 1. a lot of noise, a din. 2. a light bat used to hit balls in tennis, badminton or squash. 3. an unlawful means of making a living.

radar *n*. an instrument that sends out radio waves. These waves are reflected back off objects like aircraft or ships, and the reflection shows where the object is.

radiate *vb*. 1. give out heat and light. 2. be arranged like spokes.

radiator *n*. 1. a device that sends out heat. 2. the part of a car that keeps the cooling water at the correct temperature.

radical *adj*. fundamental, going to the root; (in politics) in favor of reforms and social change.

radio *n*. an instrument that receives radio waves and uses them to produce sounds which you can hear. *vb*. transmit by radio.

radio waves *pl. n*. invisible waves sent out by a transmitter and traveling very fast.

radish *n*. a small roundish root with a strong peppery taste.

radium *n*. a rare, radioactive metal.

radius *n*. (plural **radii**) a straight line from the center of a circle to its edge or circumference.

raffia *n*. a fiber from an African palm tree, used for weaving and matting, etc.

raffle *n. & vb*. a lottery; dispose of by lottery.

raft *n*. logs fastened together to make a sort of boat without sides.

rafter *n*. one of the crossbars of wood in a roof.

rag *n*. a piece of torn clothing or material.

rage *n*. great anger. *vb*. rave, be violent.

raid *n. & vb*. a surprise attack.

rail *n*. 1. a long bar or rod. 2. one of the long metal strips that form a railroad track.

railing *n*. a fence made of metal bars.

railroad *n*. the organization that controls a system of tracks, and the trains that run on them.

rain *n*. drops of water falling from

A radar station sends out radio signals. These are reflected back from an aircraft and show its position on a screen.

the sky. *vb*. fall or send down as rain.

rainbow *n*. an arch of color in the sky. A rainbow is caused by sun shining on rain or mist.

raincoat *n*. a waterproof overcoat.

rainfall *n*. the amount of rain that falls in a period of time.

raise *vb*. lift up; make higher.

raisin *n*. a dried grape.

rake *n*. a tool like a comb on a long handle. *vb*. use a rake.

rally *vb*. come together, arouse, recover from illness. *n*. meeting, competitive event.

ram 1. *n*. a male sheep. 2. *vb*. strike against violently. *The ship rammed the submarine.*

Rails are laid on steel or concrete sleepers. A flange or lip on the inside edge of each wheel holds it to the rail.

169

R

ramble 1. *vb.* wander about without purpose. 2. *vb.* talk in a disconnected way. 3. *n.* a walk for pleasure.

ramp *n.* a sloping floor, path, etc., leading from one level to another.

rampart *n.* fortified mound of earth.

ramshackle *adj.* broken down; derelict.

ran *vb.* past of **run**.

ranch *n.* a large farm with a lot of land for grazing.

rancid *adj.* smelling and tasting foul, especially of fats. *The butter was rancid.*

random *adj.* (at random) without purpose; haphazard.

rang *vb.* past of **ring**.

range 1. *n.* a row of mountains. 2. *n.* the distance over which a gun can fire a bullet. 3. *n.* a large area of open country. 4. *n.* stove with oven and burner. 5. *vb.* place in rows.

ranger *n.* 1. keeper of a forest or national park. 2. specially trained soldier. 3. mounted policeman. 4. senior guide or scout.

rank *n.* 1. a title or place that shows how important someone is. *General is a very high rank in the army.* 2. row, a line.

ransack *vb.* search thoroughly; plunder.

ransom *n.* money paid to a kidnapper to make him or her release a prisoner. *vb.* buy freedom.

rap *n.* & *vb.* the sound of knocking, especially on a door.

rape *n.* & *vb.* forcing a woman to have sexual intercourse.

rapid 1. *adj.* swift; fast. 2. *n.* part of a river with fast current, usually with rocks or obstructions (also **rapids**).

rapid transit *n.* rapid passenger transportation in cities, e.g. subway.

rapier *n.* a kind of sword with a slim blade, used for thrusting.

rare *adj.* unusual; not often found.

rascal *n.* a worthless fellow; a naughty person.

rash 1. *n.* lots of red spots on the skin. 2. *adj.* reckless, hasty.

raspberry *n.* a small red berry which is good to eat.

rat *n.* a rodent (gnawing animal) found in large numbers all over the world. *vb.* betray friends.

rate 1. *n.* charge or payment, according to some standard. *My rate for cleaning windows is $2 an hour.* 2. *n.* speed over a given distance. 3. *vb.* estimate, regard. *How do you rate her chances of winning?*

rather 1. *adj.* somewhat. *Our friend is rather late.* 2. *adv.* preferably. *I would rather stay at home than go out this evening.*

ratio *n.* the relationship in amount or size between two or more things. *The ratio of text to pictures in this book is about 2 columns (of text) to 1 (picture).*

ration *n.* a fixed portion, especially of food. *During the war the sugar ration was four ounces a week.*

rattle 1. *vb.* make a clattering noise. 2. *n.* a baby's toy which makes a rattling noise when shaken.

rattlesnake *n.* a poisonous snake.

rave *vb.* talk wildly without making sense; speak with great enthusiasm. *She raved about his bushy beard.*

raven *n.* a large, black bird of the crow family.

ravine *n.* a deep valley or gorge.

raw *adj.* 1. uncooked. *It can be dangerous to eat raw meat.* 2. without experience. *Many of the soldiers were raw recruits.* 3. sensitive to touch.

ray *n.* 1. line or beam of light, heat or some kind of energy. 2. a flat kind of fish.

rayon *n.* the name given to various man-made textile fibers containing cellulose, a substance found in the walls of plant cells.

razor *n.* an instrument for shaving hair from the skin.

re- 1. *prep.* concerning *Re the book you lent me.* 2. *prefix* meaning again, repeated. By knowing the meaning of the main word the sense of the prefixed word should, in most cases, be obvious, e.g. **reintroduce**, **rethink**.

reach *vb.* get or grab hold of something; arrive at.

react *vb.* respond to; change chemically.

reactor *n.* an apparatus in which atomic energy is produced.

read *vb.* look at, and understand, writing or printing.

ready *adv.* prepared. *Are you ready yet?* In a fit state; willing.

real *adj.* actual; alive; correct; genuine.

realize *vb.* come to understand. *Judy realized that she must have seen a ghost.*

really *adv.* truly; correctly. *Do you really mean that?*

realm (*relm*) *n.* another word for kingdom.

reap *vb.* cut and collect a crop, especially a cereal, such as wheat.

rear 1. *n. & adj.* the back part; at the back. *I like to sit at the rear of the classroom.* 2. *vb.* look after young creatures as they grow up. 3. *vb.* (of a horse) stand up on the back legs.

reason *n.* anything that explains why or how something has happened; power of mind to think. *vb.* try to reach conclusions by thinking.

reasonable *adj.* having good judgment; moderate; fair.

rebel (**reb**-*el*) *n.* someone who revolts against a government; someone who refuses to obey orders. (*ri*-**bell**) *vb.* revolt, organize a **rebellion** *n.*

rebuke *n. & vb.* speak severely to, reprimand.

The safety razor was invented in 1880 by King C. Gillette.

recall *vb.* 1. remember; bring back to mind. 2. call someone back.

recede *vb.* move back, withdraw.

recession. *n.* decline in activity or prosperity.

receipt (*re-seet*) *n.* an official piece of paper stating that a bill has been paid.

receive (*re-seeve*) *vb.* get something that has been given to you or sent to you; accept.

recent *adj.* not long ago.

receptacle *n.* container.

recital *n.* a performance, usually of music. *A piano recital.*

recite *vb.* say aloud from memory. *Paul can recite a poem by heart.*

reckless *adj.* careless, rash, wild.

reckon *vb.* calculate, count; estimate; suppose, think.

reclaim *vb.* 1. restore poor or abandoned land to agricultural use. 2. get back something you are entitled to.

recline *vb.* lean; lie.

recognize *vb.* 1. know that you have seen somebody or something before. *I wonder if she will recognize me after all those years?* 2. acknowledge.

recommend *vb.* advise; speak or write favorably of. *I recommend this book to you.*

reconcile *vb.* 1. make friends again after a quarrel. 2. resign oneself to.

record (**reck**-*ord*) 1. *n.* a flat disk which makes sounds when it is turned on a record player. 2. *n. & adj.* the best performance known. *She scored a record number of goals.*

record (*ree*-**kord**) *vb.* 1. write something down so that it will be remembered. 2. put sounds on a record or tape.

recorder *n.* a musical instrument made of wood or plastic, played by blowing into one end.

recording see **record**.

record player *n.* phonograph, a machine for playing records.

recover *vb.* 1. get something back. *He recovered his boot from the mud.* 2. get better. *I am glad you have recovered from your fall.* **recovery** *n.*

R

recreation *n.* enjoyable exercise, refreshment of mind and body.

recruit *n.* a newly enlisted or drafted member of the armed forces. *vb.* enlist someone.

rectangle *n.* a four-sided figure in which the opposite sides are equal to each other and all four angles are right angles.

recuperate *vb.* get better after an illness; regain, recover.

recur *vb.* (past **recurred**) occur again. **recurrence** *n.*

red *n.* & *adj.* the color of blood. *Red is one of the primary colors.*

reduce *vb.* make less. *If you reduce the price I will buy it.*

redundant *adj.* exceeding what is needed, superfluous; needlessly repetitive. **redundancy** *n.*

reed *n.* tall, firm-stemmed grass that grows near water.

reef *n.* a ridge of rock or sand near the surface of the sea.

reel 1. *n.* device for winding, e.g. fishing line; length of film on a spool. 2. *n.* Scottish dance. 3. *vb.* sway; be giddy.

refectory *n.* a dining room in a convent, monastery or some schools.

referee *vb.* & *n.* a person who controls a football or boxing match. **ref** (*abbrev.*).

reference book *n.* a book that is used to find particular pieces of information. You do not usually read through the whole book. *Dictionaries and encyclopedias are reference books.*

referendum *n.* voting on a particular issue by all voters; a plebiscite.

refine *vb.* remove impurities. **refinery** *n.* a building or equipment where oil, sugar, or metal is refined.

reflect *vb.* send back light, heat, sound or radio waves from any object.

reflection *n.* the picture you see in a mirror or in calm water.

reform *vb.* make a great political or social change; improve. **reformation** *n.*

refraction *n.* the bending of light when it passes from one medium to another.

refrain 1. *vb.* curb, restrain, keep oneself from doing. 2. *n.* regularly recurring phrase or verse at the end of stanzas of a poem.

refresh *vb.* give new energy to.

refrigerator *n.* a cabinet or room in which food is kept very cold so that it does not spoil.

refuge *n.* a shelter from danger. **refugee** *n.* person escaping danger and seeking shelter.

refund *n.* & *vb.* return money.

refuse (re-**fyuze**) *vb.* say that you will not do something that you are asked to do. **refusal** *n.*

refuse (**ref**-*yuse*) *n.* rubbish, things that are thrown away.

regal *adj.* concerning kings and queens, royal; magnificent.

regalia *n.* emblems and symbols of royalty, e.g. crown, scepter, etc.

regard *vb.* look at; take into consideration; hold in high esteem. *n.* gaze, concern. **regards** *pl. n.* respectful friendly feelings. *I send you my regards.*

regarding *prep.* concerning.

regatta *n.* a race meeting for boats and yachts.

regent *n.* a person who takes the place of monarch if the monarch is too young or too ill to rule.

reggae (**reg**-*ay*) *n.* West Indian music with a strong beat.

regime (*ray*-**zheem**) *n.* a system of government; a period of rule.

regiment *n.* a large army unit.

region (**ree**-*jun*) *n.* an area of the world or of a country with no particular border. *Evergreens grow mainly in the colder regions of the world.* **regional** *adj.*

register 1. *n.* a book in which lists of things or other information is kept. 2. *vb.* record; put in writing. *I wish to register a complaint.*

regret *n.* & *vb.* be sorry for something that has been done.

regular *adj.* happening in the same way or at the same time again and again. *There is a regular bus service between most big cities.*

regulate *vb.* 1. govern or control according to rules. 2. adjust (a watch, etc.).

rehearse *vb.* practice, particularly for a play or concert. **rehearsal** *n.* a practice performance of a play.

reign (rhymes with *pain*) *vb. & n.* period of rule (as a king or queen).

reindeer *n.* a kind of large deer that lives in cold regions.

reins (rhymes with *canes*) *pl. n.* straps fastened to a bridle to control a horse.

reject *vb.* refuse to accept of keep something because it is not good enough.

rejoice *vb.* to be happy.

relapse *vb. & n.* slip or fall back into a former worse state.

relative *n.* someone who belongs to the same family as you. *Your aunt and uncle are your relatives.*

relax *vb.* become less tight; loosen. *If you relax your muscles you will feel better.*

relay race *n.* a race in which each person in a team goes part of the distance.

release *vb.* set free, liberate; put into circulation. *The film was released first in Scotland.*

relevant *adj.* relating to or connected with the subject being discussed.

reliable *adj.* can be trusted and depended upon. *She is a reliable dentist.*

relic *n.* something that survives destruction; something belonging to a holy person kept by others as an object of reverence.

relief (*re-leaf*) *n.* 1. removal or lessening of pain. 2. help given to refugees etc. 3. carving in which the designs stand out from the surface.

relief map *n.* a map that shows where high and low areas of land are.

relieve *vb.* free; give aid to.

religion *n.* a belief that there is a god who created and controls the universe. **religious** *adj.*

relish 1. *n.* enjoyment of food. 2. *n.* a sauce. 3. *vb.* get pleasure from.

reluctant *adj.* unwilling, hesitating. **reluctance** *n.*

rely *vb.* depend on. *I rely on you to give me a lift tomorrow.*

remain 1. *vb.* stay after others. *Sue remained in the house when the others went out.* 2. *vb.* be left over after some has been taken away. *You can have the few candies that remain.* 3. **remains** *pl. n.* what is left after some amount has been taken away; a dead body.

remainder *n.* what is left over when a part has gone or been taken away.

remark *vb. & n.* comment, observe. **remarkable** *adj.* worth noticing; extraordinary.

remedy *n.* medicine or treatment for a disease. *vb.* put right.

remember *vb.* keep something in mind; recall, or bring something to mind; not to forget. *Remember to telephone me when you arrive.*

remind *vb.* make or help someone remember. *Sarah reminded everyone about her birthday.*

remote *adj.* far away from other places, times, or relations. *We spent our honeymoon on a remote island.*

remove *vb.* take away.

Renaissance *n.* a French word meaning "rebirth" and describing the great revival in learning, art, etc., that took place in Europe from the 14th to 16th century.

rendezvous (**ron-***day-voo*) *n.* an appointed meeting place. *vb.* meet at an appointed place.

rent 1. *n.* a regular payment made for the use of a house or other place or thing. 2. *vb.* have the use of something you pay a rent for.

repair *vb.* make something that is broken whole again; mend.

repeat *vb.* say or do again. **repeatedly** *adv.* again and again.

repel *vb.* drive back, turn away. **repellent** *adj.* unattractive.

repent *vb.* feel sorrow or regret for the wrong one has done.

173

R

replace *vb.* put back where it came from. *Please replace the book on the right shelf.*

replica *n.* an exact copy of something.

reply *vb.* answer someone. *n.* an answer.

report 1. *vb.* tell of something; give an account of (for publication). *n.* the account itself, spoken or written. 2. *n.* a bang.

reporter *n.* a person who obtains and writes about news for a newspaper, TV, etc.

represent *vb.* act or speak for other people.

reprimand *vb.* speak sharply to, scold. *n.* official rebuke.

reproduce *vb.* 1. make something happen again; copy. *The concert was recorded on tape and reproduced the next day.* 2. give birth. **reproduction** *n.*

reptile *n.* a cold-blooded vertebrate animal that creeps or crawls. *Crocodiles, snakes and tortoises are all reptiles.*

republic *n.* a country that elects head of state, usually a president, and does not have a king or queen.

reputation *n.* a person's qualities or character as seen and judged by others.

request *vb.* & *n.* ask for something. *He requested this tape.*

require *vb.* 1. need. *She requires some help with the costumes.* 2. insist on.

rescue *vb.* take from danger; set free. *The knight will rescue the princess from the dragon. n.* being rescued.

research (*re-***surch**) *vb.* investigate, look into, carefully. (**ree-***surch*) *n.* inquiry, scientific study.

resemble *vb.* be or look like something or somebody else. *Alan resembles his grandfather.* **resemblance** *n.*

reserve 1. *vb.* keep back to use later. *Shall I reserve a chair for you if you are late? n.* a place kept for a special purpose. *You can see some very rare birds at the bird reserve.* 2. *n.* a player

who does not play for the team unless someone else is unable to play. **reserved** *adj.* shy.

reservoir *n.* a place where a large amount of water is stored, often in an artificial lake.

resident *n.* someone who lives in a particular place, a permanent inhabitant. **reside** *vb.*

resign (*re-***zine**) *vb.* give up, especially to give up a job. **resignation** *n.*

resin *n.* a sticky gum that oozes (leaks slowly) from trees; rosin, the best known, comes from pines.

resist *vb.* oppose; go against. **resistance** *n.*

resources *pl. n.* the useful things that a person or country has. *Oil is one of our country's greatest resources.*

respect *vb.* & *n.* (have) a high opinion of; esteem. **respectable** *adj.* decent; of good solid behavior.

resort (*ri-***zort**) 1. *vb.* turn to. *He was so unhappy he resorted to overeating.* 2. *n.* vacation area.

re-sort (*ree-***sort**) *vb.* sort again.

resolve *vb.* decide, be determined to. *I resolve to get to work on time in the future.*

responsible *adj.* in charge of something. *I am responsible for the paint cupboard.* **responsibility** *n.*

rest 1. *vb.* lie down; relax. 2. *n.* the remainder. *What has happened to the rest of our group?* **restful** *adj.* quiet, soothing.

restaurant *n.* a place where you can buy and eat food.

restore *vb.* put back as it was before; repair. *Sue restores old furniture.*

restrict *vb.* keep within bounds, limit. **restriction** *n.*

result 1. *n.* & *vb.* something that happens because of some action or happening. *Joe's injury was the result of a kick at football.* 2. *n.* the final score in a game.

resume *vb.* begin again, take back. *After the interval the concert resumed.*

resurrect *vb.* bring back to life. **Resurrection** *n.* the rising of Jesus Christ from the tomb.

retail *vb.* sell goods in a shop. see **wholesale**).

retain *vb.* hold back, keep.

retina *n.* coating at the back of the eyeball which is sensitive to light.

retire *vb.* 1. give up work, usually because one is old. 2. go back; withdraw. *The rain was so heavy, we had to retire to the pavilion.*

retreat *vb.* go back from.

return *vb.* 1. give something back. *Could you please return my pen.* 2. go back, come back again. *When do you return from your holiday?*

reunion *n.* being reunited, a coming together again.

reveal *vb.* uncover; make known. *I can now reveal the secret.*

revenue *n.* the money that a government receives from taxation etc.

revere *vb.* show respect, honor for.

reverse 1. *vb.* go backward, particularly in a vehicle. 2. *n.* the opposite of something.

reversible *adj.* able to be reversed.

review 1. *n.* published opinion of a book, play, etc. *vb.* examine, criticize. 2. *vb.* & *n.* inspect troops.

revise *vb.* look over again in order to correct or improve. **revision** *n.*

revive *vb.* bring back to life or consciousness; make active again. *The Olympic Games were revived in modern times.*

revolution *n.* 1. a time when a government is changed by force, not by an election; a time when ideas and the way people live are changed by new ideas or actions, as in the *Industrial Revolution*. 2. a full turn of a wheel. **revolve** *vb.*

revolver *n.* a hand gun with its ammunition held in a revolving cylinder.

reward *n.* a present given to someone for what has been done. *We were given a reward for helping to catch the thief. vb.* give reward.

rheumatism *n.* the name given to a group of diseases which cause pain in the muscles and joints and make them stiff and hard to move.

rhinoceros *n.* a large African or Asian animal with a very thick skin and one or two horns on the snout.

rhubarb *n.* a leafy plant the stalks of which are often cooked and eaten.

rhyme *n.* & *vb.* use a word that sounds like another word. *"Egg" and "beg" rhyme with each other.*

rhythm (**rith**-*em*) *n.* the pattern of beats in music and poetry.

rib *n.* one of the curved bones of the chest.

The rhinoceros is a relation of the horse. There are five species.

ribbon *n.* a narrow piece of material used as an ornament or for tying things, as well as in typewriters.

rice *n.* a cereal grass that is widely grown for food. It grows in wet parts of India and China and in most warm climates.

rich *adj.* 1. having a great deal of money; wealthy. 2. (of food) containing a great deal of fat, cream, etc.

rickshaw *n.* small, oriental two-wheeled passenger vehicle drawn by a man on foot or bicycle.

rid (get rid of) *vb.* throw away something that is not wanted.

riddle *n.* a puzzling question. *"What goes up when the rain comes down?"* is a riddle. (*The answer: "an umbrella".*)

ride *vb.* (past **rode** past part **ridden**) travel on something, particularly a horse or bicycle.

rider n. a person who rides, particularly on horseback.

ridge n. a long narrow part higher than what is on either side.

ridiculous adj. silly enough to be laughed at. **ridicule** vb. make fun of.

rifle n. a gun that is held against the shoulder when it is fired.

rift n. a split, opening; chasm.

rig n. 1. arrangement of ships' sails. 2. equipment for drilling oil wells.

rigid adj. stiff; unbending; strict.

right 1. n. & adj. the opposite of left. 2. adj. correct; accurate; good. *Do you have the right time?*

rim n. 1. the edge of a container. 2. n. the outside edge of a circle.

rind n. the thick, tough skin of some fruits and vegetables, and of cheese and bacon, and of a tree.

ring n. 1. a circle, such as the ring in a circus. 2. a circular band of gold

or other material worn on a finger as an ornament. 3. the sound made by a bell.

rink n. a place for skating.

rinse vb. wash out in clean water.

riot n. a noisy and violent disturbance by a crowd. vb. take part in a riot.

rip vb. tear something.

ripe adj. (of fruit) ready to be eaten. **ripen** vb. grow ripe.

ripple n. small movement on the surface of water.

rise vb. come or go up; get up.

risk n. the chance of danger or loss. vb. expose to risk. **risky** adj.

rite n. the set words and actions of a (religious) ceremony. **ritual** adj. & n. concerned with rites; the rite itself.

ritzy adj. in fashion, snobby. *She wore a ritzy hat to show off to her friends.*

rival n. a competitor; an opponent. vb. compete with.

*A diagram of the Cincinnati Milacron robot, labeled to show the six degrees of freedom it can achieve. (**Yaw** means to move from a straight course).*

Elbow extension

Shoulder swivel

Arm sweep

Pitch

Roll

Yaw

river *n.* a large stream of water that flows from higher to lower ground and into another river, a lake or sea.

rivet *n.* a bolt for joining metal plates together. *vb.* join with rivets; hold the attention.

roach *n.* silvery freshwater fish.

road *n.* a wide path or highway for cars and other vehicles.

roam *vb.* wander; go here and there.

roar *n.* & *vb.* loud, deep sound like the noise a lion makes.

roast *vb.* cook food in an oven.

rob *vb.* take or steal things. **robber** *n.* a person who steals; a thief. **robbery** *n.* theft.

robe *n.* a long, loose dress or gown, sometimes worn as part of a national or ceremonial costume. *vb.* put on robes.

robin *n.* a small bird of the thrush family with rusty-orange feathers on its throat and breast. *Robins often make their homes in town gardens.*

robot *n.* a machine that can be made to do things that people do.

rock 1. *n.* a large stone. 2. *n.* a type of popular music with a strong beat. 3. *vb.* move back and forth.

rocket *n.* 1. a firework that shoots up into the sky. 2. a device for sending missiles and spacecraft into space.

rod *n.* a long, straight stick.

rode *vb.* past of **ride**.

rodent *n.* one of a group of fairly small mammals that gnaw things. *Rats, mice and squirrels are all rodents.*

rodeo *n.* performance by American cowboys of riding and other skills.

rogue *n.* a bad man; a rascal.

roll 1. *vb.* turn over and over. 2. *n.* make something into a shape like a tube. 3. *vb.* flatten with roller. 4. *n.* a small loaf of bread.

rollerskates *pl. n.* set of wheels attached to a boot for skating on the ground.

rolling pin *n.* a long tube used for rolling out pastry to flatten it.

Roman Catholic *n.* a Christian who accepts the Pope as the head of the church.

romance *n.* medieval tale of chivalry; a love story. *vb.* exaggerate.

Romance *adj.* languages based on Latin. **romantic** *adj.* imaginative, remote, mysterious.

The three-stage Saturn V rocket was used in the early Apollo flights. Each stage drops away after use.

Lunar module

3rd stage

2nd stage

1st stage

USA

R

romanticism *n.* a late 18th- and early 19th-century artistic movement.

roof *n.* the top covering of a building. *vb.* cover with a roof.

rook 1. *n.* a bird belonging to the crow family. 2. *n.* a castle-shaped chess piece. 3. *vb.* defraud.

room *n.* a space; a compartment in a building, such as a living room or bedroom.

roost *n.* & *vb.* a resting place for birds; a perch.

root *n.* the part of a plant that grows under the ground.

rope *n.* thick strong cord. **ropy** *adj.* like rope.

rose *vb.* past of **rise**.

rose *n.* a prickly shrub with showy flowers. *adj.* deep pink.

rosemary *n.* an evergreen shrub used in cooking and making perfume.

Rosh Hashanah *n.* the festival of the Jewish New Year.

rot *vb.* go bad; decay.

rotate *vb.* go around and around. **rotation** *n.*

rotor *n.* the rotating blades on top of a helicopter which serve as both the propellers and wings of a fixed wing aircraft. They provide both **thrust** and **lift**.

rotten *adj.* to be soft or bad. *Wasps like to eat rotten apples.*

rough (rhymes with *cuff*) *adj.* 1. not smooth. *My dog has a rough coat.* 2. not gentle. 3. done quickly and not meant to be exact. *Can you draw me a rough plan of the town in which you live?*

round *adj.* shaped like a circle or a ball.

round trip *n.* a trip taken to a place and then back again. *It costs less money to buy a round trip ticket.*

round up *v.* to bring together, usually cattle. **roundup** *n.*

rouse *vb.* wake up; stir, excite.

route (rhymes with *boot*) *n.* the road or direction taken to get somewhere.

routine (*rot-een*) *n.* set way of doing things.

row (rhymes with *cow*) *n.* & *vb.* noise, quarrel.

row (rhymes with *go*) 1. *vb.* use oars to make a boat move through water. 2. *n.* a line. *She planted a row of beans in her garden.*

rowdy *adj.* noisy and disorderly.

royal *adj.* to do with kings and queens. *When a king is married he has a royal wedding.* **royalty** *n.* being royal; a percentage paid to an author, etc., according to sales.

rub *vb.* 1. slide or press something against something else; polish. 2. rub out, remove marks etc. on paper, blackboard, etc.

rubber *n.* 1. a strong, elastic material made from the sap of a rubber tree. 2. a piece of rubber, or plastic, used for wiping out pencil marks.

rubbish *n.* waste matter that is thrown away.

rubble *n.* debris; pieces of stone, brick, from a building.

ruby *n.* a red, crystalline precious stone.

rucksack *n.* a bag that can be strapped on your back for carrying.

rudder *n.* a flat, upright, movable wood or metal piece at the back of a boat or aircraft used for steering.

ruddy *adj.* a healthy reddish color. *He had a ruddy complexion.*

rude *adj.* 1. bad-mannered; impolite. 2. crude or simple (now old-fashioned).

rug *n.* thick, heavy fabric used as floor covering; a mat or small carpet.

ruin (**roo-*in***) 1. *vb.* spoil completely. 2. *n.* (usually used in plural) the remains of an old building. *We visited the **ruins** of an abbey on our school outing.*

rule 1. *n.* a law; something that must be obeyed. 2 *vb.* be in charge of a country, keep under control, govern. *William the Conqueror ruled England after 1066.*

ruler *n.* 1. a straight strip marked in units (inches, etc.) used for drawing lines or measuring. 2. a person who rules a country.

rum 1. *n.* an alcoholic liquor distilled from the fermented products of the sugar cane.

rumble *vb.* & *n.* deep sound like that of distant thunder.

ruminant *n.* animal such as cow and deer which chews the cud.

rummage *vb.* search through a confused pile of things.

rumor *n.* a story that is passed around, but may not be true; hearsay. *There is a rumor that a spacecraft has landed in China.*

rump *n.* buttocks; back part of a mammal.

rumple *vb.* wrinkle, crease.

run *vb.* (past **ran**) go very fast (of a person or animal); go smoothly; control. *She runs the office.*

run across *vb.* meet someone by chance. also **run into**.

rung *vb.* past of **ring**.

rung *n.* one step of a ladder.

runner *n.* messenger; person who runs in a race; the part on which a sled slides.

runway *n.* the hard surface on which an aircraft takes off and lands.

rural *adj.* of or about the countryside.

rush 1. *vb.* move very fast. 2. *n.* a kind of strong grass that grows near water.

rusk *n.* piece of bread rebaked until it is crisp.

rust *n.* the reddish-brown crust that forms on iron and some other metals when they become damp. *vb.* become covered with rust.

rusty *adj.* rusted; out of practice. *My piano playing is rusty.*

rustic *adj.* to do with the country.

rustle 1. *n.* & *vb.* crisp sound of dry leaves. 2. *vb.* steal livestock.

rut *n.* a furrow in a road made by wheels. *The track was full of ruts and potholes.*

ruthless *adj.* having no pity.

rye *n.* a cereal grain that, with barley, is one of the hardiest grown. It is used to make flour as well as alcoholic drinks such as whisky, gin, vodka and kvass.

sabbath *n.* a weekly religious day of rest. The sabbath is Saturday for Jews, and Sunday for Christians.

saber (**say**-*ber*) *n.* a sword with a curved blade.

saber-toothed tiger *n.* prehistoric carnivorous mammal. In its largest form it was bigger than a modern lion, and had two canine teeth eight inches long in its upper jaw, for slashing at its prey.

sable *n.* a small, carnivorous mammal of the weasel family, valued for its dark fur.

sabotage (**sabb**-*oh-tazh*) *vb.* & *n.* damage something on purpose.

saccharin (**sack**-*er-in*) *n.* white crystalline substance, 300 times as sweet as sugar, discovered in 1879. It is used in the diets of diabetics and dieters.

sack 1. *n.* a large bag made of strong material. 2. *vb.* dismiss someone from a job. 3. *vb.* destroy a town captured in war.

sacred *adj.* to do with religion and worship. *The Bible and the Koran are sacred books.*

sacrifice *vb.* give away something precious, often to God. *n.* the thing that is given away.

sad *adj.* unhappy; sorrowful. **sadden** *vb.*

saddle *n.* the rider's seat used on a bicycle or a horse. *vb.* put a saddle on; burden someone with a task or person.

safari (*sa-***far**-*ee*) *n.* an expedition, usually in a hot country, at one time for the purpose of hunting animals,

S

but today for observing and photographing them.

safe 1. *adj.* protected from danger. 2. *n.* a special strong, locked cabinet where money and other valuable things can be kept.

safeguard *vb.* protect *n.* something that prevents injury.

safety *n.* being safe from loss or injury. *The cattle were moved from the flooded fields to a place of safety.*

safety pin *n.* a pin that locks its sharp point into itself by means of a clasp.

saffron *n.* a type of crocus, the stigmas of whose flowers give us the powder called saffron which is used as a flavoring in food and as a yellow dye.

sag *vb.* droop, bend, hang down (especially in the middle).

saga (**sah**-*gah*) *n.* an old story, especially one that tells of the ancient Norse heroes of Scandinavia.

sage 1. *n.* perennial herb belonging to the mint family, the leaves of which are used in cooking as a seasoning. 2. *adj.* & *n.* wise; a wise person.

said *vb.* past of **say**.

sail *vb.* travel across water in a ship or boat, especially when the travel is powered by wind.

sailor *n.* a person who goes to sea in a ship, or who sails a boat; a member of a ship's crew.

saint *n.* an extremely good person, particularly one who has been recognized as holy by the church.

sake *n.* end; benefit; purpose. *For the sake of discussion, we will say it is true.*

salaam *n.* an Arabic word meaning peace, and a form of greeting in the East.

salad *n.* a mixture of uncooked vegetables such as lettuce, tomato, or cold cooked dish, served with dressing.

salamander *n.* a small amphibian with a lizardlike body.

salary *n.* the money paid to someone

for work performed.

sale *n.* 1. the act of selling. 2. the selling of goods cheaply.

saliva (*sal-eye-va*) *n.* spit; the liquid in your mouth.

salmon *n.* (plural same) a kind of fish that is highly prized as food.

salt *n.* a chemical compound formed, with water, when a metal or other substance reacts with an acid; common table salt, or sodium chloride. *You add salt to season or preserve food. adj.* having a **salty** taste. *adj.* containing salt. *It is easier to float in salt water than in fresh water.*

salute *vb.* & *n.* raise your stiffened hand to your forehead or hat as a form of greeting or honor.

salvage *vb.* save from loss or destruction.

salvation *n.* rescue, saving the soul.

salvo *n.* the firing of several guns at the same time.

same *adj.* similar to, or identical with something. *Sally and I go to the same school.*

samovar *n.* a Russian tea urn.

sampan *n.* a kind of Chinese boat.

sample *n.* an example of something, which can be used to show what the others are like. *vb.* judge quality of.

samurai *n.* a Japanese warrior of former times.

sanction *n.* & *vb.* allow, authorize.

sanctuary *n.* a safe place for people, or for birds and animals. *In a bird sanctuary it is against the law to hunt or kill the birds.*

sand *n.* tiny grains of minerals, mainly quartz, formed by the erosion of rocks, and often forming beaches.

sandal *n.* a kind of open shoe, attached to the foot by straps.

sandstone *n.* a rock consisting of grains of sand, mostly quartz, which have been compressed.

sandwich *n.* a kind of food, consisting of meat or other filling between two slices of bread.

sane *adj.* sensible, normal, sound in mind. **sanity** *n.*

sang *vb.* past of **sing**.

sanitary *adj.* of or concerning health, especially relating to cleanliness.

sank *vb.* past of **sink**.

Sanskrit *n. & adj.* a language of ancient India.

sap *n.* the juice in the stems of plants.

sapling *n.* a young tree.

sapphire *n.* transparent blue stone, valued as a gem; the hardest mineral known apart from diamond.

sarcasm *n.* a bitter remark of contempt or scorn, often ironical. **sarcastic** *adj.*

sarcophagus (*sar-***kof***-a-gus*) *n.* a stone coffin.

sardine *n.* a small fish of the herring family.

sari *n.* a length of cloth draped around the body as a dress, and worn mainly by Indian women.

sash *n.* 1. a band or scarf, worn across the shoulder or around the waist. 2. the frame and glass of a movable window.

sat *vb.* past of **sit**.

satan *n.* the devil; the evil one in many religions.

satchel *n.* a small bag, usually of leather or canvas.

satellite *n.* 1. a moon. 2. an artificial object put into orbit around the earth.

satin *n.* cloth with a shiny face and a dull back.

satire *n.* a form of comedy in which sarcasm and wit are used to ridicule people's follies.

satisfactory *adj.* adequate; all right, or good enough.

satisfied *vb.* past of **satisfy**.

satisfy *vb.* please, make someone contented. *He wanted to satisfy his teacher, so he did his homework carefully.* fulfill; comply with.

saturate *vb.* fill something, e.g. a sponge, so completely that no more can be absorbed.

Saturday *n.* the seventh day of the week, between Friday and Sunday; named after Saturn, Roman god of harvests.

sauce *n.* a liquid mixture served with some foods for added flavor.

saucepan *n.* a metal cooking pot with a handle and sometimes a lid.

saucer *n.* a small curved plate on which a cup stands.

saucy *adj.* cheeky, impudent. **sauciness** *n.*

sauna (**saw**-*na*) *n.* a kind of hot steam bath, of Finnish origin.

saunter *vb.* stroll, walk in a leisurely way.

sausage *n.* a chopped meat mixture which is made into a tube-shape inside a skin.

savage *adj.* wild and fierce; uncivilized. *vb.* attack and bite (of animals).

Indian women wearing the traditional sari.

savanna *n.* large areas of grassy African plains. The *llanos* and *campos* of South America are other examples of savanna vegetation.

save *vb.* 1. rescue. *The crew of the sinking ship were all saved.* 2. build up a reserve of money. *We are saving up for our summer holiday.* 3. keep for future use. 4. bring about spiritual salvation.

savings *pl. n.* the money someone has saved, often kept in a bank.

savior *n.* someone who saves you from danger. *Jesus Christ is often called the Savior.*

S

saw 1. *n.* a sharp tool with teeth for cutting wood. 2. *vb.* cut something with a saw. *How long will it take to saw those planks in half?* 3. *vb.* past of **see**.

sawdust *n.* dust of wood, made by sawing.

saxophone *n.* a metal woodwind musical instrument, played by blowing into it, used mainly in jazz bands.

say *vb.* speak; tell or announce something.

saying *n.* a well-known phrase or proverb. *"Too many cooks spoil the broth" is a saying.*

scab *n.* the dry protective crust that grows over a wound

scaffolding *n.* a structure of tubes and planks used when a building is being put up or repaired.

scald *vb.* & *n.* burn with hot liquid or steam.

scale 1. *n.* one of the thin pieces of hard skin that covers the bodies of fish and reptiles. 2. *n.* a series of measuring marks on an instrument such as a ruler or thermometer. 3. *n.* a set of musical tones arranged in order. 4. *vb.* climb something.

scalene *adj.* something with unequal sides and angles.

scales *n.* an instrument for measuring how much things weigh.

scalp *n.* the skin and hair on your head.

scalpel *n.* a small knife used by surgeons.

scan *vb.* 1. read over quickly. 2. pass a beam of light over (in television and radar). 3. (in poetry) have the correct rhythm.

scandal *n.* a disgraceful fact or event which causes outrage. **scandalize** *vb.* shock.

Scandinavia *n.* term used to include Denmark, Finland, Iceland, Norway and Sweden.

scar *n.* the mark left on skin from a wound, after it has healed. *vb.* mark with scars.

scarab *n.* a type of dung beetle, considered sacred by the ancient Egyptians.

scarce *adj.* rare, uncommon, in short supply. *Because of the fuel shortage, oil is very scarce.* **scarcity** *n.* being scarce, in short supply.

scare *vb.* frighten.

scarecrow *n.* figure of person dressed in old clothes set up in a field to frighten birds away from crops.

scarf *n.* (plural **scarves**) a piece of cloth, generally used to cover the head or shoulders.

scarlet *n.* & *adj.* bright red.

scatter *vb.* go off in different directions, to throw something so that it spreads out. *Jilly scattered crumbs on the bird table.*

scavenge *vb.* feed on carrion or garbage. **scavenger** *n.* *Dogs are terrible scavengers.*

scene (*seen*) *n.* 1. the place where something happens. *Luckily, there was a policeman at the scene of the accident.* 2. a section of a stage play; place represented on the stage.

scenery (**seen**-*ery*) *n.* 1. the natural features of a place, such as hills, fields and trees. 2. the painted curtains and screen used to make a theater stage look like a real place.

scent (*sent*) *n.* a smell, usually a pleasant one; a perfume; odor of an animal. *vb.* detect.

sceptic (**skep**-*tic*) *n.* a person who doubts the truth (of religion etc.) **sceptical** *adj.*

schedule (**sked**-*ule*) *vb.* & *n.* a timetable, a plan, a scheme.

scheme (*skeem*) *n.* & *vb.* plot, plan.

schism (**siz**-*um*) *n.* a break or split in a political party or religious group.

scholar *n.* a student; a clever person who has studied hard and knows a great deal; a person who has won a scholarship (prize) at a school or college. **scholarly** *adj.* learned.

scholarship *n.* money won by someone in an exam to pay school or university fees.

school *n.* 1. a place where children are educated; its building. 2. a group of fish swimming together.

S

schooner *n.* a fast sailing ship, generally with two masts.

science *n.* 1. knowledge got by studying, watching and testing. 2. study of physical world, e.g. physics, biology or astronomy. **scientific** *adj.*

science fiction *n.* stories that are based on imagined scientific events.

scientist *n.* a person who studies a scientific subject.

scissors *pl. n.* a tool with two blades joined together, which cut when they meet.

scoff *vb.* mock; make fun of.

scold *vb.* speak crossly to someone about what they have done or not done. *The teacher scolded them for being late for school.*

scone (*skon*) *n.* a small, flat round plain cake.

scoop 1. *n.* ladle or large spoon; *vb.* to spoon. 2. *n.* an important news story found in only one newspaper.

scooter *n.* 1. a vehicle with two wheels, a base, and a handlebar. 2. a motorscooter is a light kind of motorbike with a small engine.

scorch *vb.* darken the surface of something by burning it slightly. *n.* a slight burn.

score 1. *n.* a result in a game. *At the final whistle the score was two goals to one. vb.* gain points in a game. 2. *vb.* scratch or mark something. 3. *n.* an old-fashioned word for 20 4. *vb. & n.* copy of music showing all vocal and instrumental parts.

scorn *n. & vb.* feel or show contempt; despise.

scorpion *n.* a small creature of the spider family, with a poisonous sting in its tail.

Scotch *n. & adj.* whiskey and tweed from Scotland.

scot-free *adj.* without punishment.

scoundrel *n.* rogue, a person without principles.

scour *vb.* 1. clean thoroughly. 2. rush about looking for something.

scout *n.* 1. someone who is sent out ahead of the group to look for difficulties or dangers. 2. a member of a Scout Association.

scowl *n.* a cross look. *vb.* frown at.

scramble *vb.* 1. rush pell-mell. *We managed to scramble to the top of the hill.* 2. mix up, as in *scrambled eggs.*

scrap 1. *n.* a small piece of food; a fragment. 2. *vb.* get rid of something. 3. *n.* old cars or other metal objects that have been thrown away. 4. *n.* a fight.

scrapbook *n.* a book in which to save cut-out pictures, newspaper clippings and other papers.

scrape *vb.* 1. scratch; slide along. *Our dad scraped his car on the gate-post.* 2. only just succeed. *Bill barely scraped through his exam.*

scratch *vb.* drag a sharp point, such as a needle or fingernail, over something; rub with fingernails to relieve itching.

scrawl *vb. & n.* scribble; hasty or bad handwriting.

scream *n.* a high-pitched yell, usually of pain or fright. *vb.* give a sudden, harsh cry.

screen 1. *n.* a partition; a frame covered with wood or cloth, and used to hide something. *They put a screen around my bed in the hospital when the doctor came.* 2. *n.* upright surface on which films, etc., are projected; part of television or radar on which picture appears. 3. *vb.* protect someone. 4. *vb.* show on screen. 5. *vb.* investigate a person's life and character for reliability.

screw *n.* a nail with a spiral groove called the thread which pulls the screw into the wood. *vb.* fasten with a screw.

screwdriver *n.* a tool for driving screws into walls and other things.

scribble *vb.* scrawl, write carelessly; make untidy patterns with a pen or pencil. *Our teacher scolded me for scribbling in my book.*

scripture *n.* holy writings, especially the Bible.

scroll (rhymes with *hole*) *n.* a roll of paper with writing or pictures on it.

scrub 1. *vb.* clean by rubbing with a wet brush. 2. *n.* ground covered with shrubs, brushwood, etc.

scruff *n.* the back of the neck.

scruple *n.* a doubt because of what one's conscience says.

scull *vb.* row with small light oars called **sculls**.

sculptor *n.* a person who makes statues or carvings. **sculpt** *v.*

sculpture *n.* the art of making things from wood, stone or other hard materials; the product itself.

scum *n.* impurities that float to the surface of a liquid.

scurf *n.* flakes of dead skin on the scalp.

scythe ("sc" like "s") *n.* a tool with a curved blade for cutting grass or corn.

sea *n.* the big areas of salt water which cover most of the earth; the oceans.

sea anemone *n.* a soft-bodied, tube-like sea animal.

sea gull *n.* a bird that lives near the sea and eats fish.

sea horse *n.* a small fish with a horse-shaped head.

seal 1. *n.* a smoothly furred mammal which lives in or near the sea. 2. *vb.* close something by sticking its edges together. *We sealed the letter with glue.* 3. *n.* an impression stamped on to something to show that it is genuine. *The letter was stamped with the king's seal.*

sea level *n.* land that is at the same level as the sea. It is used to measure the height of all other land. *The hill was 40 feet above sea level.*

sea lion *n.* a sea mammal that is very similar to the seal but which has small ears on the outside.

seam *n.* the line where two pieces of cloth are sewn together.

search *vb.* look for thoroughly. *n.* the act of searching, an investigation.

seashell *n.* the hard covering of a sea creature, especially a mollusk.

seashore *n.* the seacoast; the land closest to the sea.

seaside *n.* the seashore; the district bordering the sea. *We are spending a week at the seaside.*

season *n.* a time period, one of the four divisions of the year called spring, summer, fall and winter.

seasoning *n.* flavoring added to food. **season** *vb.*

seat *n.* a piece of furniture for sitting on.

sea urchin *n.* a small spiny creature that lives on the seabed.

seaweed *n.* a large group of plants that grow in or near the sea.

seaworthy *adj.* a ship that is in a fit state to go to sea.

second 1. *adj.* the one after the first. *He came in second in the race.* 2. *n.* one-sixtieth of a minute. 3. *n.* the assistant to a boxer or duelist. 4. *vb.* give one's support to; endorse. *I second that idea.*

secondhand *adj.* already used, not new. *We bought my bike secondhand from a neighbor.*

secret *n.* a piece of information that is kept hidden, confidential.

secretary *n.* 1. an office worker who types letters and makes arrangements for other people. 2. company officer who keeps records of a company.

sect *n.* a group of people who have beliefs (especially religious) in common.

A gray seal. Seals are sea mammals.

seduce *vb.* tempt or lead astray.
seduction *n.* **seductive** *adj.*

see *vb.* (past **saw** past part. **seen**)
1. observe with the eyes. *Can you
see that star?* 2. understand. *Now I
see what you mean.*

see about *vb.* make arrangements for
something to happen. *I'll see about
ordering a Christmas tree.*

seed *n.* a tiny part of a plant from
which a new plant may grow.

seek *vb.* (past **sought**) look for; try
to obtain.

seem *vb.* appear to be. *He seems
honest enough, but you can never be
sure.* **seeming** *adj.* apparent but not
real.

see off *vb.* go with someone to the
place where they start a journey.

seesaw *n.* a long plank balanced on a
central support, which rocks up and
down when people sit on the ends.

seethe *vb.* cook by boiling.

segment *n.* one separate part of
something. *Oranges can be divided
into separate segments with your
fingers.*

segregate *vb.* keep apart or set away
from others. **segregation** *n.*

seize (rhymes with *sneeze*) *vb.* grab
something firmly, or by force;
snatch. *The mugger seized the
woman's handbag.*

seldom *adj.* not often.

select *vb.* choose from a group as
best or most suitable. *Ben was
selected from his class for the team.*
selection *n.* what is selected; things
from which to select.

self- *prefix* meaning by oneself or
itself, automatic, independent.

self *n.* (plural **selves**) a person's
individuality, most often used in
pronouns such as myself, yourself,
etc.

self-defense *n.* protecting yourself
against attack.

selfish *adj.* caring too much about
yourself and what you want, rather
than about other people.

self-service *n.* a restaurant, shop,
etc., set up so that the customers
can serve themselves.

*Seaweed provides food and shelter for
many sea animals. There are green,
brown and red seaweeds.*

section *n.* one of the parts into which
something can be divided. *The apple
was cut up and I got a section of it.*

sector *n.* any part of a circle between
two radii and the circumference.

secure 1. *adj.* safe, out of danger.
2. *vb.* fix something so that it is
safe. *The guard made sure the door
lock was secure.*

S

sell *vb.* (past **sold**) exchange something for money.

semaphore *n.* a system of sending messages with flags which you hold in the air.

semi- *prefix* meaning half, e.g. **semicircle, semidetached**.

send *vb.* (past **sent**) cause something or someone to go to a particular place; dispatch.

send off for *vb.* write asking for something you want to be sent to you. *I am going to send off for that record.*

senile *adj.* old and feebleminded.

senior *adj.* older in years, or more important than others.

señor *n.* the Spanish word for Mr. or Sir.

señora *n.* the Spanish word for Mrs. or Madam.

señorita *n.* the Spanish word for Miss.

sensation *n.* being aware through the senses; feeling; a thrilling event. *The first space flight was a sensation.* **sensational** *adj.*

sense 1. *n.* one of the ways your body has to tell you what is happening around you: sight, hearing, touch, smell and taste. 2. *n.* the meaning of something. *I can't make sense of what he is saying because he is talking too fast.*

sensible *adj.* behaving in an intelligent way. **sense** *n.* such behavior.

sensitive *adj.* affected by external stimulation, e.g. light. *The film is very sensitive to color.* easily hurt; delicate.

sent *vb.* past of **send**.

sentence 1. *n.* a group of words that make sense together. 2. *n.* a punishment given to a criminal by a law court. *The burglar got a sentence of two years in prison. vb.* pronounce sentence on.

sentimental *adj.* full of feelings (sentiments), especially soft, romantic ones; overly emotional.

sentry *n.* someone whose job is to guard something at a gate, etc.

sepal *n.* a kind of leaf that forms the outside part of a flower.

separate 1. *adj.* divided, not joined together. *The jigsaw came in 100 separate pieces.* 2. *vb.* divide up, sort out. *She asked me to separate the peas from the beans.* **separation** *n.*

September *n.* the ninth month of the year.

sequel *n.* the next part, continuation or installment of a story, etc.

sequence *n.* order of things coming after one another. *A sequence of events.*

sequoia *n.* one of a family of North American *conifers* (cone-bearing trees).

serene *adj.* calm, unruffled.

serf *n.* a person in history who belonged to the place where he lived, and to the lord who owned the land. *A serf was a kind of slave.*

sergeant *n.* a noncommissioned rank in the army, air force, or marines.

serial *n.* a story that is told in parts, instead of all at one time. *We watch the serial on TV every Sunday night.*

series *n.* a number of things that happen one after the other, and which belong together in some way. *Peter had a series of colds last winter.*

serious *adj.* thoughtful, not funny; important because of possible danger.

sermon *n.* a religious speech, lecture delivered from a pulpit.

serpent *n.* an old-fashioned word for a snake.

serrated *adj.* having teeth or notches on the edge. *A serrated knife.*

servant *n.* a person who is paid to work in the house of another person.

serve *vb.* 1. work for someone. 2. sell things in a shop. 3. give out the food at a meal.

service 1. *n.* occupation of a servant. 2. *pl. n.* the armed forces. 3. *n.* a set of utensils etc. *A dinner service containing 12 plates etc.* 4. *n.* supplying what is necessary. *Water, gas and electricity are essential services.* 5. *n.* a religious ceremony. 6. *n.* (in

tennis etc.) the act of serving a ball.
7. *vb*. maintenance (of a car etc.).

sesame *n*. an herb that is used for flavoring. The seeds are also used to make oil.

session *n*. a meeting or series of meetings in court to do business, etc.

set 1. *n*. a group of people or things that belong together. *We bought a set of table mats for our brother.* 2. *vb*. become hard. *The jelly was left to set overnight.* 3. *vb*. arrange things in a certain way. *Will you set the table for dinner, please?*

set about *vb*. begin to do something.

set eyes on *vb*. catch sight of something.

set in motion *vb*. start something off.

set sail *vb*. begin a voyage.

set off *vb*. start out on a journey.

settee *n*. a sofa, a long soft seat.

settle *vb*. 1. go to a place and stay there. *My uncle went to Canada to settle.* 2. decide something. *We couldn't agree which of us should eat the cake, so we asked Dad to settle the argument for us.* 3. pay a bill.

settlement *n*. 1. a place to where people have moved, built houses and decided to live. 2. terms of an agreement.

set upon *vb*. attack someone.

sever *vb*. cut or break; separate.

several *adj*. some, usually three or more, but not many. *There were several coats left in the hall.*

severe *adj*. strict or harsh, not gentle. *The weather was very severe.*

sew *vb*. (past **sewed** past part. **sewn**) join pieces of material together with a needle and thread. **sewing** *n*.

sewage *n*. human waste carried through drains by water.

sewer *n*. a large drain for taking away sewage and waste water.

sewing machine *n*. a machine for sewing cloth, leather, etc.

sex *n*. being male or female. **sexual** (*adj*.) desires.

sextant *n*. an instrument to measure angles. used in navigation.

shabby *adj*. worn-out; thin and faded. *He always wore a shabby old suit to the office.*

shack *n*. a hut, especially a roughly built one.

shade *n*. 1. out of direct sunlight. *The dog sat in the shade where it was cool.* 2. something which protects against strong light or heat. *The lampshade was made from paper.* 3. how dark or light a color is. *My shirt is a darker shade of green than yours.* *vb*. screen from light.

shadow 1. *n*. the dark shape cast by an object when it is in a strong light. 2. *vb*. follow someone closely, as a shadow does.

shady *adj*. shaded; uncertain; dishonest.

shaft *n*. 1. a long handle, such as the one on a spear. 2. a narrow, deep hole that leads to a mine or pit.

shaggy *adj*. having tangled hair.

shake *vb*. (past **shook** past part. **shaken**) move vigorously from side to side, or up and down. *In some countries, people shake hands with friends every time they meet.* tremble, vibrate. **shaky** *adj*. unsteady, trembling.

shall *auxiliary vb*. a word that indicates determination, or that something will happen in the future. *I shall get up early tomorrow morning.*

shallow *adj*. not deep. *The water was shallow and only covered my feet.*

shalom *interj*. a Jewish greeting.

shame 1. *n*. feeling sorry or regretful for having done something wrong; guilty feeling. 2. *n*. (*casual*) a regrettable thing. *What a shame you couldn't come.* 3. *vb*. make ashamed.

shampoo *n*. liquid for washing your hair. *vb*. wash your hair.

shamrock *n*. the name for some kinds of clover.

Shangri-la *n*. an imaginary place where everything is almost perfect.

S

shan't *vb.* abbr. of **shall not**.

shanty *n.* 1. crudely built hut or dwelling, usually of wood. *This area is known as shantytown.*

shape *n.* the outline of something; what appearance it has. *The soap was made in the shape of a bear. vb.* give shape to. **shapely** *adj.* **shapeless** *adj.*

share *vb.* divide and distribute something among a group. *Annie shared her candy with us.*

shark *n.* a family of large, fierce fish.

sharp 1. *adj.* having a pointed end or fine edge that cuts things easily. 2. *adj.* sudden or quick. *There was a sharp bend in the road.* 3. *n.* a musical note raised by a semitone. **sharpen** *vb.* make sharp.

shatter *vb.* break into small pieces.

shave *vb.* & *n.* cut hair off parts close to the skin. *Most men shave their chin every day.* **shaving** *n.*

shawl *n.* a cloth worn about the shoulders for warmth or for decoration.

sheaf *n.* (plural **sheaves**) a bundle of grain stalks tied together after they have been harvested.

shear *vb.* cut the wool from a sheep.

shears *pl. n.* a pair of scissors with large blades, used for cutting heavy fabrics, shearing sheep etc.

sheath *n.* a cover for a sword or a knife. **sheathe** *vb.*

shed 1. *n.* a small hut. 2. *vb.* let things fall off or drop away. *Some trees shed their leaves in the fall.*

sheen *n.* glossiness, brightness.

sheep *n.* (plural **sheep**) a common farm animal with a woolly coat.

sheepdog *n.* a dog used to herd or guard sheep.

sheer *adj.* 1. very steep, like the side of a cliff. 2. of fine material, can be seen through.

sheet *n.* a thin, flat, rectangular piece of metal, paper or fabric; bed covering of linen, cotton, etc.

sheik (*sheak*) *n.* an Arab chief.

shekel *n.* the main unit of currency of Israel.

sheldrake *n.* a European wild duck.

shelf *n.* (plural **shelves**) a plank fixed to a wall, etc., on which to keep books or other articles.

shell 1. *n.* a thin hard outer covering. 2. *n.* explosive artillery projectile. 3. *vb.* remove shell from.

Two kinds of shark: the thresher (above) and the hammerhead.

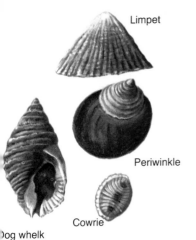

Limpet

Periwinkle

Cowrie

Dog whelk

shellfish *n.* a soft-bodied water animal that lives inside a shell for protection.

shelter *n.* a place that protects you, e.g. from unpleasant weather. *vb.* serve as a shelter; take shelter.

shepherd *vb. & n.* a person who looks after sheep for a living. **shepherdess** *n. fem.*

sheriff *n.* a law officer.

sherry *n.* a wine fortified with brandy originally from the Cadiz region of Spain.

shield 1. *n.* a large piece of metal, leather, etc., used to protect the person who carries it against attack. 2. *vb.* cover or protect something. *He used his hand to shield his eyes from the glare.*

shift *vb.* change the position of something. *Graham wants to shift the table into the corner of the room.*

shilling *n.* a coin used in several countries before decimal currency. A British shilling was worth five new pence, and there were 20 shillings in a pound (£1).

shin *n.* the front of the leg between the knee and the ankle.

shine *vb.* (past **shone**) give out a steady beam of light. **shiny** *adj.*

shingle *n.* slate or wood part for roofs and house sides.

ship *n.* a large seagoing boat. *vb.* take or send by carrier.

shipwreck *n.* an accident in which a ship is sunk or badly damaged at sea; a wrecked ship.

shipyard *n.* a place where ships are built or repaired out of the water.

shire *n.* 1. a county. 2. large horse once used for pulling heavy loads.

shirk *vb.* run away from, avoid doing. *She shirked her responsibilities.*

shirt *n.* an article of clothing for the top half of the body, with sleeves and a collar.

shiver *vb.* shake with cold or fear.

shoal *n.* a group of fish swimming together.

shock *n.* an unpleasant surprise. **shocking** *adj.* scandalous, very bad.

shoe *n.* a protective covering for the foot.

shone *vb.* past of **shine**.

shook *vb.* past of **shake**.

shoot 1. *vb.* use a gun, or a bow and arrow; wound with gun. 2. *vb.* go quickly. 3. *vb.* photograph with a camera. 4. *n.* the tip of a growing plant. 5. *vb.* kick for a goal at soccer.

shop 1. *n.* a room or building where goods are sold. 2. *vb.* buy things from a shop. **shopper** *n.*

shopkeeper *n.* a person who owns or looks after a shop.

shoplifter *n.* a person who steals from a shop.

shop steward *n.* a spokesperson elected by workers.

shore *n.* the land along the edge of a sea or lake.

short 1. *adj.* the opposite of long or tall. *Both his parents are very short.* **shorten**. *vb.* make or become short in length or time. 2. *adv.* to be lacking in something. *I am running short of envelopes.* **shortage** *n.*

shortbread *n.* thick cookie made of flour, sugar and shortening.

shortcoming *n.* a failing, defect.

shorthand *n.* a way of writing quickly by means of symbols.

shortly *adv.* soon, before long.

shorts *pl. n.* short trousers that end above your knees.

shortsighted *adj.* 1. condition of someone who can see clearly when things are close, but cannot see things farther away; nearsighted 2. lacking foresight.

shot *vb.* past of **shoot**.

shot *n.* 1. the firing of a gun. *We heard a shot in the distance.* 2. an attempt to do something. 3. injection of a drug. 4. lead pellets in the cartridge of a shotgun.

shot put *n.* an Olympic event which involves throwing a heavy metal ball as far as possible with one hand. The ball weighs (16 pounds) for men, (8 pounds 13 ounces) for women.

should *vb.* a word meaning "ought to." *I should apologize to her.*

shoulder *n.* the part of your body from your neck to your arm. *vb.* push with shoulder; assume responsibility. *She shouldered the job of bringing up her brother's children.*

shout *vb. & n.* call out or speak loudly; a loud cry. *My grandfather is a bit deaf, so you'll need to shout.*

shove *vb. & n.* push.

shovel *n.* a large spade with a curved blade to lift and toss material. *vb.* use a shovel.

show 1. *vb.* (past part. **shown**) let something be seen. *Show me what you have written.* 2. *n.* a play or other entertainment. *The artist arranged a show of his paintings.*

shower *n.* 1. a short period of light rain. 2. a special device for sprinkling water over oneself as a form of bathing.

show off *vb.* display proudly; try to make people think you do something very well.

show up *vb.* 1. expose. 2. arrive.

shrapnel *n.* fragments from a bomb, etc.

shred *vb.* tear or cut into pieces. *n.* a narrow, torn-off piece.

shriek *n. & vb.* a high-pitched scream.

shrill *adj.* high and loud (of a sound).

shrimp *n.* a small edible shellfish with a long tail.

shrink *vb.* (past **shrank**) get or make smaller. *Wool often shrinks in hot water.*

shrub *n.* a bushy plant, like a small tree.

shrug *vb.* raise or lift the shoulders. *n.* a symbol of indifference.

shrug off *vb.* brush aside; take no notice of.

shrunk *vb.* past part. of **shrink**.

shudder *vb. & n.* tremble convulsively with cold or fear.

shuffle 1. *vb.* mix cards so that they are not in any special order.

shun *vb.* avoid, keep away from.

shut *vb.* close. *Shut that door.*

shutter *n.* 1. a cover for a window. 2. part of a camera.

shuttle *n.* an instrument used in weaving for carrying thread back and forth.

shuttlecock *n.* a cork filled with feathers that is hit back and forth in the game of badminton.

shuttle service *n.* an aircraft or train that travels regularly between two places.

shy 1. *adj.* not liking to meet other people. 2. *vb.* turn away in sudden fear. *Horses sometimes shy away from strange objects.*

sick 1. *adj.* ill, not well. *Feeling sick to your stomach means you feel like you will vomit.* **sicken** *vb.* begin to feel ill; feel loathing. **sickening** *adj.* nauseating. **sickness** *n.* ill health; a disease.

sickle *n.* a reaping tool with a curved blade and short handle.

side *n.* 1. the edge, wall or boundary of something. 2. the part of your body between the armpit and the hip. 3. a team in a game, or a country in wartime.

sideways *adj.* with one side first. *Crabs move sideways along the ground.*

siege ("ie" as in "ee") *n.* a time when an army surrounds (besieges) a town or building so that people cannot get in or out.

siesta (*see-yes-ta*) *n.* an afternoon nap.

sieve (rhymes with *give*) *n.* a frame with a stiff net, used to separate small things from larger ones or to drain off liquid.*vb.* use a sieve.

sift *vb.* put through a sieve.

sigh (rhymes with *die*) *vb. & n.* breathe out loudly, usually to show that you are tired, bored or sad.

sight *n.* 1. the ability to see. *Sight is one of the five senses.* 2. something that is seen by someone. *We saw a very strange sight on the beach.*

sign 1. *n.* board with words or pictures to give information to people. *The sign said "danger."* 2. *vb.* write your own name on something. 3. *n.* a mark or clue that has a special meaning. *The footprints were a sign that someone had been to the house.*

signal 1. *n.* a sound or movement that has a special meaning, especially from a distance. *Car drivers have to signal before they turn.* 2. *vb.* send a message. *He used semaphore to signal the news.*

signature *n.* someone's name written in his or her own writing.

significance *n.* the importance of; the meaning of. *What is the significance of a dog wagging its tail?*

signor *n.* (plural **signori**) the Italian word for Mr. or Sir.

signora *n.* (plural **signore**) the Italian word for Mrs. or Madam.

signorina *n.* the Italian word for Miss.

signpost *n.* a post bearing a sign that tell travelers the direction and distance of places.

silage ("i" rhymes with "eye") *n.* animal fodder made from green crops and preserved in a silo.

silence *n.* a time of complete stillness.*vb.* make silent.

silent *adj.* without any sound.

silhouette *n.* the outline or shape of something.

silicon *n.* after oxygen the most common element in the Earth's crust. It is found in quartz.

silk *n.* a natural fiber from the cocoon of the silkworm moth. **silky** *adj.* like silk.

sill *n.* the ledge along the bottom of a window.

silly *adj.* stupid, foolish; frivolous.

silt *n.* deposit of fine soil left by a river. *vb.* become choked with silt.

silver 1. *n.* a valuable, whitish, shiny metal (symbol – *Ag*); coins made from metal of the same color. 2. *n. & adj.* a color that looks like the metal.

silver screen *n.* a screen on which to show motion pictures.

similar *adj.* like something else, but not exactly the same; of the same kind. *Robyn has a dress similar to mine, but hers has red bows instead of blue ones.*

simmer *vb.* cook in a liquid just below boiling point.

simple *adj.* 1. easy; not difficult. *This game is simple.* 2. basic; not complicated. *A screw is a simple machine.* **simplify** *vb.* make simple.

sin *n.* breaking a religious law, or doing something that is known to be wrong. *vb.* commit a sin.

since 1. *prep.* from a time past. *We haven't met since we were little.* 2. *adv.* because. *I often meet John, since we live in the same street.*

sincere *adj.* honest, true.

sing *vb.* (past **sang** past part. **sung**) use the voice to make musical sounds.

singe *vb.* burn something slightly at the edges.

singer *n.* a person who sings, earns money by singing, etc.

single *adj.* 1. just one. *You have only a single chance in this game.* 2. *adj.* unmarried.

singular *n. & adj.* 1. one person or thing, not plural. 2. *adj.* exceptional.

sinister *adj.* frightening, something that seems evil.

sink 1. *vb.* (past **sank** past part. **sunk**) drop down; decline. *A stone will sink to the bottom of a pool.* 2. *n.* a basin with drain and water supply, for washing things in.

S

sip *vb.* drink in small quantities.

siphon *n.* tube for transferring liquid, from one vessel to a lower one; once it is full of liquid, the difference in pressure at the ends of the tube ensures a continuous flow. *vb.* draw through a siphon.

Sir *n.* the title placed before the name of a knight or baronet. *Sir John Smith.* a polite way of addressing a man.

siren *n.* an instrument for making a loud warning signal, like a police siren.

sister *n.* a daughter of the same parents as someone; a nun.

sit *vb.* (past **sat**) rest on your bottom.

site *n.* a place for structures. *There was a bulldozer on the building site.* *vb.* locate or place.

situate *vb.* place, locate.

situation *n.* a place or position; a temporary state or condition. *The situation is serious.* a set of circumstances.

size *n.* measurement, showing how large or small something is.

skate *n.* a steel blade fixed to a boot for fast movement on ice. *vb.* glide on skates.

skeleton *n.* the framework of bones in the body of an animal.

sketch *vb. & n.* draw quickly and roughly; an outline.

skewbald *n. & adj.* (a horse) marked in white and patches of color other than black.

ski *n.* long strips of wood or other material fixed to boots for fast movement over snow. *vb.* travel on skis.

skid *vb.* slip out of control. *Cars often skid on icy roads.*

skill *n.* the ability to do something very well. **skillful** *adj.*

skim *vb.* 1. remove scum from the surface of a liquid. 2. pass lightly over.

skimp *vb.* give too little attention to; use too little of.

skin 1. *n.* the covering on the outside of the body. 2. *vb.* remove the skin of an animal; strip or peel off.

The human skeleton is made up of 206 bones. The central supporting part is the spine, which consists of 33 vertebrae.

skin diving *vb.* going underwater without a full diving suit and breathing line.

skinny *adj.* thin, lean.

skip *vb.* hop or jump, as over a jump rope.

skipper *n.* the captain of a ship or boat.

skirt *n.* a piece of clothing worn by women around the lower half of the body, and not divided like trousers. *vb.* go around edge or border of.

skull *n.* the bony frame of the head.

skunk *n.* a North American mammal, related to the weasel and badger, which secretes a foul odor.

sky *n.* the dome of the heavens overhead.

skydiving *n.* a form of parachute jumping.

skylight *n.* a window in the roof of a building.

skyline *n.* the silhouette or outline of things against the sky.

skyscraper *n.* a very tall building with many floors.

slab *n.* a thick slice. *This slab of marble is too heavy to carry.*

slack *adj.* 1. loose. *That rope is too slack.* 2. careless; lazy. **slacken** *vb.* make or become slack.

slain *vb.* past of **slay.**

slam *vb. & n.* shut (a door) very hard and noisily; the noise made by slamming.

slander *n. & vb.* damage a person's character by spreading lies. **slanderous** *adj.*

slang *n.* a way of using words that is thought to be less correct than other ways. *"Cop" is slang for police officer.*

slant *vb. & n.* a slope, like the one a ladder makes when it is up against a wall; attitude; bias.

slap *vb.* hit something with the flat of the hand. *n.* a blow.

slash *vb.* make long cuts in something. *n.* a slashing cut.

slate 1. *n.* a grayish kind of rock, which can be split into thin sheets for use as a roofing material. 2. *n.* a writing tablet, made of slate, formerly used in schools.

slaughter *vb.* kill, usually when many animals or people are killed at once. *n.* killing of animals for food.

slave *n.* a person who is owned by someone else, and has to work without pay, doing exactly what the owner wants. **slavery** *n.*

slay *vb.* kill violently.

sled *n.* a small vehicle used for traveling over snow or ice. *A sled has runners made from strips of wood or metal instead of wheels.*

sleep *n.* the time when you are unconscious and resting. *I average eight hours' sleep a night.* *vb.* be or fall asleep.

sleeping bag *n.* a padded bag for sleeping in, often used when camping.

sleepy *adj.* tired; full of sleep; ready for bed.

sleet *n.* a mixture of rain and snow which falls very hard.

sleeve *n.* 1. the part of an article of clothing that covers the arm. 2. a tubular cover that fits over a machine part.

sleigh (rhymes with *ray*) *n.* a large vehicle used for traveling over snow or ice. Some sleighs have engines, others are pulled by animals.

slender *adj.* thin, narrow.

slept *vb.* past of **sleep.**

slew *vb.* past of **slay.**

slice 1. *n.* a thin piece cut from something, such as a loaf of bread. 2. *vb.* cut something into slices.

slick *n.* patch of oil on water.

slide 1. *vb.* move smoothly over something. *It's fun to slide on the ice in winter.* 2. *n.* a slippery chute, often in a park, on which children climb and slide. 3. *n.* a piece of glass, film, etc., for use in a microscope or projector.

slight 1. *adj.* small, not important. *Belinda made a slight mistake.* 2. *vb.* ignore; treat with contempt.

slim *adj.* thin, slender. *vb.* to become thinner.

slime *n.* unpleasantly wet, slippery substance. **slimy** *adj.*

sling 1. *n.* a piece of cloth used to support an injured arm. 2. a loop of leather used for throwing stones,

sometimes also called a slingshot.
3. *vb*. hurl. 4. *vb*. hang or suspend from something.

slink *vb*. move away slowly and quietly (in fear or shame).

slip *vb*. miss your footing; slide.

slipper *n*. a soft shoe worn in the house.

slippery *adj*. easy to slip or slide on, such as an icy or oily surface.

slit 1. *n*. a long, narrow hole. 2. *vb*. make a cut in something.

slope *vb*. & *n*. a slanting place, an incline, especially on a hill.

sloppy *adj*. messy, untidy; over-sentimental.

slot *n*. a narrow opening in something that smaller things can be pushed through. *Some front doors have slots for letters.*

sloth (rhymes with *cloth*) *n*. 1. a tree-dwelling mammal found in tropical America. 2. laziness.

slow *adj*. moving at a sluggish pace;

A two-toed sloth.

not fast; taking a long time to do; (of clocks) behind correct time.

slug *n*. a crawling land mollusk, related to the snail, but with little or no shell.

slum *n*. an overcrowded area with old, poor-quality houses.

slump *vb*. & *n*. fall suddenly or heavily; a decline in trade.

sly *adj*. clever at tricking people in secret; cunning.

smack *vb*. hit hard with the flat part of your hand. *n*. a slap; the sound of a smack.

small *adj*. little; tiny; not large.

smallpox *n*. a very contagious disease.

smart 1. *adj*. clever. 2. *adj*. well-dressed, neat. 3. *n*. & *vb*. (cause or have) a sharp, stinging pain.

smash *vb*. break something to pieces.

smear *vb*. & *n*. daub; spread grease or paint roughly over a surface.

smell 1. *n*. the sense which tells you what scent something has. 2. *vb*. use your sense of smell; to sniff. 3. *n*. a scent, often unpleasant.

smelly *adj*. having an unpleasant odor.

smelt 1. *vb*. separate a metal from its ore by heating to a high temperature. 2. *n*. a kind of fish.

smile *vb*. turn up the corners of the mouth as a sign of pleasure or amusement; grin. *n*.

smith *n*. someone who makes things from metal. *A goldsmith makes jewelry and ornaments from gold.*

smog *n*. heavily polluted, smoky air. *The word "smog" is made up from "smoke" and "fog.".*

smoke 1. *n*. the grayish vapor given off by a fire. 2. *vb*. smoke cigarettes or other kinds of tobacco; emit smoke. *The chimney smokes.* **smoker** *n*. a person who smokes tobacco.

smolder *vb*. burn very slowly, without a flame.

smooth *adj*. even or slippery; gentle to the touch. *That floor has a very smooth surface now that it has been sanded and polished. vb.* make smooth.

smother *vb*. deprive of air; stifle by covering with a blanket, etc.

smudge *n*. dirty mark, blur, stain.

smug *adj*. highly self-satisfied.

smuggle *vb*. take things into a country secretly by hiding them. *Smuggling is against the law.*

snack *n*. a small, quick meal.

snaffle *n*. a kind of bit in the harness of a horse.

snag *n*. an unexpected difficulty.

snail *n.* a small mollusk with a soft body and a hard protective shell.

snake *n.* a long, thin reptile without legs or eyelids. *Some snakes are poisonous.*

snap 1. *vb.* break suddenly. 2. *vb.* bite at someone suddenly. *Dogs sometimes snap at unfriendly people.* 3. **snap**(**shot**) *n.* a photograph.

snare *n. & vb.* a trap for animals.

snarl *vb.* growl and show teeth, as an angry dog does.

snatch *vb.* take away quickly. *The cat tried to snatch the fish from the plate.* *n.* a sudden grab.

sneak *vb.* to move stealthily, quietly, furtively. *He sneaked away.* *n.* an underhanded person.

sneer *vb.* (at) scoff, show contempt. *n.* a scornful smile, etc.

sneeze *n. & vb.* a sudden rush of air through the nose, caused by an irritation of the mucous membrane.

sniff *vb.* draw in air quickly and audibly through your nose. *n.* act of sniffing.

snippet *n.* a small piece. *He read a snippet from the newspaper.*

snob *n.* someone who admires people only if they are rich or important. **snobbish** *adj.*

snooker *n.* a game played on a billiard table, using balls and a cue.

snooze *vb. & n.* (take) a short sleep; nap.

snore *vb. & n.* (make) a noise through the nose or mouth when asleep.

snorkel *n.* a tube for breathing air through when you are under the water.

snort *vb. & n.* noise made by forcing air violently through the nose.

snout *n.* an animal's nose.

snow *n. & vb.* flakes of frozen water that fall from the sky in very cold weather.

snowball 1. *n.* a ball of compressed snow. *The children were having great fun throwing snowballs at each other.* 2. *vb.* grow or increase rapidly.

snowdrop *n.* a green and white flower that grows in early spring.

snowstorm *n.* a heavy fall of snow with a high wind; a blizzard.

snug *adj.* warm and cozy.

soak *vb.* leave something in liquid for a very long time.

soap *n.* a substance made from oil or fat and used for cleaning things. *vb.* lather with soap.

soar (rhymes with *door*) *vb.* fly high in the sky.

sob *vb.* cry noisily.

sober *adj.* sensible, levelheaded; not drunk.

soccer *n.* a ball game played between two teams, each with 11 players.

social *adj.* 1. living together in groups. *Ants are social insects.* 2. to do with people and how they live. *My aunt works in the social services office in our town.*

socialism *n.* a politicial doctrine which places the means of production and distribution in the hands of all the people.

society *n.* all the people who live in a group or country, and the way they live and meet.

sock *n.* an article of clothing worn on the foot, beneath a shoe; a short stocking.

A single large snowflake may be made up of thousands of tiny ice crystals.

S

socket *n.* a hole into which something fits. *Jack put the bulb into the electric light socket.*

soda *n.* washing soda (*sodium carbonate*), baking soda (*sodium bicarbonate*), caustic soda (*sodium hydroxide*).

sodium *n.* a silvery-gray metal (symbol – *Na*) that is so soft that it can be cut with a knife.

sofa *n.* an upholstered soft seat for two or more people.

soft *adj.* not hard; having a shape that is easily changed; comfortable. **soften** *vb.* make soft.

soil 1. *n.* the earth in which plants live and grow. 2. *vb.* stain with dirt.

solar *adj.* to do with the sun. *Some people heat water with solar energy.*

sold *vb.* past of **sell**.

solder *n.* an alloy, usually of tin and lead, having a low melting point, used for joining (**soldering**) certain metals. *vb.* join using solder.

soldier *n.* a member of an army.

sole 1. *n.* the flat part underneath your foot or your shoe. 2. *n.* a flat sea fish. 3. *adj.* just one thing or person. *He was the sole member of the class to fail the test.*

solemn *adj.* serious, thoughtful.

solicitor *n.* lawyer.

solid 1. *n.* anything that can be touched, and is not a liquid or a gas. 2. *adj.* not hollow, with no space inside. *The ball was made of solid rubber.* **solidify** *vb.* make or become solid.

solitary *adj.* alone, lonely.

solo *adj.* on your own. *Jane gave a solo performance on her guitar.*

soluble *adj.* capable of dissolving.

solve *vb.* find the answer to a problem or puzzle. **solution** *n.* the answer.

somber *adj.* gloomy.

some *pron. & adj.* part of something; not all; not everyone; an unspecified amount.

somebody *n.* a person, particularly when you are not sure who it is. *Somebody has stolen my purse.*

someplace *adv.* somewhere.

Top-soil (rich in humus) — Sub-soil — Weathered rock

A fertile soil is rich in humus, bacteria and minerals. Humus is made from rotting vegetation.

somersault *vb. & n.* turn head over heels.

something *n.* anything; any object. *I've got something in my eye.*

sometime *adv.* at an unknown time in the future. *I hope we meet again sometime.*

sometimes *adv.* occasionally; from time to time; not often. *I sometimes play tennis on weekends.*

somewhere *adv.* at some place. *I've left my pen somewhere but I can't remember where.*

son *n.* someone's male child.

sonar *n.* an apparatus that uses sounds and their echoes to locate objects in deep water.

sonata *n.* musical composition, especially for piano, generally having three movements.

song *n.* a short poem set to music and sung.

sonic boom *n.* disturbing bang, like an explosion, heard on the ground when an aircraft flies faster than the speed of sound; caused by shock waves set up by the aircraft.

sonnet *n.* a poem of 14 lines with a fixed rhyme scheme, e.g. ababcdcdefefgg.

soon *adv.* in a short time. *I'll have to go soon.*

soot *n.* black flakes or powder left behind, particularly in a chimney, after a fire.

soothe *vb.* make someone calm when he or she is upset or angry.
soothing *adj.*

sophomore *n.* second-year student.

sorcerer (**sors**-*er-er*) *n.* a magician; someone who can cast magic spells.

sore *adj. & n.* something that hurts when it is touched, like a bruise; painful.

sorrow *adj.* sadness, grief.

sorry *adj.* regretful. *I'm sorry I'm late.*

sort 1. *n.* things grouped by a common feature; kind. *What sort of person is he?* 2. *vb.* arrange things according to class or kind; classify. *Please sort the laundry by color.*

sought *vb.* past of **seek**.

soul (rhymes with *hole*) *n.* the part of a person that is thought to live forever, especially by religious people.

sound *n.* anything that you can hear.

sound barrier *n.* the speed of sound. *When a plane travels faster than sound, it goes through the sound barrier.*

soup (rhymes with *loop*) *n.* a liquid food made from meat or vegetables cooked in water, milk, etc.

sour *adj.* sharp-tasting like lemons, not sweet; bad tempered.

source *n.* the starting point, the beginning. *This river's source is in that mountain.*

south *n.* the direction opposite north on a compass.

souvenir *n.* something that you keep to remind you of a place, person, or an event.

sovereign *n.* a king or queen; supreme ruler.

sow (rhymes with *how*) *n.* a female pig.

sow (rhymes with *so*) *vb.* (past **sowed** past part **sown**) put seeds in the ground so that they grow.

soybean *n.* a bushy plant, native to Asia, grown for its seeds (beans) which are rich in protein.

space *n.* 1. the distance between things. *How much space did you leave on the bookshelf?* 2. the blank area between written words on lines. 3. the region beyond the earth's atmosphere. *The sun, moon and stars are all in space.*

spacecraft *n.* a vehicle that orbits the earth, or travels in space, away from earth.

The Mercury spacecraft was the first American man-made satellite to carry a man.

spade *n.* 1. a tool for digging the ground. 2. a playing card of the suit called spades.

spaghetti *pl. n.* long thin rods of pasta (dried paste made of wheat flour).

197

S

span *vb*. extend from one side of something to the other. *The bridge had to span a very wide river.* *n*. distance between piers of bridge.

spaniel *n*. any of a number of kinds of dogs having feathered tail and legs and large drooping ears.

spank *vb*. hit, usually on someone's bottom, as a punishment.

spar *vb*. to take part in a practice bout of boxing.

spare *adj*. extra to what is needed. *You can use my spare pen.* *vb*. do without. *I can spare you the afternoon.*

spark *n*. a tiny glowing bit from a fire; a flash of light.

sparkle *vb*. flash with light, send out sparks, glitter.

sparrow *n*. a small seed-eating bird.

spasm *n*. involuntary and abnormal muscle contractions.

spat *vb*. past of **spit**.

spawn *n*. the eggs of fish and other water animals, such as frogs. *vb*. produce or deposit eggs.

speak *vb*. (past **spoke** past part. **spoken**) talk; communicate aloud by using words.

spear *n*. a weapon made from a long pole with a sharp point on the end. *vb*. pierce with a spear.

special *adj*. different from others, and usually better than them, exceptional. *My birthday is a very special day for me.*

speciality *n*. 1. something a person is especially good at. *Tina's speciality was cooking.* 2. a special or distinctive product.

specialize *vb*. study and become an expert in one subject, etc. *This college specializes in science.*

species *n*. a group of animals or plants that are alike in some way. *Mice are a species of rodent, and so are rats.*

specific gravity *n*. the density of a substance compared with the density of water at 39°F (4°C). If, for example, a substance is twice as dense as water, then it has a specific gravity (S.G.) of two.

specify *vb*. name or state in detail.

specification *n*. detailed description of an item or of work that needs to be done.

specimen *n*. a sample, a small amount or an example of something that shows what the rest are like.

speck *n*. a tiny amount of something, usually dust.

spectacles *pl. n*. a pair of eyeglasses worn to help you see better.

spectator *n*. someone watching a game or other entertainment, an onlooker. *The spectators cheered when Kevin scored a goal.*

spectrum *n*. when a ray of light passes through certain materials, especially glass, it splits into bands of colors called a spectrum, which looks like a rainbow.

speculate *vb*. 1. ponder. 2. buy or sell shares of property or stock in the hope of making a profit.

speech *n*. 1. speaking. 2. a talk given to a group of people.

speed *n*. how fast something or someone moves. *vb*. go fast.

speedometer *n*. an instrument for measuring how fast a vehicle is moving.

spell 1. *vb*. indicate letters of a word in the correct order. 2. *n*. magic words that are supposed to make something happen in a strange way. *The witch's spell turned the prince into a frog.* 3. *n*. a period of time. *A spell of fine weather.*

spend *vb*. (past **spent**) 1. use money to buy things. *How much do you spend on bus fares each week?* 2. stay a period of time. 3. use a period of time for some activity.

spew *vb*. throw up, vomit.

sphere *n*. a round object, e.g. a ball.

sphinx *n*. in mythology, the sphinx was a fabulous monster of the ancient world with a winged lion's body and a human or animal head.

spice *n*. vegetable products used to flavor and preserve food. *vb*. flavor with spice.

spider *n*. a small animal with eight legs. *Some spiders make webs to catch insects.*

spied *vb.* past of **spy**.

spies *n.* plural of **spy**.

spike *n.* a long thin object with a sharp point; a large headless nail. *vb.* fix with spikes.

spill *vb.* let something fall out of its container. *Did you spill the salt on the table?*

spilled *vb.* past of **spill**.

spin *vb.* (past **span** past part. **spun**) 1. turn around quickly in one place like a top. 2. make thread by twisting fibers together; make a web.

spinach *n.* a leafy green vegetable with a high iron and vitamin A and C content.

spinal column *n.* see **spine**.

spine *n.* the long line of bones down the middle of your back, the backbone; spinal column. **spineless** *adj.* lacking character.

spiral *vb. & n.* the shape a line makes when it circles around, like the thread of a screw.

spire *n.* the tall pointed part of a church or other building; steeple.

spirit *n.* 1. a soul. 2. a ghost. 3. courage. 4. *pl. n.* alcohol.

spit *vb.* (past **spat**) throw out saliva from mouth.

splash *vb.* throw water about. *n.* the sound of splashing; a patch of color.

splashdown *n.* the landing of a spacecraft in the sea on completion of a mission.

splendid *adj.* very good; very impressive in some way; magnificent. *We saw a splendid castle when we visited Mexico.*

splinter *n.* a small, sharp piece of wood or other material. *vb.* break into splinters.

split *vb.* break something into parts. *The class split up and went off in different directions. n.* a splitting.

spoil *vb.* 1. impair. *That pole spoils the view.* 2. treat a child or other person indulgently. *The old man tended to spoil his grandchildren.*

spoke *vb.* past of **speak**.

spoke *n.* radiating bar connecting the hub and rim of a wheel.

sponge *n.* 1. a sea animal with a very light, soft body. 2. a soft object used for washing, once made from the sea animal, but today usually made of plastic. *vb.* wipe with a sponge.

sponsor *n.* 1. a godfather or godmother. 2. a person or company paying for radio or TV advertising; a person or company who supports financially an athlete, etc.

spoon *n.* a device with a handle and bowl for eating liquids and other food.

spore *n.* the tiny dustlike cell from which some plants grow. *Ferns and mushrooms have spores instead of seeds.*

sport *n.* activity, pleasurable games. *Football, tennis and baseball are all sports.*

spot 1. *n.* a small area. *This is a pleasant spot.* 2. *vb.* pick out someone or something. *Can you spot your friend in the crowd?* 3. *n.* a blob. 4. *n.* a spot light.

spotlight *n.* a strong beam of light that can be moved around.

spouse *n.* husband or wife.

spout 1. *n.* the part of something, such as a teapot, where the liquid comes out. 2. *vb.* gush. *Whales spout when they get to the surface to get rid of stale air.* 3. *vb.* (*casual*) go on speaking. *He could spout poetry for hours.*

sprain *vb.* damage a joint, such as your ankle, by tearing or straining the ligaments. *James sprained his ankle roller-skating. n.* such injury.

sprang *vb.* past of **spring**.

sprawl *vb. & n.* spread out carelessly. *Adrian's books are sprawled all over the office.*

spray *vb. & n.* (squirt) a liquid in a fine mist.

spread *vb. & n.* extend; cover something. *There's no need to spread the butter so thickly on your toast.*

sprightly *adj.* light and lively. *Grandma is a sprightly woman for her age.*

S

spring 1. *vb.* move suddenly upward. *The tiger springs quickly at the goat.* 2. *n.* one of the seasons of the year, when plants begin to grow again after winter. 3. *n.* a place where water comes out of the ground. 4. *n.* a piece of metal able to return to its original shape or position after being forced into another.

sprinkle *vb.* scatter or pour out in particles or small drops. *He sprinkled salt over his food.*

sprint *vb. & n.* run at top speed, especially for a short distance. *He won the 5000 meter race by putting in a very fast sprint at the finish.*

sprout *vb.* start to grow.

spruce 1. *n.* a tree belonging to the pine family.

sprung *vb.* past part. of **spring**.

spun *vb.* past of **spin**.

spur 1. *n.* a sharp device worn on a rider's boot and used to prod the horse into going faster. 2. *vb.* prod or encourage someone. *I hope my advice will spur you into immediate action.*

spurt 1. *n.* a sudden, brief burst of effort, particularly in a race. 2. *vb.* gush or spout.

spy *vb.* find out something by secret methods. *n.* (plural **spies**) a person who does that, usually for a government.

squad *n.* a small group of soldiers or people working together; a football team plus reserves.

squalor *n.* filth, dirt. **squalid** *adj.*

squander *vb.* spend wastefully. *She squandered a week's wages on a lot of worthless rubbish.*

square *n.* an area with four equal sides and four right angles; an open space enclosed by houses. *adj.* in the shape of a square. *vb. & n.* multiply a number by itself; the result of such multiplication. *4, 9, 16 and 25 are all squares.*

squash 1. *vb.* press something so that its shape flattens out. 2. *n.* a game played by two players on a special court with a small, black rubber ball and racket.

squat *vb.* 1. crouch on the ground with your knees bent. 2. settle in an unoccupied building.

squaw *n.* an American Indian name for a wife or woman.

squeak *vb.* make a high-pitched noise like a mouse. *I must oil that door to stop it from squeaking.* *n.* a short shrill cry.

squeal *vb. & n.* a long shrill sound.

squeeze *n. & vb.* press something tightly, compress.

squid *n.* a 10-armed sea mollusk related to the octopus.

squint *vb. & n.* look with eyes partly closed.

squirrel *n.* a small gray or red rodent with a bushy tail and long hind legs.

squirt *vb.* shoot out from a narrow opening. *The toothpaste squirted out of the tube.*

St. 1. an abbreviation for saint. *St. Francis of Assisi.* 2. an abbreviation for street. *Chestnut St.*

Squirrels have sharp claws for climbing and bushy tails that help them keep their balance.

stab vb. wound someone with a knife or another sharp weapon. n. a wound.

stable 1. n. a building for horses and cattle. 2. adj. steady, firmly fixed.

stack n. & vb. arrange things on top of each other in an orderly pile.

stadium n. a large roofless building with tiers of seats surrounding a field or track, where people gather to play or watch sports, such as football, baseball, etc.

staff n. 1. a group of people who work together. *There are four teachers on the staff of this school.* 2. a long, thick stick.

stag n. a male deer.

stage 1. n. the raised platform in a theater on which people perform plays. vb. put on a play. 2. n. a point in the development of something. *What stage have you reached with your project?*

stagecoach n. a horse-drawn passenger vehicle running regularly between established stops.

stagger vb. walk unsteadily.

stagnant adj. water that is standing still and is therefore not fresh. **stagnate** vb.

stain 1. n. a mark or colored patch on something. *The teacher had an egg stain on his tie.* 2. vb. mark; change the color of something; dye.

staircase n. a set of stairs, complete with banisters, etc.

stairs pl. n. a series of steps in a staircase.

stalactite n. an icicle-shaped stone structure hanging from the roof of a cave. **Stalagmites** are similar but grow upward from the floor.

stale adj. not fresh; old.

stalk (rhymes with *walk*) 1. adj. the stem of a plant. 2. n. & vb. follow or pursue something or someone secretly.

stall 1. n. a table or a stand in a marketplace. 2. n. a division of a barn or stable for one animal. 3. vb. stopping a car engine by mistake.

stallion n. a male horse.

stamen n. the male part of the flower that holds the pollen.

stamina n. staying power, endurance.

stammer n. a speech fault in which the person repeats the sound at the beginning of words. *"I c-c-can't s-s-see."* vb. speak with a stammer.

stamp 1. vb. bang your foot on the ground. 2. n. a small label bought at a post office, which has to go on letters and parcels.

The Penny Black of 1840 was the first postage stamp with a sticky back.

stand 1. vb. (past **stood**) be upright, in place. *The statue stands in the middle of the square.* 2. n. something on which things can be displayed, like a small, high table.

standard n. 1. something by which things can be compared or measured. *This ruler is not the standard size. It's much too short.* 2. a flag on a pole, usually raised to show loyalty to a country or its government.

stand-in n. someone who acts for another person when that person cannot be there. **stand in** vb.

stand out vb. be conspicuous.

stand up to vb. defend oneself against.

stank vb. past of **stink**.

stanza n. a division of a poem, a group of lines.

star n. 1. one of the tiny shining lights you see in the sky at night. Stars are really very large, and all except our sun are many millions of miles away. 2. a famous singer or actor.

S

starboard *n.* & *adj.* the right side of a ship when you are facing toward the front, or bow.

starch *n.* an important food substance formed in plants. *vb.* stiffen with starch.

stare *vb.* & *n.* look hard or searchingly for a long time.

starfish *n.* a creature of the seabed with a disk-shaped body and five or more arms.

starlight *n.* light from the stars.

starling *n.* a common bird with glossy black, brown-spotted feathers.

Stars and Stripes *n.* the U.S. flag.

start 1. *n.* the beginning of something. 2. *vb.* begin. 3. *vb.* turn a motor on. *He was unable to start his car.*

startle *vb.* surprise someone.

starve *vb.* grow ill from not having enough food, or from not having any at all. **starvation** *n.*

state 1. *n.* how something or someone is. *The garden is in an untidy state.* 2. *n.* a country, or division of a country. *There are 50 states in the United States of America.* 3. *vb.* say in words something. *This book states that the king is dead.*

stately *adj.* dignified, grand.

statement *n.* a formal description or detailed account of something.

station *n.* 1. a place with platforms and buildings where trains stop to pick up and drop off passengers. 2. a place that provides a public service, e.g. a fire station.

stationary *adj.* standing still, not moving.

stationery *n.* the paper, pens, pencils, ink and other materials used for writing.

statistics *pl. n.* the science of collecting figures, studying them and drawing conclusions about their meaning. For example, a bus company might count how many people travel by bus to work each day to help decide what kind of buses and how many to run on its routes.

statue *n.* a model in stone or metal, an animal, etc. of someone famous.

stay *vb.* remain; live somewhere for a time. *n.* a period of staying.

steady *adj.* firmly positioned; well-balanced. *vb.* make steady, stable.

steak (rhymes with *make*) *n.* a thick slice of meat or fish.

steal *vb.* (past **stole** past part. **stolen**) take something that does not belong to you by theft.

steam *n.* & *vb.* water so hot it has turned into water vapor, or gas.

A steam engine of the 1700s.

steam engine *n.* an engine or locomotive powered by steam.

steamer *n.* a boat driven by the power of a steam engine.

steel *n.* a strong metal made from iron in a furnace.

steep *adj.* sloping sharply.

steeple *n.* a tall pointed tower on a church or other building.

steer *vb.* control the direction of a vehicle, ship, etc.

stem *n.* the stalk of a plant, the part that grows up from the ground.

stench *n.* unpleasant smell.

stencil *n.* a flat sheet of metal, plastic or special paper into which words, patterns, etc., are cut. They can be copied by passing ink or paint through the holes onto paper or other materials. *vb.* use a stencil.

step 1. one of the movements you make when you walk, run or dance. 2. one of the flat parts of a stairway or ladder, where you put your feet when you climb them. 3. a stage in a process.

step- *prefix* indicating a relationship through remarriage, e.g. **stepchild**, **stepdaughter**, **stepfather**, etc.

stereo or **stereophonic sound** *n.* sound that is put through two or more loudspeakers.

sterilize *vb.* destroy all germs with heat or strong antiseptic. **sterile** *n.* free of germs; unable to bear offspring.

sterling *n.* the money of Great Britain. *adj.* made of sterling silver.

stern 1. *adj.* strict or severe. 2. *n.* the back end of a boat or ship.

stethoscope *n.* an instrument used to listen to people's heartbeats and the sound of their breathing.

stew *n. & vb.* a meat and vegetable mixture, usually boiled slowly for a long time.

steward *n.* a man who looks after people, often on a train or plane.

stewardess *n.* a woman who looks after people, often on a train or plane.

stick 1. *n.* a wooden rod or twig. 2. *vb.* glue or fix things together.

sticker *n.* an adhesive label.

stick up for *vb.* support someone who is in trouble. *I knew it wasn't Ted's fault so I tried to stick up for him when the others blamed him.*

stiff *adj.* not easily bent, rigid.

still 1. *adj.* motionless; soundless. *Please keep still.* 2. *adv.* even so, however. *I can still hear them walking.* 3. *n.* apparatus used in distilling alcohol.

stilts *pl. n.* a pair of poles on which you can stand and walk above the ground. **stilted** *adj.* stiff, pompous.

stimulus *n.* something that makes you active or energetic; an incentive. **stimulate** *vb.*

stinger *n.* a sharp organ of some plants and animals. to protect themselves. *Wasp stings hurt. vb.* wound by pricking.

stingy *adj.* not generous, mean.

stink *vb. &* smell bad.

stir *vb.* 1. move liquid around with a utensil. *Steve forgot to stir the soup, and it burned.* 2. rouse.

stirrup *n.* a metal support that hangs on each side of a horse's saddle, into which the rider puts his or her feet.

stitch *n.* (plural **stitches**) one of the loops of thread made in cloth when you are sewing or in yarn when you are knitting. *vb.* sew.

stoat *n.* a small, slim mammal of the weasel family with a black-tipped tail and reddish brown fur.

stock *n.* 1. goods kept to be used or sold. *I keep a large stock of paper in that closet.* 2. a share in a company.

stocking *n.* a covering for the leg; long sock.

stole *vb.* past of **steal**.

stomach *n.* organ in the middle part of your body, into which food goes after it is swallowed and where digestion begins. *vb.* endure, tolerate, put up with.

stone *n.* 1. a kind of rock. *The statue was made from stone.* 2. a small piece of rock. *I've got a stone in my shoe.* 3. the hard seed of some fruits, e.g. plums, cherries. 4. a gem, a precious stone. 5. a measure of weight, the same as 14 pounds.

stood *vb.* past of **stand**.

stool *n.* a seat or chair without a back or arms.

stoop *vb.* bend the body; condescend *n.* a habitual bend in the back. *My grandfather has a slight stoop.*

stop *vb.* 1. come to a halt. *The car stopped at the traffic lights.* 2. prevent. *n.* a halt, pause.

store 1. *n.* a large shop. 2. *vb.* keep things until they are needed. *Squirrels store nuts.*

S

stork *n*. a tall white bird with a long beak and legs, and wide wings.

storm *n*. a very strong wind with rain, hail, snow, thunder, etc.

story *n*. (plural **stories**) 1. one floor of a building. *My bedroom is on the third story.* 2. a fictional narrative. *Please tell me a story.*

stout *adj*. thick and heavy.

stove *n*. an apparatus used for cooking food or heating.

stowaway *n*. someone who hides in a ship, aircraft or some other form of transport, in order to travel in secret or without paying.

straight 1. *adj*. not bent or crooked. *You can draw a straight line with a ruler.* 2. *adv*. directly. *Did you come straight home from school?*

straightaway *adv*. immediately, *n*. section of road having no curves.

straighten *vb*. make something right, correct or straight. *Henry asked me to help him straighten the carpet.*

strain *vb*. 1. push, stretch or try too hard; injure by overusing. *n*. 2. drain liquid from a solid through a cloth or net of small holes.

strait *n*. a narrow channel of water connecting two larger bodies of water.

strand *n*. a thread.

strange *adj*. odd; unusual.

stranger *n*. someone you don't know.

strangle *vb*. kill by pressing hard on the throat, choke. **strangulation** *n*.

strap *n*. a strip of leather or some other material used to fasten or hold things. *vb*. fasten with straps.

strategy *n*. the art of planning a military campaign, political or economic policy, etc.

stratum *n*. (plural **strata**) a layer (of rock, clouds, etc.)

straw *n*. 1. dry stalks of grain. 2. a thin tube for drinking through.

strawberry *n*. a small plant belonging to the rose family, with white flowers and red fruit.

stray *vb*. wander away. *The fence was broken and so the cows could stray onto the road.*

streak 1. *n*. irregular band of color.

In parts of Europe white storks nest on chimneys.

The white marble is streaked with red. 2. *vb*. rush past.

stream *n*. 1. a brook; a small river. 2. a flow of anything.

streamline *vb*. design (a vehicle, etc.) with a smooth shape to cut down wind resistance.

street *n*. a road lined with buildings, particularly in a town.

strength *n*. how strong something or someone is. *Walter did not have the strength to lift the barrel by himself.*

strengthen *vb*. make or become stronger.

stress 1. *n*. tension, strain. 2. (in mechanics) pressure or force exerted on a body. 3. *vb*. & *n*. emphasis. *I cannot stress too much the importance of a good diet.*

stretch 1. *vb*. pull something out so as to make it bigger. 2. *n*. a length of time or a distance. *Janet could see a long stretch of road ahead of the car.*

stretcher *n*. a movable bed for carrying sick or injured people.

strict *adj*. stern; exact; inflexible.

stride *vb*. (past **strode**) walk with long steps. *n*. a long step; a pace.

strife *n*. conflict, struggle.

strike 1. *n.* hit hard. 2. *vb.* stop work as a protest against the people who employ you. *n.* when people strike. *The workers have been on strike for six weeks now.*

string *n.* thin cord or rope.

strip 1. *n.* a long narrow piece of material. 2. *vb.* take off all your clothes; deprive; tear off.

stripe *n.* a band of color, especially on clothing and other fabric. **striped** *adj.*

strive *vb.* (past **strove**) try hard. *You must strive to do better.*

strode *vb.* past of **stride**.

stroke 1. *vb.* move your hand gently over something. *Carol liked to stroke her cat's soft fur.* 2. *n.* a serious illness which can result in paralysis (being unable to move all or part of the body.)

stroll (rhymes with *pole*) *vb.* & *n.* walk along slowly.

strong *adj.* powerful; having great strength; difficult to break.

stronghold *n.* a castle, fortified place.

strong point *n.* what a person is particularly good at doing.

struck *vb.* past of **strike**.

structure *n.* anything that has been built. *A house is a structure, and so is a table.*

struggle *n.* hard contest. *vb.* strive; violent effort; fight, usually using your whole body. *Jenny had to struggle to free herself from the rope.*

strum *vb.* play a musical instrument lightly with the fingers.

strut *n.* a wooden or iron bar which strengthens a framework.

stub 1. *n.* short piece left after the main part has been used or removed. *A cigarette stub.* *vb.* extinguish (put out) by crushing. 2. *vb.* bump. *Donald stubbed his toe on the rock.*

stubborn *adj.* not willing to change, or to do what other people want.

stucco *n.* & *vb.* (apply) a plaster coating to wall surfaces.

stuck *vb.* past of **stick**.

student *n.* someone who is studying, usually at a school or a college.

studio *n.* an artist's workroom; a place for recording, broadcasting, or making films.

study 1. *vb.* read and learn; to look at something carefully. *He had to study the map for a long time before he made the journey.* 2. *n.* a room devoted to study or literary work.

stuff 1. *vb.* fill something with some kind of material. *My teddy bear is stuffed with wool.* 2. *n.* anything you don't know the name of. *What's the stuff your Dad mended the cup with?*

stuffy *adj.* having no fresh air, smelling stale and airless.

stumble *vb.* miss one's footing; come close to falling.

stump *n.* the short, stubby remains of something, such as the part of a tree that is left in the ground after the rest of it has been cut down.

stun *vb.* 1. make senseless with a blow on the head. 2. astonish.

stung *vb.* past of **sting**.

stunk *vb.* past part. of **stink**.

stunt 1. *vb.* stop the growth of. 2. *n.* a difficult feat, a showy performance (often for publicity).

stupid *adj.* slow of mind; dull.

sturdy *adj.* strong, well built.

sturgeon *n.* a toothless, shark-like fish valued for its roe (eggs) which are sold as a delicacy under the name of caviar.

stutter *vb.* stammer.

sty *n.* 1. a painful red swelling on the eyelid. 2. a pen in which pigs are kept; a pigsty.

style *n.* the way something is done or made. *Tim's shirt is the latest style, but he doesn't like it.* **stylish** *adj.* fashionable; having a good sense of style.

stylus *n.* a fine point used for playing records, etc.

sub- *prefix* meaning under, inferior, lower, e.g. **subhuman, subnormal, subsoil.**

subject *n.* 1. the thing that is being talked about or written about. *John is the subject of everyone's interest.* 2. someone who is ruled by a government, or by a king or queen.

Today many submarines are nuclear-powered. They can stay submerged for a very long time and are armed with long-range missiles.

submarine *n.* a kind of boat that can move under the water instead of on the surface. *adj.* under the sea.

submerge *vb.* plunge, go or put under water.

subscribe *vb.* contribute, sign one's name to. **subscription** *n.*

subside *vb.* settle, sink back to normal. *The flood gradually subsided.*

subsidy *n.* financial help from a government to industry, farming, etc., to keep prices down.

subsidize *vb.* pay a subsidy to.

substance *n.* anything that can be seen or touched. **substantial** *adj.* solid, considerable.

substitute 1. *vb.* put in place of something else. *Peter substituted oil for butter when he cooked the onions.* 2. *n.* a player in a game who joins in for someone else. *Paul was only a substitute but he scored the winning goal.*

subtle *adj.* delicate, refined; difficult to understand or distinguish.

subtract *vb.* take away an amount from a total. **subtraction** *n.*

suburb *n.* the outlying parts of a town, usually where people live. **suburban** *adj.*

subway *n.* an underground tunnel, particularly one for pedestrians; an underground railway.

succeed *vb.* 1. achieve something you set out to do. 2. come after (a king or other important person.) *He succeeded his father as Duke of Dorset.* **success** *n.* achievement, a good outcome.

successful *adj.* able to do what you want to do or try to do.

such *adj.* of that kind. *How can you believe such stories?*

suck *vb.* pull into the mouth through suction. *Baby sucks his thumb.*

suckle *vb.* feed young at the breast; draw milk from the breast or udder.

sudden *adj.* happening quickly and without warning. *A sudden idea struck her.* **suddenly** *adv.*

S

sue *vb.* seek justice by legal action.

suede *(swade)* *n.* leather made from skin of a young goat (kid), cowhide, etc., with flesh side out.

suet *n.* fat that protects kidneys of cattle and sheep, used in cooking.

suffer *vb.* experience pain or unhappiness. **suffering** *n.*

sufficient *adj.* enough to meet one's needs; adequate; not too much.

suffix *n.* syllable(s) added at the end of a word to make another word, e.g. host host**ess**, red redd**ish**, king king**dom**.

suffocate *vb.* die from being unable to breathe. **suffocation** *n.*

sugar *n.* a sweet food.

suggest *vb.* put forward an idea indirectly; hint.

suggestion *n.* plan, thought.

suicide *n.* die by killing yourself on purpose. **suicidal** *adj.*

suit 1. *n.* a jacket with trousers or skirt that are made to be worn together. 2. *vb.* be right for a certain purpose, convenient, appropriate. *It will suit me to go now, because I am not busy.* 3. *n.* a legal process. 4. one of the four sets in a pack of cards.

suitable *adj.* correct, right for what is needed. *That dress will be very suitable for traveling.*

suitcase *n.* a large bag or case for carrying clothes, etc., on a journey.

suite *n.* a set of rooms or matched furniture. *A three-room suite.*

sulfur *n.* a nonmetallic element often found in the form of yellow crystals (symbol – S).

sulfuric acid *n.* an extremely corrosive, colorless, oily acid widely used in the chemical industry.

sulk *vb.* be in a bad temper. **sulky** *adj.*

sullen *adj.* silently bad-tempered.

sultan *n.* a king or sovereign of a Muslim state.

sultana *n.* a light-colored seedless grape grown for raisins and wines; a sultan's wife.

sum *n.* 1. the whole amount. 2. the result of added numbers.

summarize *vb.* give a short account, sum up. **summary** *n.* a brief account of the main facts.

summer *n.* the warmest season of the year, between spring and fall.

summit *n.* top, highest point, peak.

summon *vb.* call together.

sum up *vb.* state concisely.

sun *n.* The sun is the central body in the solar system and the nearest star to the earth.

sunburn *n.* red or brown coloring of the skin caused by over exposure to sunlight.

Sunday *n.* the first day of the week; the Christian day of worship; named after the sun.

sundial *n.* a kind of clock that shows the time by a shadow the sun makes on a dial.

sunflower *n.* a tall plant with a large, flat flower edged with yellow petals.

sung *vb.* past part. of **sing**.

sunk *vb.* past part. of **sink**.

sunlight *n.* the light of the sun.

sunny *adj.* bright with sunshine.

sunrise *n.* dawn, morning, the time when the sun comes up.

sunset *n.* dusk, evening, the time when the sun goes down (**sundown**).

sunshine *n.* direct rays from the sun.

sunspots *pl. n.* dark patches that appear from time to time on the surface of the sun.

super- *prefix* meaning above, over, more than, on top (of).

superb *adj.* excellent, magnificent.

superficial *adj.* on the surface.

superior *adj.* higher; better.

superlative *adj.* the best.

supermarket *n.* a large self-service shop where customers can buy food and many other goods.

supernatural *adj.* something that does not have an ordinary explanation.

supersede *vb.* take the place of.

supersonic *adj.* faster than the speed of sound.

superstitious *adj.* someone who believes in luck, chance and magic happenings is superstitious. **superstition** *n.*

supervise *vb.* oversee, watch over,

207

S

control. **supervision** n.

supper n. a meal eaten at the end of the day.

supple adj. easy to bend; not stiff. *Athletes have to be supple.*

supply vb. **supplied** past. 1. give what is needed. *I will supply you with a book.* 2. n. things that are kept to be used later. *We have a large supply of pencils.*

support vb. hold up; help; supply with a home and food; regularly watch or attend, e.g. football. **supporter** n.

suppose vb. think that something is so, although it may not be. *Let's suppose that it will take us two hours.*

suppress vb. put down, crush; (of information) conceal. *The enemy suppressed the news of the defeat.*

supreme adj. the greatest; most excellent, reliable, etc.

sure adj. certain. *Are you sure that is true?* **surely** adv.

surf n. waves breaking on the shore of a beach.

surface n. outer or upper part of something. *The astronauts landed on the surface of the moon.* vb. bring or come to the surface. *The truth will surface.*

surgeon n. a doctor who operates on people.

surgery n. treating disease or injuries by operating.

surly adj. bad-tempered, sullen.

surname n. your family name. *My name is Anne Bell, so my surname is Bell.*

surpass vb. do better than; go beyond.

surplus adj. & n. what is left over when need or use is satisfied.

surprise n. something that happens unexpectedly. *The party was a lovely surprise.* vb. attack or come upon suddenly; astonish. **surprising** adj.

surrender vb. give in. *The soldiers had to surrender when they lost the battle.* to give up possession of.

surround vb. enclose, or be all around. *Flower gardens surround our house.* **surroundings.** pl. n.

survey vb. 1. take a look at a view.

2. look carefully at a house or other building before it is sold, to check that there is nothing wrong with it. 3. measure an area of land.

surveying n. the measurement and mapping of parts of the earth's surface.

survive vb. remain alive, especially through changes or difficult times. **survivor** n. a person who survives.

suspect (*su-spekt*) vb. have a feeling that something is true, although you are not sure; doubt. *I suspect that someone has worn my bathing suit because it seems damp.* (**sus**-*pekt*) n. a person who is suspected of having done something (usually bad.)

suspend vb. 1. hang something up. 2. stop, cancel or postpone something.

suspense n. state of anxiety or excitement while waiting for something to happen.

suspicion n. mistrust, a feeling that something is wrong.

sustain vb. 1. hold up, support. 2. suffer (an injury etc.).

swallow 1. vb. make food go down your throat. 2. n. a small bird with long, slim wings and a forked tail.

swam vb. past of **swim**.

swamp 1. n. a bog or marsh. 2. vb. overwhelm by an excess; flood.

swan n. a graceful long-necked water bird with paddling feet.

swank vb. & n. (a) show off.

swap vb. exchange one thing for something else. *Will you swap your lunch for mine?*

swarm n. a large group of bees or other insects. vb. form a swarm.

swastika n. two kinds of cross, one the symbol of the Nazis in Germany, the other a religious symbol in India.

sway vb. swing slowly back and forth.

swear vb. 1. use bad language, words that many people do not think right. 2. make a solemn promise, vow. *The knight had to swear to obey his king.*

sweat (rhymes with *wet*) vb. & n. the

liquid that comes out of your skin when you are hot or nervous.

sweater *n.* a knitted or crocheted garment for the top of your body.

sweep *vb.* (past **swept**) 1. clean with a brush. 2. glide majestically.

sweeping *adj.* extensive, wide. *The government took sweeping measures to improve the economy.*

sweet 1. *adj.* having a sugary taste. 2. *n.* a candy such as a toffee or chocolate. 3. *adj.* charming.

sweeten *vb.* make sweet.

swell *vb.* get bigger, increase. **swelling** *n.*

swept *vb.* past of **sweep**.

swerve *vb. & n.* (make) a sudden violent turn; a swerving motion. *The driver had to swerve to avoid hitting a dog.*

swift 1. *adj.* fast, quick. **swiftness** *n.* 2. *n.* a fast-flying bird with long wings.

swig *vb. n.* drink in long drafts.

swill 1. *n.* part-liquid food for swine. 2. *vb.* drench; guzzle or gobble.

swim *n. & vb.* (past **swam** past part. **swum**) move yourself along while afloat in water.

swine *n.* a collective word for pigs; (casual) unpleasant person.

swindle *vb.* cheat. *n.* fraud.

swing *vb.* (past **swung**) move yourself or something else backward and forward along an arc. *The monkey was swinging from branch to branch. n.* a seat slung by ropes.

switch 1. *n.* a device for turning lights and other electrical appliances on and off. *vb.* switch on, switch off. 2. *vb.* change from one thing to another.

swivel *n.* a device joining two parts which enables either one or both parts to turn freely. *vb.* pivot, turn on a swivel.

swollen *vb.* past part. of **swell**.

swoop *n. & vb.* rush down (out of the sky.) *The eagle swooped on its prey.*

sword *n.* a hand weapon with a long blade.

swordfish *n.* a big tropical fish, with a sword-shaped bony snout.

swore *vb.* past of **swear**.

swum *vb.* past part. **swim**.

swung *vb.* past of **swing**.

sycamore *n.* a tree belonging to the maple family.

syllable *n.* one section or part of a word, which can be said by itself. *Ambulance has three syllables: am-bu-lance.*

syllabus *n.* a course of studies.

symbol *n.* a sign. *In arithmetic the symbol + means "add."* **symbolize** *vb.*

symmetrical *adj.* having the same shape and size on both sides of a central line. *All these capital letters are symmetrical, even the second one: A E H M O T X.* **symmetry** *n.*

sympathy *n.* a feeling for another person's distress or unhappiness; to be in tune with another person. **sympathize** *vb.*

symphony (**sim**-*fon-ee*) *n.* a form of long musical composition for a full orchestra, usually consisting of three or four movements.

symptom *n.* some indication, sign or mark on the body, e.g. a rash or high temperature, pointing to a disease.

synagogue *n.* a meeting place for Jewish religious worship and teaching.

synod *n.* a meeting or council of clergy (and laity) of a church.

synonym *n.* a word that has the same meaning as another word. *Looking glass is a synonym for mirror.*

synopsis *n.* a summary, especially of a story or play.

synthetic *adj. & n.* made artificially.

syringe *n.* an instrument for sucking a liquid in, and forcing it out again, in a thin stream.

syrup *n.* a sticky, sweet, thick liquid, made from sugar and water.

system *n.* a group of items forming as a unified whole; an organized procedure. *Filing system.* organs that together perform a function. *Digestive system.* **systematic** *adj.* methodical.

tabby *n.* a domestic cat.

tabernacle *n.* a tent used by the Jews in Biblical times; a place of worship; a receptacle for consecrated hosts.

table *n.* 1. a piece of furniture with a flat top supported by legs. 2. a way of arranging figures, such as a multiplication table.

tablespoon *n.* a large spoon used for serving food. *A tablespoon is often used to measure amounts in cooking.*

tablet *n.* round, compressed drug or medicine; sheets of paper glued together at one edge.

table tennis *n.* a game played on a table, using paddles and a celluloid ball.

tabloid *n.* small-sized newspaper that contains news, etc., in a condensed form and which has many photographs.

taboo *n & adj.* something that must not be talked about, touched, etc.; set apart.

tack 1. *n.* a small flat-headed nail. 2. *vb.* sew with long loose stitches. 3. *vb & n.* sail a boat into the wind. 4. *n.* a zig-zag course on land.

tackle 1. *n.* equipment for a sport or some other activity. *Dad keeps his fishing tackle in the garage.* 2. *vb.* start work on a problem. *John decided to tackle the washing alone.* 3. *vb.* throw down or stop an opponent, especially in football.

tact *n.* knowing what to say or do to avoid offence. **tactless** *adj.* **tactful** *adj.*

tactics *pl. n.* the science of using

military forces in a war. **tactical** *adj.*

tadpole *n.* a young frog or toad, at the stage between the egg and the adult.

tag *n.* 1. a small label. 2. a game in which one person chases the others, and catches them by touching or "tagging" them.

tail *n.* a projection at the back of many kinds of animal. *Some monkeys use their tails as a fifth limb.* *vb.* follow close behind.

tailor *n.* a person who makes or alters suits, coats, etc.

take *vb.* (past **took** past part. **taken**) get possession of something; catch or gain.

take after *vb.* resemble. *Doesn't Tina take after her mother?*

take in *vb.* 1. be tricked. *I was taken in by what he said, but it was really a lie.* 2. bring someone into your house. *The hotel was full, so the manager found a motel to take us in.* 3. understand. *I'm sorry but I didn't quite take in what you said.* 4. make something narrower. *The skirt was too big, but I took it in at the waist.*

takeoff *n.* 1. take to the air (of an aircraft). **take off** *vb.* 2. a parody, humorous mimicry.

take over *vb.* assume control of. **takeover** *n.*

take up *vb.* start doing something which is new to you. *My father has decided to take up pottery.*

talc *n.* a mineral with a soapy feel which is ground to a powder to make talcum powder for dusting the body after a bath.

tale *n.* a story; mischievous gossip.

talent *n.* an ability to do something well. *Nell has a natural talent for skating.*

talk (*tawk*) *vb.* speak. *n.* a short lecture. **talkative** *adj.*

tall *adj.* having greater than average height, often said of people and buildings. *Simon is not as tall as his brother.*

Talmud *n.* book of Jewish tradition.

talon *n.* the long claw of a bird of prey, such as a hawk.

tambourine *n.* a musical instrument shaped like a shallow drum, with disks around it. It is shaken, and beaten with the hand.

tame *adj.* an animal that is not wild, and is used to being with humans; uninteresting. *vb.* make tame.

tamper *vb.* meddle with.

tan 1. *n.* a light brown color. *vb.* turn brown in the sun. 2. *vb.* make animal skins into leather.

tandem *n.* a bicycle with two seats.

tang *n.* a sharp taste or smell.

tangerine *n.* a small loose-skinned kind of orange.

tangled *adj.* disordered. **tangle** *vb.* & *n.* twisted interwoven strands.

tango *n.* & *vb.* Latin American dance; music for this dance.

tank *n.* 1. large container for liquids. 2. an armored fighting vehicle with guns, which moves on treads instead of wheels; a jail cell used for receiving prisoners.

tankard *n.* drinking vessel with a handle.

tanker *n.* a ship used to carry oil or other liquids.

tantrum *n.* a sudden fit of bad temper.

tap 1. *n.* a device for turning on and off the flow of water into a sink, bath, etc., 2. *vb.* knock gently but repeatedly. 3. *vb.* take water, information, etc. from a source. *I think that my telephone has been tapped.*

tape 1. *n.* a narrow length of material used for tying or in dressmaking. 2. *n.* a strip of plastic which is used to record sound. *vb.* record on magnetic tape.

taper 1. *n.* long thin candle used for lighting lamps, etc. 2. *vb.* make or become smaller toward the end. *A church spire tapers.*

tape recorder *n.* an instrument for recording sounds on tape and playing the sound back again.

tapestry *n.* a picture on cloth, made by sewing or weaving in colored threads.

tapir *n.* a nocturnal animal of tropical America, Malaya and Sumatra which is related to the horse.

tar *n.* a dark, thick, sticky substance obtained from wood, coal, etc.

tarantula *n.* large, black, south European spider, named after the town of Taranto in Italy; it has a slightly poisonous bite.

target *n.* anything that has an object shot or thrown at it. *An archery target is usually made of straw covered with canvas.*

tariff *n.* price list; list of custom duties.

tarmac *n.* a road surface of broken stones mixed with tar (short for tarmacadam).

tarpaulin *n.* waterproof cloth, originally of tarred canvas.

tart 1. *adj.* sharp- or sour-tasting. 2. *n.* a pie with pastry underneath the filling but not on top of it.

tartan *n.* a traditional Scottish woolen cloth, woven in one of a variety of square patterns.

task *n.* a job, a piece of work. *It was her task to make the beds in the morning.*

tassel *n.* a bunch of hanging threads used as an ornament.

taste 1. *n.* the sense by which you can tell the flavor of food and drink; the flavor itself. *vb.* try food or drink to see if you like it. 2. *n.* good or bad judgment in art, clothing, etc. *I admire her taste in clothes.*

tattoo *vb* & *n.* mark or color the skin with patterns.

taught *vb.* (*tawt*) past of **teach**.

taut (*tawt*) *adj.* when something has been stretched so that it is firm. *Pull that rope until it is taut.* **tauten** *vb.*

tavern *n.* an inn or pub where food and drink are served to patrons; saloon; bar.

tawny *adj.* yellowish-brown color.

tax *n.* (plural **taxes**) money paid to the government by people and organizations.

taxi 1. *n.* a car with a driver that can be hired for short journeys. 2. *vb.* the long run an aircraft makes to or

T

from the runway.

tea *n.* the dried leaves of an evergreen shrub. The leaves are soaked in boiling water to make the drink called tea.

teach *vb.* instruct other people; give them knowledge and encourage them to think for themselves.

teaching *n.* the act or profession of a teacher.

teacher *n.* a person who instructs (teaches) other people, usually in a school or college.

teak *n.* an evergreen tree with very hard wood grown in India, Burma, and Thailand.

team *n.* 1. a group of people in a game or sport who are all on the same side. *There are 11 players on a football team.* 2. a group of people who join together to do a particular job.

teapot *n.* a vessel with a curved handle and spout for making and pouring out tea.

tear (*tare*) *vb.* (past **tore** past part. **torn**) rip something such as cloth or paper, pull apart by force; move or act with great violence, force or speed.

tears (*teers*) *pl. n.* drops of salt water which fall from your eyes when you cry.

tease (*teeze*) *vb.* make fun of someone, often unkindly.

technical *adj.* to do with machinery or how things work.

technology *n.* the study of technical ideas.

tedious *adj.* boring; tiresome because of its length or dullness.

tee *n.* place from which a golfer drives the ball at the beginning of each hole; small peg on which the golf ball is placed to drive off.

teenager *n.* a young person between the ages of thir*teen* and nine*teen*.

tee shirt *n.* (also **T-shirt**) a short-sleeved collarless, cotton undershirt; also a pullover knit sport shirt.

teeth *n.* plural of **tooth**.

teethe *vb.* cut (grow) new teeth.

teething *n.*

teetotal *adj.* never drinking alcohol.

telecommunications *pl. n.* long-distance signals by telephone, radio, telegraph, and television.

telegram *n.* a word message sent by telegraph or radio.

telegraph *n.* a system for sending long-distance messages by electric current. **telegraphy** *n.*

telephone *n.* an instrument for talking to people over long distances by turning speech into electrical impulses, which travel along wires. *vb.* use the telephone.

telescope *n.* a tube-like instrument with special lenses, which makes distant things appear clearer and larger.

television *n.* a way of sending and receiving pictures and sounds by radio waves. **TV** *abbr.* **televise** *vb.*

tell *vb.* give information to somebody. *Tell me about your trip.*

temper 1. *n.* your mood (usually when bad). *Gareth was in a bad temper because his parents refused to let him watch TV.* 2. *vb.* make a metal harder and more pliable by heating it and then cooling it rapidly.

temperament *n.* a person's character and way of feeling, thinking and behaving. *She has a gentle temperament.*

temperamental *adj.* sudden changes of mood.

temperate *adj.* a climate that is neither too hot nor very cold; moderate; avoiding excesses. *New Zealand has a temperate climate.*

temperature *n.* degree of hotness or coldness. *Temperature can be measured with a thermometer.*

tempest *n.* violent storm.

temple *n.* 1. a building used for meeting and worship in some religions. 2. flat part of the side of the head between ear and forehead.

tempo *n.* the speed at which a piece of music is played.

temporary *adj.* lasting for a limited time, not permanent. *We had a*

Microphone

Transmitter

Aerial

Camera
lens

Sound
joined
to
picture

Picture
tube

Screen

*The television camera changes light
waves into electrical "vision" signals.
With sound signals from the
microphone, these are sent out on radio
waves. The receiver changes the signals
back to pictures and sounds.*

temporary power failure today.

tempt *vb*. try to persuade someone to
do something they ought not to;
entice.

tenant *n*. a person who rents and
occupies someone else's property.

tend *vb*. 1. be likely to do
something. *This car tends to steer to
the left.* 2. look after. *Shepherds tend
their sheep in the fields.*

tender 1. *adj*. delicate, soft, easily
hurt. 2. *vb*. offer. *The minister
tendered his resignation.* 3. *n*. a small
boat in which you get to a larger
one.

tendon *n*. tough fibrous tissue that
connects muscle to bone.

tennis *n*. a ball and racket game for
two or four people, which is played
on a specially marked court.

tenon *n*. piece of wood which fits
into a hole (a *mortise*) to join two
parts of a piece of furniture, etc.

tenor *n*. & *adj*. highest natural adult
male singing voice.

tense *adj*. taut; showing mental or
physical strain.

tent *n*. a shelter made from
waterproof material, such as canvas,
stretched over a frame of metal
poles, and held up with ropes.

tentacle *n*. a long, thin, snakelike
"arm" of animals such as the
octopus.

tepee *n*. American Indian tent.

tepid *adj*. slightly warm.

term *n*. 1. a set period of time. *The
spring term lasts for 10 weeks.*
2. word or expression which is used
to describe particular ideas in
different professions, e.g. medical
terms. 3. *pl. n.* conditions.

terminal 1. *n*. a building where some
form of transportation ends. 2. *adj*.
the end; final, particularly of an
illness which someone will not

213

T

survive.

terminate *vb*. bring to an end.

terminus *n*. an end station on a bus, train or air route.

termite *n*. an insect like an ant that builds large hills of earth and mud.

tern *n*. a seabird.

terrace *n*. a level area cut out of a slope; a row of houses built as a single block.

terra-cotta *n*. brownish-red baked clay used for statues, pottery and tiles and as a covering material on buildings.

terrapin *n*. a name for a small kind of turtle.

terrific *adj*. terrifying; excellent. *We had a terrific time in Norway.*

terrible *adj*. very bad, frightening, dreadful.

terrier *n*. one of various kinds of small dog that can dig out or drive out small game animals.

terrify *vb*. make someone very frightened.

territory *n*. an area of land.

terror *n*. great fear. (*casual*) a tiresome person.

terse (*turs*) *adj*. brief, concise.

test 1. *vb*. try out something. *I want to test the car before I buy it.* 2. *n*. a set of questions to be answered; a kind of small exam.

testes *pl. n*. (singular **testis**) also **testicle** egg-shaped glands contained in the scrotum, a bag hanging behind the penis in male mammals. The testes produce sperm.

testify *vb*. give evidence under oath. *n*. **testimony**.

tetanus *n*. a dangerous disease in which the muscles become rigid.

tether *n*. a rope for fastening an animal so that it can only move within a set radius.

Teuton *n*. a member of the Germanic race.

text *n*. the main part of a printed book.

textbook *n*. a book giving information for study in a school or college.

textile *n*. woven cloth of any sort.

texture *n*. how the surface of something feels when you touch it.

than *conj*. introducing second part of a comparison. *Jill is taller than Jack.*

thank *vb*. tell someone that you are grateful to them. *Thank you for the lovely party.*

thatch *n*. a roof covering made from layers of straw or reeds.

thaw *vb*. melt (of ice or snow).

theater *n*. 1. a place where plays are performed by actors and watched by an audience. 2. an operating room where medical students may watch surgical operations performed. **theatrical** *adj*.

theft *n*. stealing.

their *pron*. belonging to them.

theme *n*. the main subject. *The theme of the book is love.*

then *adv*. at that time. *I didn't know you so well then.* after that; next.

theology *n*. the study of religion.

theory *n*. an idea to explain something. *I have a theory about why he ran away.*

there *adv*. in or to that place. *Put the box down there.*

therefore *adv*. for that reason; and so.

thermometer *n*. an instrument for measuring temperature.

thermos *n*. a vacuum container for keeping beverages or foods at a constant temperature.

thermostat *n*. an instrument that automatically controls a heating system or sprinkler system.

thesaurus *n*. a book like a dictionary, but without definitions, and with words of similar meaning listed together in groups.

thick *adj*. wide; not thin or slender. *The walls of the ancient castle were several feet thick.* 2. (of a liquid) flows more slowly. 3. an impolite word meaning "stupid."

thicket *n*. a dense growth of small trees and shrubs.

thief *n*. (plural **thieves**) a person who steals.

thigh (rhymes with *my*) *n*. the part of

your leg between your hip and your knee.

thimble *n.* a small covering, often made of metal, worn on the finger to avoid pricking it when sewing.

thin *adj.* lean, slim; not thick.

think *vb.* 1. use your brain to work out a problem; consider, reflect. 2. believe. *I think that's the right direction, but I'm not absolutely sure.*

think over *vb.* consider.

third 1. *adj.* next after second. 2. *n.* one of three pieces that make the whole thing. *There were three of us, so we each had one third of the cake.*

thirst 1. *n.* (a dry feeling caused by) the need to drink. 2. *vb.* want something to drink. **thirsty** *adj.*

this *pron.* & *adj.* (plural **these**) the one here, not a different one.

thistle (**this-**sel) *n.* one of a family of plants with prickly leaves. *The thistle is the national emblem of Scotland.*

thorax *n.* part of an insect that bears the wings and legs; (in humans) the chest.

thorn *n.* a sharp spiky projection on some kinds of plant, such as the rose.

thorough (**thur-**o) *adj.* proper and careful. *Fred gave his room a thorough cleaning.*

thoroughbred *n.* a pure breed of horse.

thoroughfare *n.* a public main road or street.

though (*tho*) *conj.* even so; even if; although.

thought *vb.* past and past part. of **think.**

thought (*thawt*) *n.* an idea or an opinion; meditation. **thoughtless** *adj.* unthinking, inconsiderate. **thoughtful** *adj.* absorbed in thought; considering other people.

thousand *n.* the figure 1000; 10 hundreds.

thrash *vb.* beat; defeat.

thread (rhymes with *bed*) *n.* a length of spun fiber. *vb.* put a thread through a hole, such as the eye of a needle. **threadbare** *adj.* with the threads showing, shabby.

threaten *vb.* warn that you will do something bad. *Michael tried to threaten his sister with a punch.* **threat** *n.*

thresh *vb.* beat the seeds from stalks of grain.

threw *vb.* past of **throw.**

thrift *n.* manage one's money carefully; not being extravagant. **thrifty** *adj.* economical.

thrill *vb.* make someone excited. **thriller** *n.* a novel or play with a lot of suspense and intrigue, usually about crime.

throat *n.* the front of your neck, and the tubes inside that take food and air into your body.

throb *vb.* beat strongly and rhythmically like the heart.

thrombosis *n.* a blood clot in the heart or a blood vessel.

throne *n.* a special chair for a king or queen, or some other important person.

throttle 1. *vb.* choke, strangle. 2. *n.* a device for controling the flow of fuel in a car, etc.

through (*thru*) *prep.* from one side to another. *The stone went right through the glass.*

throw *vb.* (past **threw** past part. **thrown**) fling or hurl an object, such as a ball.

throw up *vb.* be sick, vomit.

thrush *n.* 1. member of a family of small songbirds. 2. a disease affecting animals' feet.

thrust *vb.* push, force, shove; pierce. *They thrust their way through the crowd. n.* a stab. *A sword thrust.*

thug *n.* a gangster, cutthroat or ruffian.

thumb (*thum*) 1. *n.* the short, thick finger on each hand. 2. *vb.* flick through the pages of a book or magazine. *John thumbed through the magazine.*

thunder *n.* the noise that follows lightning in a storm.

thunderstorm *n.* a rainstorm with thunder and lightning.

Thursday *n.* the fifth day of the

week, between Wednesday and Friday; named after Thor, Norse god of thunder.

thus *conj*. and so.

thyme (*time*) *n*. an herb, of the mint family, used in cooking.

thyroid *n*. an important gland in the neck near the larynx.

tiara *n*. a jeweled head ornament worn by women.

tick 1. *vb*. make a light, repeated sound like a clock. 2. *n*. a small insect that burrows into the skin of animals and sucks their blood.

ticket *n*. a piece of printed card or paper that allows you to go in somewhere, such as a cinema, or travel on public transport. *Tom had to pay his bus fare again because he'd lost his ticket.*

tickle *vb*. touch someone lightly. *I tickled the baby's feet and made her laugh*. *n*. sensation of tickling.

tiddler *n*. a small fish or anything very small.

NEAP TIDES

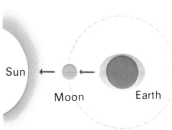

SPRING TIDES

tide *n*. the regular rise and fall of the sea. **tidal** *adj*.

tidy *adj*. neat, in order. *vb*. make tidy.

tie 1. *vb*. fasten something with string or rope. 2. *n*. a thin piece of cloth worn knotted around the neck of a shirt.

tier (rhymes with *ear*) *n*. two or more ranks or layers placed above one another. *The wedding cake had four tiers.*

tiff *n*. a minor quarrel.

tiger *n*. a large, striped animal belonging to the cat family.

tight *adj*. 1. close-fitting; difficult to remove. 2. (*slang*) drunk.

tights *pl.n*. a close-fitting piece of clothing that covers your feet, legs and body up to your waist.

tigress *n*. a female tiger.

tile *n*. a flat piece of hard material used to cover floors, walls or roofs.

till 1. *n*. a machine used for adding and storing money in a shop. 2. *vb*. dig the land. 3. *prep*. up to, as late as.

tiller *n*. the handle or lever for turning a boat's rudder from side to side.

tilt *vb*. make something slope or slant. *n*. a sloping surface.

timber *n*. growing trees or their wood; wood suitable for carpentry or building.

time *n*. seconds, minutes, hours, days, months and years are all ways of measuring time. *vb*. record time of; choose the right time.

timetable *n*. a list of times at which certain things will happen. *The timetable showed us when our train would depart.*

timid *adj*. shy, not brave.

Spring tides are caused by the sun and moon pulling together. Neap tides occur when the sun and moon are at right angles to one another.

T

A tiger – a member of the cat family.

tin 1. *n.* a soft, pale metal which is mixed with other metals, or sometimes used to coat metal objects. 2. *n.* a container for food, a can. 3. *adj.* made of tin.

tinge *vb.* give a slight color to; tint.

tingle *vb.* a sensation like "pins and needles."

tinker *n.* a person who goes from place to place mending things, such as pots and pans.

tinkle *n.* a short ringing sound like a bell.

tinsel *n.* glittering and sparkling material used for decorations.

tint *vb.* & *n.* a slight or pale color.

tiny *adj.* very small.

tip 1. *n.* the point or end of something. *You can only see the tip of an iceberg above the sea.* 2. *vb.* knock over or spill something. 3. *n.* & *vb.* give someone, such as a waiter, reward for service.

tipsy *adj.* slightly drunk.

tiptoe *n.* the end of your toe. *vb.* walk on tiptoe. *She tiptoed out of the room.*

tire *vb.* become weary. **tireless** *adj.* seemingly incapable of becoming tired.

tissue *n.* 1. any kind of very fine fabric or material. 2. a paper handkerchief. 3. the mass of cells that make up the body of an animal or plant.

tit or **titmouse** *n.* any of a variety of small, active birds, e.g. blue tit.

titanium *n.* a silvery metallic element found in various ores and used mainly as an alloy. (symbol – *Ti*).

title *n.* 1. the name of a book, play, film, etc. 2. the words used to show a person's rank, such as "Doctor."

titter *vb.* & *n.* a nervous giggle.

toad *n.* a frog-like amphibian that has a rough warty skin. It lives mainly on land.

toadstool *n.* a kind of fungus like a mushroom, many varieties of which are poisonous.

toast *vb.* & *n.* 1. a slice of bread browned on both sides by grilling. 2. drink to someone's health, success or happiness. *We drank a toast to Rob on his birthday.*

tobacco *n.* the plant or leaves of the plant nicotiana which are dried and used in cigarettes, pipes, and cigars.

toboggan *n.* a long, flat sled for sliding down snowy hills. *vb.* travel by toboggan.

today *n.* this day; the present time.

to-do *n.* unnecessary fuss.

toe *n.* one of the five digits on the foot.

toffee *n.* a sticky kind of candy made from sugar and butter.

toga *n.* a flowing garment worn by men in ancient Rome, made of a large circular piece of woolen cloth.

together *adv.* in company with someone or something.

toil *vb.* & *n.* work very hard. *She toiled all day for little pay.*

toilet *n.* a lavatory, or the room in which the lavatory is.

token *n.* a symbol; a coin or other item used to represent something else.

told *vb.* past of **tell**.

tolerate *vb.* allow to happen; endure or put up with. *I will not tolerate bad manners.*

T

toll (rhymes with *coal*) 1. *n*. money paid in some places for crossing a bridge or for using a road. 2. *n*. & *vb*. ring or sound (of) a large, heavy bell, especially one used for funerals.

tomahawk *n*. an Indian war hatchet.

tomato *n*. (plural **tomatoes**) a round, red, juicy fruit eaten as a vegetable.

tomb (rhymes with *room*) *n*. a place where dead bodies are buried.

tomcat *n*. a male cat.

tome *n*. a large, heavy, scholarly book.

tom-tom *n*. a small drum, usually played with the hands.

tomorrow *n*. & *adv*. the day after today.

ton *n*. measure of great weight. *A "short" ton is 2000 pounds.*

tone 1. *n*. the musical quality of a sound. 2. *vb*. tint (of colors etc.).

tongs *pl. n*. (a pair of) an implement similar to pincers for grasping and holding objects, especially hot ones, e.g. *coal tongs.*

tongue *n*. the flap of muscle inside the mouth that we use for tasting, swallowing and speaking.

tonight *n*. the night of this day.

tonsils *pl. n*. a pair of glands at the back of the throat, one on each side.

too *adv*. as well as; also; in addition to something. *May I come, too?*

took *vb*. past of **take**.

tool *n*. a device such as a hammer or screwdriver that helps you do a job; an implement.

tooth *n*. one of the hard, bony parts in your mouth which are used for chewing food. **toothache** *n*. a pain in one or more teeth.

top 1. *n*. the highest point of something, summit. 2. *n*. a spinning toy. *adj*. at the top, uppermost.

topaz *n*. a semiprecious usually crystalline stone of varying colors, yellow, white, blue or pink.

topic *n*. a subject of conversation, etc. **topical** *adj*. relating to what is of interest at the moment.

topple *vb*. overbalance, fall headlong.

topsy-turvy *adv*. & *adj*. upside down; totally disordered.

torah *n*. the scroll of the first five books of the Bible – the Pentateuch – used in a synagogue for religious purposes.

torch *n*. a burning stick used to give light or flame.

tore *vb*. past of **tear**.

torment *n*. & *vb*. tease, annoy, cause distress.

torn *vb*. past part. of **tear**.

tornado *n*. (plural **tornadoes**) a violent storm with heavy rain.

torpedo *n*. a cigar-shaped explosive weapon used against ships.

torrent *n*. 1. a rushing stream. 2. a heavy flow of something.

torso *n*. the trunk of a body or statue (without head or limbs).

tortoise *n*. a slow-moving land reptile with a hard shell.

torture *n* & *vb*. treating someone very cruelly on purpose.

toss *vb*. throw lightly into the air.

total 1. *adj*. complete, all of something. 2. *n*. the answer when a series of numbers is added together.

totem *n*. an emblem or symbol of a clan or family. *A* **totem pole** *is carved with emblems that tell a story.*

toucan *n*., a large bird with an enormous orange beak.

touch 1. *vb*. feel something. *I reached out until I could just touch the wall.* 2. *n*. the sense of feeling.

touching 1. *vb*. having surfaces in contact with one another. 2. *adj*. feeling of tenderness. *The film had a very touching ending.*

tough (*tuff*) *adj*. not easily cut, strong and rough.

tour *n*. & *vb*. a journey on which a number of places are visited.

tournament *n*. a series of games in which the skills of the competitors are tested.

tow *vb*. pull a vehicle, boat, etc., behind another. *Our car's broken down. Can you tow us to the nearest garage?*

toward *prep*. in the direction of something. *The car was coming* *toward us much too fast.*

towel *n.* absorbent cloth for drying or wiping off wetness.

tower *n.* a kind of tall building, or the tall part of a building such as a church.

town *n.* a large group of houses and other buildings that is larger than a village but smaller than a city.

toy *n.* a child's plaything.

trace 1. *vb.* copy something by covering it with very thin paper and drawing around the outline that shows through. **traceable** *adj.* 2. *n.* a small sign, mark or amount left by something.

trachea (**tray-**keya) *n.* the windpipe.

track 1. *n.* a series of marks left by an animal or a vehicle. *vb.* follow something by watching for the signs, or tracks, it has left behind. 2. *n.* a railway line. 3. *n.* very strong chains of steel which are used

A tortoise is a land-living reptile (above). Turtles live mainly in water.

instead of wheels on tanks and some kinds of tractor. 4. *n.* section of a recording.

tract *n.* 1. a stretch of land. 2. a pamphlet or leaflet.

tractor *n.* a strong motor vehicle used to pull farm machinery.

trade *vb.* buy and sell; exchange.

trademark *n.* a special mark or sign used to show who made something and prevent illegal copying.

trade union *n.* an organization of people who work in the same sort of job; a **labor union**.

tradition *n.* beliefs, customs, etc., which are handed down from one generation to another.

traffic *n.* vehicles such as cars and trucks, or people, traveling along roads. *The traffic is very heavy today, because lots of people are driving out into the countryside.*

traffic jam *n.* a situation when the traffic has come to a standstill or slowed down to a crawl.

traffic light *n.* a crossing signal of colored lights on a pole, which tells drivers when to go, slow down, and stop.

tragedy *n.* (plural **tragedies**) 1. a kind of play, usually with a sad ending. 2. any very sad event. *His death at such an early age was a terrible tragedy for his parents.* **tragic** *adj.*

trail 1. *n.* a series of marks that show the way to somewhere; track. 2. *vb.* pull something along behind you. 3. *vb.* (of plant) grow along or hang down to the ground.

trailer 1. *n.* a vehicle that is towed along behind another one.

train 1. *n.* a group of carriages or wagons joined together and pulled along the track by an engine. 2. *vb.* prepare for a test of skill. *The team trains three times a week.*

traitor *n.* someone who betrays country or friends.

tramp 1. *vb.* walk heavily. 2. *n.* a long walk, a hike. 3. *n.* a homeless person who wanders, or tramps, from place to place.

T

trample *vb.* tread heavily on something, thus crush or destroy.

tranquil (*tran-kwill*) *adj.* calm, peaceful. **tranquillizer** *n.* a calming drug.

trans- *prefix* meaning across or beyond, e.g. **Trans-Continental Railroad**.

transaction *n.* business that is carried out.

transfer *vb.* move from one job or place to another.

transistor *n.* a very small electronic device that is used in radios and other electrical equipment; a radio that uses transistors.

translate *vb.* change from one language into another. *Pam had to translate a poem from Italian into English.* **translator** *n.*

transmission *n.* the passage of radio waves from the transmitting to the receiving station.

transmit *vb.* pass on, send out; broadcast.

transparent *adj.* something that is clear enough to see through.

transplant *vb.* move a plant from one bit of soil to another; move an organ, such as a heart or kidney, from one person's body to another.

transport (*trans-port*) *vb.* carry people or goods from one place to another. (**trans-port**) *n.* the vehicles in which people are carried.

transpose *vb.* change the order of.

trap *n.* & *vb.* a device for catching animals.

trapdoor *n.* a door covering an opening in the floor.

trapeze *n.* a bar hung on ropes far above the ground, and from which acrobats can swing.

trapezoid *n.* a four-sided figure with no sides parallel.

trash *n.* rubbish.

travel *n.* & *vb.* (past **traveled**) go from one place to another, make a journey.

trawler *n.* a fishing boat that drags (or trawls) nets along the bottom of the sea to catch fish. **trawl** *n.* a large net. *vb.* to fish with a trawl.

tray *n.* a flat object for carrying dishes, etc.

treachery *n.* betraying the trust a person has in one.

treacle *n.* a dark kind of syrup, produced as a by-product of sugar refining.

tread 1. *vb.* (past **trod** past part. **trodden**) put your feet down on the ground. 2. *n.* the rubber and its raised pattern on the outside of a tire. 3. *n.* top surface of a step.

treason *n.* trying to overthrow a government or to kill or injure its leader.

treasure 1. *n.* a store of valuable things, such as gold and jewels. 2. *vb.* value something very highly. *Alan treasures signed photos of several stars.* **treasury** *n.* a place where valuable things are kept; the funds of a state.

treat 1. *vb.* behave toward someone in a certain way. *Caroline treats her baby brother very kindly.* 2. *vb.* use something to improve or change. *You can treat this stain with salt.* **treatment** *n.* 3. *n.* something that gives you special pleasure. *My aunt took us to the play for a treat.*

treaty *n.* a written and signed agreement between countries relating to alliance, commerce, etc.

tree *n.* the tallest kind of plant with only one thick central stem or trunk.

tremble *vb.* shake gently all over.

tremendous *adj.* of great size or power; excellent.

trench *n.* a ditch, often used in warfare to protect troops.

trend *n.* the general direction or course.

trendy *adj.* following the latest fashions.

trespass *vb.* go on somebody else's land or property unlawfully. **trespasser** *n.* person who trespasses.

tri- *prefix* meaning three or threefold, e.g. **tricolor** having three colors.

trial *n.* 1. an examination in a court of law. 2. a test of something to see how good it is. *We watched the trial of the new helicopter.* 3. a hardship, affliction.

triangle *n.* 1. a flat shape with three sides. **triangular** *adj.* 2. a musical instrument made of metal, that is hit with a small metal rod.

tribe *n.* a group of people who have the same customs and language. **tribal** *adj.*

tributary *n.* a small stream or river that flows into a larger one.

trick 1. *n.* a joke or prank; a deceitful act or scheme. *vb.* deceive, cheat. 2. *n.* a piece of "magic" done by a conjuror. 3. *n.* a round played in some card games, such as bridge and whist.

trickle *vb.* flow in a thin stream.

tricolor *n.* a three-colored flag, especially the blue, white and red flag of France.

tricycle *n.* a three-wheeled cycle.

tried *vb.* past of **try**.

trifle *n.* 1. an unimportant or small thing. 2. a sweet pudding made from cake, custard, fruit, wine and cream. **trifling** *adj.* of small importance.

trigger *n.* the lever on a gun that is used to fire it.

trigonometry *n.* a branch of mathematics concerned with the properties of triangles.

trim 1. *adj.* neat and tidy. 2. *vb.* cut something so as to make it neat and tidy. *Please trim my hair.* 3. *vb. & n.* (adorn with) small ornaments.

trinity *n.* a group of three.

trinket *n.* a small ornament or jewelry of little value.

trio *n.* three people working together, especially musicians.

trip 1. *n. & vb.* catch your foot on something and fall over. 2. *n.* a journey. *Have a good trip.*

tripe *n.* 1. the stomach of a cow eaten as food. 2. rubbish, worthless stuff.

triple *adj.* made of three parts. *vb.* make or become three times as great or as many.

triplet *n.* one of three babies born to the same mother at the same time.

triumph *n.* great victory or achievement. *vb.* rejoice in victory. **triumphal** *adj.*

troika *n.* Russian vehicle drawn by three horses abreast.

troll *n.* a goblin or dwarf, usually evil, in Scandinavian legends.

trolley *n.* an electric car for passengers that runs on tracks.

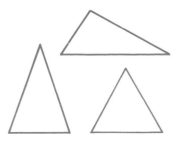

Three different kinds of triangle.

trombone *n.* a musical wind instrument made of brass.

troops *pl.n.* a body of soldiers, armed forces in general.

trophy *n.* something taken in victory especially when kept as a memorial; a prize; a memento.

tropical fish *pl.n.* fish that live in the warm seas of tropical regions, often along the edges of coral reefs.

tropics *pl.n.* the areas of land around the equator. **tropical** *adj.*

trot *vb. & n.* run with short steps like the slow run of a horse.

trouble *n.* problem; difficulty; disgrace or punishment. *Jerry got into trouble for breaking a window.* *vb.* disturb; put to inconvenience.

trough (*troff*) *n.* a long shallow container for the drinking water or feed of animals.

T

troupe *n.* a group of performers.

trousers *pl.n.* an article of clothing for the lower half of the body, divided into two sections, one for each leg; pants.

trout *n.* (plural **trout**) a silvery-brown, speckled freshwater fish belonging to the salmon family.

trowel *n.* 1. a garden tool like a small spade. 2. a flat-bladed tool for spreading mortar.

truant *n.* a child who stays away from school when he or she is supposed to be there. **truancy** *n.*

truce *n.* a period when two sides in a war or quarrel agree to be at peace.

truck *n.* a motor vehicle used to carry big or heavy loads.

trudge *vb.* plod; walk steadily with great effort.

true *adj.* correct; accurate; not false; genuine. *I hope what you say is true.*

truffle *n.* 1. edible fungus that grows underground. 2. soft candy made of a chocolate mixture.

trumpet *n.* a brass wind musical instrument, played by pressing valves. *vb.* proclaim.

trump up *vb.* invent, fabricate.

trunk *n.* 1. the main stem of a tree. 2. the body of an animal apart from the head or limbs. 3. a large box. 4. the long nose of an elephant. 5. the luggage compartment of a car.

truss *vb.* tie up tightly; bind.

trust *vb.* believe that something or somebody is good, or will tell the truth. *n.* confidence in a person.

truth *n.* correctness, accuracy; something that is true. *I'm telling you the truth.*

try 1. *vb.* attempt to do something. **trying** *adj.* exhausting, difficult to bear. *He is a trying person.*

tsar (*zar*) *n.* (variant spelling of **czar**) the emperor of Russia until 1917.

tsetse (*tet-si*) *n.* brownish fly found in tropical Africa.

tub *n.* 1. a small barrel. 2. a bath (bathtub). 3. an old, slow and clumsy ship or boat.

tuba *n.* a large musical wind instrument that gives a low note.

tubby *adj.* short and fat.

tube *n.* a long, hollow cylinder, especially for conveying liquids.

tuber *n.* the large part of an underground stem from which new plants grow. *A potato grows from a tuber.*

tuberculosis *n.* a disease caused by bacterial infection.

tuck *n.* & *vb.* fold under. *Sheets are tucked under the mattress.*

Tuesday *n.* the third day of the week, between Monday and Wednesday; named after Tiw, Norse god of war.

tuft *n.* a small bunch, cluster or clump. *A tuft of hair or grass.*

tug 1. *vb.* pull hard.

tugboat *n.* a small, powerful boat that tows larger ships in and out of port.

tulip *n.* a brightly colored, spring garden flower which grows from a bulb.

tumble *vb.* fall down suddenly.

tumbling *n.* skill or practice of gymnastic feats, e.g. handsprings, flips, without use of any apparatus. *vb.* **tumble.**

tumbler *n.* 1. a large glass without a stem. 2. an acrobat.

tummy *n.* (*casual*) stomach.

tumor *n.* a lump or swelling in the body made up of abnormal cells.

tuna *n.* a large fish, of the mackerel family.

tundra *n.* the cold, treeless plains in the arctic and subarctic regions.

tune *n.* a musical melody, especially the music that goes with a song. *He hummed a cheerful tune.*

tungsten *n.* (also called *wolfram*), a hard, heavy, gray-white metallic element (symbol – *W*).

tunic *n.* a long, close-fitting jacket, often part of a uniform.

tunnel *n.* an underground passage. *vb.* dig under the ground.

turban *n.* a head covering consisting

of a long strip of cloth wound around and around a cap. Turbans are traditionally worn in some Eastern countries, often for religious reasons.

turbine *n*. an engine with a driving wheel (or screw) which is turned by water, steam or air.

turbojet *adj*. & *n*. a type of gas turbine in which hot gases produced by the burning of fuel turn the blades of a fan whose shaft works the blades of a compressor which sucks in air and forces it into the combustion chamber.

turbot *n*. a large flat fish.

tureen *n*. a large deep bowl for serving soup, etc.

turf *n*. 1. grass-covered ground. *"The turf" is an expression sometimes used to mean "horse-racing."* 2. a piece of earth with grass attached to it, cut from the ground.

turkey *n*. a large American bird of the pheasant family, bred in many parts of the world for its delicate meat.

turn 1. *vb*. revolve; go around. 2. *vb*. change direction; face the other way. 3. your place in a scheduled order. *n*. *It's my turn*.

turn down *vb*. refuse an offer or ideas. *I wanted to turn down the job, but I needed the money, so I agreed to do it*.

turnip *n*. a plant grown for its roundish, white, edible root, which is cooked and eaten as a vegetable.

turnout *n*. 1. the number of people attending a function. *There was a big turnout for the president's visit*.

turn up *vb*. 1. arrive, usually unexpectedly. *Emma turned up just before dinner*. 2. increase something by using a control. *That knob on the radio turns up the sound*.

turquoise *n*. a blue or green semi-precious stone.

turret *n*. 1. a small tower, usually in a larger building. 2. a revolving part of a warship, tank, etc., that holds a gun.

turtle *n*. a reptile that can pull its head and limbs inside its shell.

tusk *n*. a long, large, pointed tooth on an elephant, walrus, etc.

tutor *n*. a private teacher; a person who gives individual instruction to students.

tutu *n*. the short frilly skirt worn by a ballerina.

twice *adv*. two times.

twig *n*. a small branch on a tree or bush.

twilight *n*. the dim light between sunset and nighttime.

twin *n*. one of two children born to the same mother at the same time.

twinge *n*. a sharp, shooting pain.

twinkle *vb*. send out little flashes of light.

twirl *vb*. spin, turn around and around.

twist *vb*. wind around, turn and curve.

tycoon *n*. a very rich businessman.

type 1. *n*. a kind, a sort. *Tulips are a type of flower*. 2. *vb*. use a typewriter. 3. *n*. the letters used to print words.

typewriter *n*. a machine that prints letters.

typhoid fever *n*. an infectious disease in which the intestines become inflamed.

typhoon *n*. a tropical cyclone (windstorm) that often brings rain.

typhus *n*. a severe feverish disease marked by eruptions on the skin.

typical *adj*. a good example of its kind.

typist *n*. a person who uses a typewriter.

tyrannosaurus *n*. a huge, flesh-eating dinosaur that lived more than 70 million years ago.

tyranny *n*. oppressive and cruel use of power.

tyrant *n*. a cruel, unfair ruler.

U-boat *n.* German submarine in both world wars.

udder *n.* the bag-like part of a female mammal, such as a cow, from which milk comes.

ugh *inter.* an expression of disgust.

ugly *adj.* unpleasant to look at; not beautiful or handsome. **ugliness** *n.*

ukulele (*you*-ka-**lay**-*lee*) *n.* a small guitar with four strings.

ulcer *n.* an open sore, usually with a flow of pus (infected fluid).

ulna *n.* the inner of the two bones of the forearm.

ultimate *adj.* last, final, eventual. *Our ultimate aim is to be successful.*

ultraviolet radiation *n.* light beyond the visible spectrum.

umbilicus *n.* the cord connecting the developing fetus with the mother's placenta and through which the fetus is fed. When the child is born the cord is cut, leaving the "belly button." **umbilical** *adj.* of the navel.

umbrella *n.* a fabric shade, supported by a wire frame with a handle which people carry to keep the rain off. *You can fold up an umbrella when you're not using it.*

umpire *n.* the person who sees that the rules are obeyed in certain games. *Important tennis matches have an umpire to oversee them.* *vb.* act as umpire.

un- *prefix* expressing negation, lack of, etc. used before adjectives, adverbs and verbs. If the meaning of the main word is known then the sense of the word with the added prefix should usually be clear, e.g. **unaccompanied** not escorted or accompanied. **unbalanced** not balanced. **unchristian** not in accordance with Christian beliefs or practices.

unadulterated *adj.* pure; unmixed with any other material.

unanimous (*you*-**nan**-*i*-*mus*) *adj.* when everyone agrees.

uncanny *adj.* strange, mysterious.

uncivil *adj.* rude, impolite.

uncle *n.* the brother of your mother or father.

uncompromising *adj.* unyielding; stubborn.

unconscious *adj.* not conscious, not knowing what is happening around you, unaware of.

uncouth *adj.* clumsy and awkward in manners and language.

uncover *vb.* take the cover off something, or show it.

undemonstrative *adj.* reserved. *A person who does not show feelings openly is undemonstrative.*

under *adj.*, *adv.* & *prep.* beneath.

under- *prefix* meaning below, beneath, less than, lacking in. When the meaning of the main word is known, the sense of the prefixed word should in many cases be clear, e.g. **underweight, understate.**

undercover *adj.* not in the open, secret.

underdog *n.* a loser or someone who will almost certainly lose in any fight or contest.

undergraduate *n.* a student at a university who has not yet taken a degree.

undergo *vb.* suffer, experience.

underground railway *n.* a railway which runs mainly below ground.

underline *vb.* 1. draw a line under words on a page to make them stand out, e.g. <u>Danger</u>. 2. emphasize, stress.

underneath *adv.* & *prep.* beneath. *The mechanic was lying underneath the car he was repairing.*

underpass *n.* a place where one road passes under another one.

understand *vb.* (past **understood**) grasp the meaning of something with your mind; know. *Did you understand what the teacher was saying?* **understanding** *n.* the ability to know; an agreement.

understanding *adj.* gentle, kind.

understudy *n.* an actor who takes over from the usual performer of a part in an emergency.

undertake *vb.* agree to do; be responsible for. *John undertook to look after the herb garden.*

undertaker *n.* a person who arranges funerals.

underwrite *vb.* (in insurance) accepting the risk or liability for what is insured.

undo *vb.* 1. untie (a knot); unbutton; remove. 2. reverse; bring to nothing. *This government says it is going to undo the damage caused by the last government.*

undress *vb.* take clothes off.

undue *adj.* too much, excessive. *They gave him undue praise.*

undulate *vb.* rise and fall like waves.

unearth *vb.* dig up or discover something. *Granny managed to unearth some old family photos from her desk.*

unemployed *adj.* without a paid job; out of work; not being used.

unemployment *n.* the state of being unemployed.

unequal *adj.* not the same; not equal.

unfair *adj.* not just or according to the rules.

unfortunate *adj.* unlucky.

unfounded *adj.* not based on fact. *Your doubts about my honesty are unfounded.*

unfrock *vb.* remove a person from being a priest.

unfurl *vb.* unfold and display. *The flag was unfurled.*

ungainly *adj.* awkward, clumsy.

unhappy *adj.* miserable; not happy; unfortunate.

uni- *prefix* meaning one, e.g. **unicellular** having only one cell.

unicorn *n.* an animal in stories and legends that has a body like a horse and a single horn in the middle of its forehead.

uniform 1. *n.* matching clothes worn by all the members of a group of people, such as a school or an army. 2. *adj.* unvarying, constant; to one standard. *The books are of uniform size.*

union *n.* joining together of a number of things or people. *The American colonies formed a union in 1789.*

unique (*yoo-***neek**) *adj.* the only one of its kind; having no equal.

unit *n.* a single thing, or a group of things that are thought of as being one thing.

unite *vb.* join together, combine. **unity** *n.*

universal *adj. n.* general, common, done by most people. *Art and music are universal.*

Uniforms (from left): A Russian grenadier; a Napoleonic infantryman and a modern UN soldier (American).

U

universe n. everything in existence; all space; the cosmos.

university n. a place where people go on studying after they have left high school; an institute of higher education (college) with the authority to award degrees.

unkempt adj. untidy in appearance.

unkind adj. not kind; treating others badly. **unkindness** n.

unknown adj. n. not known; unexplored.

unless conj. except. *I'm not coming unless you come too.*

unload vb. empty a load from something, such as a ship or truck; remove ammunition from gun.

unlucky adj. not lucky; unfortunate. *Anne played so well that her team was unlucky not to win.*

unnecessary adj. not necessary; something that can be prevented.

unpack vb. remove things from a container, particularly a suitcase.

unpleasant adj. not pleasant; nasty or disagreeable.

unsavory adj. offensive, disagreeable.

unscathed adj. unharmed.

unseemly adj. not suitable for the time and place; improper.

unsightly adj. ugly.

untidy adj. not tidy, nor orderly; leaving things in a mess. *Adrian's bedroom was incredibly untidy.*

until prep. & conj. till; before; till such time as. *The dentist cannot give you an appointment until next week.*

untold adj. too many to be counted.

unusual adj. not usual; strange or peculiar; remarkable. *Caroline was wearing a most unusual dress.*

unwell adj. ill; sick; not well.

unwieldy adj. awkward to handle.

unwitting adj. unaware of; not knowing.

unwrap vb. take the wrapping off something, such as a parcel or present.

up adv. & prep. in, to a higher place, level, etc.

upheaval n. great disorder, change.

uphill 1. adv. going up a hill or slope. *Riding a bicycle uphill can get very tiring.* 2. adj. difficult. *Life can sometimes be an uphill struggle.*

upholstery n. the padding and covering of chairs and sofas. **upholsterer** n.

upkeep n. cost of keeping in good repair.

upon prep. on; on top of.

upper adj. above, in a higher place.

upright adj. 1. vertical, standing tight. *We put the pole upright in the sand.* 2. honest. *She is an upright woman.*

uproar n. a violent disturbance, commotion.

upset vb. (past **upset**) 1. knock something over. *Mark upset the milk.* 2. make someone unhappy. *The bad news upset Jan.*

upshot n. the outcome, final result. *The upshot of the argument was that we agreed to do nothing.*

upside down adv. the "wrong" way up. *Sloths spend most of their time hanging upside down from branches of trees.* In total disorder.

upstage adv. back of the stage away from the footlights.

upstairs adv. adj. & n. above the ground floor of a building. *Go upstairs to your bedroom.*

upstart n. a person who has risen suddenly to a position of power or wealth.

upstream adv. & adj. in the direction opposite to the flow of the stream or river, higher up the river.

uptight adj. nervous, annoyed.

uranium n. a hard, heavy silvery, metallic element that is radioactive (symbol – U).

urban adj. to do with cities. *A city is an urban area.*

urchin n. a mischievous, shabbily dressed boy.

urge vb. encourage, drive on. n. strong force or desire.

urgent adj. so important that it needs to be attended to at once. **urgency** n.

urine n. amber-colored liquid waste that is excreted.

urn n. a vase or container for storing

the ashes of the dead; large vessel with a tap for holding hot drinks.

usage *n.* customary practice or manner of doing things.

use (rhymes with *views*) 1. *vb.* employ something for a particular purpose. *You use a saw for cutting wood.* 2. *n.* (rhymes with *juice*) the way in which something is used. *Plastics have many different uses.*

used *adj.* not new; secondhand.

used to *vb.* 1. know some experience well because it has often happened. *We are used to waiting a long time for the bus.* 2. referring to the past. *Her parents used to live in Australia but then they moved to New York.*

useful *adj.* helpful, valuable.

useless *adj.* of no use; no good to anyone. *A broken watch is useless.*

usual *adj.* the normal way in which something happens, or is done; most of the time. *Dan wore his usual clothes to the party.*

usually *adv.* in an ordinary or a normal way. *We usually go to school together.*

usurp *vb.* seize or take possession of by force or illegally (especially authority or power).

usury *n.* money-lending at a very high rate of interest. **usurer** *n.* a person who practises usury.

utensil *n.* a tool or instrument, especially one that is used in cooking. *An egg whisk is a very handy utensil.*

uterus (*yoo-ter-us*) *n.* the womb, the organ in which an unborn mammal is carried.

utilize *vb.* make use of.

Utopia *n.* an imaginary and perfect place. **utopian** *adj.*

utter 1. *adj.* complete or total, especially something bad. *The room was an utter mess.* 2. *vb.* say something, make a sound. *The kitten tried to utter a faint mew.*

utterance *n.* words spoken.

U-turn *n.* when a vehicle changes direction through 180° by turning on a U-shaped course; a complete change of policy.

vacant *adj.* empty; not filled. **vacancy** *n.* being vacant; unoccupied property or job. *There is a vacancy in the post office.*

vacate *vb.* give up, make empty, leave. *Customers are asked to vacate the premises as soon as they have finished their business.*

vacation *n.* holiday; time when courts, schools, etc. are closed.

vaccinate (**vak**-*sin-ate*) *vb.* inoculate against a disease, notably smallpox. **vaccination** *n.* **vaccine** *n.*

vacuum 1. *n.* an absolutely empty space. 2. *vb.* clean by suction, using a *vacuum cleaner.*

vagabond *n.* a person without a fixed home.

vague *adj.* not clear, indefinite, indistinct. **vagueness** *n.*

vain *adj.* 1. showing too much pride. 2. futile, unsuccessful. *They searched for the dog in vain.* **vanity** *n.*

vale *n.* a valley.

valence (**vay**-*lence*) *n.* (also called **valency**) the number of chemical bonds with which an atom or a radical (group containing different atoms) can link with other atoms.

valet *n.* a man who looks after the personal needs of his employer, hotel guests, etc.

valiant *adj.* brave, courageous.

valid *adj.* legally acceptable. *Is your driving license valid for all countries?*

valley *n.* a hollow between hills; a U-shaped or V-shaped depression in the earth's surface.

valuable *adj.* of great value or worth.

value 1. *n.* the amount of money that

V

something is worth. 2. *vb.* estimate value of; think highly of.

valve *n.* 1. a device that controls the flow of liquid, allowing it to go in one direction only. 2. one half of a hinged shell.

vampire *n.* 1. a dead person in old stories who is supposed to suck the blood of living people. 2. a small bat found in the forests of Central and South America.

van *n.* a covered vehicle for carrying things.

vandal *n.* a person who destroys or damages things for no obvious reason. **vandalism** *n.*

vane *n.* a device that revolves in the wind and indicates wind direction. *Vanes are often put at the top of buildings.*

vanilla *n. & adj.* the pod of a tropical climbing plant used to flavor ice cream and other foods.

vanish *vb.* disappear suddenly.

vanquish (*van-kwish*) *vb.* defeat, conquer.

vapor *n.* a substance such as gas, mist or smoke. *Steam is water vapor.*

variety *n.* 1. a number of different things or kinds of. *You can buy this blouse in a variety of colors.* 2. a form of popular entertainment, involving comedians, singers, dancers, etc.

various *adj.* having different varieties; several. *Michael has worked at various jobs since he left school.*

varnish *n.* a liquid made from chemicals like resins which is used like paint and, when dry, is hard, shiny, and transparent. *vb.* coat with varnish.

vary *vb.* change, become different.

vase *n.* a glass, china or pottery container, deeper than it is tall, often used to hold flowers.

vast *adj.* very large in size, amount, etc. *The circus tent was vast.*

vat *n.* a large, usually uncovered container for holding liquids.

vault 1. *vb.* jump with your hands resting on something for support. *Denise tried to vault over the fence.* 2. *n.* an underground room, often used to store valuable things. 3. *n.* an arched roof.

veal *n.* the meat of a young calf.

veer *vb.* change direction, especially of the wind; change one's mind.

vegetable *n.* a plant, especially one grown for food. *Vegetables taste less sweet than most fruits.*

vegetarian *n.* a person who does not eat meat or fish. *Some vegetarians do not eat milk or eggs either.*

vegetation *n.* all the plants that grow in a certain area.

vehement (*vee-a-ment*) *adj.* violent, energetic.

vehicle *n.* anything that is used to transport people or things from one place to another. *Trains, cars and carts are all vehicles.*

veil *n.* a covering for the head, and especially the face, in some Eastern countries.

vein (rhymes with *lane*) *n.* 1. one of the blood vessels that takes blood back to the heart from various parts of the body. 2. a layer or streak of mineral.

velocity *n.* the speed of a body measured in a given direction.

velvet *n.* a fabric with a thick, soft pile of short, raised threads all over its surface. *Velvet is used largely for curtains and furnishings.*

vendetta *n.* an Italian word meaning a feud or violent hostilities, especially between families.

veneer *n.* a thin layer of good quality wood covering wood of poorer quality; superficial appearance.

vengeance *n.* punishment inflicted on someone to pay back harm or wrong done; revenge.

venison *n.* the meat of a deer.

venom *n.* the poison of certain snakes and other poisonous animals, injected by biting or stinging.

vent *n.* an outlet or opening through which gas, etc., can escape. *He gave vent to his feelings.*

ventilate *vb.* circulate air to freshen (a room); discuss something openly and freely.

ventriloquist *n.* someone who can make the voice seem to come from somewhere else.

venture *vb. & n.* risk, dare to. *"Nothing ventured nothing gained," as the proverb says.*

venue *n.* a meeting place.

veranda, verandah *n.* a covered patio or terrace on the ground floor of a house.

verb *n.* a word for something that is done, or happens. *In "the cat ate the rat," the verb is "ate."*

verdict *n.* the decision of a judge. *The verdict was "not guilty."*

vermin *n.* (plural **vermin**) any animals, from insects to rats, which cause harm to crops, etc., or which spread disease.

versatile *adj.* having ability in different skills.

verse *n.* one section or part of a song or poem.

version *n.* one form or variant of an original book, incident, etc. *That is your version of what happened. My version is totally different.*

versus *prep.* in contest against. It is shortened to *v.* in sports, e.g. Jets *v.* Cowboys, and in lawsuits, e.g. Jones *v.* Smith.

vertebra *n.* (plural **vertebrae**) the small bones of the spine.

vertebrate *n.* an animal with a backbone, or spinal column.

vertical *adj.* straight up and down, upright, perpendicular.

vespers *n.* an evening church service.

vessel *n.* 1. a hollow utensil, especially one for holding liquids. 2. a ship or boat.

vest *n.* a sleeveless garment, usually V-necked, worn over a shirt.

vestige *n.* a slight trace or evidence of something that once existed.

vestment *n.* an official robe or gown worn for services and rites.

vestry *n.* a room in a church where vestments are kept.

vet *n.* an abbreviation for veterinarian.

veteran *n.* someone with a lot of experience.

veterinarian *n.* a doctor for animals.

veto *n.* (plural **vetoes**) the power to forbid or prohibit something. *vb.* refuse to agree to.

vex *vb.* annoy or irritate someone.

via (**vie**-*a*, **vee**-*a*) *prep.* by way of. *Today the train went via Oxford instead of Reading.*

viable *adj.* workable.

viaduct *n.* a long bridge that is built to carry a railway, road, or canal across a valley.

vibrate *vb.* move very quickly back and forth, quiver.

vicar *n.* a clergyman in charge of a church and parish.

vice 1. *n.* a very bad habit or immoral conduct. 2. *n.* a tool that holds things steady and in one place so they can be worked on. 3. *prefix* (**vice-**) in place of, next in rank to, e.g. Vice-President of the United States.

vicinity *n.* neighborhood. *If you are ever in the vicinity, do drop in.*

vicious (rhymes with **wish**-*us*) *adj.* fierce, violent, savage.

victim *n.* someone who suffers harm or danger.

victor *n.* one who defeats an enemy or opponent; winner.

Victorian *adj.* belonging to the reign of Queen Victoria.

victory *n.* success, winning. **victorious** *adj.*

vicuna *n.* a small South American camel without a hump.

videotape *n.* a magnetic tape used for recording the pictures and sounds from or for television movies and programs.

vie *vb.* compete with someone.

view 1. *n.* act of seeing; what is seen. 2. *n.* opinion. *Have you any views on this topic?* 3. *vb.* look at.

viewfinder *n.* device to help photographer aim the camera, indicating the part of the scene that will appear on the film.

Vikings *n. pl.* Scandinavian seafarers who raided and plundered many parts of Europe between the 700s and 1100s.

A Viking longboat. The Vikings were great traders as well as raiders.

vile *adj*. horrible, unpleasant.

villa *n*. a country house in Roman times; a small house in a suburban or residential district.

village *n*. a group of houses and other buildings that is smaller than a town and usually has a church.

villain *n*. a wicked or evil person.

vine *n*. a climbing or creeping plant. **vineyard** *n*. a place where grapevines are grown.

vinegar *n*. an acid liquid used for flavoring and preserving food.

viola *n*. a stringed musical instrument that looks like a large violin.

violence *n*. great physical force. **violent** *adj*.

violet 1. *n*. & *adj*. a color, like a mixture of blue and purple. 2. *n*. a small plant with violet-colored or white flowers.

violin *n*. a stringed musical instrument played with a bow. **violinist** *n*. player of a violin.

viper *n*. one of a group of poisonous snakes.

virtue *n*. goodness; morality; merit.

virtuoso *n*. a highly skilled persons especially in playing a musical instrument.

virus *n*. a tiny living particle that can carry and cause diseases.

visa *n*. a stamp on a passport allowing a person to enter a particular country.

viscount (**vie**-*count*) *n*. title of a nobleman (peer) ranking between an earl and baron.

viscountess *n*. the wife of a viscount.

visible *adj*. capable of being seen. *The ship was still just visible on the horizon.*

vision *n*. 1. the power of seeing, eyesight. 2. something seen in a dream, etc. 3. great power of imagination.

visit *vb*. pay a call on someone; go to see a place; stay with or at. *n*. a journey made in order to visit a place or person.

visitor *n*. a person who comes to see or stay with someone; a traveler who is staying in a place for a short time only.

visor *n*. the part of a helmet, usually movable, that covers the eyes; a shade, such as the flap inside a car window that protects your eyes from the sun.

visual *adj*. concerned with sight and seeing. **visualize** *vb*. imagine, form a picture. *She tried to visualize what the dress would be like without pleats.*

vital *adj*. 1. of great importance. 2. lively, energetic.

Three members of the violin family (from left): the violin, the viola and the cello.

Cello

Viola

Violin

V

vitamin *n*. one of a group of chemical substances that our body needs in order to stay healthy.

vivid *adj*. lively; bright and clear. *Dickens wrote vivid descriptions of London life.*

vixen *n*. a female fox.

vocabulary *n*. all the words known or used in a certain language.

vocal *adj*. to do with the voice.

vocation *n*. a calling (by God) to do special work; a career or profession.

vodka *n*. type of alcohol made in the Soviet Union and Poland – a strong mash liquor which has no color and little flavor.

vogue *n*. the fashion at a particular time. *Hats are again in vogue.*

voice *n*. the sound produced when you speak or sing; your ability to make such a sound.

void *adj*. 1. containing nothing; vacant. 2. having no legal force; not valid.

volcano *n*. (plural **volcanoes**) an opening in the surface of the earth from which magma (molten rock), gas and steam are forced out; a mountain formed from hardened magma. **volcanic** *adj*.

vole *n*. a small rodent that looks like a mouse.

volley *n*. 1. flight or return of a ball before it has hit the ground. *vb*. 2. a number of missiles, e.g. arrows, fired at the same time.

volt *n*. a unit for measuring electrical pressure or electromotive force.

volume *n*. 1. the amount of space something takes up. 2. a single book, particularly one of a set. 3. loudness. *I can't hear the radio properly; could you please turn up the volume?*

voluntary *adj*. doing without being asked or forced to; done without payment or obligation.

volunteer *n*. a person who offers to do something without being asked; a serviceman who joins up from his own choice. *vb*. offer one's services. *Jim volunteered to mow the lawn.*

vomit *vb*. throw up food from your stomach through your mouth; be sick.

vote *vb*. show what you want from a group of choices by supporting one of them; ballot.

voucher *n*. a coupon; a certificate.

vow *vb*. & *n*. (make) a solemn promise.

vowel *n*. one of the sounds represented by the letters A, E, I, O, U and sometimes Y.

voyage *n*. a journey, particularly by sea.

vulgar *adj*. crude, coarse, in bad taste.

vulnerable *adj*. unprotected and easily wounded; open to attack and liable to have feelings hurt.

vulture *n*. one of a family of large birds of prey which feed largely on dead animals.

Inside a volcano. Hot lava and melted rock erupt through the central vent. The mountain is made from layers of cold ash and lava.

231

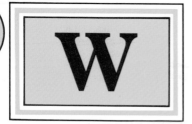

waddle *n.* & *vb.* walk in a clumsy way like a duck.

wade *vb.* walk through water; move with some difficulty, progress slowly. *The river was just shallow enough for us to wade across.*

wadi *n.* an Arabic word meaning the dry bed of a river.

wafer *n.* a thin crisp biscuit; material sliced very thin.

waffle 1. *n.* a small, crisp kind of pancake. 2. *n.* & *vb.* talk or write nonsense.

wag *vb.* quick jerky movements up and down or from side to side. *A dog wags its tail when it is pleased.*

wage *vb.* carry on, take part in. *They waged war for five years.* *n.* the money you get for working, usually paid weekly.

waggle *vb.* wave or wag; wobble. *The pilot waggled the wings of his aircraft to show he had seen us.*

wagon *n.* an open cart with four wheels; delivery truck.

wagtail *n.* one of a family of small birds with sharp beaks and long tails.

waif *n.* a homeless, abandoned child.

wail *n.* a mournful cry, usually loud and shrill. *vb.* cry in wails, lament.

waist *n.* the narrow part of the body between the chest and the hips.

waistcoat *n.* a sleeveless jacket, sometimes worn as part of a suit.

wait *vb.* stay in one place, expecting something to happen. *We will wait here until you come back.*

waiter *n.* a man who serves food in a restaurant.

waitress *n.* (plural **waitresses**) a woman who serves food in a restaurant.

wake 1. *vb.* (past **woke** past part. **woken**) stop sleeping; rouse from sleep. 2. *n.* the track left in water by a ship.

walk *vb.* & *n.* (of a person or animal) move along at a steady pace, travel on foot, advance by steps.

walkie-talkie *n.* a portable radio telephone.

Walkman *n.* a small portable cassette tape player with headphones.

walkover *n.* an easy victory.

wall *n.* a barrier made of brick or stone surrounding a piece of land; the side of a room or building. *vb.* (**in**) protect with a wall.

wallaby *n.* a kind of marsupial, smaller than a kangaroo.

wallet *n.* a folding purse in which money or papers are kept.

wallow *vb.* splash about in mud; take delight in; be helpless. *They were left to wallow in ignorance.*

walnut *n.* deciduous tree belonging to the Northern Hemisphere, grown for its fine wood and its edible nut of the same name.

walrus *n.* (plural **walruses**) a large sea animal with long tusks, which lives in the Arctic.

waltz (rhymes with *false*) *n.* a dance in three-quarter time. *vb.* dance a waltz; have easy success.

wand *n.* a slender stick used by fairies and magicians in stories to cause magic spells.

wander *n.* go from place to place without having a plan or a purpose. **wanderer** *n.*

wane *vb.* become smaller. *The moon is waning.*

wangle *vb.* get something by cunning; finagle. *Fred wangled a free ticket to the show.*

want 1. *vb.* wish for or strongly desire something; need. 2. *n.* lack of something; need (of).

wanted *adj.* sought (especially by the police).

war *n.* armed conflict between two or

more countries or groups of people.

ward *n.* 1. a room in a hospital where sick people needing similar care stay. 2. administrative division of a town. 3. *vb.* keep watch over, guard.

warden *n.* a guard in charge of prisoners in a jail.

ward off *vb.* prevent something happening.

wardrobe *n.* a cupboard where clothes are hung and stored.

warehouse *n.* a large building where goods of all sorts are kept. *vb.* store in a warehouse.

warfare *n.* the state of war.

warm *adj.* slightly hot; affectionate.

warn *vb.* tell people of danger.
warning *n.* something that tells you of danger. *There was a warning light by the bridge, so we stopped.*

warp 1. *vb.* become twisted or bent. 2. *n.* the vertical threads on a loom, used for weaving.

warren *n.* a place where a group of rabbits live together in burrows.

warrior *n.* a fighter.

warship *n.* a military ship, especially one armed for combat.

wart *n.* a small, hard lump on the skin.

wash *vb.* clean something by soaking it in water.

washer *n.* a small flat ring used to make a joint tight, such as on a tap.

wasp *n.* a flying insect with a striped body and a sting in its tail. **waspish** *adj.* snappy, irritable.

waste *vb.* use more than you need of something, or throw something away although you could have used it. *n.* unwanted material. **wasteful** *adj.* extravagant.

watch 1. *vb.* look on. *Did you watch the football game?* 2. *n.* a timepiece, usually worn on the wrist.

watch for *vb.* be on the alert for.

watch over *vb.* guard, protect.

water 1. *n.* the most common of all liquids, formed from two gases: oxygen and hydrogen. 2. *vb.* sprinkle with water; apply water to; dilute.

water boatman *n.* a water bug with long and powerful hind legs.

water buffalo *n.* a large kind of ox, used as a beast of burden in many Eastern countries.

watercolor *n.* a painting done with paint that dissolves in water.

water cycle *n.* the continuous movement of water from lakes and seas via the atmosphere to land areas and back again.

waterfall *n.* a rush of water which falls from a high place in a river or stream.

waterlogged *adj.* so soaked with water as to be unable to float.

watermark *n.* a special design impressed onto paper which can be seen when held up to the light.

water polo *n.* a game played in water with a large inflated ball and two teams of seven swimmers. The ball is thrown from one swimmer to another, and each team tries to score goals.

water power *n.* mechanical force derived from weight or motion of water.

waterproof *n. & adj.* a material that does not let water pass through it.

water skiing *n.* skiing on water, in which the person is towed along by a motor boat. As a competition, water skiing includes slalom (steering around markers), distance jumping and figure skiing.

water supply *n.* the source or means of distributing water to people, including reservoirs, tunnels, etc.

water table *n.* the level below which the earth is saturated with water.

watertight *adj.* something that water cannot get into or out of without the thing breaking; leakproof.

waterwheel *n.* a wheel that uses the force of falling water to run machinery.

watt *n.* a unit of electric power.

wattle *n.* a plant found in Australia belonging to the acacia family, which produces branches suitable for interwoven (wattle) roofs and fencing. Its golden flower is

W

Australia's national emblem.

wave 1. *n.* a moving ridge on the surface of the sea. 2. *n.* a curve or curl in your hair. 3. *vb.* signal to someone by moving your hand.

waver *vb.* hesitate, be undecided.

wax *n.* a soft, yellowish material often used for making things waterproof.

way *n.* 1. a method. *Can you show me the right way to do this problem?* 2. a path. 3. direction. *Do you know your way home?*

weak *adj.* fragile, easy to break, not strong. **weaken** *vb.* make (or become) weak.

wealth *n.* a great amount of money or property. **wealthy.** *adj.* rich.

wean *vb.* change a baby animal from drinking its mother's milk to eating other foods; free gradually from a habit.

weapon *n.* an object, such as a gun or sword, used for fighting.

wear (*ware*) *vb.* 1. be dressed in, have on your body. *Penny wanted to wear her new dress and her pearl necklace to the party.* 2. become less good through being used. *The car brakes have begun to wear quite a lot.*

weary (**weer-***i*) *adj.* tired; tired (of).

weasel *n.* a small meat-eating animal related to the badger and the otter.

weather 1. *n.* conditions in the atmosphere, which may be wet or dry, hot or cold, etc. 2. *vb.* come safely through (a storm).

weather vane *n.* a device for determining wind direction.

weave *vb.* (past **wove**; past part. **woven**) make cloth on a loom with a pattern of threads.

web *n.* a loose set of threads. *A spider makes a web with threads from its body.*

web foot *n.* a foot, like the ones on ducks and frogs, which has skin joining the toes together.

wedding *n.* a marriage ceremony. **wed** *vb.*

Wednesday *n.* the fourth day of the week, between Tuesday and Thursday; named after Woden,

Anglo-Saxon god of war.

wee *adj.* a little bit; tiny.

weed *n.* a wild plant that grows where it is not wanted, such as in a flower bed. *vb.* remove weeds **weedy** *adj.* full of weeds; (*casual*) lean and scrawny.

week *n.* the sequence of seven days from Sunday to Saturday; any seven-day period.

weekday *n.* a day other than Sunday or Saturday.

weekend *n.* the period between the end of one working week and the beginning of the next, usually Saturday and Sunday. A long weekend might include Friday and Monday.

weekly *adj.* & *adv.* every week.

weep *vb.* cry with tears coming from your eyes.

weevil *n.* type of beetle distinguished by its long snout.

weft *n.* the horizontal threads on a loom, used for weaving.

weigh *vb.* measure the heaviness of something by using scales.

weight *n.* 1. how much something weighs. *What is the weight of that parcel?* 2. a heavy piece of metal or other substance. *A deep-sea diver has lead weights on the diving suit to help descend more quickly.*

weight lifting *n.* one of the sports included in the Olympic Games in which competitors lift very heavy weights from the floor to above

Three mammals that live in the sea: a dolphin (top); an elephant seal (far right); and a blue whale – the largest animal that has ever lived on earth.

their heads.

weird *adj.* strange; peculiar; odd.

welcome *n. & vb.* do or say things which show you are pleased when someone arrives.

weld *vb.* join metals by heating or pressure or a combination of both. *n.* a welded joint.

welfare *n.* people's health and happiness.

well 1. *adj.* healthy. 2. *adv.* to do something in a good or successful way. *Emma swims very well.* 3. *n.* a deep hole for underground water.

wellington *n.* the name for a kind of high boot, nowadays a rubber or plastic boot. *Wellingtons get their name from the riding boots worn by the Duke of Wellington.*

Welsh *adj. & n.* of Wales; the people and language of Wales.

went *vb.* past of **go**.

wept *vb.* past and past part. of **weep**.

west *adj., adv. & n.* one of the points on a compass; the direction in which the sun sets.

western 1. *adj.* of Western (i.e. West European and American) countries; belonging to, or coming from, the west. 2. *n.* a film or book about the American Wild West. **westernize** *vb.*

wet *adj.* consisting of, or soaked with, liquid; rainy. *vb.* make wet.

whale *n.* a very large sea animal that looks like a fish. *vb.* hunt whales.

wharf *n.* a place where ships are loaded and unloaded.

what *interrogative adj.* used in questions which ask for a selection from an indefinite number or quantity. *What do you want?*

whatever *pron.* no matter what. *Whatever he may say, I still don't believe him.*

wheat *n.* the grain from which most flour is made.

wheel *n.* a circular structure that is revolveable around an axle. *vb.* push or pull a bicycle, cart, etc.

wheelbarrow *n.* a small garden cart with one wheel in front, pushed by holding two handles.

wheeze 1. *vb.* breathe with difficulty and making a hissing sound.

when *adv. & conj.* at the time that; at what time. *When is our next meeting?*

whenever *conj.* at every time; at any time. *Come whenever you like.*

where *adv. & conj.* in such a place; in which place? *Where did you leave your case?*

wherever *adv. & conj.* in whatever place. *I shall find him, wherever he is hiding.*

whether *conj.* if. *Do you know whether we are late?*

which 1. *interrogative adj.* used in questions that ask for a selection

from a limited number or quantity.
2. *relative pronoun* stands for a
previous noun.

while 1. *n.* a period of time. *I've been
waiting all this while.* 2. *conj.* during
the time when. *Did anyone phone
while I was out?* 3. *vb.* pass away the
time. *Joan whiled away the time by
reading a book.*

whim *n.* a sudden idea, fancy. *He
went to the circus on a whim.*

whine *vb.* 1. make a high-pitched
unhappy or distressed cry.
2. complain in a whining voice.

whip 1. *n.* a long rope or strip of
leather joined to a handle, usually
used to hit animals. 2. *vb.* beat
cream, eggs, etc., until they
thicken.

whirl *vb.* turn around fast in circles;
rush along.

whirlpool *n.* a place in a river or
ocean where the water spins around.

whirlwind *n.* a fierce wind that blows
in circles, small rotating windstorm.

whisk 1. *vb.* beat eggs with a whisk.
2. *n.* go or carry off quickly. *The
waiter whisked our plates away.*

whiskers *pl. n.* hair that grows on the
face.

whiskey *n.* distilled liquor made
from grain.

whisper *n.* & *vb.* talk in a low voice,
without vibrating the vocal cords.

whist *n.* a card game for four players
using all 52 cards and a trump suit.

whistle 1. *n.* & *vb.* make a shrill
sound by blowing through your
tightened lips. 2. *n.* an instrument
for blowing through to make a
whistling sound. *vb.* to blow a
whistle.

white *n.* & *adj.* the color of snow.

white elephant *n.* a possession that is
more trouble than it is worth.

White House *n.* residence of the
president of the U.S.

whiting *n.* a small sea fish.

Whitsun *n.* short for "Whitsunday";
a Christian festival held on the
seventh Sunday after Easter. Also
known as Pentecost, it celebrates
the day when Christians believe the
Holy Spirit comforted the apostles.

who 1. *interrogative adj.* which
person. *Who did that?* 2. *pron.* the
person that. *I know who was
speaking to you.*

whoever 1. *interrogative adj.* what
person. *Whoever would have thought
it?* 2. *pron.* any person. *Ask whoever
you like to the party.*

whole (rhymes with *mole*) *adj.* all of
something, a complete thing;
uninjured.

wholesale *n.* & *adj.* selling things in
large quantities, usually to be sold
again. *vb.* sell wholesale. see **retail**.

whooping cough *n.* an infectious
disease marked by strange and
terrible coughing.

whose *interrogative adj.* of whom.
Whose book is this?

why *interrogative adv.* for what
reason. *Why are you looking at me
like that?*

wick *n.* the thread or material put
into a candle or lamp which burns
when ignited.

wicked *adj.* bad, evil.

wide *adj.* broad; having the sides far
apart.

widow *n.* a woman whose husband is
dead and who has not married
again.

widower *n.* a man whose wife is dead
and who has not married again.

width *n.* how broad something is; the
distance from one side to the other.

wield *vb.* 1. use with the hands.
2. exercise authority, etc.

wife *n.* (plural **wives**) the woman to
whom a man is married.

wig *n.* false hair to cover a bald head
or to cover one's own hair with
different hair.

wigwam *n.* a hut used by North
American Indians, made of a frame
of poles covered with bark or skin.

wild *adj.* not tame; original or
natural state; living in a natural
way; out of control, uncontrolled.

wilderness *n.* an uninhabited and
uncultivated area of land.

wilding *n.* wild plant or animal.

will 1. *vb.* a form of the verb "to

be," indicating determination or future action. *What will you do next?* 2. *n.* intention, determination, desire. 3. *n.* a document that says what will happen to someone's property when he or she dies.

willing *adj.* ready to do what is wanted or needed.

willow *n.* one of a family of deciduous trees found in many parts of the world, generally near water.

wilt *vb.* 1. droop like a plant without water, become limp. 2. become weak.

win *vb.* gain victory in a contest or game; succeed. *n.* victory in a game. **winner** *n.*

wince *vb.* & *n.* shrink back as if in pain.

wind (rhymes with *kind*) *vb.* 1. turn the spring of a clock so that it will work. 2. wrap thread, wool, etc., around something.

wind (rhymes with *sinned*) *n.* the movement of large masses of air. **windy** *adj.*

wind instrument *n.* a musical instrument that is played by blowing into it.

windmill *n.* a mill powered by the action of the wind on "arms" called *sails.*

window *n.* an opening, usually covered by glass, in the wall of a building to let in light and sometimes air.

windshield *n.* the front window of a car.

wine *n.* an alcoholic drink made from the fermented juice of grapes.

wing *n.* 1. the part of a bird or insect used for flying. 2. one "arm" of an aircraft that provides lift. 3. side extension of a building.

wink *vb.* close one eye briefly, perhaps as a signal to someone.

winter *n.* the coldest season of the year, between autumn and spring. *vb.* spend the winter in, at, etc.

wipe *vb.* rub something clean or dry.

wipe out *vb.* destroy completely. *A bad earthquake can wipe out a whole*

village. **wipeout** *n.*

wire *n.* a long thread of metal that can be bent and twisted.

wisdom *n.* accumulated knowledge and understanding.

wise *adj.* able to understand many things.

wish *vb.* & *n.* want or desire something. *I wish it wasn't raining.*

wishbone *n.* a small bone (the *furcula*) in front of a bird's breastbone. *People sometimes break a chicken's wishbone between them. The person with the bigger piece gets a wish.*

wisteria *n.* an ornamental climbing plant with purple flowers.

wit *n.* intelligence; humor.

witch *n.* (plural **witches**) a woman in stories who uses magic to make things happen.

witchcraft *n.* the skills of a witch; use of magic or sorcery.

with *prep.* connected to; possessing; in the company of. *Robin was playing with his little sister.*

withdraw *vb.* (past **withdrew** past part. **withdrawn**) pull back from something, or take back. *Sally is going to withdraw from the match.*

wither *vb.* become dry, shrivel.

withers *pl. n.* the ridge between the shoulder bones of a horse.

withhold *vb.* keep back, refuse to give.

without *prep.* not having something. *James came to school without his books.*

withstand *vb.* still keep one's position, oppose, resist.

witness *n.* & *vb.* a person who sees something happen, particularly a crime.

wizard *n.* a man in stories who uses magic to make things happen.

wobble *vb.* rock unsteadily from side to side; waver.

woke *vb.* past of **wake**.

wolf *n.* (plural **wolves**) a wild animal of the dog family. *vb.* eat greedily.

woman *n.* a grown-up female human.

womb *n.* the organ in which the young of mammals is carried and developed until it is born, the

W

uterus.

wombat *n*. a burrowing marsupial (pouched mammal) related to the koala, and found in the wild only in Australia.

won *vb*. past of **win**.

wonder *vb*. ask yourself something; feel surprised.

wonderful *adj*. a happening that is so good it surprises you.

won't *abbrev*. for **will not**.

wood *n*. 1. a number of trees growing together in one place, a small forest. 2. the trunk and branches of trees cut up and used to make things, lumber, timber.
wooden *adj*. made of wood.

woodcut *n*. a picture printed from a carved wooden block.

wooden *adj*. made of wood.

woodpecker *n*. one of a family of tree-climbing birds found in most parts of the world.

woodwind *n*. a family of musical instruments, played by blowing through a mouthpiece and into a hollow tube. Different notes are made by opening and closing holes in the instrument.

woodwork *n*. making things out of wood; the things that are made.

wool *n*. the natural hairy undercoat of sheep.

woolen *adj*. & *n*. (cloth or yarn) made from wool.

word *n*. a unit of written or spoken speech, made up of a number of letters. *We leave spaces between words when we write them down.*

word processor *n*. automated typewriter system that displays written words on a screen so that the composition can be edited before it is printed.

wore *vb*. past of **wear**.

work 1. *n*. anything that requires effort; a job. 2. *vb*. do a job.

worker *n*. someone who works for a living.

workshop *n*. a place where things are made or mended.

world *n*. the earth and universe.

worm *n*. the common name for a large group of animals with long, thin, limbless bodies.

worn *vb*. past part. of **wear**.

worry *vb*. be upset or anxious about something or someone.

worse *adj*. not as good as.

worsen *vb*. make or become worse.

worship *n*. & *vb*. praise God.

worst *adj*. the least good.

worth *n*. the value of something.

worthless *adj*. having no value; useless; lacking worth.

would *vb*. a word that implies both possibility and the desire to do something. *I would like to help you.*

wound 1. *n*. an injury or a cut. *vb*. inflict a wound. 2. *vb*. past of **wind**.

wrap *vb*. cover something by enfolding; make a parcel. *n*. a loose garment such as a shawl.

wreath *n*. an arrangement of flowers or leaves tied together in a circle.

wreck *vb*. damage something so badly that it cannot be used again. *n*. a ship or building that has been badly damaged.

wren *n*. one of a family of insect-eating songbirds that are found in most parts of the world.

wrench *n*. & *vb*. pull or twist violently.

wrestle *vb*. fight using your body as a weapon.

wretched *adj*. very miserable or sad.

wriggle *vb*. twist and turn your body, squirm.

wring *vb*. squeeze liquid out of clothing, etc., by twisting.

wrinkle *n*. a crease on skin, cloth or other flat surfaces. *vb*. become marked with wrinkles.

wrist *n*. the joint between your arm and your hand.

wristwatch *n*. a watch that is worn around the wrist.

write *vb*. (past **wrote** past part. **written**) put down words on paper.

written past part. of **write**.

wrong 1. *adj*. incorrect. *You gave the wrong answer.* 2. *n*. an old-fashioned word meaning evil or wickedness.

wrote *vb*. past of **write**.

wrung *vb*. past of **wring**.

xenophobia (*zen-o-**foab**-ya*) *n.* a great dislike of foreigners.

xerography (*zeer-**og**-ra-fee*) *n.* a process for photocopying documents, widely used in offices.

X ray *n.* a form of electromagnetic waves which can pass into or through most living things.

xylophone **zy**-*lo-fone n.* a musical instrument made up of rows of wooden or metal bars that are struck with hammers.

yacht *n.* a light sailing boat.

yak *n.* a large kind of ox, with a shaggy black coat and long horns.

yam *n.* the edible root of various tropical climbing plants.

yank 1. *vb. & n.* pull suddenly. 2. *n.* British nickname for U.S. American. Also **Yankee**.

yap *vb. & n.* a short shrill bark, like the sounds small dogs make.

yard *n.* 1. a measurement of length (3 feet or 36 inches). 2. an open space surrounded by walls and buildings. 3. a spar slung from a mast to support a sail.

yardstick *n.* a yard measure; a standard of comparison.

yarn *n.* 1. fibrous strand used in knitting and weaving. 2. a tale.

yashmak *n.* veil worn by Muslim women over the face.

yawn *vb.* open your mouth wide when you are bored or sleepy. *n.* the act of yawning.

ye *pron.* an old-fashioned word for you.

year *n.* the amount of time it takes the earth to travel around the sun; the period from January 1 to December 31; any period of 12 months.

yearly *adj.* every year; once a year.

yeast *n.* a substance used to make bread and beer rise.

yell *vb.* shout loudly. *n.* a loud cry.

yellow *n. & adj.* the color of a lemon *Yellow is one of the primary colors.* *vb.* turn yellow.

yen *n.* the currency unit of Japan.

yesterday *n. & adv.* the day before today.

An X ray of a human hand.

yet 1. *adv.* up to the present time. *Have you finished your work yet?* 2. *conj.* nevertheless.

yew *n.* an evergreen conifer often planted in churchyards.

Yiddish *n.* the international language used by Jewish people.

yield 1. *vb.* give in, give up. 2. *n.* the amount of grain or fruit on a plant or within an area of a farm. *We got a good yield of plums from that tree.*

yodel *vb. & n.* sing(ing) in the manner of Swiss mountaineers, the voice going from normal to falsetto.

yoga *n.* a Hindu spiritual system of meditation. *The form of yoga popular in Western countries uses special postures and breathing exercises to give control of mind and body.*

yogurt or **yoghurt** *n.* milk fermented by a bacterium.

yoke *n.* a wooden harness which joins a pair of oxen at the neck for working together. *vb.* link together.

yolk (rhymes with *soak*) *n.* the yellow part inside an egg.

Yom Kippur *n.* the Day of Atonement, a Jewish feast marking 10 days of penitence and abstinence at the start of the Jewish New Year (mid-September).

Yorkshire pudding *n.* a batter of eggs, flour and milk cooked in drippings and traditionally eaten with roast beef.

you *pronoun* used for the second person singular and plural. *Could you please lend me your pen, John?* or *Can you all hear me?*

young 1. *adj.* not old. 2. *n.* baby animals. *Mammals feed their young on milk.* **youngster** *n.* a young girl or boy.

your *pronoun & adj.* belonging to you.

youth *n.* (plural **youths**) the time when one is young; a young man or woman; (collective) young people. *The youth of today will deplore the youth of tomorrow.*

Yo-yo *n.* a toy that consists of a reel or disc that winds and unwinds from a string held in the hand.

zany (**zay**-*nee*) *adj.* absurd, eccentric; strangely funny.

zeal *n.* an old-fashioned word meaning enthusiasm or eagerness.

A zebra – a wild African relative of the horse. Its stripes help to camouflage it on the grasslands where it lives.

zebra *n.* an African animal related to the horse, with dark stripes on a light body.

zebu (**zee**-*boo*) *n.* a humped ox of Asia and Africa.

Zen *n.* a sect of Buddhism that originated in Japan.

zenith *n.* point of the sky directly overhead; highest point; acme.

zero *n.* nothing; the figure 0.

zest *n.* enthusiasm, lively enjoyment; gusto.

ziggurat *n.* a type of pyramid built in ancient Babylonia, the sides of which were built in huge "steps," each story set in from the one below. Ziggurats were used as temples and observatories.

zigzag *adj. & n.* going one way and then another, like the letter Z. *vb.* move in a zigzag way.

zinc *n.* a hard, bluish-white metal element (symbol – *Zn*).

zipper *n.* a fastener with two sets of teeth that lock together. *vb.* fasten with a zipper.

zither *n.* a many-stringed musical instrument having a shallow horizontal body and played with picks and by plucking.

zloty *n.* principal money unit of Poland. The word means golden.

zodiac *n.* a name given by ancient astrologers to the band of sky through which the sun, moon, and all the planets except Pluto appear to move.

zombie *n.* a corpse said to be brought back to life by witchcraft; a will-less person, someone who behaves like a robot.

zone *n. & vb.* part of a town or larger area that is set off as distinct.

zoo *n.* a place where captive wild animals are kept for public display (short for zoological gardens).

zoology *n.* the study of animals.

zoom 1. *n.* sharp upward movement. 2. *n.* a loud low hum. 3. *vb.* focus a camera quickly from long-shot to close-up by use of a special lens.